BLOOD

OF

A GANGSTA

SOUL OF A HUSTLER

CHARLES WATSON

INTRODUCTION

It's June 10th, 1990, and Joan Mills, better known as Momma Mills, is stretched out on her queen size bed. Relaxing under her air conditioner, watching the news while awaiting her favorite soap opera, "The Young and the Restless" she hears her two grandson's downstairs arguing, and with her superwoman senses, she can sense her oldest grandson holding her front door open. While the cool air from her air conditioner seeps outside.

I know that hard-headed boy ain't holding my door open passing air out to the whole dang on neighborhood Momma Mills thinks to her self, before letting her voice roar through the house.

"Tony!!! Jimmy!! Y'all better stop all that yelling in this house! And shut that door! I ain't got no money to be supplying the whole dog on neighborhood wit air, don't make me come down there!"

Tony, being quick on his toes, ended the dispute with his younger brother by compromising.

"Jim, you can't go with me this time, but if you be cool, Imma bring you a big bag of candy back, iight."

"Iight man, I want Johnny Apple Seeds, Lemon Heads, and Now Laters, and…"

before Jimmy could go any further Tony cut him off. "Iight iight I got you lil bra."

Tony shut the door and took off running up Mound Street, laughing at his younger brother's love of candy. Tony was 10, while Jimmy is 6. Although he was four years his brother's senior,

i

there diving on the football paying the police no mind. The police gone direct they attention on y'all, and as soon as they do I'm a grab the bag and get gone."

They all gavconcerns.

"Maannn, that's just stupid, that plan will never work."

"Stop trippin Fells, you always got something to say, is you wit me or what?"

"I'm always wit you bro, but ya plan still sounds stupid."

Mills just shook his head and passed him the ball and said, "Let's do this man."

As Mills made his way across the street at full speed, Fella dove on the ball, Peko dove on him, and Shawn Shawn on Peko. The cops instantly became furious as the kids rolled in the grass laughing and playing as if they didn't exist.

"HEY! HEY! HEY! Don't you see a search going on over here? GET THE HELL OUT OF THE GRASS!!" The officer yelled. While he and his two partners focused on the playing children, Mills swooped in. He grabbed the bag, stuffed it under his shirt, and quickly walked off. The cops were only distracted for a split second, but that's all Mills needed. Once Mills bent the corner, he ran full speed all the way home. Buck rocked back and forth in the cruiser while laughing and thinking, *That's my lil nigga.*

Everyone watching the search peeped that move and acknowledged Mills courage and loyalty to Buckshot. The only ones who missed his demonstration were the distracted cops. The young hustlers dapped it up with each other while laughing at the cop's stupidity. The dope fiends and onlookers stood in awe, fascinated by the youngster's trick. Little did they know, Mills had a lot more tricks in his playbook.

Torry Mills, born 1960 in Columbus, Ohio, was the second youngest child in her home. She was accompanied by four siblings. two brothers, one older sister, and a brother just a year beneath her. They were all raised in one of the toughest neighborhoods that Columbus had to offer. Main Street was the hub of prostitution, drugs, and violence in Columbus. At the age of fifteen, Torry was not only the most beautiful female to walk the mean streets of Main Street, but also one of the toughest. The Mills were a highly respected family. None of them were soft. If it wasn't for Tony Keys, Torry's older brothers Lonny and Donny would have the neighborhood on lockdown. Tony Keys was a smooth, but ruthless young hustler. His hustles varied from robberys B-M-E's, carjacking, selling marijuana , and gambling. As treacherous as he was with his pistol, he was just as frightening with his hands. Tony Keys believed he was God's gift to women and a lot of women agreed with him. He also believed he was the toughest man to walk the earth and those who thought differently were quickly dealt with. Luckily for Torry's brothers, they were both down with Tony Keys, so they never had to experience his wrath. Tony Keys hung out on Main Street, but he lived on Long Street, which was also a reputable neighborhood on Columbus East side. Truthfully, Tony Keys hung out where ever he pleased, and no one would question his position. It was known everywhere, Tony Keys was a certified gangster. Tony's way of life differed from the rest of his family. His mother, father, and siblings were all devout Christians. How Tony had become so evil, no one knew, but ever since the age of ten, the streets had been his home.

1975, middle of the summer and Tony Keys, along with Lonny, Donny, and a few more of his goons were posted up in front of the Main Street Market on the corner of Main and Wilson. As they discussed a robbery Tony had planned for later that night, a couple females gravitating towards them, and one of them caused Tony pause. He stopped in mid sentence, as he stared at the beautiful creature headed his way.

"Who is this fine thang strutting our way? Damn, she's a sight for sore eyes." Tony said smoothly.

Lonny and Donny turned to face the females with the rest of their crew. Being the oldest, Lonny reacted like the protective older brother he was. "Torry, GET YO FAST ASS FROM OFF THE STRIP!!" Lonny demanded. "I'm just going to the store.

god lee." She snapped, rolling her eyes. "Why you have to come all the way to this store wit yo fast ass?" Donny added.

"First of all, you ain't nothing but a year older than me, so you can't tell me nothing, cause you ain't grown either." Torry replied.

"Well I am, now get yo ass in that store, get what you came to get, and get off the strip!" Lonny ordered, throwing his 18 years of age and the man of the house rank around. Lonny looked at his other sister who accompanied Torry, and although she was only a year younger than him, he scolded her as well.

"Terry yo ass know better than to have Torry on this strip. Don't make coming to this store a habit." "Iight Big Brother, calm that shit." Terry responded as they walked through the crowd of young men. Tony sized Torry up, finishing his appraisal by looking into her eyes. Tony was smooth, and although he didn't say anything, Torry heard him loud and clear. Her and Terry nudged one another with their elbows as Tony admired Torry's beauty. Once in the store they burst into laughter.

"Got damn Lon! How old is ya lil sis?" Tony asked while rubbing his hands together.

"Fifteen, and too young for you." Donny replied firmly.

"Whoa! Tone it down little main man, I don't mean no disrespect, but I'm only 17, so how could she be too young for me?" Tony shot back, now feeling a little offended.

"C'mon Keys, lets drop this subject, you're way too mature for my little sister, she ain't giving up no skins and she off limits to brothas of our kind bottom line, ya dig?"

Donny knew Tony was becoming angry, but he'd swim in those waters for his baby sister or his family in general.

"I'm offended, I mean I'm truly offended by the way you view me as some pussy hungry heathen, I thought we was pals." Tony replied with a smirk on his face. He was offended by Lonny tone of voice. He understood where Lonny was coming from, but pal or not, he was going to have Lonny's sister. He'd back off for now, because he didn't want Lonny's mind on anything but the lick he had set up for tonight, but his next encounter with Torry would be more to his liking. Tony's next encounter with Torry came sooner than he expected. A few days later, he was hanging out on Liley and Main Street with a few hustlers and small time pimps. He spotted Torry walking up Mound Street with her sister and their younger brother, Mike. Mike looked up to Tony, so Tony used that to his advantage.

"AYE, Money Mike," Tony yelled from a distance.

Mike instantly knew who it was, because Tony was the only person who called him Money Mike. Once he gave Tony his attention, Tony waved him over. He watched Mike jog his way over to him, while his sisters stood on the corner awaiting his return. After tilting his bottle of old English in the air, taking a few puffs of his cigarette, and flicking it to the ground, he greeted Mike with a dap, and his famous saying, "Whats happenin main man, whats new and exciting?"

Mike cracked a smile before responding, "Not a whole a lot, whats up with you Keys?"

Nobody called him Tony except for his mother. He didn't even allow his father to call him by his first name. Not that he didn't respect him, because he respected both his parents. He just didn't like being called a women's name. He was named after his mother, so that was something special that only they shared. Keys laughed at Mikes reply as he pulled him in closer, and asked, "What's yo sister name?"

Mike smiled and said, "Which one?"

Keys pointed at Torry while saying, "Her, right there."

"Oh, that's Torry." Mike said unenthusiastically.

"Will you tell her, I would like to take her out sometime? " Keys demanded.

"You can tell her yourself man," Mike said, before yelling Torry's name, and waving her over to where he and Keys stood.

As Torry and Terry sashayed over, they mumbled words to each other.

"I told you Keys like you girl." Terry said through her clenched teeth.

"Shut up girl." Torry replied with a closed mouth.

Terry laughed at her younger sister's nervousness.

"Stop laughing Terry, I ain't playing with you." Torry whispered as they got closer.

"Tee this is Keys, Keys this is my sister Torry." Mike said, introducing the two.

"How you doing beautiful?" Keys asked.

"I'm fine." Torry replied as she stood shyly in front of him. Keys smiled before turning up his charm.

"Any man wit eyes can see that, won't you tell me something I don't know." "Huh?"

"I asked you how are you doing? And you said you were fine. Tell me something I don't know." Keys explained.

Torry smiled as she caught on to his compliment.

"Your name is Tony Keys, right?" Torry asked him as she gained her composure.

"The one and only, but my friends call me Keys."

"Well I guess I'll call you Tony since I don't know if we're friends or not yet."

"Actually, I was hoping we could become friends,"

Keys knew he had Torry where he wanted her. The look in her eyes, along with the shifting of her weight from one foot to the other told him he had her hot.

"Tony don't you have enough *girl* friends already?" Torry asked sarcastically, emphasizing the word girl.

Keys laughed at the fact that she insisted on calling him Tony. Usually the use of the name would have offended him, but for some reason Torry's use of the name amused him. He stared into her eyes while he answered her question. "Actually I don't have any *girl*friends, I have few female "associates", but I've yet to meet one special enough to label my *girlfriend*. Until today that is, or at least that is what I hope. I wanna spend some time with you, getting to know you, becoming *your* friend. While giving our friendship a chance to grow into something more. How about we start off with a phone number?"

Keys liked a woman with a little defiance because it gave him a chance to showcase his manhood while earning the respect he deserved and demanded. He loved bedazzling women with his slick talk. He felt that in the streets, you either peep game or get gamed because the game is either in you or on you. Torry gave in to Keys allure. She gave him her phone number and walked off with her sister and brother.Keys didn't waste anytime. He phoned her that night. He offered to take her out to lunch the following day, but she denied his proposition. She was playing hard to get. She learnt from her mother and older sister and that making men wait for things like dates, alone time, and first kisses were the men's opportunity to strike. She played the waiting game with Keys for almost three weeks, before going out on a date with him. Keys enjoyed the game. He called her every night talking to her about things like her favorite color, food, type of music, etc. Game recognize game on Keys behalf, so he used this time to gain her trust. In the process he was falling for her, but he had expected that possibility from the first he sawher.

By the time school was back in season, Keys had won Torry over. They were an item and Keys didn't care who disliked it. Lonny and Donny separated themselves from Keys after a heated argument that almost went to blows between Keys and Lonny. Keys knew if he hurted Torry's brother, he could kiss their relationship good-bye, so he controlled his temper best as he could. Had it been for anyone else, he would of left him where the argument began. Lonny tried preventing Torry from seeing Keys, but her feelings for him were uncontrollable. She had given Keys her young heart, mind and soul.

The only thing she was yet to give him was her virginity. As Keys coasted in his white on white hard top 1960 Impala, he felt on top of the world. Not because he was on his way to pick up Torry from school, but because he had finally took his hustle to the next level. Some guys from New York came to Columbus with hopes of finding a gold mine. They quickly set their sights on Main Street's mean strip. They started flooding the strip with heroin and cocaine, quickly turning the strip out. Once Keys got wind of their establishments, and its benefits, he muscled his way in. What he didn't know was the New Yorkers had been awaiting his arrival. They had heard about the notorious Tony Keys since they arrived, and they couldn't wait for their chance to befriend him. Keys pulled his Impala to the curb of the school.

He turned the music down and conversated with his young homie Buckshot. Buckshot was only 7 years old, and Keys was more like a father figure to him, than a big homie. Buckshot's mother was a prostitute and a junkie. Keys took a liking to the youngster, seeing as how he always ran into him roaming up and down the strip making store runs for the pimps, hookers, and hustlers. Keys started taking Buckshot out to eat, and making sure he got home at night. Buckshot, like a hungry dog when it was fed, always found his way back to his feeder, and for Buckshot, his feeder lived on the street. Keys started spending more time with Buckshot, as he saw a lot of himself in the youngster. Buckshot was a survivor, and as dangerous as the strip was, Buckshot was most comfortable there just as Keys was at a young age. One day Buckshot lead Keys into an alley, where he retrieved a shotgun loaded with Buckshots from the side of the dumpsters. He asked Keys to hold it for him because he might need it for a man who beat on his mother and cursed him out. Of course, Keys took care of the pimp who was beating on Buckshot's mother in front of him, and from that day on, he was called Buckshot,. That was also the day Keys took Buckshot in. He cared for him like a father and tutored him in the game like a teacher or an older brother. Keys met Buckshot seven months ago, and he's been taking care of him since. Keys cut his lesson short as Torry approached the car. He hopped out so he could open the door for her. Buckshot climbing in the back seat as Torry placed a soft kiss on Keys lips.

"How yo day been baby?" Keys asked, pleased with his kiss.

"I guess it's been alright, considering I been getting dirty looks from some of yo hoochies all day," Torry replied with a hint of attitude.

Keys didn't respond. He shut the passenger door, and headed for the driver's seat. Once inside the car, he heard what he knew was coming.

"Tony! Don't act like you ain't hear me!" Torry snapped.

"I hear you, and I heard you baby, but I don't care about looks you been getting from some silly ass dames, and you shouldn't either, because everybody knows who Tony Keys belong to, I love you, and I'm your man, so fuck them silly broads, IIGHT! And I don't wanna discuss this no more with Buckshot in the car. He already hear enough of arguing from his momma and all the chumps she bring home, IIGHT!"

"Whatever Tony" Torry responded, as she turned her attention to Buckshot. "Hi Buckshot"

"Sup" he responded along with a head nod. Torry knew Keys was having sex with other women because he wasn't the type of man to be sexless for months. She wasn't stupid, and Keys knew it, but he took such good care of her that she let a lot of things slide. He took such good care of her that her mother no longer had to. Keys was truly in love with Torry and he had no problem with waiting until she was ready to have sex, but that didn't mean he wouldn't with anyone else.

Truthfully Keys knew that he'd have sex with more than one woman even if him and Torry were having sex. This was a part of him that would probably never change, although he loved Torry to much to admit it. He made sure that it was clear to every women he slept with, Torry was his woman and he wasn't leaving her for anyone or anything. He also made sure his affairs were kept secret. The ladies loved and feared Keys so much that they kept their encounters with him concealed. One day while in school, one of Keys flings couldn't take seeing Torry floss Key's jewelry or rock the newly bought clothes any longer. She felt that because she was having sex with Keys, and Torry wasn't, she should be the one sporting jewelry and receiving gifts.

"Not a whole lot main man, I just came through to holla at this sucka, Pete." Keys answered as he slapped Sonny five.

"You need ol' Sonny's assistance?" Sonny asked while flashing his pistol.

"Nah, I can handle this sucka, just keep an eye on my lady for me." Keys strolled across the street smoothly.

Pete was in front of his drug house, entertaining an audience while nodding off and turning to his right side like his body cam with a kickstand.

"Petey Westro tell me something good main man." Keys said while greeting Pete by wrapping an arm around his shoulder.

"Aw man, I'm just punching that clock, working overtime ya dig," Pete responded.

"Since you been working overtime and all that, I know you got some paper to lay on me, right?"

Pete instantly started stuttering. "Uh, oh, oh, well, well, see, see it's been kinda slow Keys, but give me a couple of days and I'll be ready for you."

"Petey, don't play with me man, I gave you that package a week ago, that's more than enough time to turn a play or two. Now if you don't come out yo nasty ass pockets with my paper, I'm a do you real dirty man." Keys pulled out a 38, revolver from his waist causing Petey's stuttering to worsen.

"Ke, Ke, Ke, Ke, Keys man, I, I, I, I swear I swear man…"

"Save that swearing for the chapel, you no good sucka. Didn't I tell you if you played with my money again, I'd kill you nigga?!"

Torry watched as Keys pointed at Pete with his gun. She had only heard of the crazy things Keys did in the streets, but she was about to see him in live and in action. Torry almost jumped out her skin when Keys smacked Pete on top of his head with the pistol, while squeezing off a shot at the same time. She thought Pete was dead as he fell to the ground. Keys had only smacked Pete, but blood leaked from his skull like he'd shot him. As Keys stood over the top of Pete with his pistol aimed, Pete's audience begged and pleaded with Keys, trying to stop what they knew was about to happen.

"Do any of you mutha fuckas wanna take his place?" Keys yelled with fury.

The crowd went silent as Keys waved his pistol while yelling at them.

"Iight then, don't put cha'self in my mutha fuckin business!" when Keys swung the pistol back on Pete, Pete balled up, while covering his head, expecting to get hit again with the pistol but instead, Keys squeezed off two shots hitting Pete twice in the chest. As Pete lay in a puddle of blood, Keys made his last announcement.

"If I hear a peep out of any of you mutha fuckas, I'll be back for you wit magician speed, and magical quickness."

Torry was in shock, she couldn't believe her eyes. Her and Keys rode in complete silence. When he pulled up in front of Torry's mothers house, he said, "Tee, you ain't see nothing and you don't know nothing."

"I know Tony." She replied

"Okay, I love you, baby, and I'll be here in the morning to take you to school."

"I love you too, Tony, and be careful okay."

"Alright baby, take this bag and put it up for me until the morning."

He handed her a bag filled with the money he'd picked up and the drugs he had left over. They kissed and Torry hurried in the house. Little did Keys know, he wouldn't be picking Torry up in the morning or any other time for a long time. Later that night while hanging out on the corner of Main Street and Berkley. Keys got ambushed by the cops. Pete had lived and told the cops who his shooter was. Keys was lucky enough to get three years after having Sonny pay Pete off. Sonny wanted to kill Pete for Keys, but Keys wanted the pleasure of taking Pete's life himself. Keys had went to a juvenile facility since he wasn't yet 18 years old, and he promised himself that when he would be released that Pete would be a dead man.

Torry's life flashed before her eyes when she heard of Keys arrest. She felt like she was dying. She had no idea how she would make it without Keys, being that she had become so dependent on him. Not only financially, but mentally and emotionally as well.

Her heart felt like it had a hole in it. Without keys, she wasn't whole. She continuously had to remind herself of Keys words, " A women who cant take care of herself and her family in her man's absence is nothing more than a child, playing grown-up games. She is more a daughter to her man, than a partner. No strong man wants a weak woman."

Keys schooled her on so many things that it was difficult for her to remember them all, but now that Keys was gone, all his lessons came back to her like she were a musician and they were old songs she had wrote. She could hear him as if he was sitting next to her.

"Tee, never become so dependent on me or anyone else that you forget how to take care of Ya'self. You don't need a man for anything, you have all the tools you need to be successful on your own and know that things like this, I have never told another woman before, because with juice like this the average female may walk out of her mans life, and possibly take everything he's taught her and use it against him. I share all my knowledge with you because I see you as my equal, and I want us to be equally strong, and I trust in you, our love, and loyalty to one another, enough to believe that you will never betray me or abandon me."

Keys words empowered Torry and she knew that she had to stay strong for her and Keys both. Keys first few months were stressful, because he had no phone privileges. Torry was too young to visit him, but she wrote him a letter everyday and he reciprocated the love and loyalty. A couple weeks before he received his phone privileges, he wrote Torry a letter telling her that he'd be calling. He gave her the exact date and time and told her that he needed to speak to her about some things, so it was important that she be home.

When the day came, Torry sat by the phone, impatiently awaiting his call. After snatching the phone up on the first ring, for what seemed to be at least a hundred calls, she dosed off angry that none of them were Keys. Never hearing the phone ring, she was awakened by her mother's voice.

"Torry!! Torry!!" Her mother yelled from upstairs. Torry jumped up as if she were late for work.

"Maam?"

"Pick up the phone child, its Tony."

Torry snatched the phone off the hook with magician speed.

"I love you Tony, and I miss you so much."

"I love you and miss you too baby," Keys replied just as quickly.

"Oh hush, the two of you don't know what love is." Her mother kidded.

Keys started laughing, then thanked her for accepting his call.

"Don't worry about it baby, you just be strong in there and hurry up home so you can get this girl before she drives me crazy."

"Alright Ms. Mills, and thanks again." Keys responded before she hung the phone up, giving the two love birds some privacy.

"What's happenin baby? You get my letter?" Torry asked breaking the ice.

"Yeah I got it." Tony answered. "So you understand what you gotta do right?"

"Yes Tony."

Tony laughed, after all this time, being called Tony by her still amused him.

"Iight then, Imma have some people get wit you for a minute, just to show you the ropes."

"I don't need no Sonny or nobody else to show me the ropes, you showed me all I need to know Tony and a lot of your people been hollering at me in the streets already." Torry replied with sassiness.

"Okay baby, then its all on you, let's make it do what it do, but this is not a game to be played lightly, you remember everything I told you and showed you right?"

"Yes Tony, just chill out, yo wife got this, you worry about what you gotta do in there and let me worry about our business out here, I got this."

"Iight baby, but be careful."

They used the rest of their phone call to talk about how much they missed one another while trading I love you's through out the conversation. When the call ended, Torry wanted to cry, but she held back her tears for Tony's sake. They had become so close, that even though Tony wasn't there, she knew he could see her and she wanted him to see his woman being strong. The next day Torry's life as a drug dealer began. She hooked up with a lot of Keys people, and bought in a few of her own.

She quickly became good at it. After two months of hustling, she dropped out of school and became a full fledged hustler. With Keys in jail, Buckshot was back roaming the streets. His hustle had changed as well. Usually he would make his money shooting dice and making store runs, but now he started selling bundles of hay for a small time pimp. Once Torry got wind of it, she quickly put a stop to his dealing with this pimp.

She knew Keys wouldn't approve of it and he purposely kept Buckshot from selling drugs. He didn't feel Buckshot was ready and neither did Torry. She looked at Buckshot as a younger brother and often let him sleep at her mother's house with her. Ms. Mills quickly took a liking to the little man child and welcomed him in her home with open arms. Buckshot liked staying with Ms. Mills, but like Keys, he was a child of the streets. He also liked keeping an eye on his mother, although their relationship was non existent. Keys taught him that no matter how much wrong his mother did, she would always be his mother and for that reason alone, she deserved his respect. He also taught him that drugs and the streets had the power to rape a person of their morals, principles, and self respect, so he excused his mothers neglect and lack of parenting.

Even at such a young age he understood that his mother had been raped by the street life and the ever-so powerful drug, known as heroin. By the time Keys came home, Torry had mastered her craft. She was all business. Being that she was easier to deal with than Keys, she widened their clientele. She had bust the game wide open for the two of them. She also had young Buckshot ready for the finishing touches that only Keys could give him. Keys came home in the summer of 78'.

Torry threw him a coming home party in which he was greeted by all hustlers, pimps, prostitutes, and several junkies. Keys was the man of the night and his time in jail only made him more confident. The females lusted after his toned frame, pretty eyes, and bright white smile while he walked throughout the party with his chest out, like a true king of the jungle. Torry and young Buckshot stuck by his side as he mingled with all the play turners and money earners.

Keys enjoyed the sight of Torry moving throughout the party with such confidence. He could feel the respect his baby had earned in his absence. She was a qualified woman and the missing piece to his puzzle. She complemented his lifestyle perfectly and after he took care of Pete, they'd locked the game down. That night Torry gave Keys her virginity, causing them to fall deeper in love. The next day Keys hit the streets bright and early. He had learned some new tricks while in jail and he was ready to put them into play.

In no time, he and Torry were closing in on the game, locking down the East side and parts of the South and North. Keys was more aggressive than before. He was shooting, pistol whipping, and applying all beat downs to all those who opposed his rule. Six months after Keys got home, Pete was found in an alley dead, from a single shot to the head. No one actually seen

Keys do it, but everyone knew he was responsible. When Torry tried to slow Keys down, warning him of the cops, and the law, He told her that he was the law and that what he was doing was serving justice. As Keys drove up Main Street checking his drug houses and street workers. He had Buckshot with him, and as always, school was in session.

"Whats the number one rule Buck?" Keys asked sternly.

"Never get high off ya own supply," Buckshot answered

"That's right, ain't nothing more backwards than a hustler using his own product, where's the money in that." Keys paused for a few seconds then threw another question at Buck. "Who can you trust?"

"No one, its hard enough trusting ya'self to do the right thing, but its iight to have a little faith in people, because no one person can accomplish great things alone."

Keys shook his head while sizing his young protégé.

"Whats rule number two?" Keys asked when he saw Buck relaxing.

"You either peep game or get gamed. Never let anyone play you like a sucka or like you ain't hip to game, and never ask for respect, demand it, and take it if necessary."

Keys was satisfied with Bucks knowledge. He pulled up to one of his stash houses and told Buck to follow him inside. Keys gave Buck his first official package. He fed him a few more grapes and told him to go to work. Buck was a natural, and why wouldn't he be, after all, the streets raised him. In 1980 Keys and Torry had their first child. Of course Keys wanted him to be a junior, but like Keys own mother, Torry wanted to be much as apart of her son's name as his father. They compromised and named their son Tony Mills.

Giving him his father's first name and his mothers last. Young Tony was a spitting image of his mother, besides the fact that he had his father's eyes, light brown skin, and good slightly thin hair. With a new born baby, Torry fell back from her hustle, only dealing with a few of her best customers. Keys on the other hand, dug deeper into the game. His violent streak kept on growing. While his hunger for more money and control grew as well, not to mention his unfaithfulness. Torry had grown tired of his cheating, but she loved him and vowed to never abandon or betray him. She knew he loved her with all his heart, but for some reason one woman wasn't enough for him sexually.

Torry had gotten so mad one time, she smacked blood out Keys mouth. He just stared at her, as she followed the slap with another one. That day she realized how deep his love for her was. To this day, she's the only person who has ever put their hands on Keys and lived. As the FAO became more reputable, Keys joined the trend and started breaking down on his number one rule, "Don't get high off your own supplies."

Keys became addicted to the nose candy. The drug only enhanced his temper, and violent streak. As the 80's moved on, Keys body count grew. He had the streets so terrified that no one would tell on him. Snitching went against the code of the streets anyway. Snitches got ditches and fakes got found in lakes, that was the motto on the strip. In 83' Torry was pregnant with Keys second child. Keys started hanging out at a new spot called "Joe' Hoes."

All the pimps, hustlers, hookers, stick up kids, pan handlers, and gangsters hung out at Joe's Hoes. It wasn't only a hang out; it was a million dollar spot. All the money on the strip came through the J-Spot, which was Joes Hoes street name. Keys leaned against his cocaine white 1980 Cadillac Coop, with white leather guts, on trues and vogue tires. He stood with a female under each of his arms and another between his legs. Young Buckshot sat on the hood of the car serving a few addicts. Keys was higher than Rick James, and just as fly. Just as the female in between his legs began to whisper in his ear, Torry pulled up out of nowhere. She jumped out her car and sprung into action like she was back in her high school hallway with Maria. Stomach protruding and all, she grabbed the female between Keys legs by her hair, snatched her to the ground, and went to work on her face. Keys stayed leaned up against the car, stoned out of his mind. He watched as Torry beat the blood out the hooker's mouth. The two ladies under Keys arms went to grab Torry off their friend, and both received backhands from Keys. He smacked both of them to the ground and said

"If I don't put my hands on her, what makes you think you got the right to put your nasty ass hands on er?"

At that moment an up and coming pimp and gangster strolled over to Keys.

"Slow ya roll lil daddy, don't nobody put they paws on my broads, but me, and these hoes are Candy's property, now check ya'self nigga." Candyman spoke with authority. Candyman was well aware of who Keys was, but his up and coming status had gone to his head. Candyman's name was ringing in the streets, and Keys was waiting for his buzz to go to his head. He had seen Candyman put in some work one day and begged for the day when Candyman would put on a pair of shoes that would be too big for his feet. Being that Candyman was a large man, standing at 6'2, two hundred plus pounds. He looked down on Keys 5'8 ½ frame. Keys pulled his 357 magnum from his waist and hit Candyman with all six shots, knocking him to the pavement. Torry stopped her punch in mid-air, jumped to her feet and tried to get Tony in the car as he stood with his gun in his hand talking to a dead man.

"I'm Tony Keys sucka, and I touch who the fuck I wanna touch. This is my strip and don't none of you mutha fuckas forget that." Keys screamed at everyone who was in hearing range.

Young Buckshot stood by his side with his 38' special drawn. Torry yanked on Keys coat as the sounds of sirens got closer.

"C'mon Tony, don't you hear the fuckin cops?" Torry yelled at him. She snatched the gun from his hands, gave it to Buckshot, and told him to get gone. Buckshot disappeared immediately. As Torry had Keys in his Cadillac and was ready to pull away, the cops closed in on them. Keys was sentenced to life in prison with no chance of parole. Torry gave birth to her second son in 84'. She gave him Tony's middle and last name, naming him James Keys. With Keys in prison, she was only half a person. They made one another whole. They were one mind, one body, one soul. Tony was the only man she had ever been with. She knew she could never love again. To love another man would be betrayal and she promised never to betray him.

Even in his absence she'd keep her promise. No man would ever be able to have her heart, because it forever belonged to Tony Keys. With Keys locked down, Torry went back to hustling full time. She formed a small army with her brothers, and a few of Keys soldiers. Buckshot was her right-hand man, and the only person she trusted. After two years of being alone, Torry allowed a man's charm to entice her. Most men who stepped to her seemed simple. They were no match for her, but when comparing another man to Tony Keys, they all seemed simple, not to mention small time.

D-man which was short for Dope man was another story though. He was smooth, tall, dark, and handsome. He was also earning top dog rank on the strip. D-man was from Alabama. He had come to Columbus a year before Tony Keys run in with Candyman. He laid the law on the strip, doing a little small-time pimping, and hustling. With Tony Keys being the top dog, and Candyman on the rise he knew his time to shine was far off, but he remained patient while positioning himself. Lucky for him, Tony Keys and Candyman were taken out at the same time. One by the other so to speak. He studied Torry for a year before he mustered up enough courage to approach her. He knew his money had to be right, his game had to be tight, and his name had to hold weight. So he stayed patient while watching her turn down one sucka after another.

When he became comfortable with his all-around status, which took two years, he stepped to the infamous Torry Mills. After a few months of work, Torry gave in to his southern hospitality. D-man was no Tony Keys, but he put it down with his style. After being with D-man for six months, Torry moved out her mother's house and bought a home with D-man. Like her mother, she refused to move out the hood that raised her, so they moved a couple streets from her mother. D-man was nice to her children, and besides the fact that he puts his hands on Torry, he treated her like a queen. D-man's status was going to his head and he started to catch the Tony Keys syndrome. He was applying pressure to all those in opposition. He became more violent by the day and his once low key position became permanent. The feds caught on to D-man's status and infiltrated their way into his organization.

Although he and Torry's business was kept separate, he brought the heat to Torry and her team as well. One day while Torry was out of town on business, the feds raided her and D-man's home. Fortunate for Torry she had left her boys with her mother. The feds found guns and drug-related utensils. The next day Torry's hotel room was raided by the feds. She was caught dirty, along with her brothers who accompanied her. Warrants were issued for many of her workers as well. The feds came to Torry first with a snitch deal. She refused to talk just as Keys had taught her. D-man on the other hand cooperated with the government. He told on Torry and her workers.

In turn, some of Torry's workers leaked information on her as well. When the feds came to Torry with another snitch plea, she still refused to talk. She was taught the code of silence, and that is what she lived by. Unlike a lot of weak individuals, Torry was prepared for both sides of her lifestyle. Tony warned her of the dark side of the game and prepared her mentally and emotionally for it. The only three realities for a person in the game is freedom, death, or prison. While a lot of people refuse to believe that the game has a flip side, Torry was a true player of the game, and she accepted the cards she was dealt. Even when threatened with losing her kids, she stood firm. D-man was a rat, a coward, and a man with a pink heart. The part that hurt Torry the most was that she didn't see through his hard exterior and recognize him for the charming soft brotha he was. Torry was sentenced to 20 years in feds, while D-man received ten years on a snitches plea. Just about Torry's whole team went down. Her brothers and sister were even dragged into the raid. While her brothers were locked down, they were also hit with some old murder raps. Buckshot was the only one from Torry's crew to escape the raid unscathed. While Torry and Tony served their time, their sons were in Ms. Mills's custody. The boys were raised right on the same street as their father and mother, where they would possibly one day be sucked in by the same strip.

CHAPTER 1

A s Mills ran into the house, he was met by his younger brother.

"Where my candy at Mills?" Jimmy asked looking at the brown bag that protruded from his waist.

"Not right now Jim." Mills answered as he dashed up the stairs to his bedroom, and quickly closed the door.

As Jimmy pouted downstairs, Mills explored inside the bag. He removed sandwich baggies filled with rocks the size of his fist. He knew what a dime and twenty rocks looked like, but these rocks were huge. Thoughts of how much money they worth ran through his mind as his grandmother screamed his name from the kitchen.

"TONY! TONY! Boy don't make me come up there."

"Ma'am" Mills yelled back while trying to find a hiding place for the bag.

Mills hid the bag in one of his winter coats hanging in his closet as his grandmother continued to scream. Mills ran down the steps at full speed. As he entered the kitchen he said,

"Grandma I said Ma'am,"

"Boy, did you tell your little brother you was gone brang him some candy back?" She asked while stirring her mashed potatoes.

"Yes ma'am, but I didn't..." she cut Mills off

"No you don't, don't stand here with no excuses, we don't lie to each other in this house, you told Jimmy you was gone buy him some candy. Now you take him to the store and do just that." She ordered.

1

Mills looked up at his brother and said, "C'mon cry baby. What I tell you about telling on people?"

"I ain't no cry baby, and I ain't no tattle teller." Jimmy said looking mad that his idol had called him a snitch.

Jimmy lived to impress his brother. He wanted to be just like Mills. As they walked out the front door, their grandmother yelled after them,

"Tony, don't let that boy eat all that candy at once. Dinner will be done after a while."

"Alright Momma," Mills replied.

He looked over his baby brother's wardrobe before they stepped off the porch.

"Tie ya shoes up, Jim." He said after fixing his shirt. When Jimmy was finished tying his shoes Mills said, "Look Jim, we brothers and brothers don't lie to each other, besides grandma and Buck, we all we got. I love you more than life, so don't ever think I'm lying to you. I ain't never told you a lie, have I?"

"No." Jim replied

"And I ain't gone start now. Now let's go get you some candy big head, and stop tattle-telling." Mills said teasing his little brother.

"I ain't no tattle tale man, I'm a Gee," Jimmy replied.

"Aight then start actin like it." Mills said while laughing at his little brother's reply.

On the way back from the store, Mills ran into Fella, Peko, and Shawn Shawn again.

"What up Mills, how much shit was in that bag bro?" Fella asked.

Mills gave Fella a funny look before replying, "Man, don't you see my Lil brother right here?"

"Aw shit, my bad," Fella said while putting his hand over his mouth, realizing that he said the wrong thing again.

Mills gave him the same look he gave him the first time. Mills, Fella, Peko, and Shawn all grew up together, but Mills and Fella were the tightest.

"What up J-pimp?" Fella said, acknowledging Jimmy by the name they made up for him because he attracted for them when Mills allowed him to tag along.

"Whats up Fella?" Jimmy replied.

"Ey Mills you know the cops took Buck to jail anyway?" Peko blurted out, seeing that Fella forgot to mention it.

"Word?" Mills replied.

"Word up" Peko shot back.

"Oh yea, Meka said for you to come see her immediately," Fella added.

"Aight man, I'm a get up with ya'll later." Said Mills. As he hurried home to drop Jimmy off. Once in front of the house, Jimmy started whining about why he couldn't roll with his big brother. As they went at it in the front yard, Ms. Mills opened the front door breaking up the debate.

"Jimmy come on in the house boy. You bout to eat dinner. Go in there and wash yo hands, and Mills you hurry back, cause dinner ah be ready in a few minutes."

"Yes ma'am." Mills replied as he ran off.

He quickly made it to Bucks apartment on Liley. Tameka's little sister Tanesha was sitting on the porch. She was four years older than Mills and by far the finest female in the neighborhood.

"What's up Lil Mills." Tanesha said greeting him.

"What's up Nesh. Ya sister here?" Mills shot back.

"Nah, she went to go pick Buck up. She said for you to stay here until she gets back."

"I thought the cops took Buck to jail?" Mills asked.

"They did, but only for some tickets, so Mek followed them down there to pay the tickets off. They should be pulling up any minute."

3

Mills took a seat on the steps next to Nesh, and sat there quietly. Mills cherished the ground Nesh walked on. He promised himself that one day she would be his. Mills thoughts were quickly smothered by the thoughts of him becoming a hustler. Nesh broke the silence by saying, "Mills, I don't know why you over there being quiet with yo bad self, and I saw what you did today."

Mills was known for being quiet. All the old heads and hustlers called him a sponge, because he just sat around soaking up all the juice they spat out. They all knew he was going to be a hell of a hustler one day.

"Mills, why you be running around with Buck anyway? I mean he like my big brother, I love him to death, and I appreciate everything he did for me, my sister, and my mother when she was living, but he's into things you're too young to be around, and he's hot too." Nesh continued to question Mills.

"C'mon Nesh, I be around Buck cause that's my big bro, and just like he take care of you and your family, he take care of me and mine. I'll do anything for my bro. He take care of this whole neighborhood, he makes sure everybody gets some money in they pocket, and although he does things around me that aren't good, he teaches me a lot of things. He holds the whole hood down Nesh."

"Whatever Mills, that's what wrong with D-Rocs stupid butt, running around trying to be like Buck, calling himself holding the hood down." Nesh said referring to her boyfriend, who was Buck's lil homie. Nesh was game tight for a fourteen year old young lady, but she's been around the game since she was born. Her mother was a dope fiend that died from an overdose. Her sister has been dealing drugs since she was Nesha's age, and on top of all that, she's been living with Buck for the last 5 years. Buck made it his duty to school everyone he allowed in his life to the game.

Not that he wanted everybody to become a drug dealer, but just that he related everything that had to do with life to the game. When he spoke of the educational system, he related to the game in a sense that, he felt the educational system taught children how to become an employee, instead of an employer, where as the game taught one how to conduct business, how to operate their own establishment and employ workers instead of becoming employed.

He said that all the educational system was good for was math and history. Math, so one could count their own paper and history, so one could know the real from the fake where the black nation and our ancestry concerned. He always got real emotional when talking about African history. He said schools portrayed black people as frivolous slaves with frivolous civilizations and culture. When in fact, the black nation had one of the most advanced civilizations, culture, and upbringing. The Egyptians, known as the ancient kemitians (which means people of the black land) were some of the most intelligent people in the world. They mastered mathematics, science, medicine, philosophy, and created the first system of salvation. He said that black people were in a wealth race with other diversity groups. He said that the black nation only owned one half of one percent of the world's economical assets, while Caucasians own 80 percent and the Jews, Hispanics, Asians, and Arabs control the remainder of the 20 percent. He would go on for hours when speaking about the history of blacks.

Mek and Buck pulled up as Mills and Nesha's conversation went silent. Buck stepped out his Blazer followed by a cloud of smoke, and Eazy E, screaming fuck the police through his fifteens. He bobbed his bald head while taking one last puff of the blunt he held in his hand and flicked it to the ground. Buck had a bald head which complemented his six foot toned frame, which he knew exposed as he stood shirtless. Buck didn't workout, his body was just one of his blessings from the creator. He did a year in juvy, in which he played a lot of basketball, and did push-ups but that was 4 years ago. Even though he did neither of the two in the last 4 years, his body stayed with him. Buck was only twenty-one, but like his mentor "Tony Keys" he was way beyond his years.

He walked towards the porch while smiling at Mills.

"T-money, C'mere lil bro, you know you saved ya big bro's ass today, right?" Buck said, calling Mills by the nickname he had given him.

Mills dapped it up with Buck before Buck pulled him in for a hug.

"You know I got something real special for you for what you did for me today. We gon shop till we drop ta morrow, iight."

"What's up lil sis?" Buck said speaking to Nesh.

"What's up Buck."

"C'mon lil bro, let's go inside, you tryna smoke a blunt?" Buck asked Mills.

"Nah bro, Momma got dinner ready, I just came to see what Mek wanted and holler at you about something important." Mills replied.

"Aw I told Mek I wanted you here when I got here, I wanted to let you know how much I appreciated you being there for ya big bro today. So what's up, what you wanna talk about?"

"Wont you drive me home bro so that I can make it there on time for dinner, and we can talk on the ride there." Mills suggested. "Aight lil bro, let me grab my car keys."

Buck ran in the apartment, grabbed the keys to his Cadillac Coupe, and hurried back outside. Him and Mills entered the Coupe and quickly pulled from in front of the row of apartments. Buck didn't waste any time finding out what Mills had on his mind.

"Whats happenin T-money, lay it on me.".

"Bro , I'm tryna hustle, I'm ready to get my own money."

Buck looked at Mills as if he were crazy.

"Man you trippin T-money, yo moms and pops ah kill me, not to mention grandma Mills."

"C'mon bro, my mom and pops ah kill you if they knew you had me smoking weed, and you know grandma would lose it, who's gonna tell em anyway? Not me, not you, and if you don't

6

put me down, I'm ah do it on my own anyway, so you might as well walk me through it. C'mon bro; I'm tryna get money."

Mills spoke smoothly, and it bought a smile to Buck's face because he knew Mills had learned it from him.

"Damn T-money, you gone use reverse psychology on ya bro like that. I gotta stop teachin you shit. You got a point though Mills, and if you that determined you leave me no choice, cause I'd never forgive myself if I sat back and let you get fucked around in the game, but understand something Mills, this shit ain't all flowers and teddy bears, this game where ya life is at stake.

Not everybody obtains wealth, and sometimes those who do still lose. Shid just look at ya moms and pops, and ya uncles and all the youngsters out here dying on the strip. I'm ah work wit you, but you gotta promise me that your not gonna make a move without me, until I say you're ready, aight." "Iight bro. I promise not to make a move without you."

As Buck pulled in front of Mills grandmother's house he thought of the mistake he may be making. He thought back to how old he was when Mills father put him in the game. Then he thought about the small-time pimp he used to work for before Mills mother rescued him, and he said to his self, *Better me than some other nigga.*

He looked at Mills for a few seconds before asking him,

"What you do with that bag T-money?"

"I hid it in my closet." Mills responded.

"Aight, don't let grandma Mills see that bag. I'll get it from you when I come through to take you and lil Keys to the mall in the morning." Buck said while holding his fist out for Mills to hit the rock. They dapped it up and Mills entered the house. The following day Mills was up bright and early. The sound of Bucks phone awakened him.

"Ring. Ring. Ring."

"Hello," Buck said with a crackling voice.

7

"Let's go, bro, its time to make it do what it do." Mills replied from the other end.

Buck looked at the clock on the night stand and said,

"Slow down T-money. Its seven O'clock in the morning. The mall don't open till nine."

"Man forget the mall, I'm tryna hit up the block. Like you always say, the early bird get the first worm, and don't nothing come to a sleeper but a dream." Mills shot back with determination.

Buck started laughing, Mill's determination and slick talked amused him.

"T-money chill baby bro, rushing things leaves room for too many mistakes and you know I'm a man of my word and I promised you we would tear da mall up, so that's what we gone do. The game ain't going nowhere. So go head and get you and Jimmy dressed and I'll be there in about two hour's aight?"

"Aight man." Mills said, sounding disappointed.

Mills went through his closet and pulled out one of his favorite outfits. He matched the outfit up with a pair of his slicked Nikes. Then he went into Jimmy's room and did the same for him. He woke his little brother up and escorted him to the bathroom. They brushed their teeth, showered, got dressed, and stood in front of the mirror putting the finishing touches on their tight fades. Mills put a little grease in him and Jim's hair, then gave their heads an equal amount of strokes. A few minutes later, Grandma Mills was yelling their names out telling them that Daylon, which was Bucks real name, was down stairs. Mills ran his hand over Jimmy's waves then told him to go down stairs. When Jimmy took off, Mills ran to the closet, grabbed the paper bag, and stuffed it under his shirt. As he headed down the stairs, he saw Buck lifting Jimmy off his feet saying,

"What's up lil Keys, you looking real fresh boy, you gone drive the girl's crazy." Lil Keys is what Buck calls Jimmy, because he's a spitting image of his father. When Mills 0hopped off the last step, Jimmy was all smiles. "What's up T-money, you ready to roll?"

"Yep." Mills replied.

"You got everything you need?" Buck asked insinuating about the bag.

"Yea I'm ready to roll." Mills said while winking his eye to let Buck know they were on the same page.

All three of them hugged Grandma Mills before walking out the door. Buck gave her a kiss on the cheek and slipped a roll in her pocket, while winking his eye at her. As they walked out the house Grandma Mills said, "Tony, you and Jimmy behave yourselves, and Daylon, take care of my babies."

"Yes ma'am." Mills and Jimmy yelled back, while Buck said,

"They're in good hands Grandma."

After spending a few hours at the mall, Buck took them to McDonalds, before heading home. When he pulled in front of the house, he parked the car and grabbed Jimmy from the backseat. He knew Jimmy wanted to roll with the big boys, so he sat him on his lap and said "Did you have fun?"

"Yep." Jimmy replied

"You better had had fun, wit all that money you had me spending on arcade games." Buck said jokingly. He continued. "Look lil Keys, me and Mills have to go take care of something, but since you been a big boy all day, we gone go to the arcade this weekend, and I'm a kick yo butt in that football game."

As Jimmy smiled at the thought of going back to the arcade, Buck pulled ten dollars out his pocket, handed to jimmy and told him to help Mills carry their bags in the house.

"Hurry up back T-money." Buck said to Mills as he filled his hands with shopping bags. Mills quickly returned. Buck headed for his apartment. It only took a few minutes to get there, since it was right up the street. Although Buck and Tameka slept at the apartment on occasions, they didn't live there. They had a huge three bedroom home on 161, where Nesh stayed with them. Buck pulled his Fleetwood to the curb, killed the engine, and he and Mills entered the apartment.

Buck was a Cadillac lover. He had just about every Cadillac that existed, from Braham to the Deville. Once inside the apartment they rushed by Bucks Pitts, Major Pain, which was a male red nose, and B-N-E, which stands for Bitch Nigga Eater, she was a black Koby with a snow white head. Buck had his dogs trained, they hid in the apartment until they seen who entered. If it wasn't a familiar face, they would jump out of no where and go for the kill.

"Pain! B-N-E! Doors!" Bucked yelled and the beautiful but vicious dogs stood on ground. Major Pain ran to the front door, while B-N-E ran to the back door in the kitchen. Buck and Mills went in the kitchen as well. Buck grabbed a plate, a razor, and a seat at the table next to Mills. He grabbed the brown paper bag from under his shirt, sat it on the table, and extracted a large block of dope from the bag. He popped a smaller block off of it, and put it on the plate. Buck had a half a kilo of cooked crack in the bag. To some people, that would be a large amount, but to Buck, it was crumbs that he looked out for his little homies with. Buck hit the small block, known in the streets as an eight ball, right in the center with the razor, splitting it in half.

He said " Watch me close Mills, cause I'm ah cut this in half up, then you gone cut the other half up."

Buck went to work on the small half. He cut it into a bunch of small rocks. He held one of the stones in his hand and asked,

"How much is this worth?"

Mills quickly responded. "That's a nick." Meaning a nickel piece.

"That's right; this is a five-dollar bop," Buck said. "Why you cut all the five-dollar pieces, what about the dimes, and twenties?" Mills asked.

"I was hoping you asked that question. Dig it though lil bro, this is a trick I learnt when I use to be on the block bustin all nighters. You cut all you work in to nickels, that way you able to look out for the geeks with little money, cause its going to be a lot of custies coming to you with 3 dollars, 5 dollars, and sometimes nothing, and you don't wanna be out there all day tryna bust down a twenty wit cha hands in order to get that small paper, or in order to look out for one of ya loyal customers who down on they luck, and need a piece to get them started ya dig."

"I dig." Mills said with a smileas he soaked up the game.

Buck continued, "If somebody comes for a dime, you give them two nickels, sometimes 3, it depend on how much money they spend with you. If they come for twenty, then you give them four nickels, sometimes 5. Another trick is this, when you put a lot of pieces in a dope fiends hands, they feel like their getting more for their money, than if you just put on stone in they hand."

Buck winked at Mills and said, "Let me see what you know how to do."

Mills grabbed the razor, and quickly went to digging into his half.

"Whoa. Whoa. Whoa, slow down T-money what you rushing for? It's an art to cutting dope, you gotta look at it, spinning it around, find that special spot, and hit that shit just right. If your really good at cutting dope, you'll cut more out of your shit than you suppose to."

Mills listened to Buck's words carefully. He started examining the small block. He spun it around, flipped it a few times and when he thought he found the spot he was looking for, he dug the razor into it , while looking up at Buck.

"Go head T-money, make it do what it do." Buck said reassuring him that he was on the right track. Mills cut his work up like a pro and looked at Buck for further instructions. Buck said, " Aight. Now T-money, what we just cut up was a eight ball, which weighs 3.5 grams you should cut anywhere from 300 to 350 out of an eight ball. So I want you to add all this up and tell me how we did." Mills went to counting the nickels a piece at a time. While he did that, B-M-E took off for the living room at the sound of the front door being tampored with.

Major pain was already hid by the steps, B-N-E tookher hiding place on the side of the couch. When Tameka opened the door, her, Mosh and D-Roc walked in. Major pain and B-N-E both rushed to D-Roc.

"Major pain, B-N-E, doors!" Mek yelled as D-Roc's body went stiff. The dogs went back their positions. Mek yelled for Buck as D-Roc and Nesh went back to arguing.

"I'm in the kitchen baby, who you got wit you?" Buck yelled from the kitchen. Mek stopped in her tracks at the sight of Mills bagging dope.

"Uh, uh, Buck? What is you doin?" Mek said.

"Chill out baby, T-money is a natural. Come over here and give me a kiss." Buck ordered.

Meka walked over and slipped her tongue into his mouth.

"Who is that in the living room?" Buck asked

"Oh that's D-Roc and Nesh. They goin at it again, cause that boy been foolin around with some lil trick." Mek answered.

"A Dee." Bucked Yelled from the kitchen.

"What up big homie." D-Roc yelled back.

"C'mere man."

D-Roc walked into the kitchen shaking his head saying, "Man, yo lil sis is a trip. Why every time a nigga don't call a bit... I mean a female pages back, they automatically assume a nigga is with another bitch."

Buck gave him a look that said: "Slow down that's my lil sister you talking about."

"My bad big homie, but you feel me doe, right?" D-Roc said apologetically.

"No he don't feel you, cause he calls all of his girls pages back." Tameka said answering for Buck.

Buck started laughing as D-Roc gave Mek a look similar to the one he just received from Buck. D-Roc was one of the youngest hustlers on the block. He was young, wild and down for whatever. All the young hustlers ran up under him. He reminded Buck of himself, besides the fact that D-Roc was hard headed.

They both started hustling at the young age of eleven. As Buck laughed, D-Roc turned his attention to him.

"Man this shit ain't funny bro, Nesh gone drive a nigga crazy."

"Stop trippen lil homie, that's the way puppy love goes. Especially when you can't keep ya lil dick in ya pants." Buck replied.

D-Roc started laughing.

"Aw that's how you gone front yo lil bro? It's cool. I got some money for you though." D-Roc pulled out a stack of cash out from his pockets. He put the money on the table and said, "That's what I owe you, and enough for another four and a half ounces."

Buck tossed the money to Mek and said, "Grab Dee, one of those Ikeas out that bag."

Buck had Mills bag his three hundred and thirty dollars in stones in three hundred dollar packs. He told Mills there was no need for him to keep more than a hundred on him at a time for the time being. As D-Roc looked at his work, Buck pushed the plate and the razor in front of him and said,

"Go head and handle ya business Dee. Me and Mills bout to step out front."

"What sup lil Mills, I see you bout to get ya feet wet boy, be careful out there." D-Roc said recognizing the process Buck was taking Mills through, because Buck had took him through the same steps 3 years ago.

Buck tossed Mills two hundred dollar packs to Mek and said, "I'll be out front wit Mills baby." Buck showed Mills how to hide his dope in his draw pocket and then they took off. They walked across the street to one of Buck's loyal dope fiend's house. As they stood in his front yard, Buck saw Lucky walking through the alley on the side of his apartment building. Lucky was a dope fiend who had been on the block since Buck was a youngster. He was the best runner the neighborhood had to offer.

"Ay yo" Buck yelled getting Lucky's attention. As Luck saw Buck, he ran across the street knowing he had a blast coming from buck.

"What's going on Buck, you pitching stones?" Lucky said hoping that he was.

"Nah, I'm out here with my lil bro, I want you to run for em, and watch out for him while he out here on the strip. You take care of him, and he gone take care of you. Ain't that right Mills?" Buck said

"That's right." Mills answered.

"Ain't that Torry and Tony Keys lil boy?" Lucky asked

"Yea, you know he ah natural," Buck answered.

Lucky said, "Aw man. He gone have all the business in no time, his momma and daddy are legends, and you know I'm ah get him rich, the same way I got you where you are now. Shit to think of it, you never thanked me for making you rich."

Buck started laughing at Lucky's humor, though Lucky's words did have some truth to them. Buck told Mills to give Lucky a couple of pieces to get him started. Mills started reaching for his package right out in the open.

"Naw, Naw T-money, don't ever do business out in the open. Yo business is yo business, not show business, feel me?" Buck said. He didn't give Mills a chance to respond before he continued. "Look around you Mills, the police can be anywhere, and they can be behind the houses over there or parked up the street in an unmarked car, shid the police can be any and everywhere. Never handle yo business in the open. Go over there on the other side of the house and get Lucky together."

Mills did as he was told, as Buck stood there joking with Lucky, Mills quickly returned and dropped two dime pieces in Lucky's hand.

"Aight youngster, you just chill, and I'm a show you how to make a million, ask Buck, he know about me," Lucky said as he got excited by the dope in his hand. Lucky took off as quickly as he came. D-Roc's right hand man, Slim, walked up as Lucky walked off.

"What up big homie. What up lil Mills." Slim said greeting them both.

"What's happenin Slim gangsta." Buck replied.

"What's up Slim." Mills added.

D-Roc came walking out of Bucks apartment as Buck talked to Slim.

"Man Nesh a trip, all she wanna do is argue. She always talking about I'm out here fucking this bitch and that bitch, but she ain't given me no play, all she wanna do is kiss and play footsies. Man I know that ya lil sis but I ain't on that shit big homie. I ain't fuckin wit no more virgins, cause they ain't coming off no skins." D-Roc said causing Slim, Buck, and Mills to burst into laughter.

"I told you, you was too advanced for Nesh man, but you kept horn doggin." Slim said while laughing.

"Man y'all niggas laughing and shit, I'm dead serious bro, Nesh the poster girl for blue balls," D-Roc said seriously, not knowing it was more his serious manner, than what he was saying that was so funny. Buck controlled his laughter long enough to throw some game under his lil homies hat.

"I feel you Dee, but if you really knew what you had, you'd put cha sex life on hold for a while, because Nesh is most definitely gone be a qualified woman. She has strong morals and principals, and she understands a hustler's lifestyle, which is uncommon in a lot of females, especially the young ladies in your age group. Nesh is gonna be real successful and you gone miss her when she gone, but I feel you, I was a young nigga before too, so I know how fascinated you've become wit sex, and ya love muscle, but I tell you what, you better strap ya Jimmy up, cause these girls out here is fast as fuck."

Slim cut in before D-Roc could reply. "Ey big homie, I got a couple dollars for you. I need two and a quarter."

"Aight baby that's what I'm talking bout, for a minute I thought you was gone stay on an ounce forever," Buck said kidding with his lil homie.

"Aw yeah big homie. I'm tryna get my money right," Slim shot back.

"Shit, you, Dee, and lil Walt should of been had ya'll paper right, what happened to the spot I had set up for ya'll?" Buck inquired.

"I'm on top of that big homie." D-Roc butted in.

"Yeah I know Dee. You been on top of that for the last month. Maybe if you keep your dick in your pants long enough, or stop shooting up night clubs, you could really get on top of it." Buck said as he headed across the street to his apartment to get Slim's package.

"Keep an eye on Mills till I get back Dee," Buck said before he got too far away. Lucky returned with a lady who wanted a twenty. Mills went on the side of the house and got four stones out of his bag. When he dropped it in the ladies hand, she whispered to Luck,

"Ain't that Torry and Keys boy?"

Mills looked at D-Roc as he stood in the middle of the street with a hand full of rocks in one hand, a blunt in his mouth, a gun on his hip, and a line of customers. Mills said to himself, *D-Roc is doing everything Buck said not to do, but he's getting all the money.*

Buck came walking out the apartment shaking his head at the sight of D-Roc. He handed Slim a baggie, and said, "That's four and a half ounces, just pay me for the extra two when you get done."

"Good looking Buck," Slim replied.

"Don't worry about it baby, we in this together, just get cha money, and go hard, ya dig."

"I dug, and good looking out again big homie," Slim said before walking off to join D-Roc.

"Let's go sit on the porch and smoke a blunt T-money." As they headed for the porch Buck said, "I don't ever wanna see you

16

handling business like D-Roc, that shit don't last long lil bro, dig me."

Mills nodded his head, yes. As they sat on the porch smoking that good green, Nesh stepped outside. She looked at D-Roc in the middle of the street and said, "Look at that stupid boy, he can't even sell dope right, he so stupid."

As Buck laughed at his little sister he saw a cop car bend the corner and yelled out, "A Dee!"

As D-Roc looked at Buck, Buck pointed to the cop car and took off running. The police car tried to pursue him, but the pursuit was to no avail. D-Roc ran through one yard, hopped a fence, cut through another yard, and disappeared right before the cop's eyes.

CHAPTER 2

Buck took control of his and Mek's power hour of afternoon sex. He rolled her over while managing to keep his thick muscle trapped inside her cave. As he plunged deeper into her from the missionary position, she closed her eyes and opened her mouth as if she wanted to scream but couldn't get a sound out. Buck looked down on her beautiful body as she made enticing sex faces.

Mek's 5'8 frame was stacked with accessories. She had a pair of thirty six double D'S with nipples almost the size of tootsie rolls and identical complexion. Her stomach was flat, especially for her 150lbs. Her hips rolled her body and fell right into her heart-shaped ass. Her jet black hair stopped just below her ears, and though Buck was mad that she cut it he had to admit that his lady was rockin that shit out.

Her caramel skin was now covered in sweat as she wrapped her legs around Buck's back while he gave her his full eight and a half.

"Oh Buck, oh shit, I'm coming," Mek yelled while meeting his thrust of his own.

"Damn baby I'm coming too," Buck said, as he felt his manhood blow up inside of her. Meanwhile Mills was posted up on Main and Wilson with D-Roc and Slim. After two months of being under Buck's watch, Mills was finally making moves on his own. As D-Roc took care of one customer, and Slim another, Mills was flagged down by lucky who rode in a car of his big money spenders. Mills left his bike leaned up against the store wall and hopped in the car with Lucky. After a spin around the corner, Mills hopped out of the car and ran up on one of his other customers. The block was booming, and Mills was charged up

18

because school was starting up in a month and he had planned to be the freshest dressed sixth grader in the school. As Mills was serving his customer, he heard D-Rock yell out "hit the dirt!" Mills looked up and saw a white bronco flying up the street with the passenger hanging out the window blasting off rounds.

"Boom! Boom! Boom!"

Mills dove to the ground as D-Roc ran to the middle of the street firing back. Slim stood on the opposite side of the street unloading on the Bronco as well. After the shots ended, D-Roc yelled,

"Get up Mills, and come the fuck on."

D-Roc ran to his 70's cutlass and hopped in the driver's seat, as Slim followed his lead hopping in the passenger's seat. Mills ran for his bike.

"Lil Mills fuck that bike. Get the fuck in the car." D-Roc yelled as he brought the engine to life. Mills looked at the bike one more time and ran to the car. D-Roc sped off while screaming, "Them hoe ass nigga's T bone and Fresh thought we was slippin Slim. We ridin on them north side niggas tonight."

D-Roc was charged up and after being shot at, Mills wondered why he was laughing and turning his music up in celebration. D-Roc pulled up in the back of Buck's apartment. They all exited the car and ran to Bucks back door. D-Roc banged on the door startling Buck. Buck grabbed his 45 Torres and yelled, "Who the fuck is it."

"Its Roc man, hurry up an open the door bro,"

Buck snatched the door opened with B-N-E and Major Payne by his side. D-Roc and Slim stopped in they tracks while Mills blew right passed the dogs, patting them on their heads.

"C'mon man y'all cool?" Buck asked, while snapping his fingers and pointing to the living room, sending the dogs on their way. After locking the door, Buck said "Why da fuck you knocking on the door like the police?"

19

"Man them hoe ass Northside niggas just came through Main and Wilson blasting," D-Roc answered, still hyped up from the shoot out.

"Y'all ain't strapped up?" Buck inquired.

"HELL YEA! Bro you know we don't leave home with out it. We dumped on dem fools. And we riding on them bitch ass niggas tonight."D-Roc said while showing Buck his empty nine millimeter.

"Slow down Dee, what I tell you about using ya head? Them niggas is expecting y'all to come through tonight. They'll be waiting for y'all, and no smart warrior walks into a trap like that, you dig?" Buck said, schooling his little homie.

"I dug, but fuck them Buck. Them niggas in violation coming through our hood like shit sweet, me, Slim, and Lil Walt, got in to it with them niggas at the skating rink last night. They started yelling that Northside, fuck Eastside shit, so we started screaming fuck the north side, this East Main. Then that big nigga, Deuce, walked up and threw some money at us talking bout tell Buck's hoe ass to buy him some. I spit in the nigga's face, and all hell broke loose. Make a long story brief; we shot that bitch up last night." D-Roc said with a smile on his face.

Buck instantly became furious. He hated Deuce just as much as Deuce hated him. Deuce was a north side O.G. He held the same rank out north as Buck held on the east side. T-Bone and Fresh was his lil homies, and right hand man. Buck kept his emotions under control, not wanting to set a bad example for his lil homies, especially Mills.

"Fuck Deuce and the rest of them niggas, Dee. We bout dis money, and we ain't gone let them or any other niggas interfere with our paper. Now you right, them niggas in violation, but there's a time and place for everything, be patient Dee. When the time comes, we gone have them niggas missing, feel me?" Buck said, trying to rationalize with D-Roc.

D-Roc agreed just to end the discussion, but his mind was already made up, him, Slim, and Walt were riding on Deuce and his crew tonight.

"Oh yea Big Homie, me and Slim need some shells, and lil Mills need a strap. Cause you know how crazy shit can be in the hood. Shit if ain't some niggas coming through blastin, you always gotta have that metal for them thirsty ass fiends that be out to rob a nigga." D-Roc said.

Buck looked at Mills. "T-money you aight?"

"Yea I'm cool bro." Mills responded.

Buck reached in the cabinet and grabbed a 32' special and a box of nine shells. He tossed the box of shells to D-Roc, and held the 32' special in front of Mills.

"Now listen Mills, this is not no toy, and it's not for show. If you pull this mutha fucka out, you use it. When you on the block, you put it in a bag, and you hide it somewhere close to you, are you ready for this? If not say so, because this is no toy, this is dangerous, and so is being in the game."

Mills assured Buck that he was ready for this part of the game and that he'd be extra careful. D-Roc and Slim loaded their weapons and headed back to the block. Buck kept Mills behind. He wanted to talk to him a little longer. For the next few days, Mills hustled on the strip doing just as Buck told him to do with his gun. He kept it concealed and knew that the day he would have to expose it, would be the day he would possibly have to take a life. Buck also told him he didn't want him hanging around D-Roc and his crew anymore.

He told Mills that no one man could accomplish great things alone. That he would one day have to form his own team. He knew Buck would feel that his friends weren't ready for the game, but if he was going to formulate a team, he couldn't think of any better draft pick than his friends who he's been down with him from day one.

21

"I got ya'll bro, but we gone slow roll it, cause I go run this move by Buck, but this is what we gone do, Pee. I'm ah let you hold the work while I sell it, and Fill, I'm ah let you hold this. To protect us while we out here getting money"

Mills pulled the 32 special from his waist and held it in front of Fella.

"Shawn Shawn , you cant be apart of this yet, you really too young, I know for sure Buck ain't gone approve of you getting down yet, but don't trip , cause when we go shoppin you gone shop wit us, and while we getting this money you gone roll wit us, so you can learn the game, like I did with Buck, its sorta like school outta school" Mills said.

Mills knew that Peko and Shawn Shawn were a two for one package. Although Shawn Shawn was two years younger. He and Peko did everything together. Their mom was struggling and her pay check barely paid the bills. Their father died in a bank robbery that ended in a shootout with the police. Fella, on the other hand, was an only child. His mother made it off her welfare checks and a lil hustling on the side. Fella position was slightly better than Peko and Shawn Shawn, but he was a product of the struggle as well.

Mills at least had Buck; his friends were on their own. Mills promised himself that he and his friends would be the flyest in Mohawk Middle School this year.

"Pee an Fells, I'm a pay ya'll for ya'll positions and we all gonna get money. After y'all know everything ya'll need to know about this game, then I'll get y'all own pack, and we can all do our thang together, but we gotta promise each other to stay loyal to one another, and never allow anything to come between us. None of that arguing over money, girls, like D-Roc and them, iight? "

" Iight" they all said in unison.

"Now let's say it together all at once." Mills said.

"Say what?" Fella asked.

"Just repeat after me." Mills answered

"I promise to stay loyal to this family and never allow anything to come between us."

Mills lead them with words, and they followed his verbal lead. From that day on they were inseperable. They hustled hard for a month straight and when school started they made jaws drop with their attire. Things were going so smoothly that Mills had forgotten to run things by Buck. Mills had slowed down with going on the Strip and started bringing money from the Strip to Mound and Berkley where he and his crew chilled at. Mills, Fella, and Peko, were turning Berkley into a strip of its own. The whole time creating a block to call their own as Buck did with Liley and Main. Like Buck, of course, Mills had Lucky to thank him for a lot of him and his crew's success. After school, one day Mills received a page from Buck. He looked at his pager and noticed Buck's code, with 911 behind it. Buck was worried about Mills. He saw Mills just about everyday, because Mills still had Buck holding all his money for him, but Buck was curious as to where Mills was making his money at.

Seeing as how nobody ever saw him on the Strip anymore. Mills called Buck back immediately.

"Ring, Ring, Ring."

"Hello," Buck said.

"What up big bro, this T-money." Mills said.

"Where you at?"

"On Mound and Berk." Mills answered.

"C'mon on around here and see me, I need to speak with you," Buck ordered.

"I'm on my way." Mills said before they disconnected. Mills thought this would be as good a time as any to fill Buck in on Fella and Peko's position, so he told them to roll with him to see Buck. When they arrived, Buck was standing in front of his apartment with D-Roc, Slim, and Lil Walt. D-Roc stood off to the side, arguing with Nesh as usual.

"What up big bro," Mill said to Buck.

"What up T-money, what's up lil Fella and Peko," Buck responded.

"Sup big homie." Peko and Fella replied.

"Walk with me Mills." Buck ordered as he strolled up the street. Mills followed behind him. Buck slowed up until he and Mills were side by side.

"Where da fuck you been at T-Money." Buck said, seriously concerned.

"What you mean bro?" Mills asked in return.

"Why you ain't been on the Strip or right here on Liley?" Buck responded.

Mills explained his relocation to Mound and Berkley, along with his new recruits. Buck was impressed with Mills leadership. He knew Mills was a natural, but he didn't think he would create his own block from the ground up, and in all actuality Mills didn't think of it, it just sort of happened, and he stuck with it. Buck didn't like the idea of Fella and Peko being in the game. He looked at them as two bad lil niggas who stole shit and stayed in trouble. He knew they had heart and would one day elevate to the Strip, but he just didn't think they were ready yet. Mills convinced him that they were, and Buck said, "Aight T-Money, I'm a let you make this decision on your own, cause I believe in a man's ability to make good decisions apart of what prepares him for the obstacles that life will throw at him, but don't ever make a move like that again without at least talking to me about it, and know that I won't sell them anything until I know they're ready. All their business will go through you."

Mills accepted the terms and promised to inform him beforehand next time. They walked back up the street, joining the rest of the crew. Fella was talking to his cousin Slim, while Peko awaited Mills return. D-Roc had done enough arguing with Nesh. He left her sitting on the porch, while he joined the fellas.

"What up lil Mills" D-Roc said.

"What up Roc." Mills shot back.

D-Roc looked at Peko "What up lil P, what's up with your lil fat ass Fella." Then D-Roc told his crew lets roll out. Slim and Walt dapped it up with Buck said peace to Mills and his crew and then they all loaded up in D-Roc's car. Lil Walt was really from Gilbert and Mound, but he's been hanging out with D-Roc ever since his main homie Black got locked up. Lil Walt and Black would hook up with D-Roc and Slim on occasions. Lil Walt was crazy; he was only thirteen and had at least three bodies under his belt. He barred none, and loved drama more than anyone. As Buck had his talk with Fella and Peko, Mills joined Nesh on the porch. "What's up Mills?" Said Nesh.

"You." Mills replied.

"What?" Nesh responded as she was caught off guard by Mills response.

"You what's up, Nesh. You always been what's up and when I get a little older, I'm a make you mine, watch and see." Mills said with confidence.

Nesh was blushing; she couldn't believe Mills was coming onto her. She had Mills by four years and no matter how handsome he was or how grown he portrayed to be, he was a child. Nesh laughed and said, "Stop playin boy, you know you is too young, who told you to say that, Buck?"

"Nah. Buck ain't tell me to say nothing. I've always had a crush on you, I just never said anything because of our age difference, but I'm telling you Nesh, you better wait on me, cause I know how to treat you."

Mills was usually quiet; Nesh couldn't believe the words coming out of his mouth. She thought his little crush was cute, so she played along.

"Oh you know how to treat me, huh? Tell me how I want to be treated then Mills?"

"Like a queen is how you need to be treated, because that's what you are to me, but I can tell you one thing, I will never treat you like D-Roc does." Buck walked up as Mills stunned Nesh with his response.

"I'm done speaking with Fella and Peko, like I told them, y'all stay tight and grounded on loyalty. I'm bout to go in, y'all wanna come in and smoke something?" Buck asked.

"Nah bro, we gotta get back to the block, it's money to be made you dig?" Mills said, hitting Buck with his own words.

Buck started laughing, because he recognized himself in Mills.

"I dug, get yo money lil bro, and call me later Aight. Buck said proudly.

"Aight." Mills replied.

Before leaving, Mills looked at Nesh and said,

"For real Nesh, wait on me."

She laughed as Mills walked off with his boys. The next day Mills school was shattered by the sound of Walt's twelve gauge. As students dove to the ground, Walt hung out the window dumping on some guys him, D-Roc, and Slim had beef with from Livingston Ave. The guys were caught off guard, but there reflexes allowed them to fire. One of Walt's slugs hit one of its targets. The boy lay on the ground shaking as blood leaked from his mid-section. Mills, Fella, Peko, and Brandy, received cold stares as they walked home. Everyone knew they were from Main Street and Walt was screaming Main Street as he unloaded the shotgun. That made Mills and his crew just as much of an enemy as D-Roc, Walt and Slim were. Mills knew he may have adopted some enemies by being on the block with D-Roc and his crew for these couple of months, so he already brought his gun to school with him, having Brandy hold it in her locker.

He hoped he wouldn't have to use it, but if it came down to one of them, or one of his, he wouldn't hesitate. Mills and his crew had also made enemies unknowingly just by the way they dressed. They wore the flyest gear in the school. Everything from, Guess, Used & Damaged to Cross Color, Karl Kani, and Exhaust. They also flossed Triple Fat Goose, and MCM leathers. They were saucy for sure.

Fella, and Peko did a little mingling mostly with some females, taking advantage of their fame, but Mills didn't socialize at all. He paid the females no attention and the guys were non-existent to him. The only person Mills talked to other than Fella, and Peko was Brandy. Brandy stayed next door to Fella on Berkley. She was beautiful, but to him, she was just one of the guys. She was a true tomboy. She wanted to get down on her hustle with Mills, Fella, and Peko, but Mills turned her down. He let her roll with them in the hood sometimes though. She would hold his pack for him, while he was on the block, and often times kept some of his money and extra dope at her house, because Mills was afraid his grandmother would find it. A lot of people thought they were a couple but, they were just really cool. Mills wasn't thinking about girls, except for Nesh and Brandy wasn't thinking of guys either. Mills didn't want to beef or party. He just wanted to get money.

The school was closed for a couple of days after the shooting. The boy who felt Walt's twelve gauge slug had lived, but he would be paralyzed from the waist down. When the school did open up, D-Roc, Walt, and Slim frequently came to school to start trouble, only making things worse for Mills and his crew. The guys envy for Mills and his crew deepened, while the girly's lust grew.

By Mills eleventh birthday and the middle of the school year, Mills and his crew were public enemy number one. Outside of school, Mills had problems as well. His grandmother was becoming suspicious of his behavior. Mills ran in and out of the house and started staying out way past his curfew. She was also suspicious of all the new things he had accumulated. He and his little brother's wardrobe had become very exspensive. Mills spoiled his little brother.

He brought him every video game and more clothes than he could wear. He hated that he spent little to no time with his little brother, but Jimmy really couldn't roll with him now that he hustled. Mills vowed never to let his little brother fall victim to the streets. He would make sure Jimmy never wanted for anything; that way he would not need to hustle. Mills was stopped by his grandmother on the way out the door.

"Tony. You hold up just a minute; I need to speak to you." She yelled from the kitchen. Mills stopped in his tracks.

"Boy you been doing a lot of running in and out this house lately, coming in past ya curfew, and popping up with all kinds of clothes, shoes, videogames, and carrying on. I know you ain't in them streets selling that stuff.".

"No ma'am. Momma you know Buck takes care of us, he buys us everything. Why would I have to sell that stuff?" Mills said, lying to his grandmother.

It hurt him to lie to her, but he couldn't tell her the truth, and he refused to stop hustling.

"You better not boy, cause God don't like ugly, and this is a house of the Lord, and I wont have the devil or the devil's belongings in my house. Do you hear me, Tony?"

"Yes Ma'am"

"Alright now, go on where you were headed, but be back in here on time tonight. You done missed your mother's call three days in a row. Don't you miss it tonight, you hear?"

"Yes Ma'am." Mills said on his way out the door.

"Oh my Lord sweet Jesus." Grandmother Mills said under her breath on her way to the kitchen. Mills headed back to the block with the thought of him lying to his grandma on his mind. He not only lied to her about not selling drugs, but he also had money and drugs hid in her house. Buck told him it was time for him to start managing his money. He told Mills he wanted him to take half of his money and work home with him. Mills had a stash of money and work hid in a shoebox in his closet. The fact that he had over twenty shoe boxes in his closet made the hiding place perfect. Mills figured he could at least take the drugs out of his grandmother's house.

He'd keep his drugs at Brandy's house, where he already kept part of them. The next day at school, Mills stood at Brandy's locker talking to her about moving his drugs over to her house. Of course she was game. Brandy was down for anything and Mills had become the brother she never had. While Mills and Brandy conversed between classes, Mills was approached by Shawn'tae. Shawn'tae, was in the eighth grade, which is a couple grades higher than Mills. She's one of the fastest females in the school, meaning she had a lot of sexual experience. She was also from the neighborhood of the guys D-Roc, Slim, and Walt had beef with. Mills knew Shawn'tae liked him because she always made little remarks whenever he was in hearing distance. Mills always paid her no attention like he did all the other girls who dug his style.

"What up Mills? Can I get you to come to my party?" Shawn'tae asked while handing him a flyer. Mills looked at the flyer and said, "I don't know Shawn'tae, parties ain't really my cup of tea."

"C'mon Mills, you know I like you, why you be acting like you scared of me? You ain't scared of pussy are you?" Shawn'tae said bluntly.

Mills hated having his courage put on Front Street. Although he was a virgin, he wasn't scared of pussy or anything else.

"T-Mills ain't scared of shit. Definitely not no pussy, you just be around niggas I know don't like me, so how I know you ain't tryna set me up, ya dig?" Mills shot back.

"Mills…I'm not tryna set you up. I'm more like tryna sex you up, but if you think I'm too much for you, I understand." Shawn'tae shot back seeing that Mills didn't like being called scared.

"I'll tell you what Shawn'tae, my pager number is 456-3600. You hit me up, and we will see where it goes." Mills said bringing the conversation to an end. Brandy rolled her eyes at Shawn'tae, as she walked off, hoping she could get her to say something smart so that she could kick her ass. Peko and Fella walked up at the end of the conversation. They dapped it up with Mills on the way to class, while joking with him about Shawn'tae being too much for him.

Later that day Mills, Peko, Fella, Brandy, and Shawn Shawn were posted up on Main and Berkley in front of the corner store. Mills pager went off and he didn't recognize the number. The number was followed by the code 69 which was also foreign to Mills. As Peko and Fella jumped in and out of cars, Mills went to use the payphone to call the number back. "Ring! Ring! Ring!"

"Hello?" Shawn'tae said answering her phone.

"Yeah, who dis?" Mills responded, although he knew exactly who it was because she was the only female besides Brandy, with his cell number.

"You called ma house, so who is dis?" Shawn'tae said sarcastically

"This T-Mills, somebody over there call a pager?"

"Damn Mills, you don't recognize a bitch's voice? This Shawn'tae."

"Aw. What's up Baby girl?" He replied smoothly.

"You what's up, I was hoping you could come over and keep me company while ma moms at work unless you scared to be in a house alone with me." Shawn'tae said knowing how to press Mills buttons.

"I told you before Baby girl, Young Mills ain't scared of shit. Where you live?"

Shawn'tae smiled at the thought of Mills coming to see her.

"1206 Oakwood. Don't be playing with me Mills." She warned.

"Damn. You right in the middle of them niggas huh?" Mills said, referring to the adversaries he'd adopted from his involvement with D-Roc.

"Mills, ain't nobody thinking about them niggas and them niggas don't be at my house, they be all the way down the street." Shawn'tae said getting angry at the thought of Mills not coming.

"Dig, I'll be over there in about a half-hour. I hope you ain't on no bullshit for the both of our sake." Mills said giving her a fair warning.

"Mills, chill out, I ain't on that type of shit." Shawn'tae replied seriously.

"Aight Baby girl, I'll be der in a minute."

They disconnected.

"Who was you talking to, bro?" Fella asked while offering Mills a blunt. Mills grabbed the weed and took a few puffs before answering.

"Man that was that lil freak Shawn'tae. I'm bout to go by her crib."

"Man you know that bitch stay on the same street a lot of them niggas hustle on, right?" Peko said joining the conversation.

"Yeah I know that, how'd you know that nigga?" Mills said playfully.

"Her address was on the flyer she passed out for her party next week." Peko answered.

"Man fuck that bro, you want us to roll with you?" Fella asked as he gripped the baby nine on his waist.

"Nah I'm cool bro. I got the other burner, but I'm a need y'all to come scoop me up when its time to leave."

"Aight bro just hit me up and we will be there with magician speed, and magical quickness." Brandy and Peko yelled out in unison with Fella, all of them mocking Buck's saying. They all busted out in laughter. Mills flagged one of his customers down as he drove by slowly. He grabbed his 32 special from Brandy and hopped in the car telling the driver where he needed a ride to. As the car neared Oakwood, Mills pulled on his hoody and gripped his gun. He saw a pack of boys all in front of the store hustling. When the car turned on Oakwood, Mills saw the faces of a few of the boys from his school as they stared into the car. None of them noticed Mills if they did they didn't show it. Shawn'tae stayed four blocks away from the store. Mills told the driver not to pull off until he gave him the signal. Mills hopped up the stairs that lead to Shawn'tae's door. He knocked three hard times. Without asking who it was, Shawn'tae yanked the door open. Mills peered into the house as she stood there with the door wide open.

She had on a pair of daisy duke shorts on, that exposed the bottoms of her cheeks, a halter top that pressed tightly up against her breast, and exposed her flat stomach. She stood in a pair of footy socks, with a pink ball hanging from the back, which matched her halter top and the bandana she had tied around her ponytail. Shawn'tae's body was banging, and she had a beautiful face to compliment it.

"Are you coming in? Or do you see something you don't like?" Shawn'tae said as she saw his eyes shoot right pass her into the house.

"Ain't nobody in here boy, gosh." Mills threw his hand up to the driver as he walked in the house.

"You wanna smoke then?" Mills asked as he finally let his eyes take in her beautiful body.

"Roll it up, nigga."

They sat on the couch smoking some good weed, and holding small talk for almost half an hour. Shawn'tae being the more experienced one took control of the situation. She caressed his thigh until she felt his half-hard penis. She was satisfied with what she felt, so she unzipped his pants and pulled his manhood out. She flicked her tongue at his penis a few times, making him fully erect. She stared at his seven inches of steal and thought, *This lil nigga packing to only be eleven years old,*

Shawn'tae was only fourteen, but she had slept with a number of eighteen-year-olds, so she knew a good size penis when she saw one. She helped Mills out of his coat and clothes. Mills layed his 32 special beside him on the couch and his gangsterism only turned her on more. When she removed her clothes, Mills became so hard; his pole started to throb. Shawn'tae was more intrigued with his two and a quarter inches of girth than she was his length. She slid a condom on to his manhood and pushed him back on the couch. She slid down on his pole and rode him like a wild bull. She moaned "Oh Mills; you got a big dick for a lil nigga."

Mills not knowing what to do just sat there and let her ride herself into an orgasm. She stood up and bent over and guided Mills pole into her cave from the back. Mills slowly went in and out of her, watching her womanhood swallow the full length of his manhood.

"Faster Mills faster." She said in between heavy breaths.

Mills started pushing in her and pulling out of her at a fast pace, and she screamed his name while yelling

"Yes, right there Mills don't stop." Mills dug as deep as he could go before his knees buckled from his first nut. He could barely hold his self up as Shawn'tae continued to back her thang up. After fifteen minutes of sex, Mills was weak. He and Shawn'tae got dressed, and Mills paged Fella. Fella called back immediately. Mills and Shawn'tae smoked a blunt while Mills waited for his ride. When Mills heard a knock at the door, he gripped his pistol, while peeking through the curtains, on to the porch. He gave Shawn'tae the go head to open the door, as he saw Fella standing on the porch. From that day on, having sex with Shawn'tae was an everyday thing with Mills.

CHAPTER 3

A whole year had passed. Mills, Fella, Peko, and Brandy were all ending their seventh grade year, while Shawn Shawn was nearing his sixth. Brandy and Shawn Shawn were hustling as well, and along with Mills, Fella, and Peko they had made Berkley a major money making strip. All of them were sitting at Lisa's smoking on some good green.

Brandy and Shawn Shawn are watching Peko and Fella play college football on the Sega genesis, while Mills takes care of a customer in the kitchen. Lisa was a smoker that had stayed on Berkley for years. She practically watched Mills and his crew grow up. She staid a few houses down from Brandy on the opposite side of the street, and now that the kids she watched grew up are in the game, she's allowing them to sell drugs out her house, as long as they keep her full of crack of course.

As Mills and his crew got their hustle on, Mills grandmother was at home acting on her suspicion. She was in Mill's room going through his dresser drawers and every other hiding spot she could think of. She made her way from his dresser to under his mattress to his closet. She searched all pockets of his coats and clothes, while wondering why her grandson kept a closet full of empty shoe boxes.

"Ooh Lord my Jesus, my arthritis is killing me and this boy got enough clothes to open a clothing store." She said while wiping sweat from her forehead. While wiping the perspiration from her face, she knocked some of the shoeboxes over. As they fell to the ground, money rolls poured out of them. She laid her eyes on all the money and immediately went to talk to her God.

"Jesus oh my Lord Jesus. I knew it, I knew it, I knew it, that boy done bought the devil in your house."

She went straight to the phone and paged Mills. Mills was now sitting now sitting in the recliner puffing on a fat blunt, listening to Fella and Peko crack jokes on one another.

"Pee I'm busting yo skinny ass. You can't fuck wit me, bro." Fella yelled out as if Peko was in the other room instead of next of him.

"You got me fucked up bro, wit yo fat ass; somebody give his pudgy ass an Oreo. I'm bout to come right back at you, wit this play-action pass."

Mills, Brandy, and Shawn Shawn all bursted out laughing as they verbally attacked one another. Mills laugh faded as he looked at his pager and saw his grandmothers number followed by 911. He grabbed the phone and walked into the kitchen, to avoid the noise. His grandmother told him to come home immediately with out explaining why.

Mills was thrown off, but he left on the spot.

"A yo. I'm bout to run to the crib, momma trippin bout something, I'll be right back, ya'll hold it down." He said before walking out the door. When Mills walked in his grandmother's house, his heart dropped. His grandmother was standing in the middle of the living room with his shoe box full of money in her hand.

"What's this Tony? I guess Daylon gave you this too, huh?" She said as she held the box in front of him.

"Momma I can…"

"I don't wanna hear it. You brought the devil in my house and lied to my face. God don't like ugly and this IS ugly as it gets. I want it out and I want it out now! You wanna be grown and run the streets? Well I'm a tell you like I told your mother, I can't watch what you do in them streets and I wont lock you in the house like some prisoner, but I wont have the devil in or around my home, now get this box and get IT out of here!!"

"Momma I'm sorry for lying, but I…"

"I don't want to hear it, Tony, you gone learn the hard way like yo momma and daddy, money ain't the rock of evil, it's the love for the money that's the demonic." She slowly strolled out of the living room, talking under her breath about her arthritis and diabetes. Mills got straight on the phone and called Buck. Buck arrived within ten minutes. Mills hurried out to the car and Buck quickly pulled off.

"Damn T-money, how you let momma Mills find ya stash? What she say? Do she know I had anything to do with it?" Buck asked one question after another, leaving no time for Mills to answer any of them.

"Damn bro slow down, you ain't giving me a chance to answer the first question." Mills said

"Aight I feel you lil bro, but if momma Mills find out I'm the one giving you drugs to sell, she'll never forgive me and I ain't even got to tell you how ya moms and pops gonna react." "Just chill big bro, she don't know where I got the shit from, she didn't even ask, she just flipped out, and said she wants it out her house." Mills explained.

"Okay so what all did she say?" Buck asked.

Mills did his best impersonation of momma Mills for Buck.

"God don't like ugly, Lord sweet Lord, Blazah blah, skip, and carrying on."

They both bursted into laughter as they headed for Buck's home on 161. When they pulled into the driveway, Buck told Mills to put his blunt out until they got inside, because he didn't want his neighbors in his business. Once they entered, Mek was yelling Buck's name from the kitchen. Mills took a seat on the couch next to Nesh, who was on the phone with her one and only home girl Tasha.

"Whats going on Mills." Nesh said as she ended her call.

"Nothing much. What's up with you?" Mills replied after putting fire back to the blunt he put out in the car. Buck came walking out of the kitchen just in time to help Mills finish the blunt.

"Damn T-Money, let me smoke with you like I cope wit you." Mills quickly passed the blunt, while laughing at his slick one liner. In between puffs, Buck said "You want me to grab the rest of ya paper, so you can see what…" He took two more puffs from the blunt before finishing. "You workin wit?"

"Yeah." Mills replied knowing his paper was shorter than it should be because of his shopping habits. Buck ran upstairs and quickly returned with a shoebox, to watch the one Mills held on his lap.

"Whatever you got in this box you should have in that box if you been following your plan. Half at momma Mills and a half here wit me."

Mills smiled at Buck's look knowing that Buck knew him like the back of his hand. Mills emptied Buck's box out first and counted his money up. He had forty-five hundred dollars which meant he should have an identical amount in his shoe box. When Mills finished counting the money in his box, he had seventy five hundred dollars total.

"Damn T-money, what you done spent fifteen hundred dollars on?" Buck asked as he calculated the differences. Mills looked at his Cross Color outfit, his Deion Sanders edition Nikes, and smiled. Buck said "Listen T-money, hard work deserves a reward, so I ain't gone beat yo ears up about yo spending habits, but know that after you reward ya'self its time to grind harder. So let's tighten up. Aight?"

"We on the same page bro." Mills replied.

"And let me ask you something, why you spending money on new threads for ya self, what you done bought lil Keys?"

"C'mon big bro, you know I'm not gone buy me something and not buy lil Jim nothing. I was raised better than that." Mills replied seriously.

Buck smiled, knowing that he played a big part in raising Mills. Nesh sat on the couch fascinated by how fast Mills was growing up. She had to admit to herself, that if he was a year or two older, she would surely take a chance with him. He was smooth, way beyond his twelve years, and she liked the way he carried himself. Nesh wasn't the only person who notice that Mills was up and coming. His name was starting to hold a little weight in the hood as well. Not only was Mills name starting to hold weight, but the name of his strip was too, and G.I. Boys wanted a piece of the pie.

The G.I. Boys were a crew of boys from Gary, Indiana. They had adopted that name since they arrived in Columbus a couple months ago. They instantly started making a name for themselves with their fancy cars and their cheap dope prices. D-Roc, Slim, and Lil Walt, brought the beef their way as soon as they migrated from across the bridge to Main Street. Although Buck was the hood's boss, D-Roc felt that he owned the turf, because Buck no longer in any work. So whenever the hood was violated, or whenever D-Roc felt it was, he did whatever it took to defend the turfs honor.

It is now only three weeks into the summer. Mills was standing on the porch as the G.I. Boys make their first move for his turf. He watched Spider, Man-Man, and lil Timmy stand on the corner of Mound and Berkley attempting to short stop his customers. As the dope fiend refused Spider's dope, and tried to by pass him on his way to Mills spot, Man-Man hits the fiend in his jaw knocking him to the ground. Before Spider and lil Timmy could get to stomping the fiend out, he bounced up and started running.

"These niggas got me fucked up," Mills said to him self, then yelled in the house telling his crew to strap up and hurry out side.

They all grabbed their pistols and ran out the front door. Mills told them what happened and started giving orders.

"Fella, you cross the street, cut through Brandy's yard, and start walking up Mound. Pee, you cut through Lisa's back yard, and come walking up Mound in the opposite direction. Shawn Shawn, you hop on the bike in the front yard, and ride right pass them niggas and go up the street and tie your shoe. Brandy, you call Buck and tell him to hurry over here. I'm a pull down on these niggas."

Everybody besides Brandy took off.

"C'mon Mills let me roll, I ain't afraid to bust my gun, stop treatin me like I'm some scared little girl." Brandy pleaded.

"Aight Bee, call Buck then follow me up the street, but you come up the opposite side. I don't want em to know we're together, and if I go down you better not hesitate." Mills ordered.

Mills took off. He walked up on the G.I. Boys and said,

"Look homie, I don't know what y'all think ya'll doing. But ya'll got the wrong strip for that shit, now I'm asking y'all nicely to get gone."

Mills had his hand on his nine that he kept in his back pocket, but Lil Timmy beat him to the draw. As Spider spoke up, Lil Timmy pulled out his own nine out.

"Lil nigga you betta get the fuck outtah here before you get hurt. We taking this strip over." Spider said with authority.

"Yea bitch ass nigga." Timmy added. Brandy crept up the opposite side of the street, and once she spotted Little Timmy's gun, she started blasting. "Boom! Boom! Boom!" The G.I. Boys were caught off guard. Lil Timmy turned for a split second to locate the shooter, and Mills pulled out his nine. "Boom! Boom! Boom!" Lil Mill's hit Timmy twice in the gut. Spider and Man-Man were drawing their weapons, as they faded away. Fella and Peko ran at Spider and Man-Man gunning. Spider faded away, as did Mills and they exchanged bullets. Spider aired the strip out unloading on everyone in sight. Man-Man ran into Shawn Shawn's 380. "Blowl! Blowl! Blowl!" Shawn Shawn hit Man-Man in the shoulder and gut. Man-Man ducked, covered the hole in his stomach, and took off running in the opposite direction.

He squeezed off a few shots without aiming. Spider took off through Peko's yard, while Mills continued to gun at him. Spider didn't make it far, he ran right into Buck, D-Roc, Slim, and lil Walt on the next street over. Man-Man thought he was home free when he lost Shawn Shawn, but Peko and Fella brought those thoughts to an end. Man-Man fell to the concrete and died instantly from several gunshot wounds. Mills and his crew stood over lil Timmy's crawling body. His gun lay a few feet away as he made a small trail of blood. Fella being the live wire was pumped up.

"Fuck this nigga, Mills."

And before Mills could respond, Fella shot little Timmy in his face. Buck pulled up in his all-black conversion van as the sirens grew louder. Slim slid the side door open, and D-Roc yelled,

"Hurry the fuck up and get in the van."

They all climbed in, and Buck quickly sped off. The street filled up with cops in no time. Detective Brown and White went door to door hoping to find a cooperative witness. They filled the scene with yellow tape and covered the bodies with white sheets. After deep scrutiny, they discovered Spider's body a block away sprawled out on the sidewalk. Detectives Brown and White were furious they couldn't get anyone to cooperate. They knew someone had to see the shooters; after all, there were over fifty shots fired.

The neighborhood asshole, Pac man, who happened to be a cop, already had his mind made up that Buck was involved in it, and if Buck was involved, so was D-Roc, Mills and their crews, as far as Pac man was concerned. Pac man relayed his thoughts to the detectives. They were also very familiar with Buck. The police and feds have been trying to build a case on Buck for years, but he moved too quiet and kept his circle tight. Buck pulled the van into Knights Inn Hotel. He purchased a room with his fake I.D. then he disposed of it. Once inside the Hotel, Buck called his homie Stone and told him that he had some garbage for him to take out. Stone knew exactly what Buck was referring to.

He told Buck he would be there in fifteen to twenty minutes. Stone was a technician with guns of all sorts. He cleaned, broke down and got rid of all weapons. He grabbed the trash bag out the trash can, wrapped the guns inside the hotel towels, and stuffed them in the bag.

"Listen, I don't want nobody to leave this room for a couple of days, don't use the phone or none of that shit. Just chill, I'm bout to get rid of the guns and make some calls to the hood, to see if anybody talked to the police. Ya'll keep ya'll eyes on the news, and wait on my page. Y'all know the hood live by the code of silence, and I do too much for everybody over there, so I doubt if anybody talked to the cops. I just want y'all to lay low, just to be safe."

As Buck gave out orders, Stoned arrived. He and Buck left together. Stone took the guns and him and Buck took off in separate vehicles. Two days had passed and no phone call from Buck. Everybody in the Hotel was becoming aggravated. Peko and Shawn Shawn laid across one bed, while Mills and Brandy occupied the other. Mills sat up, while Brandy was stretched across the king sized bed.

Fella sat at the table with D-Roc, Slim, and lil Walt smoking on some good green. While everybody's mind was on the crime, D-Roc was thinking about Brandy and if she was having sex yet.

"Whats up lil Brandy, when you gon let me open that lil thing up?" D-Roc said.

"WHAT!"

"I'm saying baby, its bout time you let Roc pop that cherry."

"D-Roc I don't know who you think your talking to like that, I ain't one of them lil bitches you be fucking wit. You better check ya'self nigga!".

"My bad baby, I do need to treat the ladies with more respect. So can I please open that little thang up?" D-Roc replied sarcastically.

Slim and Walt busted out laughing.

"Roc man you silly as fuck. Leave lil Brandy alone." Slim said in between laughs.

Brandy snapped at "D-Roc I don't know who the fuck you think you are. You got yo home boys fooled, but I know you can't fight a lick, so you betta save that shit before I open yo ass up."

"You lil bitch you better recognize who you talking to before I beat yo lil red ass in here." D-Roc said seriously.

"Bitch? Nigga, you the bitch." Brandy said firmly.

D-Roc jumped up, but slim grabbed him.

"C'mon Roc, chill out bro, she still a baby." D-Roc looked at Slim like he was crazy, but because Slim was his closet home boy he main'tained his composure. Brandy jumped to her feet as well. Mills finally heard enough.

"Bee chill the fuck out, you trippin Roc, we in here looking at a triple homicide, and y,all bugging out on each other, I told you we ain't about all that talking shit anyway Bee." Mills said with authority. His words only infuriated D-Roc more.

"Lil Mills you better watch who the fuck you talking to lil homie, I ain,t one of ya lil soldiers, so you can save that Buck routine, cause you ain't running shit and I ain't about no talking either lil nigga. You know how Roc get down!" D-Roc said loud enough for the neighbors to hear. Mills didn't respond, but that didn't stop D-Roc. "Y'all lil niggas start getting a little money and start getting besides y'all self. I ran that mutha fucking strip. I let y'all lil niggas get money, but I'll shut that shit down and there ain't nothing that Buck or anybody else can do about it. You know why, cause D-Roc says so nigga. Matta fact i\I'm bout to get out this bitch before I wring somebody's neck."

As D-Roc did what Buck told them not to do by using the Hotel phone to call for a ride, Mills pager went off. He saw the code 007 and knew it was Buck. "C'mon Bee lets go use the phone, this Buck right here." Mills said loud enough for D-Roc to hear.

"I don't need Buck's say so to do shit; I'm leaving cause I wanna leave, when I wanna leave, you know why? Cause Roc says so lil nigga." D-Roc yelled as Mills and Brandy walked out the door.

"You aight Bee?" Mills asked Brandy as they walked to the payphone.

"Yeah I'm straight, fuck D-Roc, bro," Brandy replied. Mills called Buck and got confirmation that everything was cool and that they could go home now. Buck also told Mills that the police were asking questions about him, but he wasn't sweating it, cause his money was too long to go on a cops haunch. He also told them to stay off the strip for a few days and that if the police tried to question them, say nothing. Mills and Brandy returned to the room, and D-Roc was still fired up. He had just finished one of his burst out announcements. He now stood in the middle of the room smoking a fat blunt. He didn't want anybody to think he had talked behind Mill's back, so he started talking loudly again. This time he spoke directly to Mills.

"Lil Mills you better start watching yo mouth lil homie, you starting to get a little big for your britches. I'm a let that shit you and ya lil girl friend was talking bout slide cause y'all don't know better, but you need to check ya self."

Mills didn't respond, and he gave Brandy a look that told her not to either.

"Buck said we cool, we can go home, but be careful cause Pac man lurkin." Mills said disregarding D-Roc's speech. As D-Roc was about to respond to Mills demeanor, his ride arrived. He was hushed by the sound of one of his girlfriend's horn. He, Slim, and lil Walt left Mills and his crew in the room alone. They all stayed in the room till the next morning. When Mills arrived home, he heard blues from his Grandmother. He had been gone for two days without calling, and she was both relieved and fired up by the sight of him. Mills stayed in the house for a few days.

He used the time for quality time with his little brother. They played video games and ate pizza just about every day. When Mills finally left the house, he spent every second at Lisa's house. He and his crew punched that clock over time. They hustled hard for the remainder of the summer. Most of their time was spent in Lisa's house or on her porch because Pac man's harassment was even worse than before. The incident with G.I. Boys drew Mills and his crew closer together. Mills knew the day would come when he would have to use his gun, but he didn't think he would handle taking a life or being apart of taking a life so easily. Mills was all in, and as far as he was concerned there was no turning back.

He was all in a life that would either bring hiM wealth or take his life. Whatever the outcome was, he was prepared to accept the cards he was dealt. One day after school Mills, Peko, Fella, and a few other young hustlers were posted up on Main Street pumping. Mills and his crew stood on the corner of Berkley, while the other hustlers stood across the street on the corner of Studer. Mills and his crew entered the corner store. Peko saw a customer trying to get their attention so he rushed back out the door. Mills purchased a bottle of Ever fresh fruit juice and some Now and Laters. Fella grabbed him a bag of Grippo's, a sprite, and playfully talked a little trash to the store owner. Then he and Mills walked out the store just in time to see Peko being robbed by Big Bruce. Big Bruce was a neighborhood dope fiend that had just come home from prison. He stood at 6'4, 250 pounds.

He was huge, and his face looked just as frightening. Big Bruce had Peko by the neck with one hand, while his other hand was buried in Peko's pocket. Mills sat his fruit juice down and Fella picked it up and followed Mills as he jogged over to assist

Peko, who tried to tussle with the huge man. Mills jumped in the air and smacked Big Bruce in the face with his nine. Big Bruce instantly let Peko go and wrapped his hands around Mills's neck.

"What you gone do with that lil pistol nigga, I'm Big Bruce. I eat bullets for breakfast." Big Bruce said as he tightened his grip on Mills's neck. Fella jumped in the air and broke the bottle over Big Bruce's head. He grabbed Fella by his shirt while holding Mills by the neck in his other hand. Mills stuck the nine to Big Bruce's rib cage and blasted off a shot. "Blow!" Big Bruce stumbled backwards, looked at the whole in his side, and charged at Mills. "Blow! Blow!" Mills hit Big Bruce two more times in the chest, knocking him to the pavement. As on the lookers watched in awe, Mills, Fella, and Peko took off running.

They ran straight for Lisa's, entering her house through the back door. Brandy and Shawn Shawn were quick to their feet as Mills, Fell, and Peko entered the house. While Peko explained what happened to Brandy and Shawn Shawn, Mills called Buck. Within ten minutes Buck was out front in his BMW. Mills rushed out to the car and spotted the police and the ambulance down the street in front of the store.

"What the fuck happened T-money?" Buck said as he pulled from the blazing hot street.

"Man some big ass fiend named Big Bruce was trying to rob Pee. Me and Fella tried to help, and dude grabbed me by the neck. He was choking the life out of me bro. I popped em once, but he kept coming. So I hit him two more times." Mills explained as his heart raced at full speed.

"What did you do you with the burner, Mills?" Buck asked as his mind went straight to getting rid of the evidence. Mills pulled the gun from his waist, and Buck headed for Stone's house. After dropping off the gun, Buck headed for his home on 161, where he would keep Mills hid until he knew things were safe. Mills didn't mind lying low at Bucks house; he used the time to get closer to Nesh. Buck spent most of his time at the house along with Mills. When he wasn't making runs of his own, he was checking on the hood to make sure everyone stayed quiet about Mills involvement with Big Bruce's shooting. The whole time Mills was at Bucks house, he missed school, but class stayed in session, because Buck never stopped schooling him on the game, and life perceived it.

"T-money, I want you to understand something…" Buck hit the blunt a couple times before he continued. "Any man can take a life. That don't make him a gangsta. Depending on the reason behind the man taking the life, it can make him a fool. Don't confuse being foolish with being a gangsta. I'm telling you because I don't want you to become controlled by your burner and the feeling of power it gives you. Ya gun is for protection, not flexin, be smart." Buck said as he and Mills sat at the kitchen table.

Mills sat there attentively. He knew the difference between a lesson that is supposed to be responded to and one that was just supposed to be understood and applied. Buck took a minute to speak on black on black crime.

"Mills I don't ever want you to gain gratification from taking a life, especially a black life. I mean don't get me wrong, a lot of times its brothers who put themselves in that position, and you never have to hesitate when it comes to your life or another man's life, but you gotta understand, black on black crime doesn't just happen. The way blacks treat each other, speak to one another and the whole nine. The oppressors have been programming us to turn against each other ever since slavery. Starting with the separation of us, by rewarding some with the privilege to live and work in the house, while the rest of us live in and work outside in the fields. For this reward, the house nigga as those living and working in the house were called, had to snitch and rebel against his brothers and sisters who may be trying to escape, learn how to read, steal a little food and etc. So you see why we are so quick to feud with one another.

We doin the white man's job for him by taking each other out and rebelling against one another."

Buck spoke strongly, but he always did, especially when speaking on the black man or women. They spent the majority of the night at the kitchen table. The next day, Mills enjoyed a little alone time with Nesh. Nesh had just come in from school. Mills was on the couch smoking on a blunt, and Nesh had plopped down on the other end while waving smoke from out the air.

"Dang boy, is that all you do?" Nesh said letting Mills know that the smoke bothered her. Mills sat the blunt in the ashtray and said.

"Nah, that ain't all I do, but I do a lot of it." He smiled at Nesh and she turned and smiled back.

"Mills you need to be careful because everybody at school has been talking about what you did at that store," Nesh said.

"Yeah.".

"Yeah, they talk about it like its something cool, you better watch out for those chicken heads too, cause they be saying they gone get you while you young, everybody say you up and coming." Nesh said while rolling her eyes.

"I ain't thinking about them chicken heads, my eyes is on one girl at yo school and you know who she is." Mills insinuated, causing Nesh to blush.

"Boy you is crazy." She said playfully. Their conversation was broken up by keys in the front door. Mek came walking through with both hands full of shopping bags.

"What's up Mills. What's happening lil sis." Mek said while giving Nesh a funny look that made both of them smile. Mills helped Mek carry her bags up the stairs, then came running back down the steps to use the phone. His pager went off, it was Lisa's number but it was Fella's code. He called it immediately. "Ring! Ring! Ring!"

"Yo." Fella said answering the phone.

"What's up, bro?" Mills replied. "You. Man why you ain't come out to the crib yet nigga, I told Buck I hollered at Abdullah, the Arab who owned the store, and he said shit cool. Dude ain't tell the cops shit. He already out the hospital. He found out who ya moms and pops are and felt stupid as fuck. He knows that if he go back to the joint he gone run right into yo pops, and yo pops gone kill his ass.".

"Yeah, big bro told me everything was cool a couple days ago. I had plans of coming out today, cause Grandma Mills been tripping about me missing a week of school anyway. Soon as Buck get here, I'm a have him drop me off over there aight?".

"Aight nigga, hurry up though, cause its booming bro." Fella responded.

They disconnected as Mek came downstairs telling Mills to smoke something. Mills handed her the half a blunt from the ash tray and Nesh took off up stairs headed for her bedroom to avoid the smoke. Buck walked in the house with his homeboy Butter as Mek and Mills were finishing off there blunt. Butter was the only homeboy Buck had besides D-Roc and his lil homies in the hood. Butter was his going out partner and his only friend his age. They've known each other since middle school. While Buck was heavy in the dope game, Butter was selling weed. He started out selling already rolled joints, now he was the man in the weed game, much like Buck in the dope game.

Mek and Butter didn't get along. She hated when he and Buck were together because he was single and was sleeping with a lot of females. Butter was a bonifide player. He was light skinned with good wavy hair. He stood at 6'2, an inch taller than Buck. He got the name Butter from his smooth butter like jumper he could hit from anywhere on the basketball court. A lot Mek's homegirls had fallen for Butter's smooth talk, and they all told Mek of the ten inches of blessing he had in his pants, which made her dislike him even more. Mek smacked her lips and rolled her eyes before walking out of the living room.

"Bae get off that bullshit and come give daddy a kiss," Buck said noticing her instant attitude. Mills saved Buck the argument when he told him he needed a ride to the hood. After following

Mek into the kitchen, giving her a bag of money, and joking about her attitude, Buck, Butter, and Mills were out the door.

CHAPTER 4

1993 was closing in fast and things were going good for Mills and his crew. Mills was a Valentine's baby, and it was late December, so his birthday was right around the corner. Mills caught a funny feeling in his gut as he smoked on a blunt while thinking of the new wheels he planned to cop. His instincts led him to the front window. When he peered through the curtains, he noticed a U-haul pull to a stop in front of Lisa's house. Before he knew it, men in back were jumping out the back of the U-haul.

"Oh shit SWAT!" Mills yelled as he threw his dope in one direction and ran the other. Fella, Peko, Brandy, and Shawn Shawn followed his lead as he flung his nine-millimeter under the couch, and ran upstairs. They could hear the front and the back door hit the floor, and the men in the black screaming,

"Columbus SWAT team, everybody get on the floor."

They stomped around upstairs looking for a place to hide as the SWAT team made their way up the steps. Mills and his crew all decided on a back room where they all dove on one bed. Lisa and a few other smokers decided to finish off their crack as if they were in the house alone. Mills and his crew were all brought out in handcuffs along with Lisa and the rest of smokers. If Fella had remembered to throw his dope downstairs like everyone else, he and his friends might not have gone to jail that day . Fella's mother, along with Peko and Shawn Shawn's mother, followed by Brandy's mother, ran up on the cruisers their children were in, asking questions while throwing threats at them about their children.

They all referred to Mills as their nephew, except for Brandy's mother, who told the officers he was her son. The lady's rescue attempt was to no avail. Other officers came walking out the house with drugs, guns, and cash in zip lock bags. Instead of being taken to the detention center for youths, they were all placed in separate interrogation rooms. Detective Brown and White took turns questioning the kids about the deaths of the G.I. Boys. Starting with Mills. After being left in the small room alone for hours, the detectives strolled in the door.

"So Mr. Mills, do you have anything to tell us?" Detective Brown asked playing the good cop. Mills was taught never to speak to the cops without a lawyer present, so he sat there quietly with out responding.

"He wants to act tough Brown, take the little shit to jail and book him for all three murders." White said in a very nasty tone. Mills's heart started to race, but he remained silent. "No Whitey, Mr. Mills here isn't a bad guy; he's smart, aren't you Tony, can I call you Tony?" Brown inquired.

Mills still remained silent.

Brown continued "Mr. Mills I know you don't wanna go to prison for some murders you didn't commit. All you have to do is give up your friend Daylon, or should I call him Buckshot, we know he killed those guys from Gary, Indiana. Even though the word is out that you did it, we know better than that, so whatah ya say, you wanna cooperate or you wanna take the rap for your buddy." Mills was scared, and it took everything in him to remain silent after hearing the detectives talk about the G.I. Boys. The questioning lasted for an hour, but Mills stuck to the code of silence. The detective went from room to room questioning Mills and his crew one person at a time. After five hours of questioning, the detectives had nothing. No one would cooperate. Mills and his crew didn't say a word. As far as the detectives knew, the kids didn't speak English. Detective Brown and White were furious. Mills and his crew had just made some new enemies, and their beef was far more threatening than any beef they could adopt from D-Roc. They were all taken to the detention center. Peko, Shawn Shawn, Fella, and Brandy were processed first. Mills went in last since Mills grandmother was not yet notified. When he called her, he got straight to the point.

"Momma I'm in jail, I need you to come to court for me in the morning."

"Oh Lord Jesus Tony, I knew it, I knew it, I told you God don't like ugly, sweet Jesus not my baby." Grandma Mills said hysterically.

"Mr. Mills you need to end your call." The lady processing him said. "Momma I gotta go, I love you, and make sure you come to court in the morning." Mills said before hanging up.

Mills lucked up and was placed in the same tank with Fella and Peko. Shawn Shawn was placed in a cap pad with the youngsters his age, while Brandy was stationed with the young ladies. When they went to court the next morning, every last one of them was held for seven days. They all got to see each other when passing through the halls to and from school, rec, and chow. On the seventh day they all went to court and were held for an additional fourteen days.

Back in the hood, D-Roc, Slim, and Lil Walt were on their way to the night club on the Northside. When D-Roc pulled his Bronco into the lot, heads turned as his system rattled the ground. 2-Pac's How Long Will They Mourn Me , screamed from the speakers, and everyone stared as the truck parked. D-Roc, Slim, and lil Walt stepped out the truck fly as always. D-Roc wore a simple dark green jogging suit, with some white and green Delta Forces. He accompanied his outfit with a green and white Boston Celtics fitted hat, which sat nicely on top of his French braids that hung just below his shoulders. He also had a two-inch wide herringbone necklace that his nameplate hung from outlined in Diamond chips. The herringbone was accompanied by a matching bracelet, a Figgerro necklace with an Ozzi

53

medallion hanging from it. A matching bracelet and three fingers on each hand were flooded with diamond rings.

D-Roc was a high yellow pretty boy, with no facial hair besides his light sideburns. He was often perceived as soft by those who weren't familiar with him. D-Roc was an expression of the term "Prettyboy Gangster." Slim Gangster, better known as Slim, was named after his tall, slim frame. He stood at 6'2, 175 pounds, with a small afro, which he wore with a razor-sharp line up. He was dressed in some dark blue jeans and a white tee and wore some baby blue Patton leather Georgia Bertini sneakers, and a white and baby blue North Carolina leather varsity jacket. He was also blinding the lookers with his jewels.

Lil Walt was 5'6 with a head full of single braids that hung down to his shoulders. He was brown skin with some grayish eyes that made his mean mug look scarier. Although D-Roc was the crew's leader, Walt was a bigger threat, and everyone knew it. He wore a black Guess jean outfit, with a black tee and some black low top Nikes. He had four gold teeth in his mouth, which covered up his chipped teeth, and accommodated his many other gold and diamond accessories that hung from his neck and sat nicely on his wrist and fingers. D-Roc saw Tasha and a few of her going out buddies strolling through the parking lot and waved them over.

"What's up D-Roc, Slim, and Lil Walt." Tasha said..

"What's up, baby," D-Roc replied.

"Dig baby doll, won't you and your girls carry me and my homeboy's pistols in the club for us? We got a hundred a pop."D-Roc.

"I don't know D-Roc, what if they search us?" Tasha responded.

"C'mon good looking, you know I ain't gone let nothing happen to you." D-Roc persuaded.

"Shit girl for two hundred I'll carry one of them bitches in." Tasha's homegirl said.

"Shit me too."

"And me three."

"Well there you go D-Roc, and you better be good in there." Tasha said letting him know that if she seen him talking to any girls she'd be first to tell her best friend, Nesh. D-Roc started laughing.

"Ha Ha Ha, yeah aight." He replied. They gave them their guns and headed for the club, letting the females go in before them. Once inside the club the girls walked up to D-Roc, Slim, and Lil Walt giving them hugs while stuffing their guns in there waste band. Lil Walt rubbed on Tasha's friend's ass as she hugged him and whispered in her ear,

"I'm trynna hit that tonight."

"And I'm trynna let you." She whispered back.

Slim, on the other hand, was being hit on by Tasha's friend Lauren. As they exchanged flirtatious words, D-Roc slid a few insinuations under Tasha's hat, causing her to blush, and glance at the bulge in his sweat pants.

"Damn is that his gun or is that all him." She thought.

They all went their separate ways. Tasha and her girls headed for the dance floor, while D-Roc and his boys headed for the bar. After ordering their drinks, they found an isolated corner of the club and stood there bobbing there heads to MC Breeds "Just Shake Ya Rump". As the music changed to Celly Cells "It's Going Down" D-Roc noticed the crowd departing like the red sea. T-Bone, Fresh, and several of their homeboys came walking through the crowd, and they stopped once they reached Big Deuce and his entourage. A fine redbone came walking over to D-Roc as he stared down his adversaries while sipping on his double shot of Hennessy.

"Big Deuce and T-Bone said, yo best bet is to get the fuck outtah here." The red bone said as she stood in front of D-Roc. D-Roc threw his drink in her face and muffed her to the ground.

"Tell T-Bone and Deuce I said suck my dick," He said while grabbing his crotch, and flicking T-Bone and Deuce off. Two guys appeared out of nowhere. The first guy swung on D-Roc missing his vicious blow. Slim busted him in the head with his beer bottle sending glass flying across the room. D-Roc and his boys were instantly rushed. Lil Walt pulled his nine-millimeter out and started smacking everyone in his reach upside the head. He sent one guy after another to the pavement. T-Bone opened fire in the club once he noticed Walt's gunplay. Walt fired back while ducking behind a group of females trying to escape the brawl. D-Roc started firing off shots as well. After that, the club erupted into a gun fight.

Slims long body dove through the air blasting off shots. He landed behind a table which he used for cover. All the gunmen lost their targets as the partiers ran through the club like a herd of elephants trying to escape a mouse. D-Roc, Slim, and Lil Walt tried to make it out the club before T-Bone and his boys, but fresh took aim on the front entrance. Lil Walt made it out of the club as he returned fire at no one in particular. D-Roc and Slim ran back into the club as the entrance became crowded, and innocent people felt the wrath of Fresh's high point nine. D-Roc saw T-Bone take off running for another exit. He opened fire causing T-Bone to hit the deck.

Shots rang out in the club once again as D-Roc and Slim traded bullets with T-Bone and his boys. Slim spotted a few girls running out the back exit.

"C'mon Roc; we gotta get the fuck outta here!" He yelled and grabbed D-Roc's shirt just as D-Roc was emptying his nine. They ran for the back door and made it out as bullets followed them.

"Aw shit! I think I'm hit," D-Roc yelled as they ran through the parking lot. They quickly loaded in D-Roc's Bronco and sped out the lot with the music blasting. Lil Walt hung out the window and emptied his nine on T-Bone and Fresh as they came running out the club. D-Roc headed for Grant hospital. He hopped out the car leaving his gun behind, telling Slim and Walt to get rid of them and hide the truck. D-Roc took a bullet to the shoulder blade. Lucky for him the bullet went in and out. After the doctors patched him up, he was visited by the detectives before getting a chance to leave. D-Roc refused to speak to the detectives, and his mother stood by his side. Lucky for the detectives, D-Roc had a warrant. They hauled him to the interrogation room before taking him down to the detention center.

Instead of questioning him about the shooting at the club, they focused on the death of the G.I. Boys.

"So… Mr. Turner lets skip the bullshit and talk about your involvement in the killing of those guys from Gary Indiana." Brown said breaking the ice.

"Pha ha ha ha ha ha ha ha!" D-Roc busted out in laughter. "C'mon man, you got to do better than that." D-Roc said.

"Listen here muther fucker; you think this is a god damn game? Well your little buddies have already told on you and your friend Buckshot, so we'll see how much of a game it is when your little pretty black ass is being fucked by some big dick mother fucker in the penitentiary." White said angrily.

D-Roc laughed in his face again. White was boiling hot, he already despised blacks. Now he was being toyed by one, he couldn't take it. He grabbed D-Roc by his shirt and tried shaking the life out of him while spitting in his face with every word.

"Ahh Shit!!" D-Roc yelled as White smashed his hand into D-Roc's wound. Brown grabbed his partner, but he was afraid of White. White was Brown's superior. He had been a cop for five years, and a detective for two. Brown knew his partner had a prejudice against blacks and people of color, but he valued his job too much to speak on his partner's dislike for people of color, and lack of interest in people of color's justice. He would let black murders go uninvestigated; the same as he did with the black break ins or anyother case where blacks were the victims.

Brown became a victim to his position, as most black people did when they were awarded a good paying job. A lot of black people over looked the injustice done to other black people when they worked for the people doing the injustice. Often times they viewed themselves as being superior as well. D-Roc ridiculed the detectives throughout their interrogation, and they made him sit alone for hours, before taking him to the detention center. D-Roc was famous throughout the detention center, where he'd spent months at a time feuding with his many adversaries that got hauled in. As D-Roc was escorted to D-pod, he saw Mills, Fella, and Peko sitting at a table playing cards.

He told the staff member who escorted him, to put him in the tank with his little homies.

Mills, Fella, and Peko dapped it up with D-Roc as he joined them at the table. They all noticed his arm in a sling, and almost in unison asked, "What the fuck happened to you?"

"Nothing, fuck this shit, did ya'll talk to the D.T.'s?" D-Roc asked referring to the detectives.

"Hell naw." They answered in unison.

"I mean they questioned us, but we all stuck to the gee code." Mills said.

"Aight, ya'll lil niggas make sure y'all keep it that way, cause they gone keep fucking wit us, tryna get us to rat on one another, but don't pay that shit no mind, them fake ass pigs don't got shit or we would have been in jail.".

They all kicked it until lockdown time. The next day, D-Roc went to court and was released, since his warrant was for violation of probation that he was on a year ago. The next time

Mills and his crew went to court they were all released with two years probation. After a couple weeks in the house, Mills and his crew were right back on the Berkley strip. Now that Lisa's house, which was used as their dope spot was boarded up, they were once again block monsters. Mills birthday was in a few weeks and he still wanted to purchase his first car. So he hugged the block every day after school. Mills was having a party at the residence inn, and wanted it to be live, so he made flyers which he passed out in the hood, and school.

He gave some to the older girls in his neighborhood telling them to pass them out to nothing but females at their school. When his birthday hit, Buck took him and Fella to a special car connect. Mills purchased a red 70'S cutlass, with T-tops, red and white pen striped bucket seats, chrome McClain rims, and two twelves with a punch 1000 watt Amp. Fella copped a money green box shaped Regal with T-tops, green bucket seats, chrome rims, and a sound system identical to Mills. They now trailed through the hood showing off their cars before Mills party that night . Brandy rode shotgun with Mills, while Peko and Shawn Shawn rode with Fella. They stopped in front of D-Roc, Slim, and Walts spot on Liley as they stood on the front porch.

"What up Roc? Y'all coming to my party tonight?" Mills yelled as he turned down his music.

"You gone have some hoes up in there nigga?" D-Roc yelled back.

"Fa'Sho."

"Count us in then homie."

"Aight then…peace." Mills said and threw up the deuces and pulled off. Later that night Mills party was everything he expected and wanted it to be. The females outnumbered the males two to one. The party was small but sufficient. The only guys there were from Main Street. There were no outsiders, which meant the chances of a gun play were very slim. Mills stood by the stereo playing Dj, while Fella, Peko, Shawn Shawn, and Brandy stood by the homemade bar sippin on liquor and smoking weed.

Buck was in the middle of a big dice game with D-Roc and the rest of the hustlers. Slim stood in the corner entertaining a crowd of females, while Walt stood over top of D-Roc assisting him in his shit talk. Nesh and her sister Mek shared a love seat by the door, while Tasha sat on the couch adjacent to them, with a few admirers and couch potatoes. As Mills changed the tape from 2-Pac to Biggie Smalls, he mumbled curse words under his breath at the sight of Shawn'tae sashaying over his way.

"What up Mills, you still mad at me?" Shawn'tae asked while showing Mills her tongue seductively.

"C'mon Shawn'tae, I told you I ain't mad at you, I just don't fuck with you like that, cause you run yo mouth toO much." Mills responded.

"Damn Mills, why you want everything to be such a big secret, I said I was sorry, let me make it up to you." She proposed.

"Nah I'm cool baby girl." Mills said as he brushed her hand off his thigh. Mills felt he was being watched, and as he glanced over his shoulder, he spotted Nesh checking him out. She rolled her eyes and smiled at him.

"Dig Shawn'tae, you just a lil bit too much for me, but I got somebody you should meet." Mills said persuasively. Before Shawn'tae could reply, Mills yelled out D-Roc's name. D-Roc looked up from the dice game and Mills waved him over, D-Roc held up a finger telling Mills to hold on a minute. D-Roc held the dice to his ear as he shook them.

"Nine my favorite point, cause I keeps mine on me, get em, Nena," He said as he threw the dice in the middle of the floor. He hit his point, and picked up the money from several spots on the floor.

"I need a fader not a friend, I take the shit that fold and the shit that jingle." D-Roc said as he shook the dice by his ear again. As he got a fader he let the dice roll out of his hand. The dice landed on a three and a one.

"Bet fifty you don't ten ah for nigga." His fader yelled out.

"Bet it nigga." D-Roc said as he slid a fifty dollar bill by his faders feet.

"Back doe lil Joe nigga." D-Roc yelled out as he threw the dice out his hand backwards. D-Roc hit a few nines before crapping out. He stood up with a stack of bills in his hand. He counted the money as he made his way over to Mills.

"What's happenin lil homie?" He said while giving Shawn'tae a glance over.

"Ain't shit happenin bro, I got somebody I want you to meet…Shawn'tae this is D-Roc, D-Roc this is Shawn'tae." Mills said as he gave Shawn'tae a little nudge towards D-Roc. Shawn'tae appraised D-Roc as he stood before her looking like a million bucks.

"That's how you wanna play it, Mills?" Shawn'tae asked. She grabbed D-Roc by the hand and said,

"Aight then."

As they walked off D-Roc looked at Shawn'tae's ass and said,

"I owe you one lil homie," With a big smile on his face.

Nesh watched from the other side of the room as D-Roc walked into the bathroom with Shawn'tae.

"I hope his thang fall off." She said to her sister with a hint of jealousy. Mills walked over to her to join his crew as Peko opened the door for two more females. Brandy passed Mills the blunt she was smoking on and said, "Happy Birthday Bro." Peko locked the door as the girls he let in walked by Mills, then came back to wish him a Happy birthday and get acquain'ted with the young hustler they had been hearing about.

The girls were a couple of years older than Mills. They went to Nesh's high school, where Mills name was a little heavy in the hallways, because of all the girls from his neighborhood that went there.

"What's up, Mills, Happy Birthday from me and my girl Chrissie." La'Shay said doing the talking for her and her friend. La'Shay and Chrissie were both fine. La'Shay was a brown skin beauty, while Chrissie was a cold light skin wavy, which meant a fine light skin sister with wavy hair.

"Thanks." Mills said smoothly.

"Mills my girl is kind of shy, but she likes you." La'Shay said referring to Chrissie.

Mills spotted Nesh looking again. This time they locked eyes, and Nesh stuck her tongue out while rolling her eyes at him. Mills knew Nesh was digging him and he smiled back at her.

"Chrissie you fine, and so are you La'Shay, but I'm kind of seeing somebody. Wont y'all holla at my bros. La'Shay this is Fella, Chrissie this is Peko." Mills said pointing at both of his homeboys.

Mek caught her sister exchanging looks with Mills and said, "Girl you better get him before one of these scavenger ass bitches get him."

"Mek you know Mills is too young for me," Nesh replied.

"Says who? And who says you can't get him now and put him up for later. Pssssh, girl you better quit playin, and it ain't like you coming up off of none of that lil coo coo noway." Mek said causing her and her sister to start laughing.

"Mek, you is a trip." Nesh said in between laughs.

Mills walked up as their laughter ended.

"What's up Mek. What's up Nesh."

"Shit smoke something nigga." Mek replied

"You the Birthday Boy, this is yo day. Did you get everything you wished for?" Nesh added.

"I don't know, it all depends." Mills answered.

"What do you mean you don't know?" Nesh asked.

"I mean you could answer that question better than I could." Mills insinuated.

"How can I answer it, I don't know what you wished for?" Nesh said.

"All I want for my birthday is you, so tell me…do I got everything I wished for?" Mills said while looking into her eyes.

Nesh smiled and couldn't stop blushing as she said, "Boy you is crazy."

Mills took a seat between Nesh and her sister, and that's where he stayed for the remainder of his party. Smoking weed with Mek and kicking it with Nesh. From the other side of the room D-Roc watched Mills and Nesh as he sat with Shawn'tae on his lap. Even though he was no longer with Nesh, he didn't like the fact of her being with anyone else. The next day Mills and his crew were right back on the block. They enjoyed their selves last night, as they all took a chance with smoking weed while on probation. Although they have yet to receive a urine test, they were warned that urine test were an option, and that if they were caught dirty they would be sent back to the detention center.

Everyone except for Peko made last night a one night thing. Peko became the heaviest smoker out of the crew. Peko had made his mind up; not smoking was definitely not an option for him. As the season changed from winter to spring, Berkley became a busier strip. Mills and Fella parked their cars on the strip letting their systems flood the street with hip hop while they hopped in and out of the cars, and hid on the side of houses serving different customers. While hustling on the block was cool for Mills and his crew, they wanted badly to be back in a spot.

Lucky pulled up in a truck with white man and two prostitutes, as Mills sat on the hood of his car.

"C'mere T-Mills." Lucky screamed from the passenger window. Being that the white man with Lucky was a stranger, Mills was leery about approaching the truck.

"Get out the car Luck." Mills yelled as him and his friends stared at the white man. Lucky caught on to Mills caution. He looked at his white friend and said,

"C'mon Mills he straight. This is one of my good guys,"

"Aight just get out the car, I need to holla at you about something."

Lucky got out the car and Mills met him on the sidewalk where he stood.

"Dude straight Mills, now sell me a fat hundred," Lucky said while twitching his lips and rocking back and fourth as if he had to piss.

"I got you baby, but what's up with Lolly, did you holler at her about me and my crew posting up in her crib?" Mills said.

"Mills you know Lolly will let you come over and make a few dollars." Lucky answered.

"Yeah, Yeah, I know, but I'm talking about me and my crew, and I ain't talking bout for no few hours, we trynna get this money, you know we gone pay swell." Mills said persuasively.

"I don't know Mills, you know Lolly is about her house, she don't allow anybody to sell out of there, but you and that lil dude from Studer, and she only let ya'll stay for a few hours."

As Lucky and Mills talked, Pac Man turned onto the street. Fella quickly turned his system off, and jumped out of his car. Pac Man pulled to a stop in front of Mills and Lucky. He hopped out his cruiser with his weapon drawn.

"Both of you put your hands up and don't move." His partner hopped out with his weapon on the white man and two prostitutes in the truck.

"Don't fuckin move," He said as the prostitutes moved around in the backseat. Pack Man did a thorough shake down on Lucky and Mills, then he started stepping on trash that layed on the ground around them. He knew hustlers kept their dope hid in potato chip bags, cigar packs, candy bags, and boxes, so it could blend with the trash on the ground. Lucky for Mills, he kept his dope in a cigar box across the street in Fella's front yard.

"Where's your dope Mills? You got it in your ass like your boy D-Roc." Pac Man said as he pushed Mills and Lucky up against the cruiser to frisk them once again.

"I ain,t got no dope," Mills said loudly enough for everyone to hear, because Pac Man was known for planting drugs on people if he wanted them bad enough.

"C'mon Mills you don't expect me to believe that. You're talking to one of the biggest smokers in the hood and you don't have any dope. C'mon Mills you're moving big dope for your boy Buck," Pac Man said, trying to get a certain response from Mills.

"I ain,t got no dope, man," Mills continued to say loudly. Pac Man's harassment was cut short when Fella's mother came out her house raising hell. She held her hand in her hand while saying, "Pac Man, you take your bullshit on somewhere else. These boys ain't bothering nobody, you gone quit fucking with my son and my nephews or I'm a have that fake ass badge of yours."

"Ms. Stargell I'm going to ask you to back away from my car, before you join your nephew here," Pac Man warned as he aggressively stuffed Mills in the back seat.

"Put me in the mutha fucking back seat, it ain't gone get you nowhere. What you gone do plant some drugs on me like you did the boy up the street the other day?" Fella's mother yelled.

"Ms. Stargell I'm going to ask you one more time to back away from my car and lower your fucking tone of voice, if your so called nephew doesn't have any drugs on him, than I'll let him go." Pac Man said in a nasty tone.

"DRUGS....you done searched the boy a thousand times, now I'm calling the damn precinct on your ass," Fella's mother yelled as she dialed numbers on her cordless phone. Pac Man paid her no attention, and walked over to the truck to assist his partner. After frisking the truck's passengers thoroughly and searching the truck. He tried to get the white man and the prostitutes to say that Mills had sold them drugs. Pac Man and his partner headed back to the cruiser empty handed.

They let Mills and Lucky out the back seat of the cruiser and sped off.

"Mills c'mon and take care of me so I can get the fuck from around here," Lucky said.

"Dig Luck, you know Pac Man probably somewhere watching us right now, so won't you go over Lolly's and wait on me, I'll be there in about five minutes. I'm a put something real special together for you and I'm a brang Lolly something." Mills said as he looked around cautiously.

"Aight Mills, but hurry up and you better make me famous," Lucky said, referring to the amount of dope he was expecting to receive from all the trouble, and the wait. When Lucky pulled off, Mills grabbed his work off the ground and told Brandy to follow him in her house. Mills grabbed several pieces he needed to take care of Lucky and Lolly. Then he gave the rest of his pack to Brandy. While Brandy ran upstairs to stash Mills pack, Mills wrapped his work he kept in some paper. He had intentions to go over Lolly's on his own, but he thought better of it. When Brandy came back downstairs, he tossed her the small pack and told her to stuff it and to ride with him over Lolly's.

Mills and Brandy grabbed two bikes from Fella's front yard. Before leaving Mills told his crew that if everything went as planned, they'd have a new spot when he returned. When Mills arrived, Lucky snatched the door open before they had a chance to knock. After a half hour of Mills slick talk and a few bolders of his hard white critly, Lolly was persuaded. Mills left Brandy there with a few stones, while he headed back to the strip to inform the rest of his crew of the good news, and grab more work.

When Mills arrived, Peko and Shawn Shawn were on the side of their house with a few customers and Fella was hopping out of one car into another. Fella made it back before Peko and Shawn Shawn finished with their customers.

"Dig Fells, we back in action, I got Lolly to let us open up shop in her house." Mills said.

"Word?" Fella replied.

"Word."

"So what's the plan?" Fella asked. Peko and Shawn Shawn walked up right on time.

"The plan for what?" Peko asked.

"I got Lolly to let us open shop in her crib,. This is how we gone do it, Bee around there right now holding it down wit a few stones. I'm bout to grab some more work and shoot back to Lolly's with her. Since ya'll already crackin here, ya'll stay here and let all the custy's know we at Lolly's. Then tomorrow me and Bee gone play the strip and shoot the custy's to Lolly's while ya'll post up. We'll do it like this for a couple days until everybody knows where we at. With Lucky's help, we should have that bitch boomin in 2 weeks tops."

"What about the fiends that don't know where Lolly stay?" Shawn Shawn asked.

"Every fiend know where Lolly stay lil bro. if you smoke dope, you done been over Lolly's." Mills answered

"Let's make it do what it do then bro," Fella said.

"Aight, I'm bout to grab some work and head back over there, let's get this paper baby!" Mills said playfully as he headed for Brandy's house.

CHAPTER 5

Lolly's house became a million dollar spot in no time. For the last three months, Mills and his crew did nothing but hustle and go to school. Now that school was out Brandy felt the crew could use a little time off.

"Bro lets go out tonight, we been goin hard for months, with no time off. I'm trynna get my party on." She said while snapping her fingers to the music that filled Lolly's living room.

"Ain't nothing going on sis, we getting this money, stack N grind, you know the name of the game." Mills replied.

"Shid bro, the skating rink popping tonight and you know hard work shouldn't go unrewarded." Brandy said using Buck's logic.

"Yea T-money, lightin up, ain't nothing wrong with a party now and then," Fella added.

Mills looked at Shawn Shawn. Shawn Shawn shrugged his shoulders, as if to say he was down with whatever. Peko came strolling in the living room counting the money he just received from one of his customers. As always he was smoking on a fat blunt of killer weed. He sensed the tension in the air, "What the fuck going on in here?" He asked.

"We trying to go to the rink tonight Pee and Mills is being stubborn as always." Brandy said while playfully shoving Mills.

"I know Pee agree wit me, he a block monster for real, huh Pee?" Mills said.

"I'm always down with banging a few bitches," Peko said while dapping it up with Fell, who always agreed when it came to the females.

"Well T-money, it looks like you and Shawn Shawn are out voted." Fella said. "

Aight man, look like we going to the rink. I mean I understand why you and Pee wanna go, ya'll some horndogs, but Bee ain't gone give no nigga no holler noway. She gone be actin all mean and shit. Then as soon as some nigga try to holler at her, she gone flip."

Mills started doing an impression of Brandy and they all busted out laughin. Brandy couldn't help but laugh, but she punched Mills in the arm letting him know that she didn't like the joke being on her.

Later that evening they all went home to get dressed for the night out. When they arrived at the skating rink, the first people they ran into were D-Roc, Slim, and lil Walt. Mills was dressed completely in Tommy Hillfiger. He had a pair of Tommy Hillfiger blue shorts, a white Tommy Hillfiger t-shirt, white Tommy Hillfiger ankle socks, and some low cut Tommy Hillfiger shoes. He wore a thick 14k link necklace, with a solid lion head hanging from it. On his right wrist was a matching Gucci link braclet, while his left wrist sported a Tommy Hillfigure sports watch. Unlike D-Roc, who wore a ring on every finger, Mills only wore one ring on each hand.

One of his rings was an iced out lion head, like his medallion. Mills sported a tight fade with waves drilling on the top. His light brown skin accommodated his baby face. Mills was already young being thirteen, but his 5'1 110 pound frame along with his baby face, only made him look younger. Mills was mature beyond his years, and the majority of his quietly smooth style was inherited from Buck. Peko was just as smooth. At 5'6 ½ he was the tallest out of the crew. His build was similar to slim, being that he was lean, weighing only 130 pounds. Peko had hazel brown eyes to go with his golden brown complexion. All the weed he smoked coupled with his natural sleepy eyes. Stigma made it hard for his pretty eyes to be admired.

Peko walked with a slow stroll, somewhat dragging his feet. He had natural curly hair like his deceased father, which added to his pimp demeanor. Peko stood tall in a pair of blue Guess jean shorts, a white v-neck t-shirt, white ankle socks, and some white low cut Canvass Nikes. He wore a white fitted cap with Mound and Berkely air brushed on the front of it. His short trimmed curly afro, stuck out the sides of his hat like a jerry curl. He sported 1 inch wide terquish link around his neck, with a Jesus piece medallion outlined in crushed ice. A matching bracelet rested on his left wrist. Shawn Shawn resembled his older brother in looks and style. They shared the same hazel eyes, with the same sleepy eye stigma. His hair was curly, which he wore in a tiny afro like his older brother. He was three inches shorter than Peko, and he stood next to him in black Guess jean shorts, a white Crew neck shirt, black ankle socks, and some black Canvass Nikes with a white Nike check. He wore a black White Sox baseball cap, with one inch wide hairing bone necklace, and matching bracelet.

D-Roc, Slim, and Lil Walt stood with a group of guys from East Main Street, by the food stand while the dance floor was packed with guys from across the bridge on Livingston Ave. As Mills and his crew approached D-Roc and his homeboys, Mills could feel the tension in the air.

"What up Roc."

"What up lil homie, ya'll be careful in here tonight, them Livingston niggas in here deep. I just split one of them hoe ass niggas and Slim and Lil Walt stomped him out. That's why everybody in here is clicked up in here. It's about to go down." D-Roc said while laughing at the drama that awaited. Peko tapped Mills and pointed across the room to Nesh and her friend Tasha.

"We bout to hit the dance floor." D-Roc said as he bobbed his head to the music, while charging his self up.

"Shit, we bout to hit the dance floor, too. I'm tryna get some bitches." Fella said before Mills had a chance to reply. Fella, unlike the rest of his crew was a live wire. Before getting into the game, Fella thrived on stealing bikes, beating people up, and occasional B-N-E's. His cousin Slim would have been put him in the game but he knew Fella was too undisciplined and he didn't want to hear his aunt's mouth if Fella went to jail. Fella wasn't as fat as everyone made him seem. He was just chubby, with a block head. He was big for his age, standing at 5'4, 170 pounds, give or take a few. He had brownish green eyes that attracted the ladies. He had a dark brown skin complexion, with a lighter brown birthmark on the left side of his face that stretched from his forehead to the top of his neck. He wore his hair evenly cut with two blade, and razor sharp line up. Fella wore a brown crew neck t-shirt, some black Eddie Bower jean shorts, and a pair of brown suede ACG mid cut Nikes, with a black sow. He also wore a Cleveland browns fitted cap, cocked to the back. Fella was just as flashy as D-Roc, Slim, and Lil Walt, so he not only had on his jewelry; he had on a few of Mills and Peko's extra pieces as well.

"Y'all go head man, I'm a catch up wit y'all in a minute." Mills said as he made his way over to Nesh.

"You sprung and you ain't even got none," Brandy said playfully as she noticed where Mills was headed.

"You be careful bro," Fella said as he lead the pack to the dance floor with D-Roc, Walt, and his cousin Slim. Brandy, Shawn Shawn, and Peko played the background.

"You stay close to me lil bro," Peko whispered to Shawn Shawn as they hit the dance floor. As the two different clickes had a stare off, the people on the skates started making their way off the floor.

"Whats up lil Mills." Nesh said, as Mills approached her and Tasha.

"You. What you doing out? I didn't think partying was your cup of tea." Mills said

71

"It's not. Tasha made me come since I'm bout to go to Atlanta for college, after this coming school year." Nesh replied.

"Damn you just gone leave before you give me a chance huh?" Mills asked.

"Chance for what?" Nesha asked playing dumb.

"My chance to be your man, to show you that I know how to treat you." Mills answered while giving her his smooth look.

"Boy you crazy, and I don't remember me saying I would give you a chance. But you talking like I'm a be gone forever. I'll still be coming home on the holidays and school breaks. I'm just tryna get away from all this craziness in the hood." Nesh said adamantly.

Before Mills could respond, Tasha was yanking Nesh's arm saying

"Oh girl he all in my shit," Talking about some guy she was exchanging dirty looks with across the room.

"Well go on over there girl, you ain't gone get nowhere playing who can look the longest," Nesh said.

"You right girl, I'm bout to go put my mack hand down," Tasha said while fluffing her curly hair.

"What's up Tasha, you ain't speaking tonight?" Mills said sarcastically knowing her attention was elsewhere.

"What's up lil Mills, you know you ma nigga," Tasha said before walking off and throwing up a peace sign saying,

"Peace out." In a funny voice.

Nesh and Tasha were both fine. They were by far the finest females on the set and there were some fine sisters out. Nesh stood at 5'2, with a compact petite frame. Her legs were smooth, with slight muscular build from being on the drill team. Her hips rolled perfectly off her body, complementing her small but sufficient apple bottom. She had a caramel brown skin complexion that stayed radiant. Her hair was jet black, and it hung below her shoulders. She wore it straight and perfectly cut to hang at the same length. She was beautifully dressed in some red high thigh-high shorts by Limited that squeezed her ass tight enough for it to be admired, but not enough to be slutty. Her red and white pen stripped halter top by Limited complemented her breast perfectly and exposed her flat stomach from the belly button down.

Her small feet stood in a pair of all white K-swiss with no socks. Her hair was pulled behind her ears showcasing her diamond earrings, which complemented her other accessories. She was shining from her ears down to her ankle bracelet. Tanesha Walker was fine, and she knew it. Tasha was what one would call bootylicious. She was a thick red bone with a body made especially for a strip club. She was an inch taller then Nesh, at 5'3. She weighed close to 140 pounds, with a flat stomach and lumps and bumps in all the right places. Her hair was a redish blonde color. She wore it in a curly like afro style, which she had parted down the middle letting her curly hair hang down to her shoulders. Her attire was identical to Nesh's, except for the color. She wore yellow shorts that hugged her jelly tight enough for anyone to tell she ain't have no panties on. Her halter top was yellow and white, and it clung to her jugs like magnets to metal.

As Nesh and Mills conversed, R.Kelly's song "You're the only one I want to dance with" roared from the speakers.

"Oh my God, this is my jam," Nesh said while throwing her arms up in the air and snapping her fingers.

"C'mon Mills, dance with me." Nesh said as she grabbed his hand and led him to the dance floor. She pulled Mills close to her and put his hands at the small of her back. As they rocked side to side, Mills inhaled Nesh's Vanilla Fields perfume. She felt and smelled like heaven to Mills as he buried his face in her neck. Nesh enjoyed the smell of Mills Cool Water cologne as she rubbed the back of his head and wished he were older. The song ended but Mills kept dancing. He was rocking to a whole nother tune in his head.

"The song is over Mills," Nesh said with a big smile on her face.

"Yo song might be over, but the song I hear whenever you around, don't ever end." Mills said as he staredinto her eyes. Nesh blushed as the music changed to Snoop Dogg's "Gin and Juice" suddenlyD-Roc and the Main Street boys started yelling "Main Street," while throwing their hands in the air. The guys from Livingston Avenue screamed, "Livingston Ave." in return and the floor became roudy as the boys began pushing and shoving each other. As Mills tried to pull Nesh off the floor, she spotted Tasha in a cat fight with two females.

"Uh un Mills hold up," Nesh said as she yanked away and ran to her bestfriend's aid. The guy Tasha was talking to, stood there and watched Tasha get jumped. Nesh grabbed one of the girls by the hair and went to work on her face with her free hand. Mills followed behind Nesh and arrived as the third girl jumped in the fight, busting Nesh in the back of her head. Mills grabbed the girl and pushed her out the way and went to pulling Nesh and the other girl apart. The guy hit Mills from behind, knocking him backwards. As Mills squared off with the guy, three more girls joined in the rally against Nesh and Tasha who was putting in work. Mills fain'ted the guy, causing him to flinch. Then he quickly rushed him with a flurry of punches. The skating rink turned into an old western brawl as the Main Street and Livingston guys collided. Mills was stole on again from behind as he used the guys head for a punching bag. Mills was knocked into a wall as Fella appeared out of nowhere. He sent one of the guys to the ground with a vicious hook.

Peko, Shawn Shawn, and Brandy were close behind. Brandy assisted the girls, while Shawn Shawn went to stomping off the guy Fella had knocked to the ground, and Peko took Mills position squaring off with the guy Tasha was talking to. Peko's long arms were too much, he picked the guy apart. Mills bounced off the wall and assisted Peko, by hitting the guy with a combination of quick blows. The cops quickly filled the place up and sprayed mase everywhere. Everyone who was on their feet took off running. Jumped rails, walls, and hitting side exits. Some people lay on the ground sleep or badly bleeding from head blows or a razor job.

Mills grabbed Nesh and Brandy by the shirt as they punished a girl in a corner. "C, mon we gotta get the fuck out of here." He yelled at them.

Peko grabbed Tasha, and they all made their escaped while covering their faces from the mase that filled the air. Once outside, Mills and his crew split up from Nesh and Tasha, as D-Roc, Slim and Lil Walt traded shots with the Livingston guys. They all loaded in D-Rocs old school and Walt hung out the window blasting off shots as they peeled out the lot. Mills and Brandy hopped in his car, while Fella, Peko, and Shawn Shawn packed up in Fella's ride. Mills caught the guys from Livingston pointing as his and Fella's car's as they loaded in theirs.

"Fells!" Mills yelled out as he and Brandy exchanged seats, so Brandy could drive. Fella nodded his head as Mills pointed to the guys loading in their cars. Mills grabbed his nine mm from under his seat and cocked one in the head. Fell passed his nine to Peko who rode shot gun. Brandy turned left out the lot, being trailed by two cars. Fella turned right with two cars on his tail as well. Fella hit the freeway while Brandy sped up Refugee. Brandy had a little distance on her tailers, but she had to slow down in order to make a quick left that Mills told her to make. Once she slowed down shots rang out from behind them.

The cars had closed the gap enough to take aim. They let off a few shots as Brandy bent the corner. They weren't far off her tail and the sound of their tires screeching let her know it.

"Make a quick right, right here on Kimberly Bee," Mills said as he prepared to return fire. As Brandy made the quick right, bullets tore through the back windshield knocking glass everywhere. Mills came out the window returning fire as the two cars bent the second corner behind them. "BOOM! BOOM!

BOOM!" Mills slowed the cars down as he sent bullets through their front windshield. Mills kept firing as one of the gunman behind them stayed out the window returning fire. Mills watched as one of his bullets hit the gun man in his hand causing him to drop his weapon. The car stopped and one of its passengers hopped out to retrieve the weapon, while the car behind them swerved around them to keep up with Brandy as she smashed the gas. Mills had a 350 turbo horse power under his hood, but they hadn't been on a street long enough to floor the engine.

Mills knew the neighborhood, so he knew a straight away was coming up ahead.

"Make a quick left on the next street Bee," Mills yelled out as they ducked their heads from the bullets flying in the air and through the car. Brandy made the left with out slowing down causing the car to drift. "Boom! Boom! Boom! Boom! Boom!" Mills emptied his clip as the cars turned the corner behind them. The gun man retreated back in the window and Mills yelled,

"Floor this bitch Bee!"

Brandy put the pedal to the metal. She pulled away from their tailors, putting enough distance between them that made it frivolous for them to keep shooting. She held the steering wheel with two hands as the car became more powerful by the second. They sped through a red light never noticing two cop cars parked in the stores parking lot, as they soared through the air from the hill they were driving up. The cop cars immediately pulled out the lot but not before Mills and Brandy's tailors sped by them. Now all the cars were being tailed by the police. They swerved through the curvy street in EastHaven's neighborhood. Mills directed Brandy to the freeway, hoping to lose the cops on the highway. Once Brandy made the turn on the freeway, Mills threw the gun in a nearby field. The cops had called for back up, and they awaited Mills and Brandy on the highway. As they drove in the ambush, Mills and Brandy knew their chase had come to an end.

Meanwhile Fella swerves in and out of traffic on another highway. His pursuers swerved through traffic behind him, while taking turns trying to pick his car off. Peko told Shawn Shawn to stay on the floor as he stayed low in his seat waiting for a chance to exchange fire. Fella smiled and laughed as he dodged bullets and cars both. Once he had seen the Miller and Kelton exit, he knew he had made it home free. As he sped up the ramp he said,

"Pee, soon as I make this turn on Miller, light they shit up." The two cars flew up the ramp behind Fella. Fella made a quick turn avoiding the stop sign. He stopped the car completely as the cars came speeding up the ramp. As they neared the stop sign, Peko sat up on the window seal and picked both cars apart, holding the browning nine with two hands. "Pucka! Pucka! Pucka!" Peko watched as the windows burst out and bullets flew into the vehicle. He hit the passenger of the first car in the chest and leg, while hitting the driver in the shoulder. Bullets wizzed into the second car hitting the front passenger in the leg and one of the back passengers in the arm, while grazing the driver. While Peko was emptying his clip, the back passenger of the first car was climbing out the backdoor. Peko never noticed him. As Fella pulled away, the guy came running off the side of the car firing of shots. He hit Peko in his shoulder, as he made his way back in the window.

"All shit Fells I'm hit!" Peko yelled as he grabbed his shoulder". The guy continued blasting off shots." Boom! Boom! Boom!" Fella's back window windshield came out as they turned on Fulton evading the shooter.

"Hold on pee, we gotta get the fuck out this car," Fella yelled as he heard the sirens from the police cars that were closing in. Fella pulled in front of his house. He ran in and returned with his mother. They put Peko in Fella's mother's car and she sped to the hospital as Shawn Shawn ran in the house to contact his mother. Fella hopped back in his car. He drove it to Lolly's backyard, to await him and Peko's mother with him.

Meanwhile, Mill's and Brandy are back in separate interrogation rooms, awaiting detective White and Brown. The detectives came walking in the room they had Mills in, with smirks on their faces.

"So Mr. Mills, here we are again," Brown said. Mills remained silent.

"So you're not going to talk to us again huh, Mr. Mills? That's fine because you and your little girlfriend can't get out of this one. There are bullet casings in the car that prove you guys were doing some shooting.So where's the gun."

"You're a dumb little fuck," White added while puffing on a cigarette. "That pretty little girlfriend of yours will be a bull dagger bout time she comes home and you'll done slept with more men then her smart guy," White said devilishly.

Mills was worried about Brandy. He cared about her too much to let her go to jail with him. He knew he would take out before he allowed her to go down.

"Don't worry, we're goin to go talk to your little girlfriend surely she wil tell on your little black ass."

He and Brown prepared to leave. Before walking out the door, White said, "Oh, by the way tuff guy, a couple of your buddies got shot on the freeway, their in critical condition, so some of your little enemies will be goin to jail with you and nine times out of ten they will kick your ass while your in there."

They left Mills in the room alone. This time he had a lot to think about. The first thing on his mind was Fella, Peko, and Shawn Shawn. The detectives went to Brandy's room and received the same silent treatment. Brandy was a soldier and going to jail didn't scare her one bit. She was down with her crew until they got layed down, especially Mills. After giving the detectives the silent treatment for over three hours, Mills and Brandy were escorted to the juvenile detention center. Brandy's mother handled the situation a lot better than Mills grandmother, who cried and called upon her Jesus for help. Mills had to be pulled off the phone by the authorities once again. As him and Brandy sat down waiting fro their escort, Mills told Brandy that he was taking the rap for all the charges.

"No bro, fuck that. If we go down, we go down together." Brandy pleaded.

"C'mon sis, you know I can t let you go down for no shit like this. People got shot Bee, this shit is serious and it ain't no use in both of us going down." Mills said.

"Fuck that bro, we in this together man," Brandy shot back. Their dispute was broken up as the staff members came in to escort them to their pods. A female came for Brandy, while a cool cat named Steve came for Mills. The next morning they were both held for an additional seven days. Back in the hood, Peko was out of the hospital with his arm in a sling. He, Fella, and Shawn Shawn were back in the spot getting money while Mills and Brandy faced felony assault charges. Though Peko was free right now, his situation wasn't pretty. His probation officer tightened the rules up on him. He was given a urine test today and he was dirty.

"Man this fake ass bitch done piss me today. I'm dirty as fuck bro." Peko said to Fella though he was speaking to him and Shawn Shawn both.

"I told you bro, you lil weed geek, lil baby weed fiend, knew that bitch gone lock you up," Fella said while laughing at his homeboys habit.

"Damn bro, they gone try and lock you up for that shit," Shawn Shawn said, as eh thought about being without his brother.

"Look at em, he still smoking. He hard-headed," Fella said as Peko paced the floor while smoking on blunt of fire weed. "Shid bro it's too late to quit now, I'm like the gingerbread man, them hoes gone have to catch Pee," Peko said while pausing in a run motion with his blunt hanging from his mouth. They all started laughing, but the joke definitely was on Peko, who looked silly with his arm in a sling, and smoke coming out his mouth.

CHAPTER 6

After spending a month in the Detention Center, Brandy was released, with six months of house arrest to serve. The third time Mills and Brandy went in front of the judge. They were threatened with three years. That was enough to make Mills step up and clear Brandy of all charges, besides driving no OPS, which was a violation of her probation. Brandy was furious. Her and Mills were like brother and sister. If he had to do three years, she wanted to do it with him. As Brandy sat in her PO's office waiting for her mother to pick her up, Mills stepped out his cell for rec, and noticed three new faces in his pod.

Some guys from Livingston Avenue were moved to his pod after putting in work on some guys from the North side in their pod. Them and Mills had been exchanging words and cold stares as they passed each other in the hallways. Mills noticed that the guy he had shot in the hand had his cast removed from his arm and he now only wore a bandage on his hand to support his wrist. All three of the guys gave Mills their mean mugs as they stood in front of their cells. Mills returned their mean mugs with one of his own, along with a smirk. He knew he had a fight on his hands, but he didn't care, because at his next court hearing he would be receiving and needed to release some of his anger.

To Mills surprise, he made it through the day without having to fight. The guys let a few days pass before they attacked. Mills was on the phone talking to his crew who took turns in Brandy's bedroom. As he laughed at one of Fella's jokes, he lost sight of his three adversaries. When he looked over his shoulder trying to locate them, he was hit hard. He dropped the phone and squared off with the guy who hit him. The guy's friends stood off to the side letting Mills get in a fair fight. Mills rushed the guy with a wild combination. He landed two of his punches, and the guy went under him in an attempt to wrap Mills legs up. Mills got out the way, and the guy only managed to grab one of his legs. Mills unloaded on his face, causing him to ball up in an attempt to block some of the blows. Mills felt what he knew was coming. He received a blow from his blind side. When he turned to face the second man, the third guy hit from the other side.

"Ya'll bitch ass niggas gotta jay Young Mills huh?" Mills said loud enough for his friends on the phone to hear. They listened as the phone hung by the cord and Mills battled it out with all three guys. Mills faked one guy with a right, and scooped the other off his feet. He slammed him to the ground, and beat the blood out of him. While Mills worked on him, the guy's buddies beat the blood out of Mills. The staff member had to call for back up as the youngest tore his pod up. When help arrived Mills was lumped up, and spitting blood from his mouth, while blood leaked from his nose. The guy Mills had on the ground was just as bloody, with a black eye, and a few lumps and bumps tag a along with it. The guy Mills squared off with at first also had a few speed knots of his own.

"Y'all niggas some bitches, all three of y'all can't whoop me! That's how Mound and Berk niggas get down." Mills said as he spat blood from his mouth.

"Livingston Ave. Bitch ass nigga. Fuck Mound Street, you see how we get down," The guys fired back. They were all restrained and locked in their cells, where they waited for the institution nurses. Mills was eventually moved to another pod, since his adversaries outnumbered him. Mills spent another month in the detention center before he was transferred to Circleville's Juvenile Holding Facility, where youths stay until a bed came open for them in Juvenile Institute, where they would serve their time. Back in the hood, Brandy sat on her front porch, flagging down customers as she waited for Fella, Peko, and Shawn Shawn to come and kick it with her. Brandy's ankle monitor wouldn't allow her to go further than her front yard. Lucky for her, she stayed right on the strip, so she had no problems getting rid of her work and the four and a half ounces Mills had left over her house. Peko and Shawn Shawn hopped out of a car in front of Brandy's house and quickly ran up on her porch.

"Damn nigga, it's about time y'all came to kick it with me. I ain't seen y'all in days." Brandy said.

"We just been chillin at Lolly's getting that money Bee, you know we love you," Shawn Shawn said with a smile on his face.

"Yea Bee, you know we love you, but I'm on the run and you know if Pac Man see me, I'm through, so let's go in the crib," Peko said as he looked up and down the street.

"Aight, c'mon spooky ass nigga. Where Fells fat ass at?" Brandy asked as they were entering the house.

"Nicole, I'm right here in the living room, you better watch your filthy mouth." Her mom said calling her by her middle name.

"My bad ma," Brandy said,tucking her head into her chest, while smiling at the fact she got caught.

"Whats up auntie," Peko and Shawn Shawn said in unison as they passed Brandy's mother in the living room.

"What's up nephews," She replied as they climbed the stairs headed for Brandy's room.

"Why y'all ain't answer my question? Where Fells at?" Brandy said as she plopped down on her bed.

"Aw shit, he been hanging out with D-Roc and his cousin Slim lately. Fells off the hook, they shot some night club up last night." Peko said as he pulled out a fat bag of weed.

"Fells been hanging with D-Roc. WHAT?" Brandy said loudly. "That's some bullshit, he knows D-Roc and them be into a lot of BS. They beefin with half the city. I heard they robbed some guy in front of the store the other day, took his rims off his car and everything." Brandy continued.

"Mills gone flip out when he hear that shit, huh?" Peko said as he licked his blunt shut. "You already know," Shawn Shawn said answering the question for Brandy.

"Pee you is one hard-headed brother, you still smoking weed," Brandy said while giving Peko a funny look.

"Shid, I'm on the run now Bee, they gone take me to jail when they catch me anyway, so ain't no use in me trying to stop now. Shid, truthfully, I wouldn't stop smoking anyway, I need this shit to cope." Peko said as he fired up the blunt.

"Cope with what nigga, and go by the window wit that. Me and Shawn Shawn ain't trynna be on the run wit yo ass," Brandy said while waving smoke out the air.

While Brandy, Peko, and Shawn Shawn chilled out, Fella was in a gambling house on 5th Avenue with D-Roc, Slim, and Lil Walt. Fella's forehead and hands were moist from perspiration. He was nervous because the houseman was standing over top of the dice game with a 40 caliber in his hand, while his goons stood by the door with Glock nines. This would be Fella's first robbery and the fact of pulling a gun on a man who already had his drawn was giving him bad vibes. D-Roc had a stack of bills piled up by his side, along with a stack of bills in front of him, which he needed to roll a nine to win.

He held the dice to his ear while shaking them,

"C'mon baby talk to daddy. This the lick that's gonna make ya pockets thick," D-Roc said. As D-Roc shot the dice, Lil Walt stood next to the houseman, while Slim stood by the liquor table which was close to the front door where the houseman's goons were. Fella stood off to the side talking to a couple of dime pieces. D-Roc hit his point and went to collecting his money.

As he counted the cash, he spoke loudly saying, "Hold up, Hold the fuck up, I was fading you for three hundred, I had two side bets for three hundred on a straight five, then I had two side bets for two hundred on a five or nine, six, eight, this shit ain't right."

"Don't nobody move, house straighten this shit, this shit ain't what it's supposed to be."

One of the owner's goons rushed over to the dice game. Fella crept up behind him, knowing that it was time to set it off.

"Hold on now baby. You say ya money ain't right?" The house man said trying to get his place under control.

"Hell yeah my money ain't right." D-Roc shot back.

"Well what is all this?" The house man was confused by D-Roc's outburst.

"This is a mutha fuckin robbery," Lil Walt said as he shoved one of his nine millimeters in the man's face. Before his goons could react Fella had his nine to the back of one of their head, while Slim aimed his tech nine, that he hid under his windbreaker, hanging by his shoestring from his shoulder at the goon.

"Slow down homie, before I put something hot in you," Slim said to the goon that guarded the door.

"You make a move and I'll blow ya brains all over the dice table," D-Roc swung his tech nine from his jacket and yelled

"Everybody reach for the sky, this is a mutha fuckin robbery. Get ya mutha fucking hands up nigga," D-Roc yelled at a man who was hesitant with following instructions. As Walt, Slim, and Fella took the guns from the houseman and his goons. D-Roc smacked blood from the mouth of the guy who was hesitant. Then shoved the guy to the ground and yelled,

"Everybody get the fuck on the floor!"

Everyone complied.

"Gangsta grab some bags," D-Roc yelled to Slim calling him by a name the crew only knew him by. Fella and Walt walked over top of their captives with D-Roc flashing their weapons. Slim grabbed a few trash bags and gave one to lil Walt and Fella. They removed everyone's jewelry and pocket cash, then hit the house safe and quickly dashed out the front door. After spending close to a month in Circleville, Mills was finally transferred to Guyage

Hills boy school in Cleveland Ohio. He stepped off the bus in an orange jump suit with a shaved head, his hands cuffed and his feet shackled, along with nineteen other juveniles. A hard ass J.C.O. by the name of Taylor walked back and forth as he instructed the boys to make a single file line. Taylor looked just as mean as the words he spoke. He stared all the juveniles in the face as he walked by them. Two guys behind Mills whispered to one another as Taylor passed them. Taylor quickly turned in their direction,

"Who the fuck talking in my line? I see I got group of hard-headed mutha fuckas and you will spend a whole lot of time by y'all self in that boy," Taylor warned.

He sized Mills up as he walked by.

"Man what the fuck wrong with this dude bro?" Mills whispered to the guy in front of him named Nasty Man, but everybody called him Nasty for short.

"Chill out hommie, this dude a dick head." Nasty whispered back. Nasty was a few years older than Mills, and this was his third time doing a juvy bid, he knew most of the staff at the facility. He and Mills were celly's at Circleville, and being that they were both from Columbus, they became pretty tight in a few short weeks they celled together. As Mills and the other nineteen juveniles walked up the long hallway, juveniles the size of grown men came running out of their classrooms. Some juveniles already stood in the hallway awaiting the intakes arrival. They stared at Mills and the rest of the intake with the meanest faces. Some of them threw up gang signs and some spoke with gang lingo.

"What up folks?" One of the guys said to the boys behind Mills.
"Seven foe gangsta," They replied.

Man these niggas trippin on this gang shit, get money. Mills thought. By the time they made it to the end of the hallway, and turned down another hallway, Mills had heard just about every gang yelled out. As they walked down the second hallway J.C.O. Taylor said

"At the end of this hallway, there will be a door to your right, y'all stand next to that door. They'll be a lady sitting at the desk. She'll give you your bed number and ya bed roll. Y'all make ya beds and stand next to them *quietly*, until given further instructions."

J.C.O. Taylor put special emphasis on the word quietly. When Mills finally got his cuffs removed he stepped in the dorm and scanned the room looking for familiar faces. He received another set of mean mugs, but he also noticed some faces that he'd seen before. Out a few familiar faces Mills recognized, he could only put a name with one. While all the other boys sat two, three, and even four to a couch, Black was stretched out on a couch by himself. Mills nodded his head at Black. Black returned his nod with a smile and said, "What's up lil nigga, get your shit together I'll be back there in a minute."

Mills got his bedroll and headed to his bunk. While Mills made his bed, Black walked up behind him with a care package.

"What's up, Black?" Mills said.

"Ain't shit ma nigga, here go a few things you gone need, it's some hygiene, and a few goodies in there. What yo lil ass doin in here man?"

"It's a long story bro," Mills answered.

"How much time you got?" Black asked.

"Three years." Mills said while shaking his head in disgust.

"Aw I'm a let you get yo shit together then, we got time to kick it. You only gone be in this pod for like a week though. Since it is your first time being locked up, they gone send you to the first time offender's dorm, them lil niggas down there wild'n out too, so guard ya grill lil nigga," Black said while playfully throwing a jab at Mills. J.C.O. Taylor came walking in as Black and Mills were finishing off their conversation.

"Aye! I thought I told you I wanted it quiet until I gave further instructions. What the fuck don't you understand about being quiet." Taylor yelled at Mills.

"What the fuck is dudes problem?" Mills whispered to Black. "Now you hard of hearing huh lil nigga, you gone start yo time off in isolation." Taylor continued.

"Chill out Mills. I gotchu, this nigga soft for real. He just hard on the intake." Black whispered.

"My bad Taylor man, it's my fault, I mislead him. It won't happen again." Black said smooth talking the J.C.O.

"You saying it's your fault like that makes things alright. You ain't running shit nigga, you gone make me take you in that box and bend yo lil ass up again." Taylor said as he moved towards Mills and Black. Once he got close he and Black squared off on each other and playfully threw a few jabs at one another. "Aight Taylor, I'm a put you on yo ass again." Black said playfully as he slipped Taylor punches and tapped him with a combination to the body. They both started laughing as Taylor grabbed Black. When they separated, Taylor looked at Mills and said,

"And don't think just because you cool with Black you can do what the fuck you wanna do, cause Black ain't the one runnin shit, this my pod." He looked at Black and said, "Go to the T.V. room pully, while I go over the rules with these new jacks." Taylor went over the rules and released the new jacks into the T.V. room with the rest of juveniles.

Mills walked over to Black's couch. Black petted the couch like a dog, and said,

"Have a seat lil nigga."

"Why everybody else is squeezing two, three, and four people on a couch and you got one to yourself?" Mills asked as he sat down. "Cause these niggas know, if they sit on my couch, I'm a beat they ass. I ain't bout to be sittin shoulder to shoulder with some niggas unless I'm cool with them like that, you dig?" Black answered.

"I dug." Mills said with a smile.

"And fuck what Taylor's soft ass talking about, this my pod. He don't run shit but his mouth." Black added.

Black was D-Roc, and Slim's age. He hung out on Main and Gilbert, which was a few blocks down from Liley, where D-Roc, and Slim hung out at. Lil Walt was from Black's crew. They'd hooked up with D-Roc and Slim and cause havoc everywhere they went. When Black got juvenile life at the age of thirteen for aggravated robbery and murder, Lil Walt teamed up with D-Roc and Slim. The three eventually became inseperable. Black knew Mills as Buckshot's younger brother. He, like everyone else on Main Street, bought dope from Buck. Mills was just entering the game when Black got knocked, so he never got to witness Mills transition. As Mills caught Black up on everything that he's missed in the hood, including the events that lead up to him being in jail, Nasty Man walked up. "What's up homie?" Black said, cutting Mills off as Nasty approached his couch.

"What's happenin?" Nasty responded.

"You tell me, nigga, you over here standing over top of my couch," Black said while jumping to his feet ready to rumble.

"Nah Nah. Hold up, Black. This is my homie, he cool." Mills said as he jumped in between them.

"Black this ma dude Nasty. He from Mount Vernon. Nasty, this ma big homie Black from the hood." Mills said introducing the two. Black let some of the air out of his already blown up chest.

"What's happenin bro?" Black said as he extended out his hand for some dap. Nasty dapped it up with Black and returned his greeting.

"You gotta excuse ma hostility homie, but I put in so much work on them streets, I don't even remember some of the niggas I had beef with, but if you a friend of Mills, you cool wit me, you can have a seat bro." Black said as he pointed to an empty spot on the couch. As they sat on the couch conversing, Black and Nasty hit it off. They knew a lot of the same females and Black finally remembered Nasty from the first time he visited Cuyahoga Hills Boys School two years ago.

After spending a week in the pod with Black, Mills was transferred to the first time offender's dorm. Once he walked in the unit, all the juveniles were beside their beds, on their knees, with their hands on their heads. J.C.O. Whitaker was just as mean as Taylor. He yelled at Mills, "Drop your shit on your bunk and join the rest of the dorm on ya knees. I'll let the boys tell you why they're on their knees, and the rules in this unit, that way when you break the rules, and everyone pays for it, you can answer to them, so hope you can fight."

He paced the floor up and down each isle.

"A dorm. Tell Mr. Mills here, why you are all on your knees right now." J.C.O. Whitaker ordered.

"Because a dorm that stays together pays together, Sir." The boys answered in unison.

"That's right, so if one person fucks up, everyone pays for that fuck up, so I say again, Mr. Mills I hope you can fight," Whitaker said as he looked down on Mills while passing his bunk. It took Mills a few days to find some guys he could relate to. Out of the sixty inmates the dorm housed, only ten of them were from Columbus. Twenty-five were from Cleveland, ten were from Cincinnatti and the reaming fifteen were from a mixture of Akron, Dayton, and Toledo. Out of the ten guys from Columbus, only four of them were thorough, five including Mills.

The other five guys were punked on a daily basis, and Mills quickly saw who not to hang around. Black told Mills that although there were gang bangers in Cuyahoga Hills, the color of a person's flag ain't mean nothing when they were from the same city. He told Mills it didn't matter what hood a person was from, Columbus boys stuck together, and the same rules applied to boys from every other city. B-nut, Law, Rash, and H.T. which stood for Hill Top, stuck together like glue and Mills could tell they were respected, although it was clear that Rex and the Cleveland boys owned the dorm. Mills was confused because if the guys from Columbus were to stick together, why did B-nut, Rash, Laws, and H.T. sit back and let the Cleveland boys pick on the other guys from Columbus in the block. Mills's questions were quickly answered after he stood up for one of the Columbus guys and the guy ran off when he was trapped in a corner by Rex and his homies. B-nut, Rash, Law, and H.T. ran to Mills rescue and topped the problem before it got out a hand.

Afterwards they explained to Mills how they had got into a brawl with the Cleveland boys over a few of the other guys from Columbus, and those same guys turned their backs and ran when the fight broke out. Mills quickly understood why the guys from Columbus were divided in the dorm. Mills, H.T., Rash, and B-nut were on the stage working out; while Law did what he does every time they had rec. Law was on the basketball court showcasing his skills. Law was the oldest of the five, at seventeen. He was from Southside of Columbus and could've played high school and possibly college ball if he didn't get sucked into the dope game.

Law was sentenced to five years after shooting two guys that robbed him. He had two years of the five in and he didn't have any intentions of working out. He felt basketball was the only workout he needed. Besides talking about females, and getting money, shooting hoops was all he did. H.T. was next in age, at fifteen but only because birthday was a couple of months before Rash's. H.T. was from a neighborhood called the Hill Top on the West side of Columbus.

Everyone abbreviated his name, thus calling him H.T. He was a black guy in a white boy's body. He was the gangsterest, and smoothest white boy Mills had ever seen. H.T. was also serving five years, though he was charged with aggravated robbery and carjacking. H.T. had been stealing and jacking cars since he was

91

eleven. He had a crew of carjackers and if he wasn't thorough he could've brought them down with him, but he took his time and kept his mouth shut.

Unlike Law, H.T. was halfway through his bid. Rash was fifteen as well. He was from Livingston Avenue, and although he was aware of the beef with him and Mills hood, he had been locked up before the beef got thick. Rash was sentenced to juvenile life, which was until he was eighteen or twenty-one. He had three years in on his murder charge. Like B-nut, Rash liked cracking on people, telling jokes and laughing. A lot of times his humor had him misconstrued for a local joker, but the boy's hands were cold. B-nut was only a year older than Mills, at fourteen. He was a blood from Columbus Lincoln Park project housing. B-nut was off the hook. He had no respect for authority and barred none.

Everything was funny to him. He was the kind of guy that made being in jail less strenuous,\ and stressful, because all he knew how to do was have fun. B-nut was serving four and a half years for killing his mother's boyfriend in self defense. As Mills got his set in on the weight bench, B-nut and Rash attacked one another with jokes.

"B-nut, yo lil ass always cupping with them lil ass locks. You ol fake ass Jamaican with that nasty ass chipped tooth," Rash said causing Mills to put the weights down and burst into laughter. B-nut and H.T. laughed as well, but Rash rarely won a cracking battle against B-nut.

"Aw blood, you tryna send me," B-nut said in between his laughter.

"Rash you got me fucked up nigga, I knew I seen you somewhere before too, you was that nigga at the club Teen Scene wit a halter top on and some biker shorts wit Sagittarius going across the ass in glittery letters," B-nut said while acting out the scene at the club. They all fell out laughing again.

"Mills you sure is getting a good laugh today, nigga. I ain't heard this much out of you since you been here." Rash said.

"Yeah that nigga always sittin around all quiet, like some monk meditating and shit." B-nut said while dropping to the floor Indian style, and clasping his hands together, while bowing his head like a monk. The laughter continued as B-nut put on a show.

"Nah man, I just be thinking and shit. I been here almost a month and Whitaker bitch ass ain't let me make a phone call yet." Mills said after his laughter became controllable.

"What you trynna chase down some little hood rat?" B-nut asked

"Hell nah bro, I'm trying check on ma peoples, and let um know where I'm at and that I'm aight, my grandma a trip. She probably talking to Jesus right now." Mills said. "I don't give a fuck about no females bro I'm about my money out there baby." Mills and B-nut were cut short by H.T.

"Aw shit Rex and them bout to jump Law." H.T. said as he jumped to his feet. He, Mills, B-nut, and Rash ran off the stage to join Law as he hit Rex with a combination and backed into Rex's partner B-White, who hit him with some thunder. As quickly as Law fell he was back to his feet.

"Y'all gotta jump ol Law dawg huh?" Law said as he pivoted out the circle they were forming around him.

"Boom!" B-nut yelled as he slid B-White across the floor with a treacherous hook. Guys from Cleveland came running off the stage, out of the game room, and from the bleachers. They quickly filled the floor up. Rash hit Rex with a pretty one too, splitting his lip. H.T. hit Rex homeboy Flannigan with some thunder, while Mills went toe to toe with Scooter.

The numbers quickly became too vast for the Columbus boys, but they held their own, refusing to hit the floor. The J.C.O.'s called for back up. The boys were too much for Whitaker and the rec staff to handle alone. Once their reinforcements arrived, the brawl was quickly broken up, but not before the floor was filled with blood. Although Mills and his boys were leaking, their blood wasn't the only bloodshed. The Cleveland boys had some war wounds of their own. While Mills and the rest of the boys were escorted out of the gymnasium, Black was walking up the hallway with J.C.O. Taylor and the rest of the unit.

Mills was aggressively ushered by Black and Black noticed the blood that poured from his nose and lip. Then he saw Rex and the Cleveland boys behind Mills leaving a blood trail of their own.

"You know you done fucked up right?" Black said to Rex while cracking his knuckles. Rex looked at Black confused, having no knowledge of how close he and Mills were. All the boys were placed in isolation, known throughout the institution as the box. Mills and his new homeboys were questioned first by authorities because they were out numbered and Rex was known to be a trouble maker throughout the camp. There were so many Cleveland guys involved that they couldn't catch them all.

Mills and his homeboys didn't give the staff any help identifying the stragglers. They said it was a misunderstanding over basketball, and they didn't know who all was involved. The boys spent a few days in isolation. When they were released five of the guys from Cleveland were placed in another unit, Rex included. Unfortunately for them, they were placed in the same unit as Black. Black, Nasty, and the rest of the guys from Columbus didn't waste any time avenging Mills and the rest of his homies. Unlike his crew, Rex managed to escape a hospital visit. After being moved to another unit, Rex and some other guys from Cleveland returned Black's favor by breaking some jaws and stomping out some guys from Columbus in their unit. For the next few months Cleveland and Columbus went back and forth exchanging beatings to one another. By the beginning of 94' the whole camp was placed on lockdown. They had no privileges and were escorted to and from chow, and school. As Mills did his push-ups, while finishing time in isolation, he thought of how worried his grandmother must be.

With all the beef going on he had no time to write letters to anyone, because he was either in the box, marching up and down hallways for hours with the rest of the dorm, or on his knees with his hands behind his head. After being in the camp for thirty days, Mills was supposed to receive his phone privileges, but after the constant fighting, the camps phone privileges were taken. After spending close to a hundred days on lockdown, the camp had calmed down and were steady being given the privileges back.

It was late spring, and camp has been off lockdown for three weeks, with no gang riots or city wars. As Mills and his homies occupied two couches for a movie day, the unit manager announced that the camp had finally been given back their phone privileges. Mills dashed to the phone, racing over thirty other juveniles. There were only four phones, so the juveniles were allowed only one call then they had to get back in line. Mills was happy he made it to one of the four phones first. As he dialed his grandmother's number, a lengthy line formed behind him, and boys on the other three phones. Mills grandmother accepted the call before the recording could go all the way through.

"Oh Lord, Tony, why ain't you call home?" Grandma Mills said with concern.

"Hi to you too mama," Mills responded. "Oh I'm sorry baby, but you had me worried sick," She responded understanding Mills sarcasm.

"Don't worry momma I'm aight, but why I haven't called is a long story, one I'd rather not tell," Mills said hoping his grandmother would leave it at that.

"Where's my lil brother at?" Mills continued quickly changing the topic.

"He's upstairs playing the game. Daylon bought him some new games for scoring three touchdowns in every last one of his football games last season," She replied.

"My lil bro playing football and I'm in here missing it. I'm hurt momma. I can't believe I ain't there for Jim right now." Mills paused then continued. "Three touchdowns a game, he's that good huh?"

"My baby's the bomb! But I'm a let him tell you his self," She said with enthusiasm. "Jimmy get the phone it's your brother!" She yelled. He snatched the phone off the receiver.

"What's up, big bro. I love you man, when you coming home?"

The question touched Mills, but he kept his composure for him and his little brother.

"I love you too big head, and I'll be home shortly." Mills replied not wanting to lie to his brother, but not wanting to tell him he had two years left either. Mills conversated with Jimmy for awhile and told him to put his grandmother back on the phone before the call ended. Mills gave his grandmother the address to Cuyahoga Hills Boys School and suddenly recording said, "Sixty seconds."

"Well momma the phones bout to hang up, I love you, and I'll call next weekend," Mills said.

"Okay baby, I love you too,.You be good and go to church while your down there, get right with The Lord Tony." She said adamantly.

"Yes ma'am." Mills replied.

"Okay baby. Oh, before I forget, call Brandy and Daylon, they been calling over here driving me crazy," She said before the phone hung up. Mills looked behind him and shook his head at the sight of the line he had to get back in. He quickly dialed Brandy's number.

"Hold up Pimp, I gotta use that phone, too." A guy named T-Bone from Cincinnatti said.

"I feel you homie, I don't mean no disrespect, but this call is really important." Mills responded.

"Aight Pimp, I'm a let you get this one off, but my shit is important too, dawg."

Mills, offended by T-Bones demeanor and the fact that he kept calling him Pimp, but the sound of Brandy's voice caused him to disregard T-Bone's disrespectful demeanor.

"What's up bro, why you just now calling a bitch?" Brandy said. Mills laughed before responding. "You crazy Bee, but shit been wild down here, we been on lockdown for fighting these Cleveland niggas, I keep a lump or bump on my shit sis."

They both started laughing.

"Man I miss you, bro, them bitches extended my house arrest for six more months, I been in this house sick, but I'm off this shit next week, I'm pumped. I got rid of your shit too, so you got a few stacks over here when you get out, nigga." Brandy replied.

"What's up with Fella, Peko, and Shawn Shawn?" Mills asked.

"They chillen, gettin money, and shit. You know Pee on the run for smoking weed. That's messed up too because me, Fells and Shawn Shawn bout to get off paper early." Brandy said.

"Oh Yeah?" Mills said happy to hear Brandy's voice.

"What Fells fat ass been up to?" Mills asked.

"Oh my God, What ain't he been up too. He been hanging out with D-Roc and them, and they been into all types of shit. They been robbing niggas and everything." Brandy said.

"BRANDY! Watch your mouth. I told you about all that cussing, you ain't mutha fucking grown." Her mother yelled from her bedroom.

"My bad ma." Brandy yelled back.

"Where Fells and them at now?" Mills asked concerned about Fella.

"They at Lolly's, hold on I'm bout to call over there." Brandy clicked over and called Lolly's on three way. Lolly answered the phone as Brandy clicked Mills back on the line. "

Who the fuck is it." "Dang auntie, what's wrong with you?" Brandy answered. "Brandy? Excuse me baby, Fella's fat ass get on my nerve, he always playing and shit." Lolly said sounding frustrated.

Mills and Brandy both started laughing know how playful Fella was.

"Is that my nephew I hear?" Lolly asked noticing Mills voice.

"Yeah this me auntie, what's happenin?" Mills answered.

"You, you happenin baby, when you coming home?"

"I got a couple more years left, where my bros at?" Mills said. "Peko and Shawn right here playing the game, Fella in the back wit some lil girl he bought over, he just walked in the door about a half hour ago, and he's already pissed me off," Lolly said.

"Let me speak to my bros' auntie before my call ends."

"Aight baby, you stay strong and hurry home. Here nigga, Mills on the phone." Lolly said as she threw the phone on Peko's lap.

"What's up bro, you know we miss you out here nigga," Peko said.

"Yeah bro I miss y'all too. Bee told me, Fella, been tripping." Mills responded.

"Aw man, that nigga off the hook, he in the back room wit some freak right now." Peko replied.

"Get that dude for me before the phone hangs up bro," Mills said. "Hold up, holler at Shawn while I get Fells." Peko pitched the phone to Shawn Shawn.

"What up big bro, we miss you out here, man." Shawn Shawn said

"I miss y'all too lil bro. You keeping them niggas together out there right?" Mills replied.

"Man you know these niggas off the hook, especially Fells bro, he all over the place, hold up. Here he goes right here." Shawn Shawn said.

"AHHHH! What's up nigga?" Fella said.

"I don't know you tell me, I hear you rolling with Roc now. You know dude ain't nothing but trouble bro." Mills said.

"Stop tripping bro, it ain't even like that. "Fella replied as the recording informed him that Mills had sixty seconds left.

"A my nigga don't worry, I'm holding it down out here. I hollered at them hoe ass niggas for you too, tighten they ass all the way up boy." Fella said while laughing as he remembered the bullets he put in the guys that followed them from the skating rink a year ago.

"Get money bro fuck that bullshit." Mills said. He was furious that his right-hand man was turning into D-Roc.

"Aye don't go nowhere bro, I'm bout to call right back." Mills said when the recording told him he had ten seconds. Mills hung up the phone and looked over his shoulder to see if T-Bone was conversating with one of his homies. Mills quickly dialed Brandy's number again.

"Aye hold up Pimp, I told you I need to get on that phone." T-Bone said as he caught Mills out the corner of his eye.

"This the last one homie, I'm in the middle of an important conversation." Mills said not paying T-Bone any attention.

"Nah you got me fucked up Pimp, my shit important too, if I ain't using that phone, ain't nobody using it," T-Bone said as he walked up behind Mills and hung the phone up.

"Never let anyone play you like a sucka." Echoed through Mills head as he turned to face T-Bone. Mills was already mad about Fella's decision to hang out with D-Roc. Now T-Bone was testing his courage by hanging his call up.

"So what you wanna work about this shit?" Mills said while sizing up T-Bone.

"Whatever Pimp, I know you ain't bout to use that phone again," T-Bone replied while standing his ground. Mills dropped the phone and rushed T-Bone with a hook and a jab. He landed his jab but missed his hook, as T-Bone faded away from it. Before T-Bone could fully recuperate, Mills was under him taking his body to the air. T-Bone tried to wiggle out of Mills lock on his legs, but it was too late. Mills slammed him to the ground hard and climbed on top of him. As Mills went to work on his face, B-nut, H.T., Law, and Rash came running out of the movie room.

"Beat that nigga's ass blood!" B-nut yelled.

Mills was carried off to the box while T-Bone was escorted to medical bay. Mills had already spent so much time in the box, that being locked in the cold room with no bed, or anything else to sit or lay on didn't bother him anymore.

Mills had long ago accepted the box as his second home, so once the door was slammed and locked on him, he removed his shirts and started doing push-ups, which he would do until he was tired enough to stretch out on the floor and sleep.

CHAPTER 7

Summer of 94'. Brandy is leaving her P.O.'s office with her mother. She's just had her house arrest and probation terminated. She stretched her arms out before getting into her mothers car, and saID, "Oh my God, I'm finally free. I can't wait to spread my wings."

"Okay Nicole, you take yo grown ass in them streets and get in some more shit if you want to. I'm a let your ass sit in jail next time." Her mother scolded.

"Dag ma. Go head and jinx me why don't you." Brandy said while playfully rolling her eyes at her mother.

"I ain't playing with you Brandy." Her mother responded with a sassy look of her own.

"I know ma, but I also know you ain't just gone let yo baby sit in jail either."

"Try me." Her mother shot back.

Brandy knew her mother was serious, but she also knew her mother wouldn't let her sit in jail. Brandy played with the radio until she found 106.3. She threw her hands up in the air and snapped her fingers while saying,

"C'mon ma this ma jam." As Jodeci's "Stay" screamed through the speakers. Her mother rolled her eyes as she pulled off and said,

"Your grown butt get on my nerves, you think I'm playing with you." They both laughed. When Brandy's mother turned onto Berkley, the strip was packed. Fella, D-Roc, Slim, and Walt stood by Fella and D-Roc's cars. D-Roc sat on the hood of his all white 94' Maximum, with gold flakes in his wet white pain't, soft white leather interior, a banging system, and sixteen inch gold Moe Moes. Fella sat in the driver seat of his 87' Monte Carlos playing with the deck to his system. His Monte was equipped with a wet green and gold marble pain't job, green and gold leather bucket seats, matching race car steering wheel, some chrome McClain rims with gold spinners, and a 350 turbo horsepower engine. He hopped out his car as Brandy's mother parked her car.

"What's up auntie? What's up Bee?" Fella yelled over the top of his and D-Roc's systems.

"What's up nephew?" Brandy's mother replied as she climed up the steps leading to her front door.

"What's up Fells, let me hit something nigga," Brandy said, referring to the fat blunt Fella held in between his fingers. Fella took a couple puffs before passing it.

"Feels good to be off that probation shit, huh?" Fella said while blowing smoke in the air. Brandy looked at D-Roc, Slim, and Walt as she hit the weed. She could feel D-Rocs eyes on her.

"What's up lil Brandy, you still mad at me?" D-Roc said with a big smile on his face.

"Nah we straight, that shits old." Brandy replied.

"What's up Slim and Walt." She said acknowledging them as well.

"What's happening," Slim said smoothly. Walt retuned her greeting with a simple head nod.

"What you getting into today, Bee? You tryna roll up to the coming home?" Fella asked. The coming home is a large block party held every year in Columbus on a drug-infested strip known as money earning Mount Vernon.

"I don't know...who y'all rolling up there with Pee and Shawn Shawn?" Brandy answered with a question of her own.

"Nah, I'm rolling up there with D-Roc, Slim and Walt. You know Pee and Shawn Shawn don't know nothing but Lolly's.

They act like that money going somewhere." Fella said. "They might roll up there though, cause Pee just bought a sick ass Regal." He continued.

Brandy was turned off by the thought of rolling with D-Roc and his crew. She didn't dislike them; she just knew that wherever they went, trouble seemed to follow. After all, half the city was at bay with them while the other half feared them.

"I don't know Fells, I might roll, if Pee and Shawn go but, I gotta call Buck, so I can get right feel me," Brandy said being careful not to expose her discomfort around D-Roc and his crew. Brandy said her see you laters and headed in her house. She paged Buck and put in her code followed by 911. Buck quickly returned her page. After a couple of minutes of encoded conversation, Buck told her he'd be there shortly and they disconnected. Brandy pulled two shoeboxes out of her closet and dumped stacks of money from both of them onto her bed.

She counted out fourteen thousand, not including the six thousand she had of Mills. Brandy put eight thousand aside, then put the remains back in one shoebox, and hid it in her closet. Brandy wondered if D-Roc and his crew knew she had twenty thousand dollars at her house, would they rob her and her mother? She was unsure about Slim because he was the most polished, and cool of the three, but she knew for sure D-Roc and Walt would have to have it.

She was sure the both of them had twenty thousand dollars of their own, if not more, but that never stoped them, they robbed people with less than them everyday. More or less didn't matter to them, if the person had it and they wanted it they were coming to get it! Brandy separated the seventy five hundred she was about to pay Buck for nine ounces and put half in each of her front pockets. She put the remaining five hundred from the eight thousand in her back pocket for spending cash, and headed to the front porch to wait on buck. After standing on her porch for five minutes, a candy pain'ted cherry red 5.0 Mustang with a peanut butter brown leather soft drop top gold flakes, some triple gold hundred spoke daytons, and a thunderous system bent the corner.

Computer love filled the street from the car speakers. Heads turned, mouths dropped, and D-Roc, Slim, Walt, and Fella gripped their pistols. Although the car was a big deal to everyone else, it was only one of Bucks newest toys that he'd more than likely get rid of in a few weeks. Had Buck not had the top down, Walt might have filled the vehicle with holes just for riding down the street and stealing him and his boys shine. Buck stopped in front of Brandy's house and motioned for her to come to the car. Brandy hopped in and Buck backed up to acknowledge his little homies. He turned the music off and said, "What's up Roc, Slim, Walt, and Fella."

"What up big homie." They replied in unison.

"Damn Roc, that Max clean as a bitch," Buck said complementing D-Roc on his ride.

"Yea its aight," D-Roc said modestly. Buck smiled.

"Who's SS is that with that wet ass marble pain't," Buck asked.

"Fuck this SS; I'm tryna get that bitch right there," Fella replied while pointing at Buck's 5.0.

"Shit that Monte clean Lil Fells, that's a bad ma fucka, but if you wanna upgrade, you know the name of the game Stack N Grind baby," Buck replied.

"What y,all getting into tonight Roc?" Buck continued.

"Shid, we gone slide up to that coming home a little later, why what's up?" D-Roc answered.

"Ain't nothing up, I'm probably gone roll up through with y'all, flick for T-money, dig." Buck said.

"I can dig it." D-Roc shot back.

"Call me before y'all take off." Buck said

"You got it." D-Roc replied.

Buck turned his system back up and threw up the peace sign as he bobbed his head and pulled off. When Buck brought Brandy back to her house, Fella, D-Roc, Slim, and Walt were gone. Although the strip was still packed, Brandy waste no anytime. She threw up the peace sign to Buck, and nodded at a few young hustlers who stood on the corner as she ran in her house. She took one ounce from the nine she brought from Buck and put the rest in her stash spot. She called over Lolly's to be sure Peko and Shawn Shawn were there then she headed out the house to join them. She flagged down one of her customers who slowly drove up the street as she came running out of the house. She served her customer a fifty and had him drop her off at Lolly's house. Brandy knocked on the door a few times before she heard Lolly on her way to answer the door.

She knew it was Lolly because she was cursing someone out as she approached.

"What's up, Auntie. Who done pissed you off now?" Brandy said as Lolly yanked the door open while yelling,

"Who the fuck is it? Aw shit, c'mon in Brandy," Lolly said, once she saw it was Brandy. Brandy entered the house laughing because she knew Lolly was screaming and cursing for no reason. Lolly was the type of person who was always mad about something.

"My niece here now, you niggas better tighten up," Lolly yelled as Brandy walked in the living room. Shawn Shawn sat on the couch by himself smoking on a fat blunt, while counting a stack of bills.

"What up lil Bro, where Pee at?" Brandy asked.

"What up sis. Pee ah be here in a minute, you know he don't come out till Pac-man gets off work, he at the crib wit his girl." Shawn Shawn answered.

"His girl shy, he been messing with her for about four months. He moved in with her and her mom since he on the run and Pac-man keep stalking our mom's crib. That nigga whipped too." Shawn Shawn said, causing him and Brandy to laugh.

Brandy passed the blunt back to Shawn then threw him a bag of weed that she bought from Buck. "Roll up." She said before heading for the kitchen to cut up her work. After busting her blocks down, she gave Lolly a plate full of crumbs, then dropped a couple extra twenties on the plate.

"That's why you're my favorite," Lolly said. Brandy winked at her, washed her hands and rejoined Shawn in the living room. Shawn Shawn sat back and let Brandy serve all the customers, as the back door got knocked on non stop. Shawn Shawn already made a killing. He had the spot to himself all day. Now that Mills was locked up, Peko and Shawn Shawn had the most money out of the crew, because they hustled together and combined their money. One of them was at the spot getting money at all times.

After being at Lolly's for an hour, Peko had finally arrived. It was 4 O'clock and Pac-man's shift was over at 3 O'clock, and Peko let his system rattle the house in Pac Man's absence. Peko quickly pulled up in Lolly's backyard and parked the car. Within a few minutes, he came strolling in the living room through the kitchen.

"What up lil Bro. What up light skin." Peko said acknowledging his little brother and Brandy. They both returned the acknowledgments with a what's up of their own. Peko plopped down on the couch next to Brandy, pulled a blunt from behind his ear, and sat fire to it.

"Plug the game up bro so I can bust yo ass in that Madden." Peko said as he took a few quick puffs of the weed.

As Shawn Shawn hooked the Super Nintendo up, Brandy asked Peko about the coming home.

"Shit, I don't give a fuck sis, if you wanna roll up there we can."

"Yea we might as well, I been cooped up in the house for a year bro, I'm trynna go somewhere, anywhere." Brandy replied.

"Aight, let me bust Shawn ass in Madden a few times, then we can roll out," Peko said.

"C'mon bro, you know you can't fuck wit me." Shawn Shawn replied.

"Yeah we bout to see nigga," Peko responded while laughing because he knew his little brother was telling the truth.

After losing a few games of John Madden's football, and smoking a few blunts the session was interrupted by Fells call. He informed the crew that him D-Roc, Slim, Walt, and Buck were on their way to the block party and that they'd parked in Tooney's drive thru lot. Peko and Shawn ended their fourth game with Peko up a touchdown. Although it was only half time, Peko swore his seven-point lead as a victory. They headed out the back door to Peko's sky blue 84 Regal, with a white rag top, sky blue interior, chrome trimming, and hundred spoke Daytons. Peko kept his Regal clean inside and out. The rims and the point both were sparkling clean.

"Pee this a nice ass ride." Brandy said as they loaded into the Regal.

"Shit for five large it better be tight." He responded.

Peko's pager started screaming as he popped the face on his system. He looked at the number, and said,

"Damn...this girl is crazy; she be on ma heels."

"Who dat, Shy?" Brandy said in a funny voice.

"Hell yea...how you know about my Shy?" Peko answered. "Damn nigga. Yo Shy, huh?" Brandy said inquisitively.

"Yeah. That's my baby, but she always paging me for no reason and shit. Where you at? Who you wit? I think she addicted to what the dick did." Peko said playfully. Brandy punched him in his arm.

"Nah she cool though Bee. I love her and shit, she down for Pee dawg." Peko said speaking in the third person.

"I hope so." Brandy replied.

"Shit light skin you need to get you a nigga so you can loosen up" Peko said playfully.

"Psssh. I don't need no nigga. I ain't thinking about no nigga; my mind is on my bread. Anyway with the way you and Fella treating bitches, I'm cool, I don't need no nigga lying and cheating on me." Brandy said in a sassy tone. Peko's pager started screaming again as he started the car up.

He looked at the pager shaking his head, because he knew it was Shy again.

"Hold up ya'll, let me run in here and call this girl back for she break my pager. Huh, roll up." Peko said throwing a bag of weed on Brandy's lap before hopping out the car.

"So where ya girly at lil bro?" Brandy asked Shawn Shawn while breaking open a swisher.

"My girls name is Reese, she cool, you probably know her sister Sa'sha y'all go to the same school."

"Sa'sha the head doctor," Brandy said while turning completely around to face Shawn Shawn in the back seat. Shawn Shawn started laughing.

"Yea that's her."

"Lil bro you better be careful, cause you know what they say, like the mother, like daughter, like sister."

Shawn Shawn continued to laugh. "I ain't playing Shawn, you better be wearing condoms, and thinking twice before you put yo thang in these lil girls, cause they nasty, and they will give you some shit you can't get rid of." Brandy preached.

"Yeah I know big sis, and I am being careful, but me and Reese ain't even went that far yet, she still a virgin." Shawn Shawn said.

Peko came running back to the car interrupting their conversation as he hopped in saying,

"I told y'all that girl ain't want shit, she lucky I love her." He backed out the yard, as eight balls "Mr. Bigs" shook the ground from his speakers. When Peko turned onto the crowded street heads turned as his fifteens roared. He quickly spotted Fella, and D-Roc's cars parked at Tooney's drive-thru. He pulled in and parked next to Buck's 5.0 Mustang. Buck sat on the hood of his car snapping off pictures as Fella entertained two females by the payphones, while D-Roc, Slim, and Walt held the attention of another flock of half-dressed females.

The scene was packed with ballers, and females of all shapes, sizes, and colors. As soon as Peko, Brandy, and Shawn exited the car Buck turned on them and took a few pictures. He passed Peko the blunt of expensive weed he was smoking on, and tossed Brandy one of his cameras. They both flicked it up for Mills until the cameras were empty. Buck finished his film off by taking pictures of the two girls Fella had flashing the camera. Fella waved Peko over to him and the two girls.

"What's up, bro. this Kita and Rita, they twins," Fella said with a big smile on his face.

"Rita this my bro Peko. Pee this is Rita she feeling you." Fella said as he pushed Rita closer to him. D-Roc, Slim, and Walt had enough fun with the gold diggers they were with, so they joined Buck, Brandy, and Shawn over by the cars.

"Roc, Gangsta, look at this bitch ass nigga," Walt said as he saw a white box Chevy on gold Daytons started to pull into the lot, then back out when he spat D-Roc and his crew who were known as Jack Boys. The three burst out in laughter as Walt grabbed his pager and pointed at the car like a gun, causing the driver to duck.

"HA! HA! HA! Coward ass nigga. He a hoe and a coward." Walt said loudly. Brandy watched as Peko and Fella fondled the twins, and it made her think about the conversation her and Peko had about her finding a partner of her own. She remembered him saying how much he loved his girlfriend Shy, but she watched him cheat on her with no regrets or empathy for his girlfriend at home. Being around the boys so much gave her an understanding of men that she didn't like and that made her distrustful of all men when it came to dating and relationships.

Fella and Peko joined the crew after setting up booty calls with the girls for later that night. As Buck gave Brandy a few bills to grab a couple of disposable cameras from the drive thru, a black on black Camero, with jet black tint, gold flakes, and some triple gold hundred spoke Daytons pulled into the parking lot. The driver of the Camero stared at Brandy as she walked in the drive thru. He obviously didn't know who D-Roc and his crew were because he parked right in front of them and hopped out the car blinging. D-Roc, Slim, Walt, and Fella stared at him with greed in their eyes.

Buck felt the vibe and said, "Be easy Roc, right now ain't the time for that."

"What you talking about big homie?" D-Roc said with a sinister grin on his face. Buck gave him a look that said "C'mon Roc, I know you." As Brandy stood in front of the cash register awaiting her cameras, the driver of the Camero stared a hole in her backside. Brandy was a tomboy, but she was drop-dead gorgeous and her young body screamed 100% woman! Brandy wore an airbrushed T-shirt with Mound and Berkley boss lady on the back of it, and her name going across her breast on the front of it. She had some white windbreakers, with a pair of red biker shorts beneath them. Brandy's body was well proportioned, and her ass demanded attention through her windbreakers. On her feet she wore a pair of crispy red and white Jordans.

Her skin complexion was high yellow, and her jet black hair rested on her shoulders. She wore a diamond ring on every finger, a thick herring bone bracelet, and a matching necklace with her name hanging from it for an emblem. Brandy could feel the guy's eyes undressing her from behind and after she got the cameras she turned around with attitude.

"Damn! Did you lose something?"

"As a matter of fact I did...I lost control of myself when I seen you. But I apologize if I offended you, but I think you're a very beautiful young lady, Brandy." The guy said smoothly.

Brandy was caught of guard by his response. Most guys were ignorant, and screamed out things like, "Let me kill it." Or "When you gone let me hit that?" but this guy was smooth, and he spoke respectfully, although Brandy felt violated by his wondering eyes. Brandy thought the guy was attractive as he stood before her with his shirt off exposing his genetically acquired six pack. He was dark skinned, with some blue jean Nautica shorts on, some white ankle socks, and a pair of high top air force ones. He rocked a skin tight fade with a few waves on the top.

Around his neck was a very thick Gucci link chain, with an iced out Jesus piece hanging from it. On his wrist was a matching bracelet complementing his three karat diamond rings. To top it all off his 5'7 frame toward hers at 5'3. Brandy still refused to fall for his slick talk, but before she could gun em down, his words froze her.

"Brandy is yo name right boss lady..."

Brandy looked down at her shirt, and thought of the words on her back, and said,

"Look, man, I ain't impressed by your jewelry, your car, or your money, so you wasting your time."

"Damn Brandy, why you being so mean, you too beautiful to be acting so ugly. Give a brother a chance; all men ain't full of shit. How about we start over? How you doing Brandy, my name is Chris." Chris said as he extended his hand for a handshake. B randy couldn't help, but to laugh.

"C'mon Brandy. I promise if you give me a chance I can keep you smiling." Chris said as he poured his game on heavy.

Brandy accepted his hand and said, "So where do we go from here?"

"Well I'm hoping you'll give me your number and allow me to call you and hopefully take you out sometime," Chris said.

"Let me guess; you carry a pen and paper in yo pocket for a moment like this huh?" Brandy replied sarcastically.

"Ha! Ha! Ha!" Chris laughed before saying, "Nah, not exactly, but I do have a pen and paper in my car, but I'm ah businessman, so I give my number out a few times a day feel me."

"Yeah, you felt." Brandy said with a smile on her face. Chris bought a pack of back woods and escorted Brandy back to his car. He gave her his pen and paper and emptied out one of his back wood cigars where she wrote down her number. She gave him his pen and paper back to him and said,

"Be careful with that,"

He looked at her and smiled. "Aight Brandy, I'm bout to get out of here because I see yo killers over there ain't feeling me." He motioned over to the guys. "You stay beautiful Brandy and stop being so mean." He said before pulling off.

Brandy and the guys spent a couple more hours at the block party, but as the day turned into night they loaded into the cars and left. The next day Brandy was the last one to make it to Lolly's. As she knocked on the door she noticed Fella's car parked on the street. She was happy to finally see him at the spot because she was startin to feel as if he'd just abandoned the crew and their motto which was getting money Stack N Grind! When she entered the house, Peko and Shawn were going into their Madden football as usual.

"What up Pee. What's up lil bro?" She said to Peko and Shawn Shawn.

"What up light skin." Peko shot back.

"Sup sis." Shawn Shawn added. Neither of them took their eyes off the game.

"Where Fells at?" Brandy asked.

"Shid…who knows. He ran in and right back out. Fells don't really hustle no more Bee, he on that stickup shit with Roc and them now." Peko said talking still not taking his eyes off the game.

"Yeah sis, big bro off the hook for sure." Shawn Shawn added.

"Well ain't that his car out there on the street?" Brandy asked. "Probably so, I think he left with his cousin Slim," Peko answered.

While Fella was the topic at Lolly's, he and Slim had two females they met at the club a few nights ago, at the hotel giving them the business. Fella held Lisa's legs in the air as he pushed his manhood in her with force.

"Oooh, get this pussy Fella. Yea! Right there!" Lisa yelled as Fella dug deeper. Slim plunged into India from the back. She yelled,

"Oooh Slim you got a big dick." Her moans and screams got louder every stroke. Fella was more turned on by India's screaming and moaning than he was his own encounter. The deeper Fella dug in Lisa, the more she yelled for him to dig deeper. As Slim flipped India over, Fella became competitive. He dragged Lisa to the end of the bed and put her legs around his shoulders as he stood on the floor. He dove into her with force and watched her large breasts bounce all over the place with every stroke he made. He was through trying to please her; he wanted her to scream like her homegirl in the other bed. Lisa was a freak. She grabbed Fella by the waist and tried to pull him in deeper in her with every stroke. As she moaned, her juices dripped all over Fella's balls and her ass cheeks.

Fella asked, "Who's pussy is this?"

"Yours." She yelled back.

113

"Tell me you love this Mound and Berkley dick," Fella ordered as he plunged into her at jackrabbit speed.

"I love this Mound and Berkley dick. I'm cumin again Fella don't stop. Harder! Harder!" She yelled. Fella looked down at his piece as it slid in and out of her hairy vagina.

God damn I'm giving her everything but my balls. Fella thought as his manhood swelled up with excitement. Slim was now on the bottom, guiding India by the waist as she took as much of his large piece into her cave as she could. Slim released one hand from her waist and smacked it on her ass as she closed her eyes to induce the pain and pleasure of the ride. Slim's pager started vibrating as India's body started to shake. He let her take control of the ride as he checked his pager. He saw D-Roc's girl's phone number followed by 911, and D-Roc's code. Slim had D-Roc's Maximum, but by D-Roc putting 911 in his pager he knew he was calling for more than his car. He stopped India right at the end of her orgasm.

He grabbed the phone and quickly called D-Roc. "Ring! Ring!" D-Roc answered after the first ring.

"Slim" He yelled into the phone over his girl's voice.

"Yeah."

"What up nigga, you ready to roll." Slim said.

"Man hurry the fuck up and come get me before I kill this bitch! This stupid ass hoe done stabbed me dawg." D-Roc shot back.

"I'm on ma way bro." Slim replied.

"Aiight man hurry up." D-Roc ordered.

"Fells lets ride. It's a 911 call." Slim said as he got dressed. Slim looked at India as she pulled her panties on, and thought about climbing back in her tight cave. He snapped out of the daze her body had him in and finished dressing. Slim dropped the girls off at the bus stop before heading to D-Roc's girl's house. When Slim pulled in front of Tee Tee's house, her lil cousin Stanley stood in front of the corner store, on the corner of Oak and

Morrison with a few younger hustlers. Fella stayed in the car, while Slim walked up on the porch, he noticed the door was cracked, and the house was silent. He pulled his nine-millimeter Taurus out, and peeked in the house. He walked in as he saw D-Roc sitting on top of Tee Tee with her arms pinned to the floor. D-Roc had scratches on his face and a shirt soaked with blood from the hole Tee Tee put in his stomach with a steak knife.

Tee Tee's face was covered in blood, her body was bruised, and the house was a mess. D-Rocs nine mm lay on the couch in front of him. While Tee Tee's steak knife lay on the floor a few inches away from her pinned down hands.

"Roc what up bro? What the fuck...you and Tee Tee done tried to kill each other in this bitch." Slim said as he put his gun away.

"Nah bro, this stupid crazy ass bitch done stabbed me, burned my clothes and threatened me with the police." D-Roc said. "Man lets go, bro, you bleeding badly my nig. Let's get the fuck outta here." Slim said as he scanned the messy living room. D-Roc grabbed his nine with one hand, but before he got off Tee Tee he pulled his hand back and slapped blood out her mouth. He stood over top of her with his nine-pointed down on her and said,

"I should kill this bitch bro, look at me, I'm bleeding to death." Slim was a bonafide gangster and he was down for whatever, but he didn't believe in putting his hands on a woman. His father used to beat on his mother and he had no respect for the man for that reason. He felt sorry for Tee Tee, but he was loyal to D-Roc, so he couldn't show any sympathy for the injured woman on the floor.

"C'mon man Roc, fuck that bullshit, let's go my nig," Slim hoped he wouldn't have to pull D-Roc off of the girl. D-Roc listened to his right-hand man but snatched the phone cord out the wall before walking out the door. As D-Roc and Slim pulled from in front of the house, Tee Tee made her way upstairs to the phone in her bedroom. She called the cops and pressed domestic violence charges against D-Roc. She gave the cops his full name and the description of the car. D-Roc had a feeling Tee Tee would call the cops, so he refused to go to the hospital. He and Tee Tee always got into fights, but today things had gotten out of hand, and the two really hurt each other badly.

Slim dropped Fella off at Lolly's and took D-Roc to his mother's house. Fella strolled in Lolly's being loud as usual. Peko laughed as Fella told the story of him and Lisa's encounter.

"I love this Mound and Berk dick," Fella said in a funny voice imitating Lisa, causing Shawn Shawn to join Peko in laughter. Brandy didn't find anything funny. It had been a long time since the four of them were together, so Brandy took advantage of the opportunity.

"Fells what's up wit, you bro?" Brandy said with concern.

"What you mean what's up wit me? Don't start trippin Bee." Fella said in return.

"I'm sayin you changed bro, you don't even hustle no more, you out here robbing, and shooting it out wit niggas, you know that ain't even what we about, you don't even fuck wit the family no more, we sure don't get money together no more, I'm sayin bro you changed."

"C'mon Bee, you tripping, I'm still the ole Fells, huh Pee?" Fells said looking at Peko for some backup.

"Man bro, you know you my nigga and I love you dawg, but Bee right, you ain't been about your paper or the fam lately," Peko said.

"What, man y'all trippin, tell em lil bro." Fella said moving on to Shawn Shawn for some backup.

"I don't know bro. If you getting money, you sure ain't getting it with us, and you know you been off the hook lately big bro. Man it wasn't like this when Mills was home," Shawn Shawn said putting an end to Fella's search for support. Fella was both angry and hurt. His pockets weren't hurting by a long shot, but it had been a while since he's kicked it with the crew he came up with.

"Aight man, maybe y'all right, but we all together right now, so let's do it like we use too," Fella said. He pulled out a fat bag of weed, and said, "Let's blow till we can't blow no more. Roll something fat for my nigga, T-money."

As they kicked it, money came through nonstop and they took turns serving the customers like they did in the old days. Brandy's pager went off as she served one of her customers in the kitchen. After Lolly let the smoker out, Brandy called the unfamiliar number back. A male voice answered the phone after a few rings.

"Who dis?" the male voice said.

"This Bee, somebody called my pager?" Brandy said inquisitively.

"Yeah this Chris and I hope that Bee is short for Brandy." He said sounding smooth as ever.

Brandy smiled as she said. "Yeah that Bee's for Brandy, what's up Chris?"

"You, I was hoping we could go to the movies tonight."

"Oh you were, were you?" Brandy said playfully.

"Yeah C'mon Bee, don't tell me you're turning me down already."

Brandy laughed at the sound of him calling her Bee already.

"Nah I ain't say that, but what time you talking about going?"

"The movie start at nine. I was hoping I could pick you up around eight?"

"I guess that can work," Brandy said trying not to sound to anxious about her first date.

"Well it's about seven now. Can I call you back at this number in about an hour and get your address?" Chris asked already knowing the answer.

"Yea that can work." Brandy said using a saying she picked up from Mills.

117

"Aight Bee see you in an hour, you stay beautiful," Chris said further alluring Brandy.

"See you later." She said before they disconnected.

An hour later Chris called. Fella answered the phone and asked Chris a hundred questions after he asked for Brandy. Brandy snatched the phone from Fella, gave Chris the address and quickly ended the call. Fifteen minutes later, Chris's system announced his arrival before his knock on the door. As Fella rushed to the door Brandy flew by him. Just as she opened the door, Fella appeared beside her with his Glock nine in hand.

"What's up homie, where you taking my sister to?" Fella asked Chris, who was confused by Fella's demeanor and large pistol.

Brandy rolled her eyes and smacked her lips before saying,

"Fella put that gun up and quit acting stupid. Chris this is my brother Fella, that's my brother Peko, and my Brother Shawn. Everybody this is my friend Chris, say what's up." She said while playfully elbowing Fella in the stomach.

"What up dawg," Peko said.

"Sup bro." Shawn Shawn said.

"Fella." Brandy said

"Whats happenin homie? You da dude from the drive thru huh?" Fella asked.

"Yeah," Chris said before Brandy pulled him away by his arm.

"Bye Fella." Brandy said as she and Chris headed to the car. Once inside the car Brandy apologized for Fella's behavior.

"It's cool, if I had a sister as cute as you I would be protective too." Chris responded.

"So that's where you live huh?" Chris said sparking conversation.
"No...that's a spot." Brandy replied while giving Chris a look that said

"Nigga I live better than that."

"A spot? Like a drug spot...?" Chris asked.

"Yea. What other kinds of spot is there?" Brandy answered.

"Ya brothers let you chill up in a drug house and shit?" Chris inquired.

"Let me? Pssshh! Nigga I get money too." Brandy said with a funny look on her face.

"Excuse me. It ain't every day a brother meet a female as beautiful as you, and hood too." Chris said while winking his eye at Brandy.

"My name Brandy nigga, you better ask somebody," She said playfully mimicking a skit from Snoop Dogg's album. Brandy and Chris shared their first laugh from that. As Chris pulled off he grabbed the half backwood filled with weed from his ashtray

"You don't mind me smoking do you?"

"As long as it's Chronic and you sharing, I don't." Brandy answered. Chris smiled and put fire to the weed. He hit a few times and passed it to Brandy while saying, "Beautiful that's some killer." Brandy hit the backwood and started to choke. As she coughed a few times and a few tears ran down her face, Chris let out a little laugh while putting her hair behind her ear and saying,

"You aight?"

"Yeah I'm cool." Brandy said feeling a little embarrassed.

"Don't be acting all bashful boss lady; I told you it was some killer." Chris said causing the two to share a second laugh.

As Brandy quickly passed him back the weed she said, "Where you get that from, that's some chronic. My brother Peko gone want some of that for sure."

"I got a little of it for sale," Chris said modestly. He was really the weed man and had pounds on top of pounds. Chris's pager had been screaming since they got in the car. He had put it on vibrate not wanting it to interfere with him and Brandy's date. The pager continued to go off, and Brandy said, "You better call whoever that is back cause they ain't playing." Chris smiled and looked at the numbers in his pager.

119

"It ain't nothing like that, this is about some money, you don't mind if we make a quick stop do you?" Chris said hoping to put a stop to Brandy's curiousity.

"Nah, its cool, gotta get that money right." Brandy replied.

Chris drove straight to his weed house. The door got knocked on non stop as he and Brandy smoked on some good weed. They ended up having to catch a late movie, as Chris got caught up in the non stop traffic of his weed spot. Brandy and Chris clicked immediately and they enjoyed each others company a lot. From that day on Chris and Brandy made it a point to hang out together almost everyday, even if they were just riding around smoking weed.

CHAPTER 8

I t's now late August and Mills has been isolation free for over two months. The boys are now sitting in their rack awaiting mail call. Mills rushed to the desk after hearing his name called. J.C.O Whitaker handed Mills a stack of mail and Mills walked back to his rack with over ten envelopes in his hand. The first one was a card and a few pictures from his grandmother and little brother. The next were pictures from Buck, along with a card and his new number enclosed. He had a couple from Peko, Shawn, and Fella. They sent pictures of the block party and a couple of Fella at the club with D-Roc, Walt and Slim.

He breezed through the pictures and moved to an envelope with the name Chrissie on it. He had no idea who the letter was from until he saw the picture of the girl from the party enclosed. He smiled at the sight of Chrissie and he thought of how fine she looked the night of his party. Chrissie's picture became less intriguing as Mills spotted an envelope with the name Tanesha Walker on it. He tore through like a wild animal. A picture of Nesh fell out, and he stared at her for a minute before reading her letter.

Dear Mills,

I bet you never thought you'd be hearing from me, huh? I hope you're healthy and behaving yourself in there. Me, I'm healthy, and I always behave myself. Mills, I want to apologize for what happened that night at the skating rink. I find myself feeling like you being in jail is my fault, and I feel really crappy because of that. Well Mills its time for me to go to my next class. Again I'm sorry, and I hope you liked your picture, write me sometime, I promise I'll find time to write you back.

With love,

Nesh

Mills was in a daze until B-nut yelled "Damn blood we like pictures too." Mills found his way back to reality, and said,

"C'mon homie what's mine is y'alls." He passed the pictures over to B-nut, Law, Rash, and H.T. surrounded B-nut and Mills bed. As they looked at the pictures from the envelopes Mills already had opened, Mills tore through the remaining envelopes, which were from Brandy. The first three of the envelopes were nothing but pictures. Mills stared at the picture of him sitting on the hood of his car in front of Brandy's house. Then he looked at a picture of him and Brandy in his car smoking on a blunt. The pictures bought back so many memories that touched him in his chest. He missed his crew, and couldn't wait to get back to the money. The last envelope continued a letter from Brandy.

What up bro?

Man, we miss you out here. I'm still mad at you for putting all them charges on yourself, but I know you did it because you love me. Me and mommy been babysitting Jimmy a lot lately, just to give grandma Mills a break and some time to her self. He starting to look just like you too. He's been hanging with some friend from school named Leon. I haven't met him yet, but I guess he cool. Mommy be kidnapping the boy, sometimes I think she loves him more than me, I'm smiling but I ain't joking. Oh yeah, I got pictures posted up in my locker at school, and you know all the lil hoochies be on ya heels. They be wanting to write you and shit, but I will never hook you up with none of them nasty ass bitches bro. other than that, ain't shit changed, oh Pee got a sick ass Regal, and Bella got a nice ass Monte. I'm bout to buy me something too, you know a bitch gotta go hard I know you salty about yo ride, but don't trip bro, you know you gone come harder when you get out. Well I'm gone bro but I love you and you better call me.

Your sister,

Bee, The Boss Lady

P.S. I did give this one girl named Tiffany your information, she cool though bro, and she ain't no hood rat, she cute too! Peace nigga.

Mills folded the letter up, grabbed the rest of his pictures, and joined his homies on B-nuts bed.

"Who this lil bitch right here blood, she cold." B-nut said speaking about Chrissie.

"That's this one female I met at my party; she's a little older, I never got a chance to fuck with her though," Mills said.

"Yea she nice, but who is this?" Law asked while holding Nesh's picture in his hand.

"Now that's my wife right there nigga, let me get that." Mills said playfully snatching the picture out of Law's hand.

"Now that right there is a dime," Law said speaking of Nesh.

"I would eat her pussy the first night I meet her." He continued. "

What!" Mills said with a funny look on his face.

"Yea nigga, y'all lil niggas better start eating y'alls girl's pussy. Before a young skinny fly nigga like my self come along and take ya bitch with a swift flick of the tongue." Law responded.

"You nasty booty mouth havin ass nigga, that's why yo breath always stinking and shit." Rash said causing the boys to break out in laughter.

"Yeah you yuck mouth, garbage truck mouth havin ass." B-nut added, but Law wasn't laughing, because it was never funny to the person who was getting cracked on especially when they were getting teamed up on by Rash and B-nut. While Mills and his homies laughed themselves to tears, Rex and some of his Cleveland homies were stomping Nasty out. Nasty had been moved to Rex's dorm a month ago in attempt to split him and Black up and to stop them from jumping the boys from Cleveland. Rex and his homies laid on Nasty allowing him to get comfortable before they bomb rushed him. Nasty didn't go out without a fight, and because the J.C.O in charge of their dorm was from Rex's neighborhood, the beating wasn't reported.

When Nasty came to church on Sunday to meet Black and the rest of the Columbus boys, his face told the story for him. The boys were ready to ride on the spot, but Black had a better plan. The camp was already warned that the next riot would result in immediate transfers to different camps of higher security for all parties involved. Black told the crew that it would be best to use the element of surprise.

"We gone lay on these niggas for a few months, then when we attack we going all out, we gone hit every dorm them niggas in, cause after this one we getting transferred anyway. But in the meantime let's get this money and rock these niggas to sleep."

Black pulled out a few cartons of cigarettes from under his shirt, then he tapped his partner Roscoe and motioned for him to pull out the bricks of the black and mild cigars.

"The cigarettes go for a dollar a square, that's twenty dollars pack, and the milds go for five a stick, twenty-five dollars a box. Y'all give me ten off each pack and fifteen off each box."

Black passed the tobacco out to all the Columbus boys, making sure to give them all at least one pack and one box.

Back in the hood, Brandy, Peko, Shawn, and Fella sat on Lolly's getting money as usual. Brandy and Chris had become serious over the months. While Peko and Chris had hit it off because Chris kept the best weed. Fella still had a dislike for Chris, more so because him, D-Roc, Walt, and Slim wanted to rob him than Fella actually Disliking him. As Peko sat fire to his swisher filled with Chris's expensive weed he said,

"Man that nigga Chris got the best weed on the east side for sure. This shit killer!"

"I'm glad somebody like him," Brandy said while rolling her eyes at Fella.

"Shid, that nigga Pee like whoever got weed. Let that nigga Chris run out of that weed, and Pee ah forget that niggas name." Fella said butting in.

"Ha! Ha! Ha! That's cold Fells, you got me fucked up too, nigga." Peko responded while laughing because Fella was probably right.

"Shut up Fella, Chris dig Pee, he always asking about em. Him and Pee is cool" Brandy said.

"Shid I would dig em too and ask about em, every chance I get if he spent two, three hunit a day wit me. He lucky a nigga don't take the shit from him, jewels and all," Fella said seeing how Brandy would react.

"Ain't nobody taking shit from him, Fella stop hatin," Brandy said in Chris's defense.

"Hatin? Shit you better check me out, I'm blinding shit." Fella said as he fixed his jewelry. Although Brandy and Chris haven't yet had sex, their relationship was most definitely serious. Chris showered Brandy with gifts, such as clothes, shoes, and pieces of moderate jewelry. When Brandy spoke of buying herself a car, he told her to save that money, and that he'd get her the car for her birthday, which was a few months away in December.

Meanwhile, Buck was on the other side of town in a big dice game, at the crap house known only by the ballers. No one shot dice for less than $500 a shot. Buck was up thirty-five thousand and still held the dice. This shot was worth close to ten thousand dollars. Him and another guy talked shit to one another as Buck clicked the dice in his hand.

"Bet another stack nigga." Polo said to Buck while taunting him with a stack of cash in his hands.

"That shits chump change nigga, wit a shot like mine, I can break the bank, pay attention I might teach you, something nigga." Buck said as he shook the dice.

"Teach me something? Shid nigga if I wanted to learn something I would have kept my ass in school," Polo responded.

"Well you know what they say...lose yo books, you lose yo lessons, pay me in bud nigga, straight seven." Buck said as he released the dice.

"Four tray and a three."

"You a lucky brother." Polo said as Buck picked the money up from all his bets.

"You know what I learnt Polo man? Sometimes it's better to be lucky than to be good." Buck said issuing out more slick talk than Polo could reciprocate. As Buck rounded the money up, T-Bone and Fresh walked through the door. Once they made contact T-Bone scanned the room and smiled at the fact of Buck being by his self. T-Bone and Fresh were younger than Buck, but they were all aware of who he was. Buck and their big homie Duece had been in rift with one another since the early teens. Once Buck and Deuce became hood rich, they became tied in business to even think about the beef with one another, but only because they rarely crossed one another's path.

Deuce still disliked Buck, and Vice Versa. T-Bone and Fresh took over Deuces beef, like D-Roc and his crew took over Buck's. T-Bone stepped in T-Bones path, and bumped shoulders with him very aggressively. Buck was far from a stranger to drama, and T-Bone quickly realized that, when Buck punched him in his face, knocking him to the floor. Buck quickly pulled his colt four-five out while telling Fresh,

"C'mon lil homie don't make me give it to you,"

Fresh was hesitant about pulling his pistol out, while Buck had his aimed for his head. Buck backed out the door as the crap house became a gun show. He ran to his car and made a quick getaway as T-Bone and Fresh came running out of the house. Buck cursed Butter under his breath as he thought of their agreement to meet at the crap house. Meanwhile Butter was at the hotel room, with Tameka.

"Oh my gosh Butter...shit you in my stomach!" Mek screamed as Butter shoved his 10 ½ inches of steel in her bushy entrance. They went at it with all the backed up anger, and hatred they thought they had for each other. Butter felt his self coming to his climax, so he pulled out of Mek, flipped her over on her stomach and re entered her from behind. He couldn't believe how wet her cave was. Although her hole fitted around his pole like glove, she was so wet he entered her with ease.

Mek moaned his name as they both climaxed together. When it was all over they both were hit with the guilt like a ton of bricks. Butter hopped off the bed, while Mek rolled off the other side. As they both put their clothes on in silence Mek took one last peek at his God like penis.

"What have I gotten myself into?" She thought as his half hard penis swayed back and forth while he pulled his boxers on.

"Butter we can't do this anymore," Mek said as the thought of how good Buck was to her and her little sister. She couldn't believe she was cheating on Buck. She loved him to death and he more than satisfied her in bed, she just let the stories of Butter's penis size, along with her dislike for him turn into an attraction and now the attraction had gone to far.

"You right Mek, this shit is wrong, Buck is my homeboy and this can never happen again."

Butter replied although they agreed not to sleep with each other again, they both knew they liked the sex too much to end it after   one   shot.

127

CHAPTER 9

Mills loaded money into the envelopes and dropped them in the mailbox. Then he laid in his bed, but it was difficult for him to sleep with tomorrow's agenda on his mind. After four months it was finally time for the last ride on the Cleveland boys. Black's plan had worked perfectly. Through selling tobacco, to the guys from Cleveland, they had become under the impression that the two cities had established a rapport, after all their attack on Nasty was on revenge for Black and Nasty's attack on Rex.

Mills dozed off playing out his actions for tomorrow's battle. When Mills woke up the next morning, the clock seemed to stand still. He had been moved from first time offender's dorm, to G dorm, which was right across the hall from H dorm, where Rex and the majority of the Cleveland boys bunked. Black pulled some strings and got moved to the H dorm because he didn't like Nasty being in the dorm all by himself, nor did he like the idea of Mills being across the hall alone. The rest of the guys from Cleveland bunked in the E dorm which was right below G and H so the attack would be easy once the guys from Columbus met and split into groups.

When the clock hit ten o'clock, Mills slipped out the door while the J.C.O wasn't looking. As he crept down the steps he was met by Black and the rest of his homies. Everyone already knew the plan, so the groups split up. Black, Nasty, Mills, Rash, B-nut, Law, H.T., Roscoe, Big dawg, and Doughboy headed upstairs to the H dorm, while Big train, Tim Tim, Lee Ray, B-knight, Tone Capone, Strong arm, D-mac, White side, Tee streets, and Lil Bobby stayed at the bottom of the stairs awaiting the signal to raid the E dorm. Black and Nasty entered the dorm

128

like any other day. Several of Rex's homies sat in the television room, while several of them layed in bed still sleep. Rex, B-white, Flannigan, and several other guys from Cleveland were deep in a dice game. The laundry room was packed with more of Rex's homies as well. They sat in there smoking weed and black and milds, while talking loudly about one of Cleveland's night clubs. As Black and Nasty walked up on the dice game Rex spotted them coming.

"What's up Black, you and Nasty trynna lose some of that money on these stones?" He said as he shook the dice.

"Yea, who got last shot?" He responded as he and Nasty joined Rex and his homies.

"Young Flannigan got last shot after him," Rex said as he rolled the dice, hitting his point. When he bent down to pick up the money, Black hit him with a vicious uppercut, lifting him up into an over right hand that sent him right back down. B.White reacted quickly. He hit Black with a stiff right that barely affected him. Nasty knocked Flannigan to the ground with a left hook, then squared off with another guy. Black pivoted to the wall as B. White and another guy rushed him. B. White was too small to handle the two-piece Black delivered sending him to the pavement. Black faked the other guy and went under him. The guy never had a chance, his feet were almost touching the ceiling as Black lifted him into the air. Black slammed him so hard; he woke the guys who were sleeping. The J.C.O ran to the back to break up the fight, but he was surprised by the troops that came running through the door.

Part of them bombed on the guys in the T.V. room, while the others ran to the back to assist Black and Nasty. By this time Rex's homies had come running out of the laundry room and the sleepers were out their bed fighting in their boxers, and socks. Although the Columbus boys were outnumbered two to one the element of surprise evened out the odds. Mills ran to Nasty's rescue as he was being cornered by three guys. With a leaping hook, Mills sent one guy to the floor. As he squared off with another guy, he was hit from behind. As Mills fell into the wall, B-nut rushed Mills attacker with a combination. H.T. ran to Blacks aid. He split three or four guys with the lock he held tightly in his hand. Rash danced around with one, looking for an entrance.

When he found it he slipped under the guys lazy job, and layed him out with a combination. Law was running around from one guy to the next hitting people from their blind sides. It didn't take long for blood to fill the floor, nor for the J.C.O to call for back up. Big Trav, and his group of soldiers hid behind the doorway that led to the steps, until every J.C.O. rushed by them on their way to assist the J.C.O in H dorm with the royal rumble he had his hands filled with. As soon as they passed, Tim Tim and Lee Ray walked in E dorm to the back of the unit where the Cleveland boys hung out and set it off. Tim Tim punched B.G. in the face with a vicious blow knocking him out his seat as he entertained the rest of his buddies.

Lee Ray slid the person closest to him, then rushed another guy. They were quickly swarmed, and the blows they endured were worth it, as Big Trav and the rest of their back up came charging in the dorm. Big Trav was huge for his age, and he put every guy he hit down with one blow. He grabbed one guy by the throat and slung him into a wall as the rest of his homies went to work. The J.C.O didn't know what to do, as his dorm was being torn to pieces. He called for back up, but all the troops were upstairs in H dorm trying to separate the juveniles up there. Tee streets ran around the J.C.O's steel chair clobbering everyone in his path. By the time the J.C.O's back up came, bodies were laid out all over the place, while some of the boys were still slugging it out. A lot of the boys were hospitalized, but all those who weren't were immediately transferred to different juvenile prison camps. Mills, B-nut, H.T., and Black lucked up and got transferred to TYKO. Rash, Law, and a lot of others were transferred to Indian River. Big Trav, Tim Tim, and Lee Ray were sent to Riverview, with a handful of Cleveland guys who survived the storm. A lot of the others were transferred to Buckeye Boys Camp. Peko was at home with his girlfriend Shy.

Last night Peko learned that he was about to become a father so he stayed home a little later than usual. Had it not of been for Peko waking up in a horny rage this morning, Shy would be in school, but instead she was in the shower rinsing off the smell of morning sex. Peko lay stretched out on the bed smoking a fat blunt. He had just returned from meeting one of his personal customers up the street and little did Shy know he was ready for round two. Shy walked into the room with her towel wrapped around her. Shy was beautiful, her reddish brown complexion complemented her reddish-brown hair color. She wore her hair in a style known as a mushroom, with the back longer than the rest. The sides hung just below her cheekbones, while the backstopped in the middle of her back. Her mouth was mesmerizing; she had pearly white teeth, with a pair of luscious lips, which managed to stay gleaming, even without gloss. Her flat stomach accentuated her hips that rolled off of her body, sticking out like stop signs, while her back side looked like the softest place on earth, as it protruded from under her towel.

"Oh, my God Peko, why you always smoking?" She said as she fanned the room with her hand.

"Cause I can't think sober," Peko replied.

"Every time somebody see you, you got a cigar in ya mouth, that is not attractive," Shy said while fixing herself in the mirror.

"Give me something else to put in my mouth then," Peko replied as he sat his blunt in the ashtray.

"That's why I'm pregnant now, you and that dirty mind of yours." She said while blushing. Peko walked behind her as she went through her panty drawer. The sight of Shy's apple bottom had Peko half excited, and Shy felt his excitement as he poked her with it from behind.

"Peko don't start that; I'm trynna get dressed," Shy whimpered in a sexy voice that turned Peko on. Peko put his hand under her towel, and caressed her inner thigh while saying, "C'mon baby, you know I can't get enough of that gushy stuff."

Shy turned around to face Peko. He looked at her seductively through his funny colored eyes.

"Pee don't look at me like that, you know that turns me on." She said while rubbing on his earlobe, which she knew was his spot. Peko removed her towel as he slid his tongue in her mouth. He moved from her lips to her breast. He teased each one with his tongue; then he nibbled on her nipples.

"C'mon Peko let's do it." She whispered in a sexy voice. Peko picked her up and carried her to the bed. Once he laid her down he went back to work on her breast. Peko and Shy had never done oral sex, but they watched enough porno's to know what to do. Peko replayed the porn in his mind and kissed on Shy's inner thigh. As Peko opened Shy's lips to get a better view of her clit, she became afraid of the pleasure she was about to feel.

"Peko Noo!" Shy whimpered as he flicked his tongue at her clit. As he picked up the speed, her cries of no became cries of yes! Peko stuck his fingers in her cave, as he licked her pearl tongue and the pleasure was too much for her to bear.

"Oh my God! Peko I'm bout to cum!!" She yelled as she tried to get away from his tongue. Peko locked her in and licked her dry as she exploded in his mouth. As Shy's body shook from the end of her climax, Peko quickly removed his clothes. His manhood was pulsating as he watched the end of Shy's orgasm. She stopped him as he tried to enter her. She rolled on top of him and kissed him gently, starting at his forehead. As she made her way down his stomach, his manhood poked her in her throat. Peko was blessed for a fifteen-year-old. He had close to eight inches of steel, along with two and a half inches of girth. Shy put his head in her mouth while rubbing her tongue across the tip of it. She knew her boyfriend was packing because of how it felt when he was in her, but now that she held it in her hand she was astonished by the size.

She had to admit the taste wasn't bad either. She slowly took as much of him as she could. She worked her mouth in an up and down motion, while occasionally using her tongue to assist her. Meanwhile, Brandy was at the Days Inn hotel with Chris, about to lose her virginity. Chris had Brandy stripped down to her bra and panties, as he worked his tongue from her mouth to her ear. Her high yellow skin looked radiant as Chris looked down on her. Chris removed her bra and her pink nipples were about to explode. Chris took the left breast in his mouth and sucked on it like a baby while satisfying the other. Chris was really careful and gentle with Brandy. He wanted her first time to be memorable. As he removed her panties Brandy stopped him.

"Hold up Chris, I don't think I'm ready," She said holding his hand from pulling her panties off. Chris had never been with a virgin before, but he talked many females out of their panties, so he didn't panic.

"Listen, Brandy, if you don't want to do this, we don't have to. I love you and I'm willing to wait, but understand I am only a man and being in a nonsexual relationship is very new and hard for me. I know you're probably scared and doubtful about how things will be after we have sex, but you have to trust me. You love me don't you?" Chris said while turning up his charm and pouring his game on heavy.

"Yes," Brandy replied.

"Do you trust me?" Chris asked knowing that if her answer was yes, her virginity was his.

"Yes, Chris but…"

Chris cut her off, "There is no buts baby, either you trust me or you don't." Brandy thought for a moment. Everything Chris had told her he'd do, he did. He told her he would get her a car for her birthday, and he did. He told her that if they were together she wouldn't have to hustle, because he'd take care of her, and he did although it didn't stop her from getting her grind on. Most importantly he both loved and respected her.

"You bet not hurt me, Chris." Brandy said as she allowed her panties to come off. Chris removed all his clothing and slipped out of his boxers. His love muscle was at full attention, and Brandy looked at the large piece before her and thought,

What did I just get myself into?

Chris hovered over top of her while taking in the beautiful sight beneath him. Brandy's body didn't have a scratch on it and the hair on her vagina matched the hair on her head. It was very soft and silky looking. Chris gently kissed her on her thigh as he opened her legs. He sucked, licked, and gently bit on her inner thighs, blowing on her vagina as he switched from one thigh to another. As he opened the entrance to her love box, she said

"Chris no, I ain't ready for all that!"

"It's gone feel good trust me," Chris said as he looked at the muffin with hunger in his eyes. Brandy's love box was pinker than bubble yums chewing gum and Chris licked his lips before tasting her. He licked around her cave before going to her clit. He wanted her to relax her body before he took her to ecstasy. He stuck his tongue in her hole, and twirled it around for a minute then he pulled out and went to work on the clit. Chris licked her at rapid speed causing her to run from the feeling.

"Chris please nooo!" Brandy yelled as she became wetter, hotter, and hornier than ever before. Chris locked her in, as he nibbled on her clit. When Brandy started cumming, she grabbed Chris's head, while locking her legs around his neck. Brandy's juices squirted out of her fountain and Chris drank them up. Chris entered her slowly, causing her to close her eyes, bite her bottom lip, and suck the air through her teeth. Chris put half of his manhood in her and stroked her with that for a while; Brandy was so wet and tight that the feeling was driving Chris crazy. As Chris pushed more of himself in her, she clawed his back while moaning his name. Once Chris had all of himself inside of her, he stroked her with slow motion. As Chris dug deeper into Brandy's hole, she dug her nails deeper in his back.

When Brandy yelled she was cumming, Chris sped up his motion bringing himself to a climax as well. When he pulled out of Brandy she was still shaking as blood stained the sheets, and she stared at the ceiling in shock from both pleasure and pain of her first sexual experience.

After being in isolation for two weeks, Mills and the others who rode to TYKO juvenile prison camp with him were released to population. All the boys were placed in different units and rarely saw one another except for when passing in the hall and chow. For the past two days Mills watched his surroundings closely. He noticed one guy keeping a watchful eye on him. The guy didn't look familiar at all, so Mills focused the majority of his attention on this guy in particular, being careful not to be too obvious. The guy came and went as he pleased. He also made a lot of handshakes and hugs while holding brief conversations. Mills wasn't for sure what the guy was doing but he was far from game shy, and to one as aware as Mills, it was clear that the guy was making money moves. While at recreation one day the guy approached Mills.

"What happenin lil homie, what city you from?"

Mills slowly made his way up from the weight bench, because the sitting position made him feel vulnerable. The guy recognized game and tried to put Mills at ease.

"No need to go on the defense homie, my name Mario, my friends call me Rio, I'm from Columbus, I just thought you looked familiar." Mario extended his hand for a shake.

T. Mills I'm from Columbus, too." Mills said while accepting Rios's hand, but still staying on the defense.

"T.Mill, huh? I been noticing you watching me T.Mills, am I in any kind of trouble that I don't know of?"

"I been meaning to ask you the same thang," Mills responded. Rio laughed because he knew Mills had noticed him peeping him out.

"How old are you, man? You look kind of young," Mills was confused by Rio's easiness. He was not comfortable holding such a lengthy conversation with a stranger, and he felt it was time to end this one.

"Listen, bro, I don't mean no disrespect, but you sure are asking a lot of questions to a nigga you don't know." Mills said.

"Asking questions is the only way to get answers homie, think about it. How else does a person get to know someone?" Rio replied.

He had a point, but Mills wasn't sure he wanted to get to know the guy.

"Listen, man, it was nice meeting you, but I think that's enough conversating for one day."Mills said.

Rio smiled.

"Communication breeds understanding but too much of anything can be bad for you, so I guess I'll catch you some other time Mills," Rio said as he walked off. Mills watched as Rio strolled over to the J.C.O that ran their unit.The two kicked it like they were buddies while taking a glance at Mills. Mills didn't know what it was, but there was something familiar about the J.C.O. Later that night Mills replayed him and Rio's conversation in his head. He remembered Rio calling him Mills before walking off, but he was sure he had introduced himself as T. Mills.

There was something unsettling about him and Rio's encounter and tomorrow, he planned on getting to the bottom of it. The next morning Mills watched Rio as he made his rounds, issuing out daps and hugs. The moment Mills caught Rio by himself he pulled down on him.

"What up homie?" Mills said as Rio walked out his cell

"Not a whole lot, what's up wit you?" Rio shot back.

"I don't know, you tell me seeing as how you know more about me then you led me to believe." Rio smiled. He called Mills by that name purposely last night hoping that he would catch on to it.

"I don't get what you mean man what do you mean man, what do I know," Rio said continuing his mind games. It was Mills turn to smile and he did sinisterly, because game recognized game.

"Well seeing as how you called me Mills before leaving yesterday when I told you my name was T. Mills you obviously know something, considering that's the name I go by in the streets. So tell me…what is this all about?" Mills said as he played the wall.

"I don't get what you mean my nig, yo last name is Mills, and that's what I called you," Rio said trying to sound innocent.

"Dig bro, two can play the game you playing, I got a phone call to make so I'm bout to pull out, but from one hustler to another, you should handle your business a little more discreet than you do, Stevie Wonder can see through yo dap, and hug front. Peace." Mills said walked off leaving Rio with something to think about this time.

Later that day second shift came on; Mills watched Rio and the J.C.O with the familiar face closely. Mills wasn't stupid or slow to the game, so he knew that there was more to Rio and the J.C.O's relationship than they led on. While at rec later that day, Mills was approached by Rio as he watched the J.C.O spray shots from all over the basketball court as he ran circles around some of the best ballplayers in the unit.

"So you back for more already?" Mills said as Rio took a seat next to him on the weight bench.

Rio laughed, "Nah homie, the game is over, the J.C.O Butter is real cool with your brother Buckshot. Buckshot told him to holler at you, but he wasn't sure you were who you are, so he had me holler at you, he wanted me to talk to you yesterday, but I was having too much fun playing mind games with you," Rio said.

"Is that right?" Mills said obviously bothered by Rio's mind tricks.

"C'mon lil homie ain't nothing wrong wit a little mental sparring match, it keeps you on your toes, you dig," Mills and Rio kicked it until rec was over. Once they got back to their unit, Rio escorted Mills to J.C.O Butter's desk.

"What's happening shorty?" Butter said to Mills.

"Not much, Rio tells me you know my big bro Buckshot." Mills replied.

"Yeah that's my ace; don't tell me you don't remember me, all that fire ass weed I sold your brother. I think you were at the house the day I came by, Buck said you were laying low because you popped some dope fiend who tried to rob you of yo shit." Butter said.

"Aw shit, that is you. I knew I remembered you from somewhere, I think Buck took me to yo crib wit em one day too, off of Brice road? Mills said.

"Ssshhh!" Butter said looking around to see if anyone was listening. "Yeah that's me, and damn boy you getting big as fuck, how long you been down?"

"Almost two years. I got one more to go, man." Mills said while shaking his head in disgust.

"Don't look so down shorty, that year gone fly by, you down here wit family now, I'm ah make sure you aight. Buck told me to tighten you up, so I'll have something for you when I come tomorrow. You stick with Rio, that's my lil homie, he been down here for a while he gone show you how to move around and Buck said to call home when you get the chance'" Butter replied.

Rio walked off to handle some business as Mills and Butter kicked it with each other. By the time Rio returned, Mills had his photo albums at the desk, letting Butter run through them. Butter looking at an inmate's picture or kicking it with them wasn't unusual, because he vibed with the juveniles like he was one of them. He was only twenty-five, and he loved talking about females and sports which was all a lot of juveniles wanted to talk about as well.

Meanwhile, Brandy, Peko and Shawn were bringing in the spring with five figures counting. As they sat in Lolly's house pumping, Buck had pulled his casket gray 94' Lexus coop on the side street as Mek takes his 8 ½ inches into her hot wet mouth. Oh shit Mek let me pull over. Buck said as he pulled behind a dark blue celebrity. Mek didn't stop. She played with the head of his pole slowly licking around it, then picking up the speed as she played with his pee hole. Buck jerked as she made her way down to his balls, then back up before slowly taking his manhood deep into her throat.

Buck layed his seat back as he played with Meks clit from the back. She moaned with pleasure as her vagina became drenched with her juices. Buck pulled his fingers out of her and stuck them in his mouth. Mek couldn't take it anymore; she climbed on top of him, and easily slid down his pole. She slid up and down while looking Buck in the eyes and moaning along with heavy breathing.

"Buck, I wanna have your baby," She whispered as she picked up the pace. Buck gripped her ass, spreading her cheeks so he could penetrate deeper.

"Let's have a beautiful little girl" Buck whispered through deep breaths.

"Buck I'm cumming, I'm cumming! I'm cumming! I love you boy." She grunted out as she climaxed and the juices ran out of her.

As spring slowly slid into season D-Roc, Slim, Walt, and Fella rode up Cleveland Avenue thinking about Slim and Fella's MVP vans that they had just come from checking out. After going on a robbing spree, throughout the winter, the crew was ready to come hard with their vehicles for the summer. D-Roc had been laying low at Walt's and Slim's house for the last few months because even though he and Tee Tee had made up, and were back sleeping together, he still had an outstanding warrant for domestic violence. With the sun beaming down on this late March afternoon, D-Roc couldn't resist the chance to break his Maxima back out for the ladies.

"Ay Roc check out theses chicks beside us bro," Walt said from the back seat. D-Roc looked to his right and motioned for the females to roll down their window. The car was loaded with three fine females, who the guys argued about since there were four of them and three females. The females all rolled down their windows, as D-Roc and his crew bedazzled them with the sun reflecting off their jewels.

"Follow us," The females yelled as they hopped over two lanes to get into the turning lane. D-Roc swerved around a couple cars and squeezed in front of another one, trying to keep up with the car full of chicks. He never noticed the police cruiser a few cars behind them as he caused a traffic jam. When D-Roc bent the corner behind the females, the police cruiser cleared traffic to catch the white Maxima. The females pulled over and watched D-Roc pull right pass them as they noticed the cruiser on his heels. The chase was on. D-Roc had pistols, along with powder and marijuana, he bent a few corners, and once out of the sight of the police, the guns, and drugs went out the windows. The police cruiser quickly made its way back to the view and D-Roc pulled over like it was nothing wrong. The cops hopped out the cruiser with their guns drawn screaming at everyone to step out of the car with their hands up. They all did as they were told. The cops held them still until back up arrived. They were all placed in the back of a cruiser, as the cops ran I.D. checks on them. Although D-Roc's Alias came back clean, he was taken down for fleeing a traffic violation. Once downtown, he was fingerprinted and identified. The next morning he was held without a bond, due to him being a flight risk.

Slim, Fella, and Walt sat next to the bondsman with D-Rocs mother as he was escorted back to a cell. Later that night Peko sat in Lolly's counting the cash he made for the day. Shawn was at his girlfriend's house, while Brandy was with Chris. Peko took advantage of his time alone in Lolly's he ran through a few ounces in seven hours. At 11:30 pm, he sat on the couch smoking a blunt, with five thousand dollars stacked up on the table in front of him. He called Shy to inform her that he was on his way home. Ring! Ring! Ring!

"Hello." Shy said with sleep in her voice.

"What's up baby you ain't wait up on me?" Peko said.

"Peko you know I gotta go to school in the morning." Shy replied.

"I know but I left my key and I'm on my way home and I need you to come let me in so get up."

"Pee why you wait so late to tell me you left your key, now you want me to get up out my sleep and sit up till you bring yo butt home?" Shy said.

"Yeah you know how yo mom be tripping about me waking her up by knocking on the door at night," Peko replied.

"I know, that's why I gave you a key boy!" Shy exclaimed.

"Stop tripping Shyrah, you know I'm a wake you up so I can get me some of that gushy before I go to sleep anyway," Peko said.

"You ain't getting nothing if you don't hurry up." Shy replied. Peko laughed.

"I ain't playing with you Peko, you better hurry up." Shy said yawning.

"You can't stop me from getting what's mine girl, I'm on my way though aight?" Peko said.

"Alright. I hate you." Shy said.

"I hate you too," Peko said as they used the word hate to replace the word love. They came up with that way of telling one another they loved each other, from a make up session they had after a heated argument. She whispered the words I hate you in Peko's ear during make up sex. They disconnected. Peko stuffed his money in his pockets, slid his gun under the couch and relit his blunt that he let go out on the conversation with Shy. Peko usually took his gun with him, but for some reason his instincts told him to leave the gun behind tonight.

As Peko walked out the back door he had a funny feeling in his gut. He scanned the dark backyard as he unlocked his car door, and out of no where a black truck pulled up blocking him in, as men in black ran out the truck's sliding door. Peko took off towards the house. When he heard the men yell,

"Columbus SWAT team get the fuck on the ground." He ran back off the porch and headed for the front of the house, but was stopped in his tracks as the men in black filled the front yard as well. Peko shot back towards the backyard, so he could leap the neighbor's fence, but never made it as the men in black boxed him in.

After months of rolling with Mario, Mills had the camp's movement down pact. He had also become cool with some more of the J.C.O's on behalf of his relationship with Butter and Mario both. Mario was known all through the camp. He was sentenced to juvenile life at the age of fourteen and for the last five years of his life he's been living in TYKO juvenile prison camp. Like Mills, Rio was a young hustler. Even now at the age of nineteen all he thought about was different ways to get money. In Rio's mind, he had the dope game down to a science. Rio was serving juvy life for murder. He and Law's case was very similar, Rio was robbed at a dope house but the robbers never searched him for a gun. As the robbers ran out the door headed for their get away car, Rio came up behind them clapping with his gun. One guy made it and the other took a shot to the back which instantly paralyzed him, as another bullet struck him in his neck. He died before the ambulance arrived.

Mills walked up the hall with his drawers full of weed. He had to do most of his hustling through Black, B-nut, and H.T. since Rio had their side of the camp on lock, and Mills didn't want to step on his new homie's toes. Mills stopped by H.T.'s unit, then B-nut's. He gave them both an ounce of good green, for a grand a piece. Only asking for a grand was showing love, because when broke down, one could make anywhere from two to three grand off of one ounce. Mills made a few other stops, so he could take care of a few customers Rio hooked him up with and then he headed for the rec department where Black was at.

He didn't spot him, which meant he was in the weight room. J.C.O Hudson was one of Butter's homies and Mills nodded his head at him while pointing to the weight room. Hudson knew Mills was looking for Black. He held up five fingers, which let Mills know he had five minutes. Mills rushed to the weight room and caught Black off guard throwing up two hundred pounds on the chest machine. When he spotted Mills he hopped off the machine and motioned for his workout partner to take over.

"What up T-money?" Black said as he and Mills embraced each other.

"Not a whole lot, let's step outside the door for a minute, Hudson only gave me five minutes." Mills said.

Mills and Black shared a few words, and when they felt no one was looking Mills passed him the last ounce of weed. Black quickly stuffed it. He and Mills embraced one another as they said their see you laters and Mills got gone. He held up a fist at Hudson, showing appreciation and saying see you later at the same time, as he walked out the gym. When Mills made it back to the unit Rio was on the phone, in what seemed to be a deep conversation. As Mills headed to his cell he was stopped by a guy from Akron named D-boy.

"Hold up Mills," D-boy said as he passed Mills up and asked for fifty. D-boy whispered give me fifty while passing Mills fifty dollars in a handshake.

"I don't know what you talking about homie." Mills said as he wondered how D-boy knew about his business.

"Rio told me to holler at you," D-boy said as he felt Mills putting a spin move on him. Mills looked over at Rio, who gave him thumbs up.

"Aight homie just give me a minute. I'll be right back." Mills said as he walked off in his cell. A few minutes later he came out his cell with fifty cuffed in his palm. He dropped the paper the weed was wrapped in on the floor next to D-boy's feet and kept walking. He headed to the phone next to Rio and dialed Brandy's number, and quickly got through.

"What's up nigga, you ain't call to wish a bitch happy birthday or nothing?"

"My bad Bee, but yo bro can't stay out of isolation, I'm in a whole nother camp and everything now." Mills replied.

"Yeah I know, Buck told me they transferred you to the place on the Westside. At least you closer to home." Brandy said. "Yeah I like it better here anyway, what's up with the fam though?" Mills inquired.

"Damn you ain't heard about Pee yet?" Brandy asked.

"Heard what about Pee?" Mills replied.

"He got caught in a SWAT raid at Lolly's a few weeks ago. He ain't have no drugs or nothing on him, but you know he had that warrant. His P.O. talking about making him do six months for probation violation, so he'll probably be down there with you in a few months. That's fucked up cause he got a baby on the way too." Brandy explained.

"What! Bro got a baby on the way, you bullshittin," Mills said enthusiastically.

"His girl like three months pregnant," Brandy said.

"Damn a lot has changed." Mills replied. Mills and Brandy talked for a few more minutes. Then he had her call his grandmother. He conversed with his grandmother for a while, since his little brother wasn't home. When Mills call was over, Rio was ending his second call.

"I see ole girl got you pissed off again huh bro?" Mills asked Rio as he watched him slam the phone down.

"Lightweight man, fuck that bucket head though, lets go smoke something. I got some new numbers for you anyway." Rio said.

Rio liked to break drugs down to grams and come up with the best prices to sell them for. He wanted a price that would make both the supplier a lot of money and sow up the whole strip, so every other day he came up with some new prices, sale schemes and projections. He called this doing numbers. Mario was a few years older than Mills and a lot of things he said made since, so Mills loved listening and trading ideas with him. Mario wasn't necessarily the smartest guy, but he was sharp because he asked a lot of questions and paid attention when someone was speaking.

When they entered Mills's cell, his celly was laying back on his bed reading a book.

"What up Junebug?" Rio said to Mills celly. His name was Julius Braxton but people called him J.B. for short. Rio and Mills joked with him saying that the J.B. stood for Junebug and always called him Junebug because he was Mills June bug and the name just stuck with him.

"What up Rio?

"Sup Mills?" June bug said as he put the book away. He knew it was time to get high whenever Rio walked in the cell with Mills, so he played his position by stuffing the bottom door with towels and opening window. Rio pulled a fat top joint out of his pocket and set fire to it. He hit it a couple times and passed it to Mills. After making it around the room three times, the joint was gone; Mills threw a small bag of weed in June Bug's lap and told him to roll another one up. While June bug rolled another one up, Mills asked Rio about his new numbers.

145

"Oh yeah peep this, say you cop a brick for twenty-six gee's, a brick is a thousand and eight grams, you turn that thousand and eight to twelve sixty, that's straight mack, some of the best dope in the city for sure, you sell twenty-eight grams for seven hundred, that's thirty one fifty a brick, that's a profit of fifty-one fifty, five thousand, one hundred and fifty dollars, now here's where the flip come in at, ounces are being sold for seven-fifty to nine hundred dollars a pop, and a lot of that shit niggas be selling ain't mack.

They turning one into one and a half, greedy niggas you feel me?"

"I feel you."

"You selling ounces for seven hundred, which is at least fifty dollars cheaper than the cheapest Dee around and you got the best in quality, you sowing up the whole strip lil homie no lie, you gone run through those forty-five ounces and days tops, that's thirty thousand a month all profit!!! Three hundred and sixty thousand a year all profit!! Let's say you run through a brick in three days instead of five; this is just for a little extra motivation, something more to reach for, ya dig? If you run through a brick every three days that's fifty thousand a month all profit!! That's six hundred Gee's in a year all profit!! You could be a millionaire in two years, can you buy that?" Rio asked, seriously. Mills shook his head in agreement. Rio was helping Mills take his hustle to a whole other level, and Mills loved every minute of it because it sort of reminded him of the talks Buck and him used to have. Mills had a little over a year left in Juvy before he was released.

He planned on soaking up all the game he could because once he touched turf again; it was back to the money.

CHAPTER 10

L's and young Pimp stood in the apartment complex's doorway as cars rode up and down Miller Avenue. L's ran out to catch one of his big spenders as Liley walked up to the complex.

"Where you going little L's? I need some shit," Liley said as L's ran by her.

"Holler at my homie." L's shot back while pointing at Pimp, as he hopped in the white man's car.

"What's happening baby, you got the same shit L's got?" Liley asked as she approached Pimp.

"Yeah I got that, what you need?" Pimp asked while scanning the scene.

"I got seventeen dollars, I'm trynna get twenty."

"I got you step inside," Pimp said as he pulled his pack from his draw pocket. He gave Liley a fat twenty and pocketed the seventeen dollars. "Boy you is fine, if you were a little older mmmm." Liley said causing Pimp to smile.

"I might have to introduce you to my daughter." She continued as L's walked up.

"Damn what about me, Liley?" L's said butting in.

"Mm mm you is too bad and too fast for Leslie," Liley said as she walked off.

"That's cold." L's said while laughing.

"You better get her daughter bro, I'm telling you Leslie is cold, and she got a fat ass," L's whispered to Pimp. Liley smoked dope, but she kept her self up. She was cute, but everyone could tell she was the one back in her day. Her daughter Leslie was a hustler's wife for sure. She was beautiful and her body matched her face. Although she was only thirteen, all the hustlers whistled at her and watched her as she walked down the neighborhood streets. She didn't give any of them the time of day. Her and L's were cool, mostly because they grew up together. If L's wouldn't have treated all the girls in the neighborhood so disrespectfully, Leslie might have given him a chance, but L's was wild, and every girl that he had sex with, he dissed afterward and moved on to their friend.

"C'mon man we got to get out here in the open where we can be seen or else all the geeks gone go up the street." L's said as he stayed ducked off in the apartment hallway.

"C'mon bro you know I can't be in the open like that, if one of my big bro's homies catch me out here pumping I'm ass out, not to mention my big bro Buck, or my grandmother, maaan shid," Pimp said with a funny look on his face.

"I feel you bro, I gotta look out for my mom, it's like she knows I'm out here doin something, but she hasn't caught me yet and I ain't trynna find out what will happen if she does. Feel me.

"You know I feel you bro" pimp replied.

L's stated splitting a swisher so he could feel it up with weed. He didn't smoke as much as he would like because Pimp didn't smoke, and he didn't like smoking alone.

"What up Pimp, you gone blow this one with me?" L's said as he filled the swisher.

"Hell nah man, football season is coming up this summer and that shit ain't good for my gas. I don't know about you, but this hustling is temporary for me, I'm going to the pro's baby," Pimp said while doing the Heisman pose.

Pimp and L's spent the rest of the day pumping out the apartment hallway. L's real name was Leon Pittman. He's a couple years older than Pimp, but because of Pimp's skill in football they played on the same football team. They also went to the same junior high school. L's was in the eighth grade while Pimp was in the sixth, but he and L's kicked whenever L's came to school. L's was known throughout the school and his neighborhood as a live wire. He didn't do much fighting, but he was known for letting his gun go. He started selling dope two years ago. And now that Pimp was his role dawg, he had a partner, and he was ready to take his hustling to the next level. It took Liley a few weeks to bring her daughter around, but the more she dealt with Pimp, the more she liked him for her daughter.

Pimp and L's stood in front of Big Looney's house with Big Looney, lil Looney, and the rest of L's big homies. Liley pulled up hanging out the passenger window of a black escort.

"C'mere Pimp," She yelled.

Pimp walked up the car.

"What's happening, Liley, how you doing today?" Pimp said as he leaned in the car.

"Ain't nothing happening, baby, I just wanted to introduce you to my daughter Leslie,"

Liley looked in the back seat where Leslie sat.

"Leslie this is…boy what is your real name?" She said directing her attention back to Pimp.

"Jimmy," He replied.

"Leslie this is Jimmy, Jimmy this is Leslie."

"Hi," Leslie said.

"What up," Pimp replied.

"Isn't he the bomb?" Liley asked her daughter.

"Mom!" Leslie said in a don't embarrass me voice.

"Alright but y'a,ll can at least exchange numbers or something."

"Mom!"

"Okay," Liley replied.

Pimp was laughing as the two went back and forth.

"Excuse my mom; she can't help her self." Leslie said to Pimp.

"Don't worry about it. I would like to call you sometime Leslie, if thas cool with you?" Pimp smoothly replied.

He and Leslie swapped pager numbers then Leslie and her mother drove off.

"So what's up, you knock her or what?" L's asked as Pimp returned with him and the rest of the fellas.

"C'mon man, my name ain't Pimp for nothing." Pimp's answer caused everyone to burst out into laughter. L's hit the blunt one more time before passing it. He choked as he couldn't hold back his laughter long enough to blow the smoke out his mouth.

"Man you tryna send me bro" He said while beating on his chest. The laughter stopped as L's and the crew took off running for the customers that pulled in front of the house and walked down the street. When they all came back they went back to joking with L's and Pimp. As they all shared a laugh at L's expense, that moment was broken up again. This time it wasn't money that interrupted their laughter, it was the shots that rang out from the Detroit Boy's pistols. Big Looney had a rift with the Detroit Boys because they were moving in on his territory.

A few days ago Big Looney and his little brother and homies did a drive by on the Detroit Boy's drug house and now the Detroit boys were returning a favor. They drove up the street with shooters hanging out of every window. Big Looney, lil Looney, and Hawk ran for cover while returning fire. Pimp dove to the ground as L's popped up from behind a car letting off shots. L's emptied the ten shots from his baby Glock. The Detroit boys sped by the house continuing to dump off shots in return. As the smoke cleared, L's noticed Lil Looney on the ground shaking as blood leaked from his abdomen. His gun lay a few feet away from him. Big Loon then got lil Loon.

"He hit!" L's yelled. Big Looney and Hawk came running to lil Looney's aid.

"Get the car started; we got to take him to the hospital," Big Looney said. Hawk ran across the street, and hopped in Looney's old school and brought the car to life. Big Looney picked his little brother up and carried him to the car.

"Lil L's grab those straps over there and get out of here. I'll get with you later." Big Looney ordered as he put his brother in the back seat. L's grabbed big Looney and his little brother's guns from off the ground, and he and Pimp ran up the alley headed for L's house.

D-Roc, Slim, Walt, and Fella are parked down the street from Chris's house, watching him and Brandy have it out. They came to rob the place but were interrupted by Brandy. As she pulled up in her all-white 93 Probe with pink rally stripes, and chrome sixteen-inch Moe Moe's. Brandy thought she would stop by and surprise Chris with an afternoon booty call, but instead she found him getting his freak on with some hoochie.

Brandy went upside the girl's head before Chris got a chance to get her under control. When Chris pulled Brandy off the girl he carried her outside.

"Get yo nasty ass hands off me!" Brandy said as she yanked away from Chris and stormed to her car.

"Hold up Bee, let me holler at you baby, it ain't what you think." Chris said as he ran after her. Chris snatched Brandy's keys out her hand as she went to put them in the ignition.

"Give me my muthafucking keys Chris," Brandy screamed.

"Hold up baby I don't want you leaving like this, fuck that bitch I love you, she ain't nothing." Chris pleaded.

"No fuck you, Chris, now give me my keys before I start acting a fool out here." Brandy said as she reached for her keys.

The girl came running out of Chris's house as him, and Brandy tussled for the keys.

"Aw shit ain't that bitch India lil cuzz?" Slim said as India jumped off Chris's porch and took off up the street.

"Hell yea that's the freak," Fella said. Then he and Slim burst into laughter. Brandy started throwing blows at Chris's face, as he tried to restrain her. Brandy's punches were a little too much for Chris to continue enduring, so he smacked her full force and then grabbed her by the throat. The keys now lay on the ground as Chris tried shaking the life out of her.

"What the fuck is wrong wit you girl, putting yo mutha fucking hands on me like that?" Chris yelled. Brandy wasn't an easy woman to restrain and she continued to fight Chris. Fella didn't like what he was seeing and rather Brandy liked it or not, Fella was bout to bring it to Chris the gee way. Fella hopped out the van and ran down on Chris. When Brandy saw Fella she knew it meant trouble for Chris. She didn't know where Fella had come from or what he was doing there, but she loved Chris, and she didn't want to see him hurt in the way Fella was going to hurt him. Brandy spotted the big boy Glock in fella's hand.

"Fella no it's cool!" she yelled.

Chris never spotted Fella running up the street from his blind side and when he turned to see who Brandy was yelling at, he felt the butt of Fella's Glock nine. Chris dropped to one knee and Fella continued to beat the blood out of him. As Brandy tried to stop Fella, D-Roc, Slim, and Walt ran up. D-Roc snatched Chris up by the neck and put his forty-five Smith and Wesson to his temple while saying,

"Get the fuck up nigga. You make one more move and I'll blow ya brains out."

Slim and Walt ran straight in the house with their weapons drawn. Brandy was confused. She didn't know whether to help Chris or grab her keys and get out of there. Fella was like a brother to her, even though they seemed to be growing apart, she still loved him.

"Bee get yo keys and get the fuck out of here," Fella said as he ran behind D-Roc who escorted Chris into the house with his four fif still pressed against his head. Brandy was crying, and her heart raced, but she did what she was told. Brandy wasn't frightened by the situation because she was no stranger to gangster shit, but she loved Chris and the fact that his life was in the hands of some killer scared her. By the time D-Roc and Fella made it into the house, Walt and Slim had assured them the house was empty.

"Where the fuck is the shit at nigga?" D-Roc asked Chris as Fella slammed the door closed.

"Its upstairs man, just please don't kill me," Chris whined.

"Gangsta, Walt lets go, the shit upstairs," D-Roc said.

"Fells watch the door bro," D-Roc ordered as he, Slim, and Walt escorted Chris up the steps.

"Is anybody else in this house?" D-Roc asked as he peeked in the two bedrooms with open doors.

"Nah man, ain't nobody here but me." Chris answered through his bloody mouth. D-Roc knew there was weed in one of the rooms because it reeked so bad he could smell it once he got to the top of the steps. Chris told them it was in the room directly in front of them. The door to the room had different locks on it, but Chris willingly handed over the keys. Slim quickly unlocked all the locks. When he pushed open the door two Pitbulls came charging at him. He let off a couple rounds, but one of the guard dogs was too fast. He grabbed hold of Slim's arm and shook it until his gun hit the floor. Boom! Boom! Boom! Walt knocked the other dog out the air with his top of the line nine. The dog let out a whimper as it hit the floor. Walt grabbed the other dog by its tail, as it hung by slim's arm. He shoved the nine in the dog's throat and let off nine rounds into the dog's skull. The dog died before it hit the ground. Slim grabbed his pistol off the ground and backhanded Chris with it.

"Bitch ass nigga, I should kill yo stupid ass." Slim yelled. D-Roc followed Slim's smack across the face with one of his own. He let Chris's body fall then stood over top of him with his Smith and Wesson aimed at his head.

"Just give me the word gangsta, and I'll finish this bitch nigga off." D-Roc said.

"I'm sorry man, please don't kill me I got kids," Chris begged. As Fella heard the shots, he started to climb the steps, but the knock at the door stopped him. He peeked out the window and saw a gold Cadillac with triple gold hundred spoke Daytons parked in front of the house. A guy stood on the porch draped in gold and diamonds. Fella knew he should have just let the guy leave, but his greed took over him. Fella opened the door with his gun behind his back.

"What up bro?" Fella said to the guy on the porch.

"What's happening man, is Chris here?" the guy said.

"Yeah he upstairs, C'mon in." Fella said as he stepped to the side to let the guy in. The guy fell for his trick and walked in the house checking his pager. Fella shut the door and aimed the gun at the guys head.

"Don't move unless I say so, or I'm a send you to meet Jesus." Fella said while moving closer to the guy who stood frozen like a statue.

"Get on yo knees and put yo hands on your head, bitch." Fella ordered. The guy did as he was told. Fella stripped him of his jewelry, cash, and car keys. Upstairs, Slim and Walt had hit the jackpot. They opened the closet door and found a small safe and four duffle bags full of blocks of compressed weed.

"Jackpot baby," Walt yelled with a devilish grin on his face. D-Roc ordered Chris to get up and walk over to the closet. Chris did as he was told. Once they moved the safe and duffle bags of weed out the closet, D-Roc pushed Chris in the closet and told him if you open this fucking door while I'm still in this house, it'll be the last door you open bro, you hear me?" Chris shook his head yes.

D-Roc slammed the door in Chris's face. Slim and Walt grabbed the duffle bags, D-Roc picked up the safe, and they took off. When they got down stairs Fella had the guy face down on the ground.

"Where the fuck was that nigga at?" D-Roc asked as Slim yanked the door open.

"He was coming to buy some herb." Fella said with a smile on his face.

"Well do something with that nigga and let's cut." D-Roc said.

'Ya'll go head, I'm a follow y'all niggas ride. I gotta have his rims." Fella said as he rushed the guy into the bathroom. D-Roc, Slim, and Walt Ran out the house and Fella was right behind them after telling the guy to get in the tub and count to a hundred. Fella laughed as he ran to the guy's Cadillac. He fumbled with the keys for a moment until he found the right one. Once he got the car started Slim pulled up along him to make sure he was cool, then pulled off. Fella pulled out right behind him, making a smooth get away.

CHAPTER 11

After two months of being involved with Leslie, Liley decided to let Pimp pump out of her house. Of course, he and L's were a package deal, but Liley didn't mind because L's always looked out for her, even when her money was funny. As Pimp sat on the sofa across from L's who was blowing a fat blunt, Leslie came strolling into the living room.

"Pimp I need a few dollars so I can grab a few things for dinner tonight." She said while taking a seat on Pimp's lap. Pimp gave her a ten-dollar bill. She walked out the front door as the back was being knocked on. L's rushed to it because he knew a knock on the back door meant money. He peeked through the window before opening the door. Once he saw magic Mike, who got the name from making a hustler's dope sack disappear so quickly. He put his baby nine in his back pocket and opened the door.

"What's up fool?" L's said as Magic Mike walked in.

"Not you, I'm looking for Pimp," Magic Mike said while twitching his mouth from left to right, and rocking his body back and forth.

"Don't start that shit Mike; you know it's all the same dope in here." L's said.

"C'mon L's you know I fucks wit Pimp, why you gotta give me a hard time?" Magic mike replied. L's pulled out his baby nine from his back pocket while saying,

"You lucky you watched me grow up nigga or else I would pistol whip yo ass Mike."

"Pimp! Come get this nigga Mike before I shoot em in his knee cap." L's yelled. Pimp came walking into the kitchen laughing because he knew L's was giving Mike a hard time like he always did.

"What's up money mike?" Pimp said while dapping it up with him like he was one of the fella's instead of a smoker.

"Sometimes you, sometimes me, all the time us," Pimp said.

"Let me get like sixty in bricks," Magic Mike replied with his usual slick talk. Pimp dropped three fat stones in his hand.

"C'mon pimpin you got moe love for Magic Mike than this," Magic Mike said even though he was already satisfied with the boulders he held in his hand. Pimp always gave Mike extra, so he knew he was spoiled. Pimp dropped another stone in his hand that was half the size of the other three. Magic Mike shuffled his feet while singing a song. "Late night candlelight fiend with a crack pipe, it's only right."

"Get yo ass out of here Mike, this ain't no soul train ma'fucka." L's said while snatching the door open and laughing at Mike's performance. As he walked out he looked at L's and said,

"That's why I deal wit Pimp because you is an evil mutha fucka." L's tried to kick him in his ass before slamming the door on him. Pimp and L's laughed as they headed back into the living room. Magic brought entertainment along with a few dollars. Leslie came rushing in the front door with tears in her eyes, immediately putting a stop to their laughter.

"What's up Les, what's wrong?" Pimp asked as she ran into his arms.

"What the fuck happened?" L's added.

"That punk Monster just slapped me, cause I wouldn't let him feel my ass, I tried to fight him, but he threw me on the ground and kicked me in my ass in front of his homeboys." Leslie explained as shameful tears streamed down her face. Leslie wasn't a soft girl. She wasn't one to do a lot of fighting, because she didn't want to mess her pretty face up, but the few fights she got into with neighborhood girls she had been victorious. Monster, on the other hand, was supposedly the toughest youngster on Oak Street. He was a few years older than L's and Pimp, bigger as well and his fighting record was flawless. He didn't bar L's, but he didn't try him either, because it was known that although L's would fight, more than likely he was issuing gunplay. That was the reason big Looney and a lot of older hustlers liked him. L's grabbed Pimp's 380 Lugar off the couch, handed it to him, and said,

"Let's roll bro, that nigga Monster got me fucked up."

Leslie knew L's was off the hook and she wanted Monster touched, but not like what L's had in mind.

"No L's it ain't that serious." She pleaded.

"Just chill Les, that nigga knows you fuck wit Pimp so he basically saying fuck all of us and he got it twisted," L's said as he and Pimp headed out the front door. Leslie ran up the steps calling her mother because she knew things were about to get out of control. As Pimp and L's marched up the street to the corner store, Monster stood in the middle of Stanley and the rest of his homeboys, while rubbing his hands together in anticipation.

"What up homie? Put yo hands on me like you did my girl." Pimp said strongly.

"Lil L's you betta tell this lil nigga who he fucking wit and who I am, fore he get his ass beat." Monster said calmly, still rubbing his hands together.

"I ain't better tell him shit," L's said as Pimp pulled out his chrome 380. All of Monster boys stepped back in the sight of the gun. Monster stood his ground though his heart was racing.

"Damn L's you gone brang this nigga to the hood and just let him shoot ah nigga you grew up with?" Monster said.

L's drew his baby nine, letting his actions speak for him. Pimp stopped L's and passed him his 380.

"Hold this L's I'm bout to beat this niggas ass." L's placed Pimp's gun on his waist while keeping his in his hand exposed to the world as if it were legal. Monster laughed at the sight of Pimp as he stepped in the middle of the street.

"I'm bout to beat the fuck out of you, bro," Monster said as he met Pimp in the middle of the street, that now served as a boxing ring. Monster was bigger and stronger than Pimp, but like his father, Pimp was naturally good with his hands. The two squared off, toe to toe. Monster stalked Pimp looking for the quick knock out blow, but Pimp never stayed still. He was bouncing around, shuffling his feet, while switching his style up with every movement. Pimp fain'ted Monster and got the response he was looking for. Monster threw a wild blow, and Pimp was under it sliding into his chest as he delivered a three-piece combination that Monster shook off.

"You hit like a lil bitch." Monster said as he spat blood from his lip. He rushed Pimp with two sloppy hooks and once again Pimp was under them. This time he delivered a right uppercut, right hook, and left hand straight down the pipe. Monster staggered back leaking from his mouth and nose. Once again he shook Pimp's blows off.

"Lil nigga you know something, huh?" Monster said. Pimp answered him with a leaping hook that swelled his eye up instantly. Leslie and Liley watched as Pimp went to work on the neighborhood bully. L's stood on the side with his homeboys. They all were astonished by Pimp's performance. L's knew Pimp had some go in him, but the way he threw his hands today made L's think Pimp should be in a boxing ring instead of football. L's had a sinister grin on his face. Hell yea my boy a tiger, I knew he had that killer instinct in him, its really on now. He thought as he started coaching Pimp on. Monster had finally got his hands on Pimp, but it wasn't for long. Monster grabbed hold of Pimp's shirt, but Pimp slithered out his shirt and went back to work on his face.

"That's enough man, C'mon L's break that shit up," Stanley said while trying to pull Monster out the ways of Pimp's flurries.

"Don't nobody touch my boy." L's said as he flashed his gun. "C'mon man you know it ain't like that L's." Stanley said while throwing his hands up in the air.

"You cool Pimp?" L's asked Pimp as he stood in the middle of the street with his shirt off.

"Yeah I'm cool," Pimp answered.

"You touch my girl again nigga, I'm a stomp a mud hole in yo ass. That goes for all you niggas." Pimp continued as Monster stood there looking like the elephant man from all kinds of speed knots from Pimp's quick hands. Leslie was already feeling Pimp, but to see the pretty boy go from smooth to hardcore in honor of her, sent her head over hills. Liley was proud of both Pimp and herself. Pimp for defending her daughter against a young hustler that was feared by many and proud of her for picking such a winner for her daughter.

Slim and D-Roc bobbed their heads to crime boss as he screamed from Slim's four twelves. Fella and Walt trailed behind them bobbing their heads to C.B.O's straight killer as it harmonized through Fella's four twelves. Slim and Fella had their vans out of the shop for two days and they've yet to park them for longer than an hour. Slim's MVP was candy green, with gold flakes in the pain't, a peanut butter brown rag top to accommodate his triple gold hundred spoke Daytons. Gold grill, bumper and door handles. The inside was plushed out with peanut butter soft brown leather seats, matching floors, ceilings and doors. The dashboard, steering wheel, and radio deck were all decked out in wood grain marble brown. Slim flashed his gold diamonds as he mean mugged all the onlookers.

The top of his mouth had Slim spelled out in diamonds, while the bottom spelled gangsta in even more diamonds. Slim wore a gold Rolex on his left wrist, with a couple of gold diamond bracelets on his right wrist, that matched the chains around his neck. He wore two nice sized diamond rings on each finger, and the sun complimented them as he controlled the wheel with both hands, swerving from one side of the street to the next. D-Roc rode shotgun with even more jewelry on. His teeth were cluttered with gold diamonds, while he wore a huge Rolex chain around his neck with crushed ice all through it. The chain hung just below his chest, while the iced out cross hung from it, stopped at his belly button. On his left wrist he had a gold Movado timepiece, with a diamond ring on every finger. On his right wrist he wore a thick gold Rolex bracelet flooded with diamond chips.

He had a ring on each one of his fingers. His long cornrows hung on his back as he bounced to the sound of crime boss while smoking on a fat blunt of expensive hydro. His eleven four-shot Taurus sat on his lap ready for action if it occurred. Slim's Glock nine rested under his leg. Behind them, Fella and Walt blinged as well. Fella's truck was identical to Slim's except that his color was raspberry blue with gold flakes and all three accessories. Fella had a fitted hat cocked to the back as he showcased his gold and diamond grill. He had the whole top row flooded while the bottom only had four teeth in the front of his mouth blinging. Walt had his whole mouth filled with 14 karat gold while only two fangs at the top and bottom of his mouth were iced out. He and Fella were draped with plenty of other accessories as well.

Both cars were bedazzling both inside and out. Walt shook his single braids as they hung all in his face, resting on his shoulders. He had twin Glocks on his lap, while Fella carried a p. 94 Rouger. As Walt looked through his rearview mirror he noticed the vans being chased by three gunmen. One directly behind the van, while two chased the vehicle on the opposite side of the street.

"Oh shit we getting dumped on," Walt said while tapping on Fella's leg and pointing to the rearview mirror. The music was up so loud that neither Slim, D-Roc, Walt, nor Fella could hear the sound of shots. Walt hung out the window and returned fire. D-Roc noticed Walt hanging out the window, as he thought he heard gunshots. As he tapped Slim and pointed to the gunman on the side of the vehicle, he was sprayed on by two gunmen running off the side of a house. He leaned towards Slim while recklessly blasting several shots. Both vans picked up their speed leaving the gunmen further behind. Walt continued to let off rounds at the gunmen behind them as the wind blew his braids in his face. When he passed the house where the two gunmen were hiding, he aimed both his nines and traded gunshots with the gunmen as well. Fella followed Slim as he swerved right and they both made a quick left turn leaving Mt. Vernon and the gunmen in the wind.

As the season gravitated towards fall, Mills paced the hallways awaiting the intake. Mills was out of place because he didn't have a pass to be out the unit, but he was cool since Butter was the J.C.O in charge bringing in the intake. As Butter lead the long line of juveniles up the hallway, Mills spotted who he was looking for and a big smile covered his face.

"What's up, bro?" Mills yelled to get his attention.

Peko's poker face instantly changed to a smile.

"T-money what's up bro?" he replied. Butter was cool unlike the other J.C.O in charge of the Cuyahoga Hills intake. He didn't mind the juveniles talking as long as they weren't too loud; Butter saw one of the ranking authorities coming, so he gave Mills a look while nodding in the authorities' direction. Mills peeped game. Butter pulled him over to the side to avoid him being stopped by the administration.

"Mr. Mills do you have a pass to be out here in the hallway?" Butter asked. Mills flashed him a piece of paper as the administration walked by.

"I'm back from med bay," Mills answered. Butter winked and quietly asked which one of them was his homies. Mills showed him Peko and Butter told him he'd make sure they got a chance to kick it with each other later, but now he needed him to go back in his unit. Later that evening butter gave Mills a pass to Peko's unit. Peko was placed in the same unit as B-nut and Mills couldn't wait to introduce them to each other, as he hurried to their block. Mills entered the unit with no problem since Butter called the J.C.O in charge of the unit in advance.

"What up blood?" B-nut said to Mills as he scanned the room looking for Peko. Mills laughed before replying because even though he wasn't in a gang, he always acknowledged him like he was. Mills didn't mind though, because B-nut used his blood lingo on everyone, even opposing gang members, which was naturally the cause of his fights.

"What up bro?" Mills said as they embraced each other.

"Shit blood, jus kicken it," B-nut replied.

Mills spotted Peko walking out of the bathroom as he and B-nut conversed.

"C'mon bro, I want you to meet somebody," Mills said as he locked eyes with Peko and flagged him down. They met in the middle of the floor with a strong embrace.

"Got damn bro, you getting big as fuck," Peko said as he stepped back to take a look at Mills.

Mills smiled. "Shid bro, look at you, you as tall as a fucking tree," Mills said as he looked at Peko's now 5'10 frame. They both laughed.

"Oh shit...bro dis ma nigga B-nut, he family...B-nut this bro Peko, he was in a lot of my pictures," Mills said as he stepped to the side so the two could dap it up.

"What's up bro," Peko said as he and B-nut shook hands.

"Shid I ban't ball it, I heard a lot about you dawg, blood talk about you, Fella, Shawn, and uh what's her name... Brandy." Peko said.

"Yeah Brandy all the time it all loves blood." B-nut said. Peko was lost by his lingo and Mills could tell by the expression on his face.

"You'll get used to it, B-nut crazy bro, or should I say, brazy." Mills said as he smiled and elbowed B-nut in his rib cage.

They kicked it for a while in which Peko told Mills he only had a couple months left to serve, Mills wasn't too affected by his short amount of time he had with one of his closest friends, because he had only eleven months himself and B-nut was right behind him with eighteen. H.T. was down to four months and Black was at twenty. Before leaving, Mills told B-nut to lace Peko up with hygiene and goods then slid him a half-ounce of weed to Peko while hugging him. Peko looked at his hand and quickly closed it.

"What am I supposed to with this, bro?? He asked as he nervously scanned the room.

"Do what you do best, B-nut got you," Mills said with a big smile on his face. Yea I got you blood, we bick it like that everyday, my head in blood's right now," B-nut said. M

ills laughed as he took off. Back in the hood Brandy and Shawn continued to grind and stack. Although they didn't have a drug house, their pager rewarded them just as much money as the drug house could. On top of that, just sitting on either one of their porches was enough to make the strip do Nino Brown numbers. Their only need for a spot was to hide from Pac Man and his cop buddies that continuously harassed them.

As usual the strip was packed on a late September evening. Brandy and Shawn sat on Shawn's porch smoking a blunt while watching baby tone, Lil Scoob, and a few other young hustlers fight over money that strolled up and down the strip. A car pulled in front of Shawn's mother's house and got swarmed by Baby Tone, Lil Scoob, and three other youngins. As the driver turned their service down, the passenger stepped out the car yelling Brandy and Shawn's names.

"Is that Lisa?" Brandy asked Shawn.

"I think so," He answered, as he stood up trying to get a better view.

"Y'all better not be acting like y'all don't remember yo Aunt Lisa after all the shit y'all put me through," Lisa said as she stood in front of the house with her hands on her hips. They hadn't seen Lisa since they got her house hit by SWAT. Lisa's house was their first dope spot and not only did Lisa watch them grow up; she kept her mouth closed when the police questioned her about the drugs and guns found in her house. As a result, she went to prison while Mills, Peko, Brandy, and Shawn all got probation. Brandy and Shawn rushed off the porch after realizing it was Lisa.

"What's up auntie?" Brandy said.

"How long you been home," Shawn added.

"Bout four months, I just got me an apartment down the street on Oakwood and Fulton," Lisa said.

"Auntie you know we looking for a place to post up at," Shawn said not wasting any time.

"You know y'all welcome nephew, I'm at 325 oakwood, but right now, I'm trynna get something fat for this twenty dollars I got," Lisa responded not wasting time with what she wanted as well.

"Keep yo money auntie, you know yo money ain't no good here girl," Brandy said while placing her hands on her hips and playfully rolling her eyes. Lisa smiled, but she figured she'd be leaving with something free anyway. After all she had just done two years in prison for them. Brandy and Shawn dropped a couple of stones in her hand and told her they'd be by her apartment later. Just like that, Brandy and Shawn were back in a spot. As soon as Lisa pulled off, Pac-Man bent the corner with his door cracked ready to jump out his cruiser and snatch up anybody who looked nervous. Brandy and Shawn hurried back up to the porch, where they could run in the house if need be. As Baby Tone and Lil Scoob tried to walk off, Pac-Man threw his car in park in the middle of the street and rushed the two youngins. Lil Scoob took off in one direction, while Baby Tone shot off another. Too bad for Pac-Man because he was without a partner and the youngsters were through one yard and over a fence before he could decide which one to chase. The other youngins on the strip disappeared as well, leaving Pac-Man to stare off with Brandy and Shawn.

As he got back in his cruiser, he yelled out Brandy, Fella, and Shawn's mother's addresses through his loud speaker. Then they said all their children were drug dealers and one day they were going to rot in jail. Later that evening Brandy and Shawn stopped by Lisa's. Although Lisa only had an apartment for a month, she already had a little traffic coming in and out. With the help of pagers, Brandy and Shawn had Lisa's apartment doing numbers in no time. As fall closed, winter prepared to open, Peko was finishing off the last couple of weeks of his six-month sentence.

Mills made his way over to Peko's unit every chance he got. They also spent every Sunday together in church, along with Black, B-nut and H.T. Mills enjoyed his time with Peko, but he was happy to see him leaving. Not only did Peko have newborn child to go home to, but the quicker Peko left, the closer Mills was to following behind him with his own freedom walk. Mills and Peko had already discussed all the business they needed to discuss, so they spent their last Sunday together reminiscing, and laughing at B-nut's wild stories. Later that night while Peko lay in his bed unable to sleep, D-Roc Slim, Walt, and Fella were dodging bullets from T-Bone, Fresh, and Big Dueces younger brother Mike's Glock and four fives. They ran through the club's parking lot ducking behind cars, as they rushed to their vehicles.

When they finally made it to their artillery, more of T-Bone's and Fresh's crew had opened fired from across the street. D-Roc grabbed his mini mac ten off the passenger seat and returned fire on them. Slim focused on getting the van started, while Fella did the same thing with his van. Walt stuffed one fifty round clip in his pocket, before spinning around with his chopper in his hand. Walt ran off the side of the van letting lose rapid fire from the A.K. He sent everyone diving for cover as he swung his body back and fired, letting the chopper chop everything in sight. As the last bullet hopped out the A.K., Walt ran back in the van. Slim and Fella were already whipping out their parking spaces. D-

Roc dove in the van while Slim, covered him with his twenty one shot top of the line nine. Fella did the same with his desert eagle as Walt hopped in the van with him.

As the vehicles sped out the lot, bullets riddled the van, knocking windows out and grazing Fella on the shoulder. Walt quickly popped the second clip in the A.K. and swung back into action. Slim dumped shots into the club, sending bouncers and party goers diving to the floor as he and Fella whizzed by the club. Police sirens filled the air as bodies lay stretched out from the club entrance to the parking lot.

By the time the police and medical squad arrived, D-Roc and his crew were gone.

CHAPTER 12

A fter spending his first few weeks, including Christmas at home with his newborn daughter and girlfriend, Peko was right back to the streets. Shawn had hustled hard for both of them while Peko was locked up. Now Peko was returning the favor, as Shawn spent time with his now pregnant girlfriend and his new dark brown hardtop 5.0 Mustang. After hustling hard, Peko told him that he had to reward himself, and he did. His Mustang had peanut butter brown rag top matching interior, dark tinted windows, some sixteen-inch hundred spoke Daytons, and two fifteens in the trunk, along with some killer horsepower under the hood.

Peko had been home for four months and he was ready to cop him a mean vehicle. He wanted to have a nice ride to match his little brother's Mustang and Brandy's Benz by the time Mills came home. Mills was down to four months and the streets anticipated. With three months left, Mills stopped selling weed and focused on rounding up the money owed to him. Two weeks prior to him being released, he had all his money except two hundred dollars which was owed to him by a guy named Tyson from Cincinnati. Tyson boxed growing up as a child. He had three golden gloves titles and would have boxed for the Olympic gold medal if he wouldn't have killed a guy from a rival neighborhood.

Tyson had been in TYKO for four years and he quickly earned the title of a champ in the juvenile prison as well. Very few people stood up to him and even fewer attempted to fight him. For that reason, he liked to throw both his weight and rank around. It had been three months since he got four fifties from

Mills, with an agreement to send the money within a month. Every time Mills asked him about his money; he blew Mills off with some drag game. Mills was starting to understand Tyson's motives.

He promised himself this would be his last time asking for his money. He walked over to the table where Tyson sat playing spades with a few of his homies.

"Aye Tyson, Let me holla at you for a second, big homie," Mills said as Tyson dealt the cards.

"Hold up dawg, let me finish this hand," Tyson said, while fixing his cards.

Mills didn't says anything, he sat back until the hand was over. When Tyson's homie started dealing another hand, Mills spoke.

"Tyson, let me holla at you for a minute bro," Tyson knew Mills wanted to talk about his money, so he tried blowing him off with the waiting game.

"Hold up lil Mills let me finish this game dawg," He said while putting his hand together.

"And how long is that gone be?" Mills said as he became more frustrated by the second.

"We just started, gimme a minute man," Tyson said now becoming aggravated.

"C'mon man you know what I need to holla at you about bro, it ain't gone take but a few seconds," Mills responded.

"Damn man, I said gimmie a minute. You starting to act like my bitch, naggin me and shit," Tyson said with authority, causing his homies to burst out laughing.

"Yeah, aight," Mills said as he walked off.

Five minutes later Mills returned with a metal mop ringer. Before Tyson's homies noticed Mills, he was behind Tyson swinging the mop ringer hard.

"Ty watch out dawg," his homie yelled as he jumped up from the table. It was too late, Mills sent blood flying across the room as he connected Tyson in the back of his head. Mills didn't stop with one swing, he continued to beat Tyson in the head until he fell out of his seat and balled up on the ground. Mills continued to beat the blood out of him while saying,

"Do I still remind you of yo bitch?"

Butter let Mills get his funky off for a few minutes before calling for back up. Rio dropped the phone in the middle of his conversation and pulled Mills off of Tyson's bloody body. Mills spent his last two weeks in disciplinary isolation. Leaving the way he came, on lockdown.

Buck leaned up against his 500 Benz on all Chrome Lorenzo's while checking the time on his bejeweled presidential Rolex. He shook his head in frustration because Jimmy was twenty minutes late for the time they had set to pick Mills up. Peko, Shawn Shawn, and Brandy stood on the porch, while grandma Mills worked her magic in the kitchen. Jimmy had a dope fiend drop him off around the corner from his grandmother's house. He speed-walked home as his pager screamed for attention. He looked at the screen and saw one of his fiends codes with the number one hundred behind it. He cursed under his breath knowing that one of his big spenders were on the way over Lily's.

The pager continued to sound off as he got closer to home. He turned it off as he heard Peko saying "There go Jimmy right there."

Buck turned around as Jimmy jogged across the street.

"What's up big bro" Jimmy said.

"I don't know you tell me? Where you been at, you know we had to pick Mills up this morning." Buck said as he opened the passenger door for Jimmy and walked around the car to the driver's side.

"I stayed over my friend L...I mean Leon's house last night, i'm sorry bro," Jimmy said as they ducked off inside the spaceship-like vehicle.

"Don't ever say you sorry, lil Keys, that's an ambiguous word, and it's usually used negatively for a person who is worthless. Never use that word in reference to an apology. Just say you apologize. Furthermore your apology is accepted, but don't make being late a habit." Time is a man's most precious commodity, and the only way to stay on time is to arrive early, feel me lil daddy?" Buck said as he held his fist out for Jimmy to hit the rock. Jimmy smiled because just like Mills and everyone else, he loved hearing buck drop his knowledge.

He hit the rock as Buck pulled away from the curb. Fifteen minutes later, they were pulling into Tyko's parking lot. When Buck and Jimmy entered the lobby they approached the only desk insight. An attractive young lady sat behind the desk pretending to enjoy the conversation she was involved in over the phone. She was happy to see Buck awaiting her service because it was her excuse to end the phone call, which she quickly did while rolling her eyes, clearly showcasing her exasperation.

" I apologize how may I help you?"

The young lady asked with a hint of both boredom and frustration.

"Well first let me apologize for any stress I may be adding to your day and I hope helping me doesn't cause you to work too hard, but I'm here to pick up Tony Mills. He is being released today." Buck answered while pouring his charm on real heavy.

Buck's mannerism brought a smile to her face. As she picked up the phone to call Mill's unit, she gave Buck a once over. The VVS diamonds in Buck's presidential Rolex almost blinded her as she tried to sneak a better peek at it. Once again the young lady was rolling her eyes as the person on the other end of the phone avoided her.

"Oh my God, some people just don't let up. I apologize for the way I have been acting, but I'm having a real bad day. Tony Mills will be out shortly, thank you for being so understanding." The young lady said as she smashed down the phone on the receiver.

"Don't worry about it Miss...." Buck said while pausing so she could state her name.

"Tonya," she said. Quickly recognizing game.

"Tonya that's a pretty name and with all due respect, you too beautiful to let a bad day at work cause you to feel so ugly. Sometimes we gotta put up with things we don't want to, to reap the benefits we need to live the type of life we like living," Buck said while glancing at his Rolex.

Jimmy smiled as Buck charmed the attractive young lady. As they exchanged words, Buck took a sneak peek at Tonya's frame as she stood up to press a button on a wall. Buck had to admit if he were not so committed to Tameka and their baby they had on the way, he would show Tonya what it felt like to be with a real nigga. Bucks thoughts were interrupted as Mills snuck up behind him and playfully delivered a hook to his ribs. Buck quickly spun around. He grabbed Mills up for an embrace while saying,

"Damn boy, you done got big as fuck!" Mills grabbed Jimmy up next, hugging him so tightly he almost cut off his circulation.

"You talking bout I'm gettin big, look at lil bro." Mills said as he rubbed his hand over Jimmy's waves and threw a few punches at him. Tonya watched as the three attractive young men reunited. She blushed as dirty thoughts traveled through her mind.

"Tonya you take it easy, don't let cha job get the best of you baby girl. After the dark comes the light," Buck said while giving Tonya a wink. Tonya waved bye as the three young men walked out the door. Mills was intrigued by Buck's 500 Benz. The jet black vehicle was roomy and the plush leather was inviting.

Mills promised to get himself one of these spaceship-like vehicles, once he brought his plan to life. Buck pulled out the lot with the sound of Jay-Z's Reasonable Doubt blasting from his speakers. As Buck turned onto grandma Mills street, Mills looked at the fancy cars parked in front of his grandmother's house and wondered who they belonged to. As Buck parked the car Peko, Shawn Shawn, and Brandy came rushing out of his grandmother's front door.

He instantly knew who the cars belonged to. *Damn, my homies gettin it like this?* Mills thought as he took a second look at Peko's burgundy and gold 96 Impala with the peanut butter brown rag top, dark tinted windows and sixteen-inch hundred spoke Daytons. The gold flakes in Peko's candy pain't sparkled as the sun hit them from an angle. The sun complemented Shawn Shawn's Mustang and Brandy's 350 Benz as well, as they both sat pretty on clean rims. Mills wasn't fully out of the car before Brandy rushed him with a big hug. Mills squeezed lightly.

"Punk don't be actin like you ain't happy to see me." Brandy said while playfully punching Mills in his rock hard chest. Peko and Shawn Shawn stood in the front yard with their arms crossed as Mills, Brandy, Buck and Jimmy crossed the street.

"Y'all niggas perped out acting like y'all ain't miss my bro," Brandy said.

Peko and Shawn Shawn stood firm.

"Ahhh"!! Peko and Shawn Shawn yelled out as they rushed Mills with tight embraces. They all laughed as grandma Mills swung her front door open.

"You better come up here and give me some love while you down there giving all my hugs away," Mills ran up the steps and squeezed his grandmother tightly while planting a big one on her cheek.

"You know I love you momma," Mills said while embracing her.

"I love you too baby, don't leave me no more now you go on down there with your friends and show them how much you appreciate them watching over your grandmother and baby brother in your absence. I got some fried chicken and thangs goin on in here and the food will be ready in a few." Grandma Mills said as she walked back in the house.

Peko flashed Mills with a fat blunt of hydro as he rejoined them.

"C'mon Pee, you know we can't do that with Jim right here." Mills whispered.

"Aw, my bad bro, later for that," Peko said as he cuffed the blunt out of Jimmy's sight. Jimmy shook his head at Mills attempt to keep him sheltered from drugs.

If he only knew, Jimmy thought as Mills wrapped his arm around his shoulder.

"Whats up lil bro, what you been up to?" Mills said.

"Not much just goin to school, and playing football," Jimmy replied.

"Whats up wit the lil girlies?" Mills asked while playfully squeezing his biceps tighter around Jimmy's neck.

Jimmy just smiled. "Uh huh, I knew you had the girlies big head," Mills said while playfully delivering a blow to his little brothers gut. Buck interrupted their moment. As he ended a call on his cell phone.

"Dig lil bro I gotta go take Mek to the hospital for her monthly checkup. I gotta make sure your lil niece growing inside her is healthy. If I don't make it back today, call me in the morning so we can discuss that business. Aight" Buck said.

"Aight big bro, I love you man, Tell Mek I said what up." Mills said.

"I love you too boy, get you some Pu..." Buck looked at Jimmy and stopped in mid sentence.

"You know what to get tonight. Get lose boy, cause tomorrow it's back to the money." They embraced, and Buck said his see you laters and call mes to the rest of his little homies, then pulled out as Buck turned off the street.

A four-door, white Bonneville with a golden brown rag top, gold grill, gold bumper, gold door handles, gold Daytons, dark tinted windows, and a thunderous system hit the corner on three wheels. Behind it was a 70's Cutlass, with gold candy pain't, a gold grill bumper, Door handles, and dual exhaust pipes along with dark tinted windows, a booming system, and som triple gold hundred spokes. It too was on three wheels. The show wasn't over as two more mouth dropping vehicles bent the corner on three wheels. A drop-top six four Impala coated with wet green candy pain'ted and chrome hundred spoke Daytons to accommodate its chrome grille, bumper, and trimmings. It also had a system that could wake the dead.

Although the top was down on the Impala, Mills could not see inside because the driver had all the dark tinted windows rolled up. Behind the Impala was a Regal, with a white and gold marble pain't job, triple gold hundred spoke Daytons, dark tinted windows, and a glass breaking system. All the cars dropped to the ground in front of Mills. Two of the vehicles pancaked side to side and front to back, while the other two bounced off the ground like basketballs. As the cars pulled to the curb, Mills looked at Peko, Brandy, and Shawn Shawn for an answer.

"Thats Fells and D-Roc and them," Peko said motioning for Mills to turn his attention back on the vehicles. Slim got out the Bonneville, D-Roc, stepped out the Cutlass, Fella rose from the Regal, and Lil Walt from the Impala. The foursome looked like rap stars as they gravitated toward Mills with their jewelry blinging.

"Welcome home bro," Fella said, while puffing on a fat backwood filled with green.

175

"Put that shit out Fells, you see Jim right here and my grandmother in the house, you trippin bro," Mills said. Then he told Jimmy to go in the house. Jimmy felt the tension in the air and he wanted to stay by his brother's side, but he did as he was told. Fella used the ground to knock the fire off the end of his blunt, then pulled Mills in for a hug.

"Damn baby you on swole," Fella said. Out of D-Roc, Slim, and Lil Walt, Slim was the first to speak to Mills.

"What up Lil Mills you looking good boy, welcome home," Slim said while pulling a wad of cash from his pocket, peeling back five hundred dollars bills, and offering them to Mills.

"I'm straight Slim, I appreciate it though big homie.

"What up Roc, Sup Walt," Mills said as Fella's now 5'9 frame swallowed his at 5'6.

"What's happenin Lil Mills you lookin good baby, I guess I can't offer you nothing seeing how you turned the Slim gangsta down," D-Roc said as him, and Mills exchanged daps.

"Yeah you must got a hell of a stash hid somewhere homie," Walt added with a devilish grin, he used for a smile. Although Mills knew what Walt was insinuating, he gave a fake chuckle to accommodate the one D-Roc and Walt shared.

"Dig I don't mean to be rude, but I need to holla at Fells on the one on one tip…take a walk with me Fells," Mills said while leading the way up the street. Fella exchanged daps with Peko, Brandy, and Shawn Shawn as he passed them. They conversed with D-Roc, Walt, and Slim while Mills and Fella stood on the corner talking.

"Listen Fells, fuck all that shit that been goin on while I was locked up, I know Slim yo cousin and I ain't asking you to turn ya back on ya family, but I'm home now, are you gone get back to getting money with cha ace or what?" Mills said.

"I'm sayin bro, we all can get money together, we all grew up together, we from the same hood, I don't see what the problem is," Fella responded.

"C'mon bro. Them and us is like water and oil. We just don't mix, them niggas ain't to be trusted, and I'm sayin bro, I don't knock how no nigga get his money, but I don't want them problems. That type shit put too much bullshit in the game. So I'm sayin though, are you gone get money wit the crew you came into the game wit, or is you gone keep living life on the edge?" Mills asked.

"What is this Mills, an ultimatum or some shit?" "Pee and Bee came at me wit that same bullshit, like ya'll trynna make me choose a side. If y'all fuck wit me, y'all gone fuck wit me no matter who I roll wit," Fella said loud enough to turn heads.

"C'mon bro, why you being so loud, This me, T-money yo Ace, from birth to the turf, we like brothers, and I'm always gone have ya back, but I ain't fuckin wit Rock and them, so now what?" Mills said adamantly.

Fella was frustrated. He loved Mills, Peko, Brandy, and Shawn Shawn as well, but he refused to be put in a position where he had to choose between his block kin, and his family by covenant.

He dug in his pockets and extracted a thousand dollars from his roll of bills, and held them out to Mills.

"Here you go I ain't trying to argue wit you right now, but we ain't kids no more, and I ain't taking no ultimatums from nobody," Fells said.

"I'm cool bro keep yo paper, but never lose sight of what's real," Mills said.

Fella laid the money on the ground in front of Mills and said, "You got my number bro, as he walked off." Mills was frustrated as well because he never expected his conversation with his ace to end the way it did. As Fella, D-Roc, Slim and Walt lifted their vehicles off the ground, and pulled off; Grandma Mills called

Mills and his friends in for dinner. Mills enjoyed his meal with his family along with laughter and small talk. As dawn sat in, Peko, Shawn, and Brandy took off, while Mills spent some quality time with his little brother, and grandmother. Mills eventually dozed off and woke up in an empty room. Jimmy had left, and his grandmother had gone to her room for some sleep of her own.

Mills grabbed the phone and paged his little brother and then made a booty call he promised Chrissie he would. Ring! Ring! Ring!

"Hello." Chrissie said.

"What's up girl," Mills responded smoothly.

"Mills?" Chrissie said with inquiry. "

The one and only." Mills shot back.

"I thought you forgot about me," Chrissie said.

"After all the letters and calls we shared how could I do that?" Mills asked with allure.

"You know how niggas in jail be making false promises and shit." Chrissie said.

"Hahaha," Mills laughed because Chrissie had a valid point.

"Dig chrissie, I'm a man of my word. Now is you gone come get me or what? Mills said.

"I don't know; you don't sound too enthused about spending the night wit me…do you want me to come and get you?" Chrissie asked in a seductive voice. Mills laughed again because he peeped her game.

"Girl you better quit playing wit me," Mills said.

"I'm sayin Mills, do you want some of this cat as much as I want you?" Chrissie teased.

"If I didn't baby I do now, you gone let me beat it up?" Mills said joining her in the game she obviously wanted him to play. They enticed one another a little longer; then Mills gave her his grandmother's address. She said she'd be there in half an hour which was just enough time for Mills to jump in the shower, and get fresh. Chrissie arrived at 12 o'clock pm. She hit the horn on her drop top Lebaron and Mills quickly ran out before her horn woke his grandmother. His eyes went from her face to in between her legs. Chrissie was a thick mixed breed with long sandy brown hair.

Her hazel eyes almost matched her hair color. Her breast almost hung out the bottom of her cut off white beater, while her nipples were protruding through it. Her flat stomach fell right into her wide hips that went with her ass in perfect harmony. She wore a pair of cut off daisy dukes that her pussy hung out of. As Mills looked at the muff between her legs and admired her thighs, she leaned over and kissed him on his cheek. Mills wore a wife beater, some green sweats, and a pair of white high top air force ones.

Mills wife beater fitted him perfectly, and Chrissie had become moist while admiring the cuts and rips of his frame. Mills leaned back in the seat as Chrissie turned up the music. Twenty minutes later, Chrissie was pulling into her apartment complex. Once inside the apartment Mills sat fire to a blunt he had put out in the car. Chrissie clocked on the lights and said,

"This is it; this is my little home." Chrissie's parents had money so Mills expected nothing less than the expensive furniture she had, but it was a women's own will to keep a clean house. Buck had told Mills a long time ago, that a man could tell a lot about a person by the way they took care of their house, especially a woman. Although Chrissie was fine and had a bright future, Mills knew she could never be more than a playmate, because she had too many miles on her, and too many men knew where she lived. At nineteen Chrissie had been with enough men to last her a lifetime. She took Mills on a tour of her house and ended the tour in her bedroom.

"So what do you think?" Chrissie asked Mills as he looked around her bedroom.

CHARLES WATSON

"I think your apartment is nice and ya room has one hell of a view." Mills said as he looked at her body and licked his lips.

Chrissie smiled as she walked to Mills and kissed him gently on his lips. Mills didn't resist; he accepted her tongue as she slid it in his mouth, and twirled it around. That was all it took for Mills to rise to the occasion. His pole rubbed up against her leg as it attempted to poke a hole through his sweat pants. Chrissie felt his manhood against her leg and she grabbed a handful of it. She wanted to taste it, and she didn't waste any time removing his clothes or hers. She laid Mills back on the bed and crawled up on his body until she met the tip of his manhood with her lips. She kissed the head softly and then flicked her tongue at it. She licked it down, then up using her tongue to explore his whole penis. She took his balls in her mouth; Mills lifted to take a peek at her. She made eye contact with Mills as she went back to work on his piece.

Mills body tensed up as he exploded in her mouth. It didn't take Chrissie long to bring his piece back to life, and once she did, she used her mouth to put the condom on. Chrissie turned around and straddled Mills pole from the back. He spread her cheeks open as she bounced up and down on him. Her juices rained down on him as she stuffed all of his manhood inside her. Mills switched positions to stop himself from busting too quickly. He bent her over and spread her cheeks apart, and her neatly shaved peach came to view. Mills watched her lips grip his penis as he entered her slowly. He started slowly moving with rhythm, allowing her to rock with him. She sucked her teeth while moaning, oooohhh! Mills that's my spot!! Mills dug deeper while pounding harder and faster causing her to grab a handful of sheets, while biting down on her bottom lip.

Oh! Oh! Oh! Oh! Oh! She screamed as Mills slammed her with rapid speed. Before the night was over they had tried multiple positions, and brought one another to several climaxes. After a half an hour of hard morning sex and some breakfast, Chrissie took Mills home. Mills didn't waste any time showering and getting dressed. He threw another wife beater on with some black sweat pants, and some grey black and white Jordans that Peko had bought him. He slapped a coat of grease on his waves and brushed them a few times, dapped his self with some Michael Jordan cologne, and made a quick call to let Brandy know he was on his way over her house, and out the door.

While walking up Mound Street, he noticed all the young hustlers standing around, flagging down cars and chasing money down. He smiled as he realized that all the new faces were in clientale. As he reached Berkley he finally saw some familiar faces. Chris and Var stood on the corner of Mound and Berkley, with a few hustlers.

"What's happening Chris. Sup var," Mills said while exchanging daps and hugs with them.

"What ya'll niggas been up to?" Mills asked.

"Shyd man trynna get this money, but shit ain't been getting right since Buck left the hood. Its like the rest of these niggas don't wanna see a young hustler blow, they taxing for they work, two twenty-five courts, nine faces for an ounce, and that shit only be half decent. Pee look out for a nigga wit that crit when he can, but you know he rocks wit his shit, he a block monster forreal." Chris said.

"How much paper ya'll got right now?"

Shid me and Var got about five hundred right now, but we still got a few hundred in stones left." Chris said.

"Hold that shit bro, I'm bout to be right in a couple hours, I'm a throw yall niggas some love, we bout to eat bro, just fuck wit me." Mills said, sellin his product without having it.

"How long you gone be, bro?" Chris asked.

"I'm bout to go get me a pager then I'm headed for that work, about two, three hours tops." Mills answered.

"Man we gone be right here bro, lil Scoob and them probably need some shit too," Chris said.

"I got yall bro, and Ima put something with it, for making yall wait." Mills said before exchanaging more daps and hugs before taking off again.

As Mills approached Brandy's house, he noticed Brandy standing on her porch with a dark skin beauty. As he climbed the steps on Brandy's porch, he and the girl sized each other up.

"What's up, bro?" Brandy said.

"I can't call it what's up with you?" Mills replied.

"Not a damn thing, just chilling with my girl and you better go in there and holler at mommy because she was talking shit all night about you not coming by here to see her yesterday" Brandy explained.

"Aw shit," Mills said as he walked in the house.

"Damn girl he is even finer in person," Brandy's friend said.

"Why ain't you say nothing to him, wit yo scary ass?" Brandy said.

"Cause he act like he ain't even know who I was,"

"Psshh! Bitch how he supposed to know who you are, when you ain't send him a picture," Brandy said.

"I know Bee but... she stopped as Mills came walking out the door. Mills was laughing at something Brandy's mother said when Brandy blurted out,

"Nigga don't be acting like you don't know who my girl is,"

"What!" Mills said.

"You heard me. This is Tiffany, the girl from my school that was writing you," Brandy said.

"Damn my bad Tiffany, but you never sent me a picture so you can't hold nothing against me," Mills explained.

"I won't," Tiffany replied.

"For the record though, I think you fine as hell," Mills said while seducing her with his eyes.

"Feelings mutual," She replied with a hint of seduction in her voice. As Mills and Tiffany caught up, Buck arrived. He looked up and down the street as he climbed the steps to Brandy's porch.

"What up Buck, why you looking so paranoid?" Brandy said.

"What's happenin lil sis, ain't no yellow cab drove by here has it?" Buck replied while scanning the street.

"Nope," Brandy answered with a puzzled look on her face.

Mills and Tiffany finished up their small talk and exchanged numbers, and then Tiffany was gone.

"What's up T-Money who's ya lil thang thang?" Buck asked with a smile on his face.

"That's Brandy's home girl, Tiffany, she nice huh?" Mills said with a smile on his face.

"She a cute dark skin, but I like mine with a lot more meat on they bones." Buck said.

"Yellow cab at nine o'clock," Brandy interrupted.

The cab stopped in front of Brandy's house and Buck signaled for a young lady in the back seat to get out. She rose from the car with a figure that was to die for. All eyes were on her as she opened Brandy's gate and joined Buck on the porch. Brandy and Mills were confused because Buck always talked about men who abused or mistreated their women. He watched his mother be abused and mistreated and vowed to never treat a woman like that. Buck was committed to Mek and everyone knew that. So who was this flawless dime standing on Brandy's porch Mills and Brandy thought?

"T-Money, Bee, this is Porcha, Porcha this is my lil brother Mills and my lil sis Brandy," Buck said.

"How ya'll doin?" Porcha said in her southern accent.

"What up," Mills and Brandy said in unison.

"Bee take Porcha in the house and grab that thang for Mills," Buck ordered. While the ladies went in the house Buck assured Mills that he and Porcha were just cool.

"C'mon lil bro you know I ain't cut like that. Mek know about Porcha, she do a lot of picking up and dropping off for me, loyal female and friend, and a man can never have too many of them in this game you dig?" Buck said.

"Like a shovel." Mills shot back. Porcha and Brandy walked out the house as Mills and Buck shared a laugh while exchanging daps.

"Guy talk huh? Shawty," Porcha said while slapping him on the back of his arm.

"You know it," Buck shot back. Porcha kissed him on the cheek and sashayed back to the cab. Mills watched her ass bounce like a ball as she walked away. He shook his head while talking under his breath. Buck laughed as Brandy let her thoughts fly.

"Walk nasty then bitch," Brandy said loud enough for Mills and Buck to hear her.

"Yall crazy and I gotta go. I got a few more people waiting on me," Buck said as he and Mills laughed at Brandy. Buck took off, and so did Mills. He gave Mills the keys to his old weight house on Liley, so Mills went there to cook up his product. When he finished he hit the strip to let Chris, Var and a few other homies know that he was back in business, and just like that his vision was coming to life.

CHAPTER 13

By the beginning of fall Mills had things on lock. His prices were cheaper and his product was better than anyone else's on the strip. Mills now rode shotgun in Brandy's Benz as she headed for Buck's house. Mills pager had been sounding off the whole four hours he had Brandy chauffeuring him around, and she was starting to get irritated by it.

"Mills you need to put that damn pager on vibrate...matter of fact you need to get a fucking cell phone,"

"You got your nerves Bee, your shit be screaming too," Mills replied.

"Yeah my shit be all about money, you got them lil hoochies blowing up yo shit,"

Mills burst into laughter.

"You trynna send me now sis, my shit be about money too, I can't help it if hoes be addicted to what the dick did,"

Brandy couldn't help but to join him in laughter, while playfully punching him in his arm.

"You got nerves Mills, you got me driving all the way out here, after you done had me on a tour all day today, just so you can catch Nesh's call, that girl got you whipped and she ain't even gave you no coochie."

Now Brandy was laughing by her self.

"That's cold Bee, you trynna send yo bro for real, I got you though."

Brandy pulled in Buck's driveway teasing Mills all the way in the house. Once inside, Brandy sat on the couch with Tameka, while Mills followed Buck into the kitchen. They sat at the table discussing business until Nesh called. Buck told Mills he wouldn't be staying in the game much longer and that he wanted Mills to take his position. Mills gladly accepted the challenge and dollar signs ran through his mind as Buck told him he would be taking him to his connect. Buck's daughter was due in a few months, and by the summer of 97, he planned to clean his hands. He told Mills the dope game wasn't a game to be played for a long period of time.

A person had to set goals and get out because only a fool thought they could sell forever. He told Mills the sooner he knew what he wanted from the game the sooner he would be able to achieve it. Buck had survived in the game, while a lot of others thrived in it. At the age of twenty-seven, with exception of a two-year juvenile bid, he's made it through the game without being caught. Before being interrupted by Nesh's call, Buck touched the topic of D-Roc and those of his kind, because what they have is never enough.

As long as there is someone with more, they would never be satisfied. He told Mills that even though he raised D-Roc, he could feel bad vibes around him. He finished up by telling him that he had seen Walt's car parked down the street from his house a few nights ago, and because of that, he wouldn't be staying there much longer. Mills knew D-Roc wasn't to be trusted, but he never thought he would turn on Buck...

Nesh's voice made Mills realize how much he needed a cell phone although she was still playing the age card with him, he wanted to hear her voice more often and he could tell that her feelings were mutual. After finding out Nesh was coming home in April for spring break, time seemed to fly by. It was now a week before Mills seventeenth birthday. He sat on his weight house waiting for H.T. to come pick him up, so they could go pick up B-nut together. H.T. also told Mills he had something he wanted to show him. He wouldn't tell Mills what it was, but he told him he would sure like it. H.T. pulled in front of Mills spot with his system on blast. Mills looked out the window as H.T. sound system shook the ground in his apartment. When Mills came out the apartment, he was all smiles. H.T. Acura legend was mean.

The platinum gray vehicle had a white rag top, dark tinted windows, and some chrome hundred spoke daytons. The inside was decked out as well. Mills leant back on the plush white leather, with grey pen stripes, while he and H.T. reminisced and caught each other up on their life to date. When H.T. pulled in Lincoln Park project housing, he and Mills didn't know rather to get out the car or pull back off. Gangsters of all sizes stood in front of B-nut's girlfriend's apartment, some of them flashed pistols, while others threw up gang signs. A few bangers inched closer to the car trying to get a better look at the passengers. H.T. rolled down his window and guns came out from everywhere. As he asked for B-nut, B-nut came running out of one of the apartments telling his homies to be bool.

"What up blood." B-nut said as he slid in the back seat.

"What's up bro, you trynna get us killed out here nigga." Mills said.

"Yea fool, you tripping," H.T. added as he quickly pulled off. B-nut burst out into laughter.

"Y'all niggas ain't got nothing to be scared of blood, y'all family. Ha ha spooky niggas."

They all started laughing just like old times.

"So what's happening baby, what the money and jets looking like?" Mills asked.

"Shid blood its money out there, but niggas be fucking shit up, with bullshit ass work, a nigga sold me some flim flame the other day. My friends said that shit made them throw up dawg. I'm a send that nigga when I bee em doe." B-nut explained.

"Man what yo money looking like bro?" Mills asked seriously.

"It ain't too good homie; I got bout nine faces in my name and a few stones or some more bullshit work. I got a banging ass spot blood, but I can't get no good work, blood me," Mills and H.T. couldn't help but to laugh at B-nuts lingo. B-nut was a blood for real, whereas a lot of youngins were faking and breaking with their set.

"Look bro, I got something real sweet for you, quality shit, and love on the price. I told you we was gone get this money when we got out nigga, shit bout to be lovely for me, which means its bout to be lovely for you." Mills said while reaching in the back seat to give him some dap.

"Shid I feel you bro, but blood need some help like yesterday," B-nut said.

"Well I'm a day late, because I'm bout to get you together today, as soon as we come from wherever white chocolate taking us," Mills was referring to H.T. who they said was a black man in a white man's body. H.T. cranked his system up as one of his favorite songs came on, and Mills threw a bag of expensive weed on B-nut's lap, with a pack of Backwoods.

"Roll up bro," Mills said before the music got too loud. Halfway through the fat blunt, H.T. was pulling in a two-door garage. Once the garage door opened and went back down to the ground, the garage was completely black. H.T. exited the car, and a few seconds the garage was illuminated. H.T. stood next to an all-white 98 Eddie Bauer Edition Expedition truck.

Mills and B-nut rose from the Acura in awe.

"That bitch pretty as fuck top," Mills said to H.T.

"I knew you'd like it homie, I got a special price just for you. I can get any rims you want, for this bitch, candy pain't, system the works, you name it. I can make it happen," H.T. said while opening the driver's door, motioning for him to get in. Mills sat behind the wheel and instantly became one with the truck.

"I want this bitch top," Mills said.

"I knew you would, that's why I let you see it before anyone else," H.T. explained.

"I want rip gold hundred on this baby, with gold flakes in the same wet white pain't, with fifth trip gold hundred on the back of this bitch, I want everything trimmed in gold from the door handles to the windshield wipers, I want the windows tinted, and king kong in the trunk," Mills said, leaning back on the plush white leather. H.T. was all smiles as Mills zoned out picturing himself on the road in the truck.

"Man that shit sound slick blood, but you gotta get the red rag top with blood pain't on this bitch and come through damu riding." B-nut said loudly.

They all burst out laughing as B-nut leant back in the passenger seat, using the dashboard for a steering wheel, showing Mills how to gangster mob.

"Aight aight, c'mon I got something else to show y'all niggas." H.T. said while waving them over to a large metal box sitting in the corner of the garage. It took Mills a minute to part himself from the car, but he eventually joined B-nut and H.T. at the box.

"Before I open this box, that truck with all the shit you want done to it would normally be about 40k, but because you family it'll only be thirty stacks and im ah lay that bitch out for you...now is y'all sure y'all ready for this shit?" H.T. asked with a sneaky smile on his face.

"Man open the box white boy, you looking really silly right now blood, like the riddler man on Batman, wit yo cracker box built ass," B-nut said playfully squared off with each other.

"Aight aight blood I ain't gone start capping on you dawg." B-nut said while laughing and blocking H.T.'s two-piece combination.

"Mills you over there laughing like shit sweet wit yo lil Tevin Campbell looking ass."

Now the joke was on Mills and H.T. and B-nut shared the laugh. H.T. finally gained his composure and opened the box. He reached inside and pulled out two AK's. He handed one to Mills and the other to B-Nut. They both fell in love with the choppers. H.T. pushed the lid wide open so Mills and B-Nut could look at the rest of the merchandise. The box was filled with artillery. Mills reached in the box and grabbed two P 89 Rougers. B-Nut grabbed a mack ten with a thirty shot clip, and H.T. lifted up a few choppers and grabbed two bulletproof vests.

He held one out for Mills and the other for B-Nut, and said, "Try these on." They spent a few minutes at the gun shack, and was ready to leave after Mills put in his order for some artillery and vest for him and his crew. H.T. and B-Nut had already met Peko in Tyko, but Mills wanted them to meet Brandy and Shawn. After calling Peko and finding out that they were all at Lisa's, he gave H.T. directions to their next destination. A half hour later they pulled in behind Pekos Impala, and killed the engine. Lisa opened the door after a few knocks if one didn't know Lisa, they would never believe her to be an all out dope fiend.

Because Brandy, Peko, and Shawn kept her geared out with her hair and nails done. They treated her like family, showing their appreciation and loyalty. Peko and Shawn sat on the couch smoking a fat blunt, while Brandy served one of her personal customers in the kitchen.

"What the fuck is up blood!" B-nut said while smacking Peko on his leg. Peko was so deep into the video game that he didn't notice B-Nut when he walked through the door. Peko jumped off the couch and pulled B-Nut in for an embrace. The two had become tight during their ninety days together in Tyko.

"What's up dawg," Peko said.

"Shit just bickin it blood, trynna get this money, blood me," B-nut replied.

"What up H.T." Peko said, acknowledging him with a warm greeting as well.

"I can't call it homie, I see you rolling good out there, when you ready to upgrade holler at me," H.T. said advertising his services. Brandy came out of the kitchen with her nine in her hand. Her beauty froze H.T. and B-Nut both. They both stared at her with admiration and lust. Brandy sized both of them up quickly giving them once over. She thought they both were attractive, but not dark enough to her liking.

"Well y'all already know Pee, soo...this is his lil bro Shawn Shawn, but you can call him Shawn, and this is Brandy, but y'all can call her Bee. Bee and Shawn this is B-Nut and H.T. they family," Mills said pointing at B-Nut and then pointing at H.T. identifying them with their names.

They all spoke to one another, and then had seats. They spent a few hours smoking some killer weed and sharing small talk. Mills told stories about many brawls, he, H.T. and B-Nut had gotten into with guys from other cities. Peko gave H.T. and B-Nut his number before they and Mills took off. The three drove a few streets over to Mills's spot, where they went inside and smoked more blunts and took some pictures to send to all their homies who were still doing time. Before they left, Mills gave H.T. a ten thousand dollar down payment on his truck and artillery. Then gave B-Nut four and a half ounces for $3150 and told him to give him a call when he was ready for more. Mills birthday closed fast. His intentions were to have a birthday and welcome home party for himself instead he put it off for his next birthday. He now rode shotgun in Peko's Impala bobbing his head to Master P's crack house.

While puffing on some expensive hydro weed. He, Peko and Shawn had been fitted for some gold teeth, a few weeks ago, and Mills received the call that they were ready. Instead of getting them done professionally, they kept the money in the hood, and ordered their teeth from Leroy, who had learnt his craft from the best in Atlanta at the grill maker. Leroy worked in his mother's basement, so Peko turned the music off as he pulled into the driveway. Leroy was letting a few people out as Mills and Peko were walking in.

They quickly entered the house and received some of Leroy's southern hospitality. Leroy led them to the basement, where he had three bad red bones awaiting his return. The young ladies gave them looks of approvals as they stood in the middle of the floor Mills with a mouth full of gold and diamonds.

"Yo shit sweet bro." Mills said while snapping his own grill in. Unlike Peko, Mills only had two iced out gold teeth in the center of his mouth. With his bottom four teeth covered in gold and diamonds. Mills flashed Peko with his five thousand dollar smile.

"How you love tha,t nigga?"

Before Peko could answer one of the females said,

"Mmhmm I can love that,"

Mills and Peko turned around finally looking at the girls in their face. Peko tried to avoid an encounter with the beautiful young ladies, because he was just piecing back his relationship from his prior unfaithfulness. Mills was just being overly confident, playing mind games with the ladies. He saw the girl appraising him the whole time, so he intentionally avoided eye contact with her, just to see how long she could go with out receiving attention.

"I think that's a real good look for you," The girl said as Mills locked eyes with her.

"Good looking out and the feelings mutual," Mills replied.

Leroy butted in.

"My bad buddie, let me introduce ya'll to each other. Mills and Peko this is Catlin, Cat fo shawt, Deedrah, or course Dee fa shawt and this is my shawty Lin. Cat, Dee, and Lin this is Peko and Mills.

"Hi." the ladies said in unison.

"What's happenin?" Peko replied.

"How ya'll ladies doing?" Mills added.

"Well I'm doing fine now but I'd be doing a lot better if I knew we had a date scheduled for sometime this week," Cat said to Mills.

Cat was cold. Mills could tell she had a nice body by the way her hips and thighs filled out her spot on the couch. Her complexion was light enough to pass for white, but enough tints to notice her African-American genes. She had green eyes, full lips that shined from the lip gloss she had on them and her hair was jet black, cut in a short style like the lead singer from Total. Her nails were freshly frenched manicured. She wore a simple white DKNY sweater, tight black DKNY jeans and some black and white and purple DKNY gym shoes. Mills was digging her flavor for sure, and as they hit it off, Deedrah had her eyes locked on Peko's tall frame.

"Peko don't tell me you ain't man enough to know when a woman is feeling you," Deedrah said while rising from her seat to show off her curvaceous figure. Deedrah was a stallion, being a few inches shorter than Peko's 6'1 frame. Her complexion was near a redish color, complementing her long reddish brown hair color and hazel eyes. Her long sleeve white shirt from Gap hugged her body showing off her handful of titties and iron board flat stomach. Her hips rolled off her body, falling into her ass that could cause a traffic jam. Her long thick legs were double-jointed, making her stand firm like a horse. As Peko stared at the gap between her legs, it took everything in him to turn down her proposition.

"First off baby, let me tell you, you cold as ice and as much as I would like to take you out, I can't, cause I got a woman and a child at home, and I'm trying my best to behave for the both of them dig me?" Peko said while licking his lips, and staring her down with his chick magnets.

"Aww that's so sweet, a man tryin to be faithful, if only there were more men like you," Deedrah said.

CHARLES WATSON

If she only knew, Peko thought. Mills and Cat exchanged numbers, Leroy gave Peko Shawn's grill, and he and Mills were off. April came quickly and as much as Mills anticipated Nesh's return. He anticipated his first encounter with Buck's connect even more. Buck pulled off highway 270 and turned onto a road that seemed to never end. As he pulled his 500 Benz up to a large fence, he rolled down his window and spoke into an intercom. After stating his name the double gateway opened up to the huge estate's lengthy driveway, parted, and Buck pulled through. As he followed the series of curves that led to the mansion's doorway, Mills drooled over the extensive land, and humongous home that came into his view.

Buck pulled behind a casket grey Rolls Royce and two men in black with fully automatic weapons approached the car, they helped Buck and Mills out the car, and escorted them in the huge mansion. After going up a hallway, down another, then another, they came to a stop in front of some double doors. The men in black gave the door a secret knock, and the left door swung open. Buck and Mills were searched thoroughly before going further. As the door closed, a Puerto Rican man with two beautiful Puerto Rican females in his arms came strolling in the room. The women were flawless, and they were wearing nothing but bikinis. The man said something in Spanish, tapped them on their butts, and sent them to a room on their left.

"Capaso." The man said while taking Buck's hand in his. "Capaso," Buck replied and the two hugged.

"Chico, this is my lil brother Mills, the one I've been telling you about," Buck said while placing his hand on Mills shoulder. "Capaso, I've heard a lot about you, all true, I hope," Chico said to Mills.

"Me too," Mills shot back with an amicable smile. Chico pulled Mills in for a hug, and said, "Don't worry, everything is fine, what I have you have, familia of Bucks is familia of mine, lets have a seat." Chico waved the body guards off as the attempted to follow behind. "Familia." He said to the guards, while nodding his head assuring them that he could be left alone with Buck and Mills. Chico spent a half hour discussing business with Mills and Buck, while the other three hours they spent watching basketball on the huge flat screen that covered almost the whole wall and smoking weed. The beautiful ladies traveled in and out of the room as they bought appetizers and refreshments. Before leaving, Chico hugged Buck and told him to enjoy life and bring his God daughter around some time, then hugged Mills and whispered in his ear, "welcome to the family." After that the body guards reappeared and escorted them to their car.

Mills shook his head with intrigue as he stared at all the expensive vehicles in the circular parking space. A Rolls Royce in front of him, Bentley on his left, Lamborgini to his right, and a Continental with you can't see me tint parked in front of the mansion's front door. Mills palms became moist as he thought about Bucks retirement next month. He would receive ten bricks for 13.5 a piece upon Bucks departure from the life and according to how fast he moved that product, his supplies could increase, which would naturally cause the price of his product to decrease. Mills was up and coming and he could feel himself becoming richer by the moment. For the next couple of weeks, Mills just coasted.

He was slowly but surely working Peko into taking over his position with smaller weight, while searching for a house to serve as a weight house for his new position. Peko and Shawn had enough money to move some large weight of their own, but they loved the profits they made from moving their work rock for rock. Peko didn't mind taking over Mills position in Bucks old weight house, because his little brother would still be going piece to piece out of Lisa's. It was like controlling two sides of the game at once, which meant more profit for them, and he could always love that.

Nesh's arrival had been pushed back a month, which Mills didn't mind, because his truck would be ready for the road by then. Mills rode shotgun in Brandy's Benz while Shawn rode shotgun in his brother's Impala. Leroy had rented a night club in the hood for his birthday party and stopping through his party was on everyone's agenda. The parking lot was packed as Brandy and Peko pulled into the last two parking spaces on the street, or across the street from the club, as they piled up at the doorway. Although Mills and his crew couldn't get in with their weapons, that didn't stop them from wearing their vests. As they slid by security at the door, they instantly spotted Leroy and his girl Lin at the bar. Lin made Mills think of Cat, who he hadn't heard from since their encounter at Leroy's basement. She hadn't called him and he was too caught up in business to contact her. Leroy saw Mills as he spotted Peko's tall frame sliding through the crowd. He quickly waveed them over. They all exchanged daps and hugs with Leroy and respectfully acknowledged his girlfriend.

Leroy embraced Shawn now sporting a 5'9 ½ frame and whispered in his ear, I see that grill was a perfect fit. Shawn showcased his grill with a big smile. As Mills and his crew mingled with Leroy and Lin, Cat and Dee came gliding towards them. They walked with a rhythm as they bounced to Biggie and Total's One More Chance. Peko grabbed his dick as he took in Dee's body. The white body suit she wore complemented her anatomy so well, that Peko could feel his piece growing in his hand, as she purposely rubbed her ass up against him.

Cat wore a pair of casual white Capri pants by Fendi, a matching white blouse and purple sleeveless v'neck sweater by Fendi, with some purple Fendi slip ons. Her earrings were blinging, while complementing the other pieces of jewelry she stayed in. She walked up to Mills and placed her soft manicured hands around his neck, and spoke directly into his ear.

"Hi stranger." Her breath smelled like sweet juicy fruit, while her hair smelled fruitier than a fruit basket. Mills was digging her, and he could tell the feeling was mutual. He smelled rich with his polo cologne, and he looked hood rich standing in his Coogi sweat suit, and all white patton leather Adidas forms. His grill was blinging while his 3 karat diamond earring blinged and his 360 waves made the club sea sick. An hour into the party and the goons arrived. D-Roc and his crew shoved their way through the crowd, braids swinging, chains dangling, grills, watches, bracelets, and rings blinging. The females loved the gangsters and they didn't hesitate showing their intrigue. Mills and Fella had seen one another a number of times since their encounter on Mills first day home, but they were both too stubborn to speak and settle their differences. Word had been circulating through the hood that D-Roc and his crew had intentions on robbing Mills.

Mills didn't know how true the rumor was, but he knew D-Roc and his crew had started snorting coke and anything was unexpected from them, especially after Buck believed he had seen them watching his house. The further Fella fell into D-Roc's trap, the more Mills started to distrust him. As they approached Leroy at the bar, they gave Mills sinister grins. Mills could tell they were high off of blow by the way they continued to massage their nose, while giving Leroy some birthday dap.

Mills didn't understand how things had become so complicated between him and his childhood friends, especially his main roll dog. It was as if they didn't want to see Mills doing good, or maybe it was they didn't want to see Mills doing better than them. D-Roc and his crew had money in large amounts of their own, or at least they should with all the robbing they had been doing. Mills brought Fella into the game basically sharing everything he had with him. Now that Fella has made for himself, and being accepted by a crew that he idolized, he flipped the script, on his homie from day one. They say money is the root of evil, it's the love for it that is. Never fall victim to greed or street fame. Bucks words ran through Mills mind as he and Fella exchanged looks again without saying a word to one another.

As the party whined down, Dee stuffed her phone number in Peko's hand while whispering in his ear, "What ya girl don't know won't hurt her." Peko had tried with everything inside him all night and decided that he had to hit that gushy at least one time, or he'd drive himself crazy. He gave her number to Shawn as he did with all the other girls numbers he cheated with because he knew Shy would be searching him thoroughly for phone numbers or any other evidence of cheating.

When Mills and his crew made it outside they spotted D-Roc's g-ride. A young hustler named Terry was leaning in the window of the all black four door Bonneville and Mills knew what was taking place. Though the scene looked harmless, Terry was being robbed and it became clear as he was shoved out the window with all his jewelry missing and his pockets inside out. Terry was a flashy young hustler who was known for keeping a few thousand dollars on him at a time. He was from Main and Kelton and looked at D-Roc and his crew as his homies, which made him easy bait for the well known jack boys. The Bonneville slowly rode by Mills and his crews, with Brotha Lynch blasting from its twelves. The windows were tinted, but they were rolled half way down so Mills could see inside. Slim and D-Roc rode shot gun, while Fella and Walt bobbed their heads in the back seat. Mills could see all of Terry's belongings on D-Roc's lap, along with a big hand gun. In the back seat, Walt had an ounce of powder on his lap. He gave Mills his mean mug while making a gun with his fingers and pointing it at Mills and Peko while jerking his hand as if he was letting off shots. As Mills attempted to flag the car down, Slim turned into traffic and sped up Main street.

CHAPTER 14

Mills strolled through H.T.'s car garage in astonishment, as he looked at all the vehicles being worked on. Some hung from the ceiling, others were at ground level. Some were finished, others were primed down. A few were missing doors and interior, while others were without engines. H.T.'s crew went to work, while he sat in the passenger seat of Mills truck with the door wide open.

H.T. tossed Mills the keys, as he approached the truck with a smile on his face.

"Hop in homie," H.T. said while snapping his fingers at one of the workers, and motioning for them to bring him something. Mills examined the truck as he walked around to the driver side. The white candy pain't, had gold flakes neatly sparkling through it. While the 18' inch trip gold hundred spoke Daytons fit the truck perfectly and had a special sparkle of their own. The fifth wheel on the back of the truck complemented the gold door handles, and windshield wipers, while its reflections reflected off the dark tint on the back window. Before Mills hopped behind the wheel, he checked out the interior, which was soft white leather, with gold pen stripes.

The dashboard, and steering wheel were all white, while the rugs and the roof , and the doors were gold. The kenwood deck was white and gold marble matching the remote that H.T.'s homie handed him. Instead of the seats having Eddie Bauer edition on the head rest it said T-money edition in gold letters. Mills put the key in the ignition and bought the truck to life. H.T. hit a few buttons on the remote and Tupac's Picture Me Rolling blasted from the speakers. He threw the remote on Mills lap, and held out his hand for some dap. Mills hit his rock and H.T.

hopped out the truck, telling Mills to call him later. Mills bobbed his head, to the music as one of the garage doors ascended. He backed out, threw up a piece sign, and pulled out into the road, while cranking up his system up another notch. Mills was pumped. Not only did he have the sickest truck the streets had seen but Nesh would arrive at the airport in less than 24 hours and two days after that he'd be receiving his first ten kilo's from Chico.

It was the beginning of May, the sun was shining, Mills had only been home now for ten months and he had close to a hundred thousand in his stash. Minus the five thousand he carried in his pocket to pay off the money he owed on the Presidential Rolex he had on layaway flooded with diamonds. After picking his Rolex up, he decided to give Cat a call. The night of Leroy's party he spent the night at her house and for the past two weeks, he's been hitting that cat at least three times a week. He liked Cat because she wasn't looking for more than what he was willing to give her. After informing her about his feelings for Nesh, she was still cool wit just being friends with benefits of course. As Mills dialed her phone number, he pictured their last time together. Thinking about how her soft luscious lips wrapped around his pole had him aroused. Ring! Ring! Ring!

"Hello."

"What's up girl, you thinking about daddy?" Mills said smoothly.

"Of course, daddy been thinking about mommy?" Cat responded. Mills laughed. "Does a bear shit in the woods and wipe its ass with a furry white rabbit?" Mills said mocking Tupac, as Whats Ya Phone Number played in the background. Cat laughed as well.

"You hungry?" Mills asked.

"I am if it means I get to spend some time with you," Cat said.

"I'm on my way to come get you; I'll be there in 10 minutes," Mills replied.

"I'll be waiting," Cat said seductively.

"Peace," Mills said before disconnecting. Shortly after Mills pulled in front of Cat's house. He killed the music because she lived in a peaceful neighborhood, way out in the suburbs. Mills gave her a call and she quickly came out. Mills looked at her thighs as she gravitated towards the truck in a mini skirt, that he knew she wore for easy access. Cat fell in love with Mills's ride at first sight, but when she stepped in the truck the bling from his Rolex and earrings made her weak in the knees. Mills hid his eyes behind a pair of Cartier frames, but the smile on his face showed that he was pleased to see her. He kissed her on her cheek, before pulling off, and turning Scarface's Mary Jane. Mary! Mary! Mary! Mary! Mary! I'm happy just to hear ya name Mary Jane! Blasted from the speakers as he relit his Garcia Vega filled with hydro. He took a couple of puffs and passed it to Cat. She took a few puffs and placed it in the ashtray.

As Mills turned the music down to ask her why she placed it in the tray, she leaned over, unzipped his pants, and slid his already half-hard penis into her mouth.

"Damn Cat, I thought you said you wanted some dinner," Mills asked as she used her tongue to play with his head.

"I do, but I can have my desert first." She replied while looking him in his eyes and sliding her mouth down his pole. Mills just leant back in his seat and enjoyed the warmth of her mouth. She felt so good it was hard for him to keep his eyes on the road, but he managed to swerve around a car making a left turn at the last minute. The next day, Mills arrived at the airport at twelve o'clock on the nose. He continuously glanced at his iced out time piece, because Nesh was over fifteen minutes late. As he searched through the crowd of people coming out of the airport's doorway he spotted Nesh. She had only become more beautiful with time. She wore a two piece Coogi outfit. Her skirt stopped at her mid thigh, showing off her muscular, yet feminine legs, that looked smooth as cask and cream.

Her skin complexion was mocha brown, and the radiation like Ra the mighty sun god. She wore her sleeveless Coogi vest open, showcasing her flat stomach, as her white halter top stopped at the top of her belly button, her jet black long hair hung 3 inches below her shoulders, and she had it pulled behind her ears to show off her two karat diamond earrings that Buck bought her. Her compact petite frame was flawless, like that of a goddess. Mills quickly relieved her of her bags. His 5'6 frame towered her 5'3. Her bath and body wash made her smell like peaches and cream, and Mills loved every second of their embrace. Nesh was taken aback by how much Mills had grown. His white tee fitted him perfectly, exposing his toned frame, that Nesh was loving as he wrapped his muscular arms around her. As they walked towards the truck, the sun hit the waves, and his bling just right. The Rolex was blinding all those who looked, while his diamond studded smile nearly melted Nesh as he helped her into the truck, carefully closing the door. He threw her bags in the back seat, and quickly pulled away from the illegal place he was parked.

"I hope that look you giving me is a good one?" Mills said while pulling into traffic.

"It is, I'm just tripping off how much you grown," Nesh replied.

"Nothing stays the same, Nesh, I'm a young man now, and I remember, and meant everything I told you when I was a youngin."

"Is that right?" she replied.

"C'mon Tanesha Tyreka La'nette Clemons, you know how I feel about you, I'm just waiting for my chance," Mills explained.

Nesh liked Mills confidence, and maturity, but the fact still remained that he was seventeen, and she'd be twenty one in two months. Their age difference had always been a problem for her, that and the fact that she didn't want a man who lived Mills lifestyle. She lost her mother and father to the dope game. Her mother smoking it and her father selling it, and she refused to let herself fall for a man who had so many possibilities of being taking away from her. Death and prison was the end result for majority of the people in the game. She looked at Mills expensive earrings, watch, and shiny grill. Then she examined his expensive vehicle.

She was happy to see Mills doing well for himself, but she knew that he had only gotten deeper into the game that she feared. The same lifestyle she had tried to evade, by going to Atlanta, Georgia for college.

"I see some things don't change," Nesh said while tapping Mills wrist. Mills looked at his watch and a smile was his only response. Nesh shook her head and harmlessly rolled her eyes. Mills knew what Nesh was getting at, but the discussion was one he'd rather not have, especially at their first encounter in over three years. Mills called Peko to avoid the topic, before Nesh brought it back up because it wasn't like her to not speak her mind. He also wanted to make sure that Peko, Shawn and Brandy were all at Brandy's house, where he asked them to be. Mills told them he wanted them at Brandy's so he could bring Nesh by, which was true, but he also wanted to surprise them with his new truck.

Mills cranked the music up and let Nesh enjoy the scenery for the rest of the ride. When he hit Main street, Nesh felt as if she never left. Everything was the same. The strip was crowded with prostitutes, smokers, and dealers. Pimps and hustlers of all kinds. When Mills turned onto Berkley the street was packed from beginning to end. All the hustlers had their cars out, with their systems on blast, as they chased down the money and hollered at the pyt's that walked nasty up and down the strip.

Mills system sounded off as he neared Brandy's house. Heads turned as Master P's ice cream man filled the street. Mills hid behind his tint, as on lookers drooled over his mean machine.

D-Roc, Slim, Walt, and Fella stood in front of Fella's mother house. D-Roc had his raspberry blue 97 Explorer parked at the curb. The Explorer was mean, with gold flakes in the pain't, tinted windows, and some gold hundred spokes. His explorer was a smaller version of Mills Expedition, but not only was the truck smaller, but his rims were too. D-Roc leant up against his truck with Tasha standing between his legs. Tasha had on just as much shine as D-Roc and a brand new Honda Elantra to match his truck. Tasha hadn't talked to Nesh in over a year.

Not that they weren't still cool, just that they were living in two different worlds. As Mills pulled up the street, letting his system slap, D-Roc and the jackboys mouths watered. The truck put D-Roc's to shame, and D-Roc nor his crew liked it. Had the truck not pulled in front of Brandy's house the jack boys would of shot it up. Nesh couldn't believe she was seeing Tasha and D-Roc hugged up. Although she was over D-Roc, the sight didn't sit right with her. Tasha was her bestfriend and the same person who called her every week for her first year away, telling her something new about D-Roc and his sex life. She talked about him like a dog, now she was with him. Snakes came in many different shapes and forms, sometimes in the form of a friend.

Mills stepped out of the truck leaving his system on blast as ice cream man screamed from his speakers, a few females yelled, "I like ice cream." Mills smiled, showing off his grill, while throwing up a peace sign to the females and young hustlers who acknowledged him. Mills was going to make Nesh's visit quick so he kept the car running with her in it, but after seeing D-Roc and Tasha shining, he knew it was only right that Nesh shine with him. He opened her door and helped her out the truck, after telling her to kill the engine and grab the keys. Peko, Brandy, and Shawn sat on the porch laughing and joking about the look on D-Roc and his crews faces, while D-Roc and his crew grilled Mills with hate and envy. Fella didn't really show hate, but no emotion was just as hateful. As the saying goes, sometimes silence can be so loud. Mills Rolex shined from where he stood all the way up the block, and D-Roc hated it, although his shine was on ten as well. Mills held Nesh's hand as Tasha yelled her name out, and came running over to her. D-Roc's mouth dropped as he stared at Nesh's beautiful face and frame. She looked flawless, fresh, and innocent.

Tasha dragged D-Roc along with her, holding tightly on to his hand. *Fake love*, Nesh thought as Tasha wrapped her arms around her. As Tasha went to explaining her and D-Roc, Nesh stopped her. Its okay Tasha me and D-Roc haven't been together for years. I just don't want you to think... Nesh cut her off again. Don't worry about it girl. She looked at D-Roc and said, "Hi Derrick." D-Roc eyed her hand as it stayed locked inside Mills. Nesh hadn't realized that Mills still held her hand, but she liked the fact that he did.

"What's up Tanesha?" D-Roc shot back with a smirk on his face. Mills was too busy talking to his crew, but he turned around in enough time to catch Tasha staring at him while licking her lips seductively. *I should have been sucking his dick.* Tasha thought as she appraised Mills from his head to his feet. Nesh caught a glimpse of Tasha's flirting as she waved at Slim, Walt and Fella. Nesh was looking for Mills to through a signal back at Tasha, but instead he brushed her off.

"What up Roc?" Mills said as D-Roc sized him up.

"Shit I see you finally got what you want," D-Roc said nodding at Nesh and Mills holding hands. Nesh knew D-Roc was directing that towards her, but Mills didn't give her a chance to say anything.

"I wish man, Nesh is a queen, it will probably be a long time before she gives me a chance," Mills replied. Nesh loved Mills come back and the way he quickly ended the conversation speaking to Tasha. Mills looked at Slim, Walt, and Fella as they stood in the yard checking him out.

"What up Slim, Walt, and Fella?" Mills said while throwing up the peace sign. They nodded their head and went back to flirting with Tasha's friends. Fella took another look at Mills as if he wanted to say something, but he quickly turned away as Mills locked eyes with him. The meeting and greeting ended as Buck called Mills asking him where he and Nesh were. Mills put Nesh on the phone. D-Roc and Tasha walked off, while Mills and Nesh climbed the steps to Brandy's porch. Two days later Mills sat in his new spot with his first ten kilos. He knew getting rid of them wouldn't be a problem, because he already had six of them gone with Peko, Brandy, and Shawn.

They'd but one, and he give them on consignment. He had Chris and Var buying nine ounces each, which was enough for half a brick. He'd give them the other half on consignment. Then he had B-Nut, and his big homie Bear Bear. B-Nut was buying half a brick, while Bear was buying a whole thang. He'd showed Bear Bear some super love on the price for his one, and take the money B-Nut had for his half a brick, and give him the other half on consignment. That would leave him with one kilo, which he'd break down into four nine ounces an look out for young hustlers with potential like Lil Scoob and Tone.

Ten days tops he'd be back at Chico with the $130,000 he owed him, and $130,000 of his own to recoup with. After ridding himself of ten kilos, Mills headed for Buck's house to pick up Nesh for their movie and a dinner date. Buck had upgraded his living conditions. He had a small estate of his own. His home was worth 1.5 million. He had nine foot ceilings, six bedrooms, a large dinning room, living room, sitting room, and a special game room for his alone time. He had transformed one of the bedrooms into a library. The stairway in the living room had a series of curves which ascended up to a balcony that over looked the living and sitting room. On the other side of the balcony, were identical steps that led to the sitting room and hallway that led to the spacious kitchen. Buck had a survaliance system installed with cameras in every room, so he could monitor in and outside his house at all times.

When Mills arrived, Nesh and Mek were seated on the couch with Buck's and Mek's beautiful daughter who lit up the sight of her uncle Mills. Mills spoke to Mek, kissed Nesh on her cheek, and grabbed Daylonna off the couch. Daylonna slobbered on Mills face as he held her in the air swinging her around like a helicopter.

"You love your uncle Mills don't you girl...I know you do," Mills said as he brought her in for one of her slobbery kisses.

"Buck up stairs in his reading room, he wanted to talk to you before you leave, Mills," Mek said.

"Mills sat Daylonna down on Nesh's lap. Mills jogged up the lengthy steps and walked in on Buck as he was reading one of his books by the reputable black activist, Marcus Garvey.

"What up T-Money?" Buck said as he swung his feet off the desk they were propped up on.

"What it is big bro?" Mills said.

"Have a seat, an I'm a tell you," Buck said while motioning to the chair that was adjacent from him. Mills took a seat while Buck fired up a blunt he had in his ashtray. Buck hit the green, held up a picture of Marcus Garvey and asked Mills

"Do you know who this is?"

"Nah." Mills said.

"This is Marcus Garvey, he's one of the first black activists to fight for black's freedom. He's a bad man, in a good way of course. He was the first black man to come up with nation migration back in Africa to establish our own country. He believed that blacks would have been better off segregated, that we have a chance to become an entity economically. He believed we should build our own economy by establishing our own business in the black communities. So we can provide jobs for our own people, circulating the money amongst one another, instead of giving all our money to the white man. The majority of unemployed people are black. That's because blacks own very little, closer to no businesses, therefore we always look for help with employment from diversity groups other than African Americans. Black on black crime is at an all-time high T-Money, shid we killing each other in the streets, not only with pistols either, but with drugs as well.

We are so busy competing with one another and taking from one another, that we have no time to compete with anyone else, or take from anyone else."

Mills sat attentively while Buck shed light. Mills was lost, but hungry for understanding.

"Im telling you this T-Money because what I'm about to do is give back to the community that I've gained from. I wanna be able to help people climb up that economical ladder. Im doing good, so why shouldn't I help my brothers and sisters succeed in life. Now I can't force anyone to succeed, they have to want success, it's like the saying goes, you can lead a horse to water, but you can't make him drink. I'm bout to create opportunity, and want you to be a part of this. The thing is you can be both negative and positive influence at the same time. The dope game ain't forever T-Money and you are now in a position where you can start setting goals, such as a quota you want to meet before leaving the game.

Sooner is always better. Because the longer you remain a participant of that lifestyle, the more susceptible you are to making negative consequences that come with that lifestyle. I ain't gone beat yo eardrums up, but I just thought I should enlighten you on a few things. When I was young and off the hook thinking I owned the world, an old wino pulled my coat and enlightened me about our history. How I was helping bring my family down, he hip me to our brother Marcus Garvey, Carlos Cook, and George Jackson. Those brothers were some gangsters, Mills. The library is always open, you should come pick up one of these books sometimes, you'd be amazed at what you can learn outside the class room.

They said if you wanna hide something from a black person; just hide it in a book. If you wanna find out what's hidden pick one up. Now get up out of here and enjoy ya night out with that young black princess down there. You know she headstrong boy, you better be ready to conversate on her level." Buck smiled as he dropped Marcus Garvey books on Mills lap and left the room. Mills spent a few minutes scanning the books pages, then placed the book back on Buck's desk and headed downstairs.

Nesh was awaiting him with her purse in her hand, and I'm ready to go face. After kissing Daylonna and saying their see you laters to Buck and Mek, Mills and Nesh were gone.

CHAPTER 15

On a hot early July afternoon, the corner of Oak and Morrison was packed. D-Roc and his crew were parked in front of Tee Tee house talking to his little cousin Stanley about two young hustlers they have been hearing about. Pimp and L's had Oak Street on lock. Since they've been pumping out of Liley's house everyone's money has slowed up. After Pimp beating up Monster, his name was floating through the streets. Without knowing it, Pimp and L's were becoming ghetto superstars and a lot of people did not like it.

D-Roc and his crew had a perfect view of Liley's apartment, and as Pimp and L's came walking out the front door, D-Roc started laughing.

"These the lil niggas you are talking about Stanley?" D-Roc asked with a big smile on his face.

"Yep, that's them niggas right there, don't be fooled by them lil niggas, they in that bitch eating," Stanley said seriously.

"Aw man, this shit is goin to be easy, like taking candy from a baby." D-Roc said once again laughing at the easy lick Stanley put him upon.

"You mean, these lil niggas everybody been talking about?" D-Roc asked. "Yep, "Stanley said.

"So which one of these niggas got out on Monster?" D-Roc asked still laughing.

"That one right there," Stanley said pointing at Pimp. As Pimp and L's crossed the street heading for the corner store, Fella thought his eyes were deceiving him. He almost burned himself with the blunt as he threw half his body in the front seat to get a better look.

210

"Man that's Mills little brother," Fella said shocked at the sight of before him.

"I was just about to say that shit, but I though I was tripping." D-Roc said.

"Hell nah, I ain't tripping that's lil Jimmy." Fella said.

"Ha! Ha! Ha! This might be the sweetest lick we done ever hit," D-Roc said laughing once again.

"Nah Roc, we can't hit this one bro, I help raise that lil nigga," Fella said.

"Aw shit, here Fells go with that superhero shit; you can't be everybody's superman," Walt said.

"Shid looks like somebody already beating us to the punch," Slim said while pointing in Liley's apartment. Three men with black mask were forcing their way into the apartment, while the forth was in the getaway car.

"There goes the neighborhood." D-Roc said while shoving a mountain of powder up his nose. Pimp and L's came walking out the store. Check this shit out. D-Roc said as Pimp and L's came walking out the store and the three masked men came running out the apartment. Pimp and L's thought their mind was playing tricks on them as the masked men ran from the car. L's dropped his bag and opened fired immediately. Pop! Pop! Pop! As L's nine sounded off. The mask men returned fire. Pimp pulled out his 380 and joined the gun fight. The masked men hopped in the car and floored its small engine. As they sped by Pimp and L's traded shots with its back seat passenger. They chased the car down, emptying their clips in to the vehicle. The cars back window came out as it recklessly bent the corner on Morrison.

"Hell nah, them lil niggas goin out dumping," D-Roc said as he burst into laughter.

"Mills lil brother got more heart than him," Walt said quickly joining him in laughter.

"Ya'll niggas silly as fuck," Slim said while adding a little giggle.

Pimp and L's ran into the apartment. Once inside, Pimp rushed to Leslie's aid as she cried at the bottom of the stairs.

"What's wrong Leslie, you aight?" Pimp asked.

"My mom, they beat her half to death cause she wouldn't tell them where the dope and money was," Leslie said while wiping her tears away.

"Where Liley at?" Pimp asked. Leslie was still in shock.

"Where the fuck is yo mom Les?" L's asked aggressively. Leslie pointed up stairs as she choked on her own tears. L's shot up the steps with Pimp behind him; Liley lay on her bedroom floor bleeding to death. Her eyes were swollen shut and blood leaked from her skull.

"Got damn man!" L's yelled, as Liley moaned from the pain of a simple touch.

"C'mon Pimp we got to get her to the hospital!" L's yelled as Pimp stood in the small state of shock of his own. They carefully lifted Liley's body and carried her down the steps.

"Leslie grab yo moms car keys and hurry the fuck up," L's ordered as he and Pimp rushed Liley out the back door. By the time Liley was carefully placed in the back seat, Leslie was running out with the keys. She hopped in the back seat with her mom, while L's drove and Pimp rode shot gun. L's helped carry Liley in to the hospital, then rushed back out the double doors to get rid of their guns and see what the streets knew about the robbers.

When L's returned, Leslie sat at Liley's bed side as she rested with tubes running in and out her body to an IV tank. L's called Pimp in the hallway, so he could inform him of what he found out.

"Word is that the Detroit Boys was the robbers." L's whispered. "Word." Pimp said.

"Word," L's said then he continued.

"You know we gotta handle that, bro. If not, niggas gone think shit sweet, like they can just take from us with no consequences,"

"Nough said." Pimp replied with anger and rage in both his voice and eyes.

Liley was able to leave the hospital after a week of medical aid. Her face was still slightly swollen and her ribs were fractured, but she was expected to recover fully. Neither Liley nor Leslie wanted to go back to their apartment, especially after Pimp and L's shooting the Detroit Boys dope spot up. Pimp and L's put them in a hotel room at the Days Inn, until Liley Section 8 voucher was transferred over to the house she had been waiting to move in on Long Street. Pimp and L's wasn't happy when they found out Liley was moving out their million dollar spot, but little did they know, Long street would not only be their new home, but it would be a place they would never forget. After three weeks of laying on the Detroit Boys, Pimp and L's finally had their movement down to the science. They hid in bushes across the street from the Detroit Boys dope spot waiting for them to come out the house in their most fly threads headed for the strip club as they did every Friday night between 11 and 12 o'clock pm.

L's checked the time on his pager as the vibration startled him. It was fifteen minutes after twelve. L's cursed under his breath as his plan started to seem fruitless. At that moment, the Detroit Boys came walking out the front door laughing and talking loudly about which stripper they would be sleeping with by the end of the night. It was only three of them, but that was enough to make the hour spent in the bushes worthwhile. As they loaded into the two-tone Lexus, L's and Pimp pulled their guns out but paused as L's said,

"Chill for one minute bro, let em get all the way in the car, then we gone run up on they shit,"

The front passenger was the first in the car, then the back passenger. The driver stood outside the car talking for a couple minutes and then he too loaded in the vehicle. Before he could bring the car to life, Pimp and L's sprang from the bushes blasting off shots. Pimp ran half way to the car and stood in the middle of the street with his hood on, picking the front seat apart. L's ran all the way up on the car. As the windows came out, glass flew everywhere. Pimp emptied his clip quickly. He had touched the driver and front passenger up pretty good, but they were still alive and moaning as they tried to get as low as possible. L's stuck his Glock inside the car and finished all three of the Detroit boys off with his last six shots from his sixteen round magazine.

His gun clicked a few times before him and Pimp took off running through a dark alley. The driver and front passenger met death instantly, as for the guy in the back seat, he fought for his life while climbing out of the car and falling hard on the pavement.

After being hooked up with some of Bucks loyal clientele, Mills was running through his first thirty kilos with ease. Mills finished up his grind a little early because tomorrow would be a long day for him. Not only was it Nesh's birthday, but he had to pick Black up from Tyko tomorrow morning. Mills had been spending a lot of time with Nesh since she had been back home and the more time they spent together the more in love he fell with her. She still hadn't given in to Mills, but Stevie Wonder could see Mills wasn't the only one falling. Mills had a special surprise for her tomorrow and he couldn't wait to see her reaction to it. He had tickets for Martin Lawrence's stand up comedy at Nationwide Arena, then he had reservations for dinner at one of Columbus's finest restaurants, but no matter how much Nesh loved Martin or seafood neither one of them could top his surprise birthday gift.

The next morning Mill's was up bright and early. He showered, groomed himself, and slid into a pair of dark blue

Nautica jeans, a v-neck white tee, and some high top white on white A-1's. After grabbing his grill from his jar of cleaner beside his bed, he ran them under water, snapped them in his mouth, put on his Rolex, and the two karat diamond earring, then rushed out the door talking to Brandy on his phone. Twenty minutes later he was pulling into Tyko's parking lot. He strolled through the door blinding Tonya with his shine from his diamonds. Mills and Tonya flirted with one another until Black arrived.

Black was already fit, but he had become huge. His chest pertruded from his shirt, while the shirt sleeves clung to his arms like a bear hug. He sagged his pants slightly, but it was still evident that they were too small for his running back type legs. His cornrolls hung down his back as they zig zagged from the top of his head. When they embraced one another, Mills could feel Black's strength as he squeezed the life out of him. As they walked out the door Black admired Mills success, from his jewels, to his ride. Mills had sent him pictures, but to see his little homie balling out of control in the flesh was inspirational. As they pulled out the lot, Mills fired up a hydro, filled backwood and passed it to Black. Master P's Ghetto Dope blasted from his system all the way to the City Center Mall.

After taking Black shopping and to the cell phone shop, Mills headed for his weight house. While Black showered and got dressed, Mills got rid of a few kilos and collected some of the money he had in the streets. Brandy stopped by to drop off twenty thousand dollars she owed Mills and before she left, Black came walking down the steps. Brandy stared at the dark piece of chocolate that gravitated towards her and felt a real attraction for the first time since Chris.

"Black this is… Brandy" Black said cutting Mills off.

"How you doing Brandy, I been waiting along time for this day," Black said while extending his hand for a formal greeting.

"What day is that?" Brandy asked.

"The day I got to meet you, Mills ain't been delivering you my messages?"

"No," Brandy said bashfully.

"That's cold Mills," Black said.

"My bad bro, you know I gotta short term memory, but dig... you can catch her up on all that shit, cause she gone be taking you to your mom's house," Mills said.

"What!" Brandy said butting in.

"Yeah sis, you know it's Nesh's birthday today, I gotta go pick her up and show her that surprise I was telling you about, you and Black need to get acquain'ted anyway, cause he's been feeling you for a long time now, and I know you like em cause he's your type, so don't front." Mills explained.

"Who the hell you think you is, match maker nigga?" Brandy said with sass.

"Nope, but, you know I wouldn't plug you wit a nigga who's not official..." Mills replied as he dug in his pocket and extracted a wad of cash. He handed the cash to Black and said, "Bro this is about four gees, just something for you to put in yo pocket, I got some heavy for you, but we'll get into that tomorrow. After you spend some time with yo mom, by the way tell her I said hi and sorry I couldn't stop by." Mills grabbed a bag full of money from the table and kissed Brandy on the cheek and said, "Good looking sis, y'all a good look for each other, too."

He gave her the key to the house and told her to lock up. As he walked out the front door, Brandy and Black stood there speechless. It took Mills forty five minutes to reach Buck's house. Mills and Nesh didn't waste anytime getting back on the road. Forty five minutes later they were turning into Elaine's far eastside apartment complexes. He pulled to the side of the road and grabbed a blind fold out of the glove box.

"Mills what are you doing, and where are we going?" Nesh asked.

"It's a surprise; now turn around so I can blind fold you," Mills replied.

"You know I don't like surprises Mills, now please just tell me what my present is...please," Nesh pleaded.

She tried melting him with her puppy dog look, but it was to no avail. Mills blind folded her and pulled into sudden square housing units. He helped Nesh out the truck and into a dark apartment.

"Mills where are we?" Nesh asked as she stood in the dark apartment. Mills hit the switch on the wall and illuminated the apartment. He removed her blind fold, and she stood in awe, as she looked at the beautiful living room, filed with plush white Italian leather, fish tanks, luxiourous lamps, and glass tables. Mills took her on a tour of the apartment starting with the kitchen. As they climbed the steps Mills held her hand while guiding her through darkness up stairs. The upper level only had two rooms. A master bedroom , and a comfortable bathroom. They started the tour in the dark bedroom. Nesh was confused. Mills said he had a surprise gift for her, but here they were in a strange apartment. Mills found the lamp next to the bed and lit the bedroom up. A dozen roses and a huge teddybear holding a large card that read Happy Birthday Nesh in big bold letters sat on the bed.

"Awe Mills this is so sweet, I've never been given roses before," Nesh said as she grabbed the roses from the bed and smelled them.

"You ain't gone read ya card?" Mills asked as he anticipated Nesh's reaction and it was becoming unbeaable.

"Of course I'm going to read my card, thank you for everything Mills," Nesh said before planting one on his cheek. Nesh grabbed the card from the teddybear and opened it wide.

Nesh,

I've been in love with you since the very first time I've laid my eyes on you, and I promise to treat you like a queen if you ever gave me a chance. This apartment isn't befitting for a queen, but I wanted you to have a place of your own to call home, when you visited. This place is yours, no strings attached.

Happy birthday my queen

T-Mills.

Nesh was speechless as she lowered the card to look at Mills.

"Happy Birthday beautiful." Mills said while holding the keys to the apartment in front of her. Nesh jumped in his arms as tears of joy poured down her face. That night, Nesh gave her virginity to Mills, and from then on they were inseparable. After becoming one with Mills, Nesh knew going back to Atlanta wasn't an option. She quickly had all her credits transferred to Ohio State University. When school started back up in September she wanted be both on time and on point.

As August closed, D-Roc and his crew cruised up Mt. Vernon letting Nas "If I ruled the world" scream from the fifteens in his Explorer. Mt. Vernon and Graham was packed and as D-Roc pulled his truck to the curb on the side of the store, guys took off running in all directions.

"Now that's what I call respect. That's the type of respect we supposed to have every fucking where we go, when we roll up, clear the mutha fucking set."

Walt said intrigued by the fear they put in people's hearts. Slim stood outside the truck emptying a backwood, while D-Roc hung out the window talking to a few females. Walt and Fella hopped out the truck to catch another flock of females that admired the truck as they walked by. When Slim walked in the store he noticed a smoke grey Taurus driving by slowly. The windows were tinted so he couldn't see inside, but he flashed his Glock 40, just to let the passengers know he wasn't slipping. The car kept on going and Slim walked in the store thinking clown ass niggas must be sweating my bro's truck. When he walked out he laughed at Walt palming two girls asses at the same time. He stood outside the truck with the passenger door swung open while he rolled his weed. He was so focused on rolling the backwood to perfection, that he never noticed the Taurus pull out the alley with a gunman hanging out the window. By the time he lifted his head up it was too late.

"Roc it's a hit!" He yelled while draining his Glock, but he never got a chance to shoot, the gunman continued to dump off slugs into his frail body. One of the slugs tore through Slims face, while the other gunman squeezed off rapid-fire into the truck and Walt and Fella as they dashed for cover. The mack elevens tore the truck to shreds. Fella ran behind the truck shielding himself as he let his forty-four bulldog bark back. Walt shielded himself with one of the females while blazing back with his 32 hot Glock. D-Roc managed to open his door, and hit the dirt. He let off rounds from his eleven shot four-five while lying stretched out on the sidewalk.

The Taurus sped off while its gunman emptied all of their clips in return. As the gunman ducked back in the window and the Taurus turned up an alley, Walt threw his female shield to the ground and chased after the Taurus letting off rounds. D-Roc ran to his aces aid, but it was too late, Slim was gone. Fella knelt down by his cousin's side, with his lifeless body held tightly in his arms, while D-Roc stood over top of the both of them with a face full of tears. He dropped his four-five to the ground while repetitiously saying,

"Not my dawg."

D-Roc's truck was a done deal. All the windows were out. While both the exterior and interior were riddled with bullets. Walt returned quickly. He shook his head, as Slim's blood-drenched Fellas clothes.

"Fells! Roc! C'mon man we gotta go!" Walt said as the police sirens became louder. Neither Roc nor Fella moved. Walt grabbed their guns off the ground and hopped behind the wheel of D-Rocs car that now looked like Swiss cheese.

"Slim gangsta gone man, hurry the fuck up, let's go, before the cops get here." Walt yelled as he cranked the truck up. The sirens became louder, causing D-Roc and Fella to come to their senses. They hopped in the truck, and Walt smashed the gas. Meanwhile Pimp and L's sat in Liley's new house on Long and 22nd awaiting their cab. L's aunt Peaches had finally found them a new dope spot. Peaches was a smoker and a prostitute. Despite her flaws, she was a moneymaker, and any dope spot she touched turned into a gold mine. Before running out to the cab, Pimp kissed Leslie and told her he would be back later. L's cracked a few jokes on Liley and Leslie both as he ran out the door laughing. Nobody actually knew who killed the Detroit Boys, but every finger pointed at Pimp and L's. Oak and Morrison was on fire now that the Detroit Boys were taking their loss out on whoever they could find, so Liley's move was right on time. The cab ride to Oak and Sherman only lasted five minutes. L's aunt Peaches answered the door with nothing but a shirt on that stopped at her waist.

Pimp stared at her bush between her legs as she motioned for them to come inside.

"Damn auntie put some fucking clothes on." L'said.

"You ain't gave me enough dope yet to be giving out orders nephew, I run this mutha fucka," Peaches said.

Two more half-naked women occupied the living room, while another came walking out of one of the back rooms. The two hookers in the living room were smoking dope straight out a pipe. L's pulled his dope sack out and passed a few rocks out and said, "Everybody get the fuck out of here smoking that shit, from here on out all dope gets smoked in the back rooms!" L's dropped three stones in his aunt's hand and as she led the pack into the back rooms. L's smacked one of them on the ass as she wiggled her naked behind while following Peaches into the room. Pimp fanned the smoke out the air while covering his nose and mouth.

"You smell that?" Pimp asked L's as he moved around the house as if the room wasn't filled with crack smoke.

"Yeah I smell it, it smell like money." L's said as he came out the kitchen with a plate and a razor.

"Have a seat Pimp; this is home baby, we bout to get rich, the money follows trust me," L's explained.

Pimp plopped down on the couch next to L's, who obviously didn't mind sitting in the same spot as a naked prostitute. Pimp and L's spent the remainder of their summer getting money. Unlike L's, Pimp was approaching a new school year which meant he'd be missing a lot of money. After explaining this to L's, L's agreed to sell both of their packs while Pimp went to school. Pimp was the brother L's never had, and the two shared a special bond, that was unbreakable.

CHAPTER 10

Slim's funeral was stacked. It looked more like a block party than a death ceremony. The parking lot was filled to the capacity with fancy cars,and saucy mourners. Detective White and Brown in an unmarked car were parked up the street. They snapped off shots as all the Main street ballers, and gangsters came to show their respects to one of their most reputable products.

D-Roc, Fella and Walt sat in Walt's fire orange 96 Caprice on gold hundreds. Walt sat behind the wheel with his door wide open as he, D-Roc, and Fella snorted coke like it was legal. Mills pulled into the lot and parked next to Tameka's Lexus truck. When he and Nesh exited the truck, he spotted D-Roc, Walt, and Fella a few cars down. He told Nesh to go ahead and he would catch up with her. As he walked over to Walt's Caprice, he acknowledged a few hustlers from around the way, who stood by their cars smoking weed. When he reached the Caprice he noticed the large Desert Eagle forty-four on his lap.

He also caught a glimpse of Fella in the back seat filling his nose with coke.

"What up Walt, what's happenin Roc, I know this is a difficult time for y'all right now and I feel y'all pain, Slim was cool as fuck," Mills said before looking in the back seat at Fella and asking him for a minute of his time. Walt shoved his Desert Eagle in Mills face while saying, "Get the fuck away from my ride homie, you ain't give a fuck about Slim and you don't give a fuck about Fella either, push on before I twist yo bitch ass cap." Mills was furious and Walt could see it in his eyes as he stared down the barrel of Walt's Desert Eagle without flinching or saying a word.

222

Mills was frightened. He knew Walt would pull the trigger, but he refused to leave without checking on his ace. Walt jumped out the car, but before he could jump into action Fella spoke up.

"Walt chill out bro, not at Slim funeral," Fella said.

"You betta tell this nigga to get the fuck away from my ride, with that fake love shit, for it be his funeral next," Walt shot back. Mills looked at Fella who still had not gotten out the car and he turned to leave. Fella stepped out the car and yelled after him. Mills turned around.

"Hold up!" Fella yelled out while walking towards him.

"What's up bro?" Fella said.

"Dig bro I just came over to check on you and to let you know no matter what this bullshit is we goin through, I'm still yo nigga, and if you need me I'm here for whatever. If you know who took ya cousin life, and you wanna ride I got cho back. My loyalty to you is eternal. You be careful and you know how to contact me," Mills said admanently. He hugged Fella for the first time in a long time, and before he walked out, he used his suit jacket to wipe the powder from Fella's nose.

"Call me bro, I'm here for you," Mills said before walking off.

Mills walked in the funeral home, just as the ceremony began. Brandy, Black, Mek, Buck, Peko, Shawn and Nesh sat in one row. Mills squeezed in next to Nesh and they all sat in as the minister was handing the floor over to Slim's mother. Her words were concise, due to barely being able to hold herself together. As "This Is For My Homies filled the funeral home's speaker, everyone visited Slim's casket to have their last look at Slim gangsta. Slim had so many different women that the young lady pregnant with his child didn't know whether to be mad at him or mourn him.

A number of females filled Slim's casket with tears, and his baby's mother patiently waited her turn. She cried her heart out while waiting her alone time with her unborn seeds sire. All hell broke loose by Slim's casket as one of the females continuously kissed Slim on his lips while trying to climb into the casket with him. Slim's baby mother lost it. She grabbed the girl by her hair and went to work on her face. As the girl gained her composure, she went to exchange a blow with Slim's baby mother, her little sister jumped in, then one of the girls home girls jumped in to assist her, and Slim's funeral turned into a royal rumble. Slim's mother, along with Fella's mother and some other relatives started pulling the girls apart from each other, but somehow they managed to lock back up.

D-Roc, Walt, and Fella had to come down to the casket and regulate the situation. As they manhandled the women, the rest of the funeral made an exit. Those who weren't going to the burial peeled out of the lot, while others awaited Slim's hurst. On the way to Slim's burial D-Roc received a disturbing phone call.

"Yeah what up?" D-Roc said answering his phone as tears poured down his face.

"Ya boy look real good in a casket, huh?" The caller said humorously. "

Who the fuck is this?" D-Roc yelled into the phone while sniffing up his tears.

"This the nigga you love to hate, hahaha! Aye I ain't know gangsters cried. Hahaha!" The caller laughed.

"You a dead man, bitch ass nigga! Enjoy all the laughs now, cause when I find out who you are, you a dead mutha fucka!" D-Roc yelled.

Walt and Fella asked in unison, "Who the fuck is that?"

"Ha ha ha! Y'all niggas ain't no killers and I hope yo homeboy Slim run into my dogs in hell so that they can bite em in his ass, ha!ha!ha!" The caller said as he hung up laughing in D-Roc's ear. D-Roc continued to yell threats into the phone long after the caller disconnected.

"Roc, chill the fuck out!" Walt yelled as D-Roc screamed into the phone at the top of his lungs.

"Man that was some snitch ass niggas talking about he killed Slim, talking some shit about we ain't nothing but some dog killers and he hope Slim sees his dogs in hell so they can bite him in his ass... man I'm telling you, bro, when I find out who that clown nigga is, I swear to God I'm a kill em." D-Roc yelled.

Walt didn't need anytime to think. He knew exactly who it was. He and Slim had only killed two dogs in their lifetime and those dogs belonged to Brandy's old boyfriend, Chris! He calmed D-Roc down and explained his logic to him and Fella. Once Walt reminded them of Chris's dogs rushing out of the room, it hit them over the head like a ton of bricks. Chris was from Mt. Vernon and he was behind Slim's death and the attack on them last summer, while they flossed their MVP's up Mt.Vernon, it had been so long ago, when they jacked Chris and shot his dogs, that they had forgotten about him, as reality sat in D-Roc clenched his big boy nine mm Taurus and said,

"That nigga a dead man!"

"Like yesterday," Fella added. After school Pimp skipped his grandmother's house and went straight for the spot. He strolled through the kitchen and walked in on L's getting sucked up by some fine redbone prostitute named Roxi. Roxi was completely naked while squatted like a frog and treated L's piece like it was a blow pop.

"Aw shit man!" Pimp said as L's palmed the back of her head while he squeezed in and out of her mouth.

"Where is you going bro?" L's said as Pimp walked out of the living room. L's laughed as Roxi swallowed his juices. He pulled his pants up and chased after Pimp in the kitchen.

"Ha! Ha! Ha! Aye you silly as fuck bro," L's said as Pimp made faces like what he was doing was nasty.

"No, you silly, you in there getting yo dick sucked by a nasty ass dope fiend slash prostitute. You trippin bro." Pimp replied.

"Shid, ain't nothing wrong wit getting yo dick sucked, you better get hip, dope fiends got the best cap and pussy." L's explained.

Pimp burst into laughter because his partner's rationale sounded stupid.

"Pussy is pussy bro." Pimp said.

"Shid how would you know? You ain't had no pussy but Leslie's lil young ass coochie, pussy whipped nigga," L's shot back with an explosion of laughter of his own.

"Aight, aight!" Pimp replied. Not wanting to talk about his and Leslie's sex life.

"I know aight nigga," L's said while playfully grabbing Pimp in the headlock.

"I need some swishers bro, let's go to the store." L's said after releasing Pimp from his headlock. Oak and Wilson was packed as Jeezy, and Lil Breezy and a few of their homies stood in front of the store unlike down on Oak and Morrison, Pimp and L's got along with the hustlers on Oak and Wilson. L's had grown up with a few of them as well and they respected each other's gangster.

"What up Jeezy, sup Lil Breezy, Truck, Domi, what y'all niggas bout to get into?" L's asked.

"Shit just pumping, trynna get that bread." Jeezy shot back.

"I can dig it." L's said as he and Pimp walked in the store.

Meanwhile, Mills, Brandy, Peko, and Shawn sat in Peko's spot blowing on good green and talking about Dee's fatal attraction to Peko.

"Man I'm telling you, bro, dat bitch Dee been tripping," Peko said.

"What's up wit her bro?" Mills replied.

"This bitch be calling my phone and pager all hours of the night and shit, leaving lil freaky messages, Shy almost heard that

226

shit one time and you know she gone lose it if she catches the kid cheating again," Peko explained.

"Ha! Ha! Ha! You just had to hit that nigga; you should of followed yo big head instead of your little one," Mills said.

"You laughing and shit bro, but this shit is serious man, this bitch trynna compare her self to Shy like I'm ah leave my family for that trick!" Peko continued.

"That's what you get nigga from not being able to keep yo dick in yo pants, y'all niggas kill me, y'all can have a good bitch, yet and still y'all out in the street cheating with a slut," Brandy said. Shawn was in tears as Mills and Brandy teamed up on his brother. Peko couldn't help it, he had everything a man wanted in a woman with Shy, but he still cheated. Having sex with other women was like a sickness for him.

"Man, I'm ending that shit this week bro, for sure," Peko said. "That's what you said last month Pee, that lil bitch gone bend over and you gone be through. You got a sensitive dick head nigga." Brandy said.

"Aw, that's cold," Peko said as Mills and Shawn shook off their laughter.

"Enough about that bitch," Brandy said, "Have yall heard about them lil niggas Pimp and L's?"

"Yeah I heard them lil niggas killed those Detroit Boys on Miller and Oak. Them lil niggas name is in the streets like a mutha fucka." Peko added.

"Who is the lil niggas? Mills asked.

"Shid if I know," Brandy said.

"They some lil niggas, mess wit one of my girls homegirl, lil sister, them lil niggas is all she talks about," Shawn added. They stayed there smoking and kicking it until the sky turned black.

As night fell, D-Roc, Walt and Fella sat in Walt's basement filling India's nose with powder, and her lungs with chronic. Fella remembered India running out of Chris's house the day they robbed him and figured she was still one of his booty calls. After picking her up, getting her high off cocaine, weed, and liquor he got her talking. They tricked her out of all the information on Chris she knew. They had her right where they wanted her and they delivered the killer blow by offering her a thousand dollars to set him up. She quickly agreed, thinking she was only setting him up to get robbed. All it took was one call and Chris quickly accepted her booty call. After finding out he was home alone, she ended the call, telling him she'd be there in twenty minutes. Fella loaded his nine-shot Moss Burg pump up, while Walt loaded his twin Desert Eagles, and D-Roc checked his twin Smith and Wessons.

Once they were ready for action, Fella told India it was time to roll.

"Y'all gotta give me my money first," India said with greed. Fella pulled a roll of bills from his pocket, counted out a thousand dollars and threw the stack on her lap. She counted it then said,

"Alright let's roll."

Little did India know she would never get to spend that money. The ride to Chris's would be the final ride. It only took ten minutes for Walt to reach Chris's apartment in Poindexter village. It was a quarter till midnight and the g-ride blended right in perfectly with the darkness of night. Fella stood to one side of the porch with his pump ready for action. D-Roc and Walt stood on the opposite side with their automatics behind their legs. India nervously knocked on the door.

Chris yelled out, "Who is it?"

After the third knock on the door, with his tech nine clenched by his side.

"Come in, why you standing there looking stupid?" Chris said with a big smile on his face. As he held the door open for India, Fella bounced off the wall and hit him in the chest with a pump. Blow!! The sound of the pump and the sight of Chris's insides jumping out his body scared India half to death. She tried to back out the door way, but Walt slumped her with a shot to the back of her head from his Desert Eagle. Fella kicked the door open wider as Chris's young black koby pit stood by the couch barking. He hit the puppy with a pump, slumping it instantly.

D-Roc stood over Chris, while repeatedly delivering numerous shots from his twin Smith and Wessons. Walt dug in India's pockets and took Fella's thousand dollars back before they darted off into the night.

CHAPTER 17

Pimp had a funny feeling as he walked to the store. He didn't know why, but his intentions were telling him to be alert as he walked up Oak Street. The street was clear which was strange for a crack strip. Pimp fixed his fifteen shot nine-millimeter as it slid around his waist. He gained a sense of security from the feel of his steel. His pager sounded off distracting him for a few seconds it took for the old school galaxy to turn on to the street. Pimp looked up in just enough time to dive out of the way of the first shot. He landed behind the car parked by the curb, and the gunman continued to let off rounds.

Bullets tore through the car as Pimp fumbled his nine. He didn't know how he was going to get out of this ambush, but he knew whatever happened, he was going out blazing. The shots stopped for a few seconds, but Pimp could hear the gunman reloading their weapons. It's now or never Pimp thought to himself. As he rose to his feet and back-peddled through a field while unloading his clip at his attackers. The driver of the Galaxy had no choice but to pull off as his nine-millimeter shells thumped up against his ride. One of the gunmen managed to reload quick enough to trade a few shots with Pimp as he dumped shells into the Galaxy.

L's was pulling up in front of the spot as Pimp ran up the steps. L's never heard the shoot out because his system was too loud. He knew something wasn't right, because Pimp still had his nine out as he ran in the house. L's quickly killed the engine and ran in behind him. Pimp sat on the couch with his hand covering his shoulder that was bleeding.

"What up bro, what the fuck is going on?" L's yelled as he became frantic at the sight of his main nigga bleeding.

230

"I came out the store and got dumped on by some niggas in a blue Galaxy!" Pimp said as L's assisted him with removing his shirt.

"It's only a graze," L's said as he spotted the small gash Pimp was bleeding from.

"Stand up and check yo self for any other holes bro," L's said with anger in his voice, and tears in his eyes.

"Who the fuck was it, I swear to God we gone kill the mutha fuckas!" L's said while pulling and AK from under the couch.

"I don't know who it was bro, they wore ski masks and I ain't never seen that car before," Pimp replied.

"Fuck man!" L's yelled with anger in him. He seemed to be more touched by the situation than Pimp. Although Pimp was a year younger, he was always the calmer one of the two.

"Just chill bro, as I've always heard my big bro say everything in the dark comes to light," Pimp said while assuring his partner that he was alright. Meanwhile Peko was sitting in front of Dee's apartment, thinking of the words to say to her. Peko flicked his roach to the ground as he knocked on the door. Dee opened the door wearing some thin cloth high rider shorts, with a matching sports bra. Peko could tell she ain't have any panties on and he was already becoming aroused. Dee's body was to die for and she knew it. This was Peko's third time visiting her this month.

Everytime he had come over to break up with her, he got hypnotized by her body and turned it into a booty call. Peko was so high, he was eating stars and the drugs made his little head easy to influence. He could feel his manhood growing in his boxers, as he stared at the deep gap between her legs, but he snapped out of his horny rage before he walked through the door.

"What up Pee?" Dee said after running her tongue over her soft luscious lips.

"Not a whole lot." Peko replied. Dee locked the door behind him while grabbing his hand.

"Hold up Dee, Im a cut to the chase, cause I see where you trynna go with this, and I ain't trynna go there." Peko explained.

"You mean to tell me you don't want to have recess on the playground?" Dee said while putting one of Peko's hands on her ass.

"Dig Dee, I told you I got a girl and a family, and you starting to get beside yourself wit calling my phone all hours of the night and tryna compare ya self to my family. This shit is over, this ain't no ass call, this is goodbye," Peko said adamantly while pulling his hand from her ass.

"Alright Peko I am tired of fighting for something I can't have anyway, but we can at least end this on a good note, right?" Dee was back in Peko's face. She grabbed a handful of his half-hard penis while whispering in his ear.

"Looks like somebody doesn't want to leave," Dee said.

She pulled his manhood through his boxer hole with ease, due to his low hanging jeans. She squatted and cocked her legs open so he could get a good look at her muf in between her legs. She flicked her tongue at the head of his penis a few times then wrapped her mouth around his pole. Peko couldn't control himself, his full nine inches grew in her mouth and he stopped resisting. Dee pulled his pants down to his ankles and pushed him back on the couch, Peko was quickly mesmerized as she slid off her tight shorts.

She slid down on Peko's pole and rode him like a wild bull. Dee was so wet, her juices drenched his boxers, as she slammed down on him. Peko did like being dominated, nor did he want to cum yet, so he stopped her long enough to bend her over the couch. Peko had let Dee trick him a few times before into having sex without a condom. She said she didn't like the way they felt and swore she was on the pill. Peko never trusted her, but her love muffin was so good that he always gave her game.

He pulled his boxers down to his knees, put his pole halfway in, adjusted his position, pushed her cheeks apart, then slammed his large penis in her cave, at rapid speed. Dee was a freak and she loved pain. She backed into every one of Peko's strokes with force while biting down on her bottom lip and looking at him over her shoulder.

"Oh Peko, don't stop I'm bout to cum!" She yelled. P

eko was in the act of exploding himself, but as he tried to pull out of her, she wrapped her hands around his waist holding him in her while she backed up on him, until he released his fluids in her.

"What the fuck is you doing, Dee! That's the shit I be talking about, that's why I'm through fucking with you, I know you be tryna get pregnant bitch!" Peko said while fixing his clothes.

"I ain't gotta try, I already am nigga and it's yours, now tell yo precious bitch Shy dat!"

"Shiiid no you ain't!" Peko screamed.

"Yes I am!" Dee replied.

"It ain't mine, bitch you be fucking outta both draw legs!" Peko said.

"Yeah nigga it's yours and you gone take care of me and my baby," Dee replied.

"Imagine that, you car hoppin ass hoe. Come thirsty once a month bleeding bitch!" Peko screamed back at Dee. "

Yea I'm a car hopper and I hopped my ass right in yo car and yo stupid ass got me pregnant and you gone take care of us, too." Dee said.

"Imagine that." Peko said as he walked out the door. It only took a few days for that which was in the dark to come to the light. Jeezy's girlfriend Ty'eisha learned from one of her homegirls that the Galaxy belonged to the Detroit Boys. Ty'eisha immediately informed Jeezy and he didn't waste any time telling Pimp and L's. He startled Pimp and L's as he ran up the steps.

Pimp grabbed his nine, while L's rushed to the window with his mack eleven.

"Be cool Pimp, it's Jeezy." L's said as he snatched the door open.

"What up bro?" L's said as Jeezy stepped in the house.

"Them coward ass Detroit Boys is what's up," Jeezy replied.

"What's up wit em Jay?" Pimp asked.

"That's who dumped on you in the Galaxy last week, my lil flame's homegirl fuck with the niggas, and when she heard them talking about it, she got my girl and the rest is self-explanatory. Them niggas on Linwood and Fulton right now bringing spring in with a bbq, slipping ya dig," Jeezy explained.

"Like a mutha fucka," L's said.

"Strap up Pimp, let's go get these niggas," L's said, while running back to the room. Pimp grabbed his AK from under the couch, as L's came running back into the living room with one of Peaches trick's car keys in his hand. He threw the keys to Jeezy and said, "We need you to grip the wheel."

"Say no more my nig, lets ride." Jeezy replied.

L's tucked his Mack under his shirt while throwing an extra clip in his back pocket. Pimp wrapped his AK up in a towel and they ran out the back door. In a matter of minutes they were creeping up on the house from the back side. Jeezy crept up real slow, letting the car cruise. Pimp scanned the back yard, noticing more females than males. He spotted most of the Detroit Boys in the front of the house and the side drinking and smoking.

"Pull up in front and hit the brakes, Jay," Pimp ordered from the back seat.

L's never gave the car a chance to make it to the front. As they passed the guys on the side of the house, "L's rose out the window and yelled, "Aye aye! What up bro." They turned to look, and L's opened fire, with the Mack. Pimp let the chopper go as the guys hit the deck and some returned fire. Pimp kept his head tucked tightly in the car while chopping down everything in sight, watching everyone diving for the ground. As they hit the ground, L's aimed for the dirt. Mills was driving up Fulton in the opposite direction. He had his system blasting, so he never heard the artillery sounding off. He pulled to the corner of Fulton and Linwood and noticed a car directly across the street, splashing with heavy artillery. He pushed Nesh's head down and quickly bent the corner. Jeezy turned right behind him, as Pimp and L's emptied their clips. As Pimp pulled his chopper back in the window he noticed the car in front of them was his brother's. He hit the floor as Mills made another quick turn and floored the engine up the street. Jeezy kept the pedal to the medal as he sped across Mound Street and swerved through traffic crossing Main.

After hearing of the three dead bodies and seven wounded at the house on Linwood, Pimp and L's were laying low. Pimp spent most if his time at home, while L's bounced around from place to place. Mills had been seeing very little of his little brother. He spent most nights with Nesh at her apartment.

His business destracted him from his grandmother as well. Had he been around more often he would have noticed the change in his brother's behavior and his grandmother's health. Grandma Mills was stubborn and stuck in her ways. When Mills offered to get her a new car she refused along with him getting her out of the neighborhood. She said she would live in her house until death did them part. She was old fashioned and worked for everything she had. Trading it in for something newer was not an option. Her old home, her old car was as good as it got for her. She hid her cancer from her grandsons because she didn't want to worry them or be put in the hospital, no matter how bad her health was.

She felt that when it was her time to go, there was nothing she could do to stop it. In a way, she was ready. After stopping by his grandmother's and seeing Jimmy home again, Mills decided this would be a good night to spend the night. While Mills and Jimmy played NBA Live on Playstation, D-Roc and his crew were driving up his grandmother's street, as they passed Mills truck, Walt let off a few shots into Mills truck. Mills jumped to his feet at the sound of the gunshots.

"Stay right here Jim, I'll be right back,": Mills said as he ran out the room. Mills ran outside his grandmother's house with his gun ready for action. He caught a glimpse of the back of the car as it turned off the street. Jimmy followed Mills down the steps with out him knowing it. He peeked through the window, with his nine tucked under his shirt, ready to back his brother up if needed. Mills circled his truck, checking out the damage. Most of the windows had been shot out and a line of holes trailed up the driver's side of the vehicle, leading to a large hole in the hood of the truck. Mills knew his engine was totaled, so he didn't waste his time checking it.

As he ran back in the house, Jimmy took off up the steps meanwhile D-Roc and his crew were back in Walt's mother's basement. Fella didn't like what had just taken place back at Mills grandmother's house. He would never agree to doing anything to harm Mills especially his grandmother's home.

"Fuck that lil Fells, who you wit, us or him? Nigga it's us against the world. D-Roc said as Fella yelled at him and Walt.

"For real Fells you starting to get on my nerves with saving that nigga, you can't be his soldier for life," D-Roc continued knowing that would press Fella's buttons."

"Fella ain't nobodies soldier, I'm a fucking a gee from my teeth to my feet, but its lines you just don't cross and even though we ain't fucking with each other no more, I'm a never bring harm to Mills, we go too far back for that," Fella explained.

"Man fuck that nigga bro, he ain't eating with us, break bready wit us or play dead out this bitch, and that goes for Mills, Buck and whoever else ain't breaking us off!" D-Roc screamed.

CHAPTER 18

It had been a few weeks since Mills truck had been shot up. He didn't have any proof but he knew D-Roc and Walt were behind it. Instead of feeding into their jealousy, he decided to make them more jealous, by buying another car. He was now with H.T. lookin at a 97' Lexus. Mills pushed his rental through traffic while smiling at the thought of D-Roc's face when he saw his new car.

Mills pulled in behind Peko's Impala as he paced the sidewalk, while yelling into his phone. All of the windows were busted out, his tires were flat, and key marks trailed around it, stopping at the front of his car.

"Yo stupid ass Dee! Why the fuck you fuck wit ma car!" He yelled into the phone.

"Fuck yo car nigga, what about me and my baby," Dee replied. "Bitch fuck you, and that ain't my baby. You so stupid that's why I ain't given you shit, you think you did something by fucking up my ride, wait to you see my new one I replace it with. You dumb ass bitch," Peko screamed.

"I'm stupid huh? We ll you stupid too cause you let a bitch like me get the number to yo house and I left yo Shy a little message too, so say goodbye to yo happy home, rookie," Dee replied as she slammed the phone down on Peko. Mills stood to the side of him as he dialed the number back.

"Fuck man!" He screamed repeatedly.

"Pee chill the fuck out bro, you letting this bitch drive you crazy," Mills said while grabbing his shirt.

"Man this bitch a batty bro, look at my window on the driver side," Peko said. Mills walked around the car and reached in the window and pulled out a brick. Attached were pictures of an ultrasound and a piece of paper that read congratulations.

"So what bro, just because a bitch is pregnant don't mean it's yours," Mills said as he walked back around the car with the brick in his hand.

Man that ain't even half of it bro, that bitch said she called my house and left Shy a message on the machine. Bro Shy gone wig out if she finds out I'm cheating again. She pregnant wit my second child and we getting our relationship right on track. I don't need this shit right now bro," Peko explained.

"Well, what you waiting for bro, call the crib and see if she got the message, if not run home and erase the message." Mills replied. "Damn good thinking bro, I don't know what I would do with out you." Peko said as he quickly dialed the number to he and Shy's apartment. Shy snatched the phone up on the second ring. "Hello." Shy answered in an irritated tone.

"What up bae," Peko said.

"Don't what up bae me Peko, I'm through playing yo games with you, come and get your shit and take it to yo other baby mama house," Shy said.

"That ain't my fucking baby Shy and me and her only happened once, it was a mistake you know I love you bae," Peko explained. "Apparently not enough and I'm tired of being cheated on, so just come get your stuff, before I get pissed and start fucking shit up. I'm not playing with you!" Shy screamed.

"Hold the fuck up bae, you acting like you the only one hurt behind this shit, I'm hurt too," Peko said. Shy slammed the phone down as he tried to use reverse psychology.

"Shy! Shy! Shy!" His yells were no avail; the only response he got was a dial tone. Pimp sat on Leslie's bed waiting for L's. It was early July and the beginning of a sick drought. L's had some good news for Pimp. L's was over a half-hour late and Pimp was becoming uncomfortable. He'd paged L's several times and L's had yet to page him back. Pimp called a cab and went downstairs to await its arrival. Liley sat on the couch with her new man friend. They were both nodding off while scratching like they had been bitten by a thousand mosquitoes. Pimp didn't really like Liley's new friend, because every time he came around Liley ended up getting higher than Rick James. Pimp didn't have enough knowledge of any other drug other than crack or cain, but he knew the drug Liley and the man were high off of was neither one of the two.

He caught her injecting herself with a needle one evening, but before he could question her, she passed out. Pimps cab arrived quickly, and he was out the door. He wanted to keep an eye on Liley until Leslie got home from school, but L's came first, and his gut was telling him that L's needed him. When the cab turned down Sherman, Pimp's intuition was verified. Peaches, Roxi, and a few other hookers were being walked out the house in handcuffs. Behind them were a few smokers and several tricks. The whole house was surrounded by men in black, while regular uniformed police assisted them with taping off the street.

Onlookers crowded the sidewalk as the men in black tore through L's car. They ripped out speakers, dashboards, carpeting, and the whole nine. Pimp stopped the cab a block away and watched the scene for a moment, searching for L's in the back of numerous police vehicles. L's was the last person escorted out in cuffs. Pimp's heart raced as his only friend was being taken away from him. He directed the cab back to Liley's house. He went back up in Leslie's room and called L's mother to inform her of the bad news. Pimp's situation had gone from bad to worse. Not only was he suffering a drought but his right-hand man was gone.

L's was in the juvenile detention center for a month and a half before receiving a year sentence for CCW and trafficking a gram of crack to an undercover. In that month and a half Pimp had been sold plenty of garbage work. Liley's man friend had been hearing Pimp, Leslie, and Liley talking about the drought, and the garbage he's been getting. He had been watching Pimp closely for the past few months, and he liked his style. Pimp was quiet, watchful, attentive, strong and about his grind. He wanted to talk to Pimp but, Liley told him Pimp wasn't big on strangers. After telling Liley, he had a connect with some good product for Pimp, she agreed to introduce him.

Late one evening, Pimp came strolling through the front door as Liley and her man friend watched television. The first thing Pimp noticed was that they were sober.

"What up lil Suppenin OG," Pimp said as he walked through the living room and headed for Leslie's bedroom.

"Sup son, let me talk to you for a minute," Liley said. Pimp stopped in his tracks.

"What's goin on?" Pimp asked.

"I wanna introduce you to my friend Sonny, he says he know where you can get some good shit at," Liley explained. Pimp didn't say a word. He was puzzled because he always heard Buck say, in the streets very little people offer their help, without wanting something in return. Liley said, "Pimp, this is Sonny, Sonny this is Pimp."

"Sup." Pimp replied.

"What's happenin youngin." Sonny shot back.

"Liley won't you give us two men a few minutes alone," Sonny said. Liley headed into the kitchen.

"Have a seat yougin," Sonny said, while patting on the couch.

"I'm cool." Pimp said.

"How old are you main man?" Sonny asked becoming more interested in a young prospect before him.

"Check it out O.G. I don't mean no disrespect, but what exactly is this about? Is this about me, or is it about you hooking me up with some good product? Pimp asked.

"Actually youngin its about both, I like yo style, and no matter how things may seem, its a lot of money out here and because of my habit I can't get it no more, I ain't always have this monkey on my back, but that's neither here nor there, I see a lot of the young me in you. You got a lot of potential to go far in the game and because I care about Liley, and she care about you, I felt the least I could do was hip you to a few tricks," Sonny explained.

"And what does being hipped to new tricks cost me? And where do you profit from it?" Pimp asked. Sonny smiled at Pimp's wittiness.

"That's a good question, because very few people give, without the intention of receiving and in this case, all I wanna receive is the satisfaction of seeing money made. You see I've taken a liking to few different youngsters and I've offered them the same opportunity, but because I am a heroin addict, they feel it's nothing to be learned from me, but a wise person knows, a lesson lies within everyone. Even if the lesson is learning about that person. You dig what I'm saying youngin?" Sonny explained.

Pimp could relate to Sonny's situation. He thought of everything he learned from Magic Mike, who was an all and out dope fiend that all the hustlers disrespected, including L's. Pimp still had his guard up, but he lowered his defenses a little.

"Fourteen, I'm fourteen," Pimp said.

"Come again?" Sonny replied.

"I'm fourteen, you asked my age," Pimp said.

Sonny smiled. "I guess that's our icebreaker, huh." Sonny said.

"I guess so, so what's up wit them tricks and that connect?" Pimp said.

"Tell me something young Pimp, what do you know about heroin?" Sonny asked.

"Heri what?" Pimp replied.

Sonny was surprised by Pimp's ignorance to the oldest drug known to man.

"You got me on that OG, im lost," Pimp said.

"Listen young Pimp, the money you making from crack, can't even compare to the money you can make form heroin. You right here in the middle of Mount Vernon and Long Street. And you don't know about dog food? Listen Pimp, this is the heroin capital because heroin is capital around here. If you give me thirty days with showing you about this heroin and you don't make more money than you can estimate making off that crack, I'll plug you wit some of my guys from California that never ran out of food that never runs out of cocaine, and despite my habit, they love me, and owe me plenty of favors, so whatever you buy I can have them front you the same thing."

Pimp pondered the proposition for a moment, weighing the pros and cons of accepting and denying the proposal.

"So when does our thirty days start?" Pimp said bringin a smile to Sonny's hard face.

It had been about three months since Shy learned of Peko's involvement with Deedreah. Peko was back to living on Berkeley living at his mother's. Shy had calmed down and started talking to him once again, but Peko didn't leave her much of a choice. He purposely left pieces of his clothing and jewelry at he and Shy's apartment so he would have reasons to stop by other than his son. After a month, Shy was giving in to his apologies, and after two months she was allowing him back in between her legs.

She still hadn't allowed him to move back in, nor had she allowed them to become a couple. Peko wanted Shy back, but for now, he enjoyed benefits of having both baby mothers. He finally accepted Dee and their baby. Dee didn't mind being second place to Shy. Peko had a key to her apartment and a key to her muffin between her legs and Deedrah didn't mind him coming and going as he pleased.

Peko pulled his Deville into Grant hospital with a smile on his face, as two nurses stood by the door admiring his vehicle. H.T. had the Cadillac loaded. It had wet purple candy pain't with the rag top, chrome grill, bumper, and trimmings, with a dark tint, and some chrome eighteen-inch blades. The interior was leather, with purple penstripes, and the trunk was on boom boom! Peko flicked the last of his hydro filled blunt to the ground as he entered the hospital. His heart was racing as he thought of Shy pushing his daughter out on her own. As the elevator skipped from one floor to the next, Peko prayed he was on time.

Meanwhile, Shawn was pulling away from Lisa headed for Grant hospital as well. As Shawn stopped at the corner, he saw the men in black pull in the back of Lisa's apartment. He drove up the street, as a U-HAUL pulled in the front of the apartment. Men in black hopped out and Shawn felt kind of bad for Lisa as he turned onto Main Street. Ten minutes later, his phone was ringing.

"Yeah what up? Whats up nephew? Its Lisa, you got some big spenders waiting on you. Shawn rolled down his window and tossed his phone out into traffic. Not today Lisa, baby. Shawn thought with a big smile on his face. He was smiling, but he couldn't believe Lisa had tried to set him up. He never expected such disloyalty from her, but then again, he was living a lifestyle where no one could be trusted. Mills pulled out of H.T. garage in his money green Lexus. The vehicle was fully loaded, with gold flakes and peanut butter brown rag top, you can't see me tint, some eighteen-inch golden Lorenzos, and king kong in the trunk. The interior was all beige, soft leather seats, flat screen TV in the dash board, with a VCR built into the floor next to the automatic shift handle. As Mills road up Mound Street, he thought about stopping at Brandy's, but quickly changed his mind when he noticed Berkeley filled with police and detectives. Fella's house was surrounded, while detective White and Brown escorted him out in cuffs. The sound of Mills phone snapped him back to reality, as he sat at the corner causing traffic to pile up behind him.

"Hello?" Mills answered his phone while hittin the gas.

"What's up bro its Bee."

"What up Bee, what the fuck is goin on at Fells crib?" Mills said. "You ain't seen the news this evening?" Brandy inquired.

"Nah, why?" Mills replied.

"Bro they charge him with Chris and that girl's murder. They just snatched him out of his mom's crib," Brandy answered with a cracking voice. Mills had no response. He parked in front of his grandmother's house with thoughts of him talking to Fella at Slim's funeral. He wondered if Fell would have called him to ride with Chris would he be in cuffs this evening too. Thoughts of his sick grandmother and his baby brother being left alone ran through his mind. Brandy's voice bought him back to reality as she screamed his name through the phone. Mills conversed with her as he entered the house and climbed the steps leading to his room. As he passed his grandmother's room, he noticed her laid on the floor next to her bed.

"Momma!" Mills yelled as he ran to her aid. He body was pale, and she fought her life with each short breath she took. Mills quickly dialed 911. Pimp was in his first heroine spot with Sonny when he received the call about his grandmother. In thirty days time Sonny helped Pimp make his first fifteen thousand dollars, which was almost as much as he'd stacked from hustling crack in three years. It didn't take Pimp long to make the switch, that Sonny promised would one day make him rich. Mills wanted to pick up his little brother, but Pimp quckly told him he'd meet him at the hospital. When Pimp arrived, Mills was seated in the waiting area. Pimp rarely saw his brother cry, but today he couldn't hold it back. Mills wrapped his arms around his brother, as he apologized for not paying closer attention to him and their grandmother. Being the man of the house he blamed his self for his grandmother's health. The dope game had separated him from his only blood family. The game had separated his mother and father from him and his baby brother. And now it was doin the same thing to him, his younger brother and grandmother. He now understood what it meant to be in too deep. Though Buck and Nesh both talked to him about leaving the game, he still hadn't given it much thought. It seemed like the deeper he got in the game, the harder it became for him to leave. It wasn't like a person trying to kick an old cigarette habit. All and main'tain strength through the struggle. He had reached a status where quiting had to be agreed on and planned ahead of time.

He couldn't just give hundreds of thousands of dollars worth of dope away, and say he was finished. Mills knew he had to have a talk with Chico and it had to be done sooner than later because he didn't want his baby brother falling victim to the game. He was walking in his mother and father's footsteps, and he refused to let Jimmy walk in his. Little did Mills know, he was three years late. Shortly after Mills and Jimmy had a seat the doctor arrived. He didn't know how to tell the young boys that their grandmother was dying, but they had to know. The doctor was subtle, but that didn't stop the tears. Their grandmother had no longer than a month to live and there is nothing they can say or do to change that.

When they entered their grandmother's room, she was wide awake. They both stood in the middle of the floor, as they tried controlling the tears that ran down there faces from the sight of their grandmother hooked to a respirator, with tubes running in and out of her.

"Come on over here and wipe those tears from y'all faces unless they are tears of joy," Grandma Mills said. The boys took baby steps as they gravitated towards her.

"I raised you boys to be strong, don't be coming in here acting weak. I've lived my life and served my purpose which is walking in the name of the Lord. I'm going to heaven and that's my utopia. So be happy and praise the Lord for chosing your grandmother as a house guest." She let out as much as a laugh as she could without coughing up her guts, but the boys were hurt, even if they wanted to, they couldn't muster up a laugh. They both spent the night at their grandmother's bedside. Mills mind raced the whole night. He wondered "Why God always chose the best people to die while allowing the worst people to live?

Here D-Roc and lil Walt was killing people every day with no remorse and God allowed them to live and keep taking lives, his grandmother was pure and non judgemental she served the Lord every day of her life, and God took her over all the evildoers. Unlike grandma Mills, Mills was not religious, but he wondered if the lord was trying to send him a message by taking all the people he loved.

For the first time since he was a child, Mills conversated with the All mighty one before dosing off into a light sleep.

CHAPTER 19

It didn't take Black and Brandy long to decide they were made for one another. They were everything the other wanted in a mate. Their relationship became serious quickly. Brandy was slowly but surely pulling away from the game, while Black was cutting deeper into it. Lil Walt was his protégé before he got locked down and he thought he'd be able to get his young killer back on his team, but Lil Walt made it clear that he was a jackboy for life which Black wasn't getting back into.

It wasn't that Black needed Walt, because once he showed his face on Mound & Gilbert the block was his, it was just that Walt used to be like his little brother. Though he was still crazy as ever, Lil Walt was all grown up now and black had to respect it. He hoped the rift between Mills, Walt and D-Roc didn't escalate into gun play because no matter how tight he and Walt were, his loyalty resided with Mills. Black pushed his new jet black Intrepid up mound street, headed for his number one money machine, that he was letting his new protégé, Lil Mark run. Lil Mark was a baby when Black went back down, but now he was a buck wild teen, with all the potential in the world. All he lacked was guidance, which black was now providing for him. Black wasn't the flashy type. Though he dressed expensively, he wore no jewelry and his car had no rims or beat in the trunk.

Beside the tint on the windows, the car was exactly the way it looked when he bought it. He was talking to Brandy on his phone as he pulled in front of the row of apartments he had mark cranking out of. As he stepped out the car, he spotted two men with pistols running out of his machine. It was dark, so he didn't recognize their faces, but he got their attention as he let his 40 cal chase them down. Pow! Pow! Pow! The jasckers blasted back. Pop! Pop! Pop! Black continued to dump off shots from his gun. He knew he hit one of them, when he saw one guys

247

body spin and fall to the ground. His partner helped him up, while blasting off shots and dragging him around the corner. Black took off towards the corner as Lil Mark came running out the front door with his nine in hand. The guys were pulling off in a brown Taurus, by the time black reached the corner. Brandy was still on Black's phone screaming his name as he screamed on his young protégé.

"What the fuck happened Lil Mark?"

"That was them bitch ass niggas Pook and Doke, they wanted some work, I let um in and I turned my back for a second to lock the door and they upped on me," Lil mark explained.

"Where the fuck was ya gun at bro?"

"The niggas come and buy work all the time so I put my pistol in my back pocket, while I was locking the door them niggas took it from me, when they upped on me."

"Damn Mark, what I tell you about slippin like that bro, you don't trust nobody but me, never put yo strap down, I don't give a fuck who you serving. Is anything left in the house?"

"Nah bro, they took everything, like ten grand and a half a slab, don't worry about it bro, I'll make all that up for us bro," Lil Mark said, feeling sorry he let his big homie down.

"Fuck that money and dope Mark, we can always get more money and dope, but you only have one life and ain't no getting that back. When its gone, its gone. This is a thinking mans game, start using your head lil nigga, cause thirsty ass niggas ah take yo life for a little of nothing out here. Lock that door and let's go before the rollers get here," Black ordered after lacing his young homies shoes.

After hitting a easy lick for a brick of cane, ten pounds of hydro, and fifteen thousand cash, D-Roc and Walt moved through traffic in their g-ride, headed for Lil Walt's mother's basement, which served as their head quarters. Fella on the other hand, sat in the county jail without a helping hand from one anyone besides his struggling mother. After all the robberies he had nothing to show for them besides ten thousand dollars two lady friends that he couldn't get a hold of. Fella thought he'd be able to count on D-Roc and walt for some lawyer money and to sell his cars and jewelry for him, but everytime he had his mother call them they fed her some bs. It only took them a couple weeks to change their numbers completely. Fella had his mother give the most reputable lawyer in Columbus the ten grand he had stashed and after a few short weeks he was receiving his second visit from Clyde Claytor.

Clyde was known through out the system as a shark. He could make cases disappear for the right amount of money, but he wasn't the type of lawyer to show any remorse for a person who was short on paper. Fella knew his ten grand wouldn't be enough for Clyde's representation, but he knew it was enough to get Clyde started until he could find a way to come up with more cash. Fella walked in the small room assigned for him and Clyde's visit. He sat in a chair across the table from Clyde, who was on the cell phone with another client.

He quickly ended the call and reached across the table to give Fella a firm shake while saying, "Mr. Stargel,l how you feeling today?"

"I'm aight Mr. Claytor, tell me something good,."

"Please just call me Clyde and I do have some good news for you, but I also have some bad news for you, which would you like to hear first?"

"I've heard enough bad news for one lifetime, give me the good," Fella answered.

"Well the good news is, I've found out who the prosecutions only witness is and without her testimony, they have no case. Have you ever heard of the saying without a snitch a case can only barely exist and can hardly be prosecuted? Don't answer that." Clyde said before continuing. "That's a tru saying by the way. Now for the bad news, the ten grand you gave me isn't goin to be enough for my representation, I'm going to at least need twenty more thousand. This is a double homicide case, so I'm gonna have to work my ass off to get you some rhythm. Those numbers you gave me to contact your buddies for some more cash have been cut off, I talked to the guys once, they said they don't know you. Our first court hearing is in February, so that gives you almost ninety days to come up with some more cash."

Clyde shuffled through some folders, while Fella sat in silence.

I cant believe those money hungry mutha fuckas. Fella thought.

"Do you smoke?" Clyde asked, breaking Fella from his trance.

"Yeah why?" Fella asked with a hint of attitude.

"Here you go, stuff these," Clyde said while secretly sliding fella a pack of New Ports across the table. "Well Mr. Startgell, you have my number, you can collect call me if you have any questions or requests or new information,"

Clyde shook Fellas hand before walking off.

"Aye Clyde, you never told me that witnesses name," Fella said before walking out the door.

"Oh, Lisa Pittman," He said before walking out the room.

The name echoed in Fellas head. Now that he knew why Lisa hadn't been excepting his calls. Lisa had turned on him. He never told her about his case, but after killing Chris and India, Lisa had started acting funny. She was real jumpy whenever Fella came around. India told her she was going to kick it with Fella and his boys the night she died and it didn't take Lisa long to put one and two together. As the guards escorted Fella back to his tank, the only thing on his mind was killing Lisa if he ever got free. Clyde told him without a witness, his case barely existed and the only way to get her out the way now was by death.

Soon as he reached his tank, he got on the phone. D-Roc and Walt were the only ones who could help him out now. He'd kept it gee when the detectives interrogated him. The least his supposed to be homeboys could do was get rid of the witness for him. He may not of been able to count on them for no cash, but he knew he could count on them for a 187, or so he thought. D-Roc and Walt sat on the couch getting high off weed and coke they just jacked for. Walt's mom screamed down in the basement telling him to pick up the phone. When he heard the voice on the phone he instantly became paranoid.

"What the fuck I tell you about calling my phone nigga!" Walt yelled in the phone.

"Slow the fuck down bro, ya'll been playing me real fucked up, changing y'all numbers and shit. I thought we was family, now I need y'all niggas help, its fuck me huh?" Fella yelled back.

"Who the fuck is that?" D-Roc asked.

"Listen my nigga, I ain't gone tell you again, don't call me or Roc's phone or my mommas phone either. Niggas you said you a gee, now gee the fuck up, do yo time nigga and remember yo momma healthy out here bro, keep it that mutha fuckin way," Walt saidbefore hanging up.

Mills had been spending more time with his little brother the last few weeks. Jimmy didn't mind spending time with his brother. The shopping and kicking it was beyond cool, but he didn't want to chance being spotted by someone who knew him by the name that was ringing so loudly in the streets Mills was being overprotective of his brother and between being with Mills and spending a few hours out the day with his grandmother, his business was being neglected.

Mills hadn't talked to Chico, but he knew by the year 2000, he wanted to be out the game, assisting Buck with enriching the black community, putting his baby brother through college and starting a family with Nesh. 1999 was less than forty days away, so Mills knew he had to talk to Chico soon. Mills gave Chico another year of hard grinding, then plug him in with Peko, who could move just as much product as him. Nesh was more than happy to hear Mills speak of leaving the game. She worried her self to death when he was out in the streets. She didn't bother him much with talk about retiring from the game. He always seemed to have a lot on his mindand she didn't want to aggravate him. With his grandmother's health, him neglecting his little brother, and worrying about D-Roc and Walt, he stayed in a small state of despondency.

Mills, Nesh, and Jimmy werepulling into Grant Hospital for their daily visit with grandma Mills. Last week the doctor informed Mills that her condition was getting worse and it would probably be best for her if he agreed to let them pull the plug. Of course Mills refused. He only took that information as an indicator to spend more time with her. When they strolled into the hospital they received the horrifying news. Grandma Mills had passed away twenty minutes before their scheduled arrival. Mills and Jimmy broke down immediately. They refused to have her taken away without them seeing her first. They ran to her room and fell into her arms as if she was alive. No one could take them off of her body. Jimmy came to his senses first. His heart ached, but it went cold, as his tears dried up on his face. At that moment he promised to never let any of his love ones be taken away from him again, nor would he allow his self to be taken from them. After his grandmother's funeral, mills found him self too effected to be in the streets. He spent a few weeks leading up to New Years in the house being consoled by Nesh. After missing Brandy's birthday, Mills owed her some quality time, so when she spoke of bringing in the New Years with a New Years Eve party at the hottest club in the city, he couldn't refuse. After telling Buck, Peko, and Shawn, they decided to bring in the New Year together.

Peko stopped by Deedrah's apartment to check on her and his child before he got dressed for the New Years Eve back tonight. As always his visit turned sexual and he sat in her parking lot smoking on a fat blunt, while thinking how beautiful it was to have two good looking baby mothers. Several doors down, he noticed a woman standing in the door way being sexed by a familiar face. As they stepped further out the apartment, Peko almost burnt his self with his blunt. Oh shit! He said to his self as he recognized not only the male figure but the female as well. Butter was shoving his tongue down Mek's throat, while grabbing a handful of her ass through her floor length mink. Peko wasn't sure he was seeing things clearly, until Mek pulled out the complex in the brand new Mercedes truck that Buck bought her for Christmas. He dialed Mills number immediately. The phone rang several times but no answer. He left a voice mail, "Y-Money this is Pee, call me as soon as you get this message, it's an emergency." Peko said while driving into traffic.

Meanwhile, Brandy stood in front of her mirror, with nothing besides a pink lace bra and some matching boy shorts. Black's man hood rose in his boxers as he watched Brandy groom her self in the mirror for the New Years Eve bash.

"Stop Black," Brandy whispered seductively as he pressed his half excited pole between her cheeks while sucking on her neck. "C'mon Bee, we gone make it quick," Black persuaded.

"Baby no, cause we gone be late for the party and we ain't been out since you came home."

"I don't ever have to go out, as long as I got you bae," Black said as he grinded on her from behind. She broke loose and ran around the room, while black chased her with his pole now at full attention. While they played hide and go getty in the bedroom, Lil Mark waited for them in the living room. He flipped from one music video to the next, while smoking on a fat hydro filled backwood and talking on his phone.

Buck sat in his game room watching the Buckeyes play Iowa Hawkseyes. When Tameka walked through the door, Buck was screaming at the television. "Cmon on man tighten up defense, watch the back door!"

"Whats up baby," Mek said as she sat on Buck's lap and rubbed on his bald head.

"My stomach bae, I'm starved," He responded while planting a big kiss on her lips.

"Baby I don't have time to cook, we gotta get dressed for the bash tonight."

"I can't go nowhere on an empty stomach, now go in that huge kitchen of yours and throw ya man something together,"

Tameka playfully smacked her lips as she headed for the kitchen. After the game Buck headed for the kitchen as well. He was talking loudly on the phone to Butter, as he joked with him about the money he had just won from his Buckeyes second half blow out. Mek was preparing his plate of fried chicken, mashed potatoes, mixed vegetables, and his favorite side, baked beans, when he finished his phone call. Aye bae me Butter gone ride together, you can take the Benz out tonight, I'm a tell Mills you gone pick Nesh up so she can ride wit you."

"Mmmch! No buck we said we was rolling together tonight, why that nigga always got to tag along and fuck up something, wit his trick ass," Mek said with an attitude.

"Bae I'm not going through this Butter shit wit you tonight. That's my only homeboy, he's like a brother to me and ya'll gone start this year off getting along with one another and that's the end of this conversation," Buck paused for a moment as he looked at Meks upset face. "Now come on over here and enjoy some of this dinner with yo man and that face ain't gone get you yo way tonight."

Mek stomped over to the large table where Buck sat. Buck grabbed her by the waist and pulled her to him and said, "Give me a kiss and quit pouting, you too beautiful to be making such an ugly face."

Mills phone was filled with messages as he and Nesh finished their third round of sex. Nesh slid up and down on his pole, bringing both of them to their fifth climax of the day. She collapsed on top of him as his man hood shrunk inside her. Both of them were worn out. They had two hours until they were to meet everybody at the club, and they decided to spend one of those hours sleeping. Nesh set the alarm clock on the phone and decided to check their messages as well. the only message on the phone was Tameka, informing Nesh on the change of plans. Mills noticed the light on his cell phone blinking, informing him of his messages. He disregarded the messages. Nesh curled up against him and he rolled over with nothing on his mind but his queen. Except for Mills not returning his call, Peko's night was going perfectly. He got to enjoy the inside of both his baby mothers caves. Then he and Shy had a talk he had been awaiting. She agreed to give them another chance. Although she said they would take things slow, Peko was happy to be back home. As he pulled away from their condo, he knew tonight had to memorize, because it would be his last night as a single man.

Shy was everything he wanted and needed in a women. Tomorrow was their starting over point and he refused to fuck his happy home again. He let Too Short's freaky tails blast from his speakers as he took the highway all the way to his brother apartment. Peko puffed on the finest dro as he admired his expensive attire and bobbed his head. He had on a purple hooded three quarter length mink, over top a crispy white tee which cordinated with his white Murray sneakers with a purple gator toe. His dark blue denim jeans were fresh off the rack. His grill was on gleam, his neck and wrist were on freeze, and both his pinky fingers were on bling.

His eyes were covered with Christian Dior shades, while an all-white Yankees fitted cap sat lightly on his head. He rapped along with Too Short, until he pulled in behind Shawn's car. Shawn's girlfriend Reese answered the door after a few knocks. She was cold blooded, at 5'2 she was 130 pounds of pure stallion, her stomach was flat as an ironing board. While her breast and badonka donk stood out like a red t-shirt at a crip gathering. Her hips rolled off her body in perfect harmony with her legs and apple bottom. Her complexion was golden brown almost matching her hazel brown eyes. Her hair was reddish brown and it hung to the middle of her back.

Peko shook his head as Reese sashayed back to the couch where she sat Indian style, while watching tv. Peko's nephew came running out of nowhere. He wrapped his self around Peko's leg, while slobbering on his pants leg.

"Boy where yo clothes at?" Peko said as he lifted him into the air. He had nothing but spider man draws on, as he stole Peko's hat and took off running. Lil nigga give me ma hat.

"Shawn Jr. give yo uncle his hat back and go get yo daddy and tell him to put some pajamas on you,"

Shawn Jr ran right into his sire. Shawn gave his brother his hat back and carried his son to his mother. He kissed the both of them and told Reese he'd be back kind of late., then he walked out with his brother. Shawn wore tan hooded three quarter length mink with over his navy blue sweater. His navy blue Sean John jeans had tan stitching, coordinating with his sweater, jacket and tan Timberland boots. His eyes hid behind a pair of Gucci frames and his grill was on chill.

His iced out Cuban link chain hung down to his belly button, with a iced out cross hangin to his belt. On his wrist was a matching bracelet, and Malvado timepiece that was iced out. Shawn andReese had a fairy tale relationship, they broke each others virginity, and he hasn't been with anyone else since. Shawn has been taking care of Reese since they were thirteen and she trusted him with her life.. Shawn could bed multiple women like his older brother but he was committed and Reese knew it, that's why she never gave him any problems about going out or coming home late. Shawn wasn't going any where and neither was she.

D-Roc and Walt sat outside the club, behind their dark tint in their g-ride macking on honeys, snorting coke, and stalking victims. They knew all the ballers would be at the New Years Eve bash and they had dollar sign in their eyes. Keisha and Iesha didn't know who D-Roc and Walt were, but when they walked up to their car, all the bling satisfied them. After exchanging numbers, the girls were off and it was just in time. They eyed the money green Lexus LS as it pulled into VIP's parking area. The Lex was nasty and they couldn't wait to see who was driving it. Mills stepped out the Lex with Rio, who had been out for five months, but too heavy on his grind to show his face. Mill blessed Rio with some cash and heavy weight when he got home,and just like Mills knew he would, Rio quickly locked his neighbor down with the same math that took Mills to the top. Mills and Rio were the last to make it up to the club out of their entourage. They killed the parking lot as they stepped out the Lex in their minks. The gold flakes sparkled as Mills leant up against his car while Rio flagged some honeys down. Mills wore a money green hooded three quarter length mink over top of his thick white tee, with some navy blue denims, and white Murray sneakers with green gator toe. His presidential Rolex lit up the parking lot as the diamonds and bezels bedazzled their audience.

Both of his ears were chunky with three karats of flawless diamonds. His gold Cardiar frames, had summer tint and they complimented his grill nicely. The other piece of jewelry Mills wore was a five karat pinky ring. Rio wore a royal blue hooded three quarter mink over his white tee, some regular denims, and white Murray sneakers with a royal blue tip. His grill was on showcase as well, as his vampire fangs entertained the females he had flagged down.

"Look at this lil bitch Walt, who the fuck he think he is? Sweet ass nigga.," D-Roc said as Mills and Rio rolled through the lot headed for the club's door. Walt was listening, but his attention was else where.

"Aye Roc ain't that that nigga Deuces lil brother right there?" Walt said while pointing at the midnight blue Lexx on chrome blades pulling into the opposite end. D-Roc watched the Lex park a few cars down on the opposite side.

"Yeah, that's that lil niggas ride, I hope his fat ass brother wit em,"

"Looks like yo wish came true, bro lets get them clown niggas," Walt said while pointing at Mike and his brother.

Mike and Deuce had on enough jewelry to start their own jewelry store. They were blinging and the show was their's to steal. D-Roc and Walt crept up on the side of a few vehicles leading to Mike's Lexus. Mike was talking to a female, while Deuce yelled at some one on his cell phone. They were both slipping, but when Walt shoved his Desert Eagle in Mikes face, while shoving the female out the way, their awareness came to life. It was too late though, because D-Roc had his nine mm Taurus in Deuce's face. Deuces looked like he wanted to try D-Roc, but Walt's voice brought him to his senses.

"Yo fat as try anything stupid, I'll blow ya lil bro's shit in the trunk of his Lex. Now both yall bitches come up off the loot and that shine," Walt said with a sinister smile on his face.

D-Roc took advantage of Walt's control. He smacked Deuce across the mouth with the Taurus. "Bitch ass nigga, strip for I put something hot in yo fat ass,"

Mike and Deuce did as they were told. They placed all their valuables and cash on the trunk and hood of the car. The parking lot party goers were amazed at the sight before them. Walt knew the girl he mugged was probably informing some of Mike and Deuce's homeboys of what was taking place, so he rushed D-Roc as he beat Deuce in the head with his pistol. They filled their pockets wih their goods and Walt smacked Mike to the ground with his Desert, while shoving him on top of his brother.

"Y'all bitch ass niggas beTter enjoy that lil shit while y'all can, cause I be to see y'all," Deuce said.

"What the fuck you say? Walt asked.

"You heard me nigga, y'all clown ass niggas dead," Deuce answered as blood leaked from his mouth. Walt fired off a few shots hitting Deuce and his little brother in their upper bodies. Everyone in the lot dove for cover as Walt fired off a few more shots to distract the onlookers as they hopped in the g-ride and sped out the lot. Som of Deuce's homeboys pulled up, as him and his little brother laId in their blood on the side of the Lex. They helped Deuce and Mike into the car and sped off, telling Keisha and Iesha to inform T-Bone and fresh aboutwhat happened.

Inside the club Mills and Rio were just climbing the stairs to the VIP section. Buck and everyone had two tables occupied. Across the room T-Boneand his crew occupied one with Moet.

"Look at Buckshot hoe ass over there slipping. We been sitting here for an hour and he still ain't noticed us," T-Bone said.

"It would be real fucked up if we crash they lil party why they over their partying with they lil wifeys and shit," Fresh added, causing the crew to burst into laughter. Keisha and Iesha stopped the laughter as they hurried across the floor, with the bad news. T-Bone and his crew flew out the club and headed to the hospital. Keisha never had the chance to tell T-Bone who had done it. Mills and Rio joined the rest of the crew , quickly ordering a few bottles of Moet. Mills finally caught the secret looks Peko had been giving him all night. So he followed him over to the bar. "What up bro?"

"damn bro, why you ain't call me back or answer your phone? This shit crazy man straight up!" Mills could see the seriousness in Peko's face and tone, so he didn't waste anytime with small talk.

"What's going on bro, talk to me,"

" Listen bro, this shit about to sound stupid, but its real like a hundred dollar bill, trip, that nigga Butter and Mek is fucking, no lie!"

"What! Get the fuck out of here bro, you wiggin out!"

259

"Nigga I ain't wiggin, I said real as a hundred dollar bill, I was at Dee's earlier today visiting her and my baby, and I saw Butter slobbing Mek down in the doorway of his apartment.I though I was wiggin out then, but then I watched her get into her Mercedes Buck bought her, just watch the looks they keep giving each other. I know when some cheating is going on c'mon bro, I'm like the poster boy for it." They both started laughing.

"I'm laughing bro but I'm serious, look at um," Mills ordered a drink for him and Peko, while they watched the affair. Mek and Butter exchanged variety of looks. When no one was looking Butter would tease her with his tongue and she'd roll her eyes. By the end of his drink, Mills had seen enough. He was furious because he knew how Buck felt about Butters. That was his only homeboy, he trusted the dude almost as much as he trusted Mills. They came up together from being knee high. Mills watched Butter and Buck toast with bottles of Moet.

Over the table Buck was telling Butter how he loved him so much and how this was their year to change the game. They embraced one another and pulled Buck to the side.

Meanwhile T-Bone and fresh were at the hospital. Mike and Deuce were in bad shape, but expected to live. Keisha and Iesha walked through the doors as T-Bone flipped on everyone who couldn't tell him who robbed his boys. After the girls told him of their encounter with guys in the Bonneville named D-Roc and Walt, the descriptions they received of the robbers fit perfectly. T-Bone thought of Buck and his crew back at the club and the only thing on his mind was take one of mines I take one of yours. He rounded his boys up and went back to the club. Mills told Buck about Butter and Mek's relationship, along with what Peko had seen. Buck was lost for words. He treated Mek like a queen and loved her unconditionally. He never cheated on her or put his hands on her. As far as he knew their sex life was beyond fine. He had a thick eight-inch pole that he knew he worked like a fifteen-year-old and the dish between her legs was his favorite meal, so there wasn't anything he could think of that she had to cheat for.

Butter was his main man, from grade school on up. They were like brothers and he and Mek couldn't stand one another. Mills had him watch the table from a distance as Peko had him do. It didn't take Buck long to notice the signs. His blood boiled as Butter rubbed Mek's hand. And he watched her kick him under the table. Tears took over his face as he stormed back to the table. Without saying a word he grabbed Butters by his sweater and drug him across the table. He slammed Butters liquor soaked body to the floor and mashed his face repeatedly with his fist.

"You disloyal mutha fucka, I should kill you, y'all been playing me like a fool. I trusted you." Buck said as he beat the blood out of Butters face. Everyone jumped up out of their seats, as Moet and liquor poured from the tabletop. Mek couldn't believe what she was seeing and hearing. Buck was on to her and Butter and his rage was evident. Butter was finished, but Buck snatched him off the ground and threw him on the table. He grabbed Mek by her throat and held her over Butter's bloody body.

"You two disloyal mutha fuckas deserve each other. I treat you like a queen, bitch, and this is the thanks I get."

"Nesh wanted to help her sister, but she was frozen by the thought of her sister cheating on Buck. After he took care of them for ten years. Buck bought his hand back and backhanded Mek across her face as she attempted to put up a fight. He brought his hand back for another one, but Nesh grabbed his hand. He turned with intentions of knocking Nesh down, but he looked at her faced an it reminded him of how much he loved her. Bouncers came from everywhere and sent buck right back into his rage, Mills grabbed Nesh as Buck snatched his arms away. Buck wanted to pop Mek one more good time, but instead threw her on top of the table with Butter.

One of the bouncers grabbed Buck by his shoulder and caught a right to his chin. The bouncer hit the pavement and the rumble began. Bouncer number two hit Buck from behind and Mills teed off on him with a flurry of punches. Bouncer number three and four were being molly whopped by Peko, Shawn and Rio. Bouncer number five picked the wrong one, Black had him in the air, and sent him crashing down on the table. Bouncer number six took a bottle of Moet to the head from Brandy as he was rushed by Black from his blind side. Mills told Brandy to get Mek and Nesh and get out them outside as the bouncers flooded VIP with mace. Black grabbed Lil Mark off bouncer number four and told him to watch out for Brandy. As Mark headed out the door, the fella went back to work. When the mace became too strong and began to tear through the fellas eyes and skin they dashed for the steps. Ounce outside, Buck and Mek went back at it. Peko and Shawn sat in Peko's Lac with the doors open trying to clear their face of mace. Black was doing the same thing in Brandy's Benz, as Lil Mark stood guard with his Glock.

Mills vision was blurry as he and Rio headed for the car. Mek and Buck screamed at one another. Mek was begging for Buck's forgiveness, and b-Buck for the first time ever, called Mek every dirty name in the book. He was pissy drunk and could barely stand still. He swayed back and fourth as he spat out all kinds of disloyal bitches and ho's. Mills couldn't see very clear but he caught two gunmen walking across the parking lot with their pistols drawn. They were headed right for Buck and the rest of his crew. Mills grabbed his twenty one shot top of the line nine and took off running across the lot while screaming Buck's name. By the time Buck heard Mills, it was too late. T-Bone and Fresh were firing off shots. Buck could of dove for cover but instead he shielded Mek and caught three of T-Bone's slugs to the chest. Lil Mark spotted the gunmen and opened up on them with his Glock. Lil Flip and a few more gunmen came out of nowhere covering T-Bone and Fresh. Mills let his gun cut lose. Peko hit his stash box and rose wit his four fifth. The gun fight was on. T-Bone and his crew retreated, but Mills chased them down dumping with his nine. Mills watched his slug rip through T-Bones shoulder, knocking him to the ground. Fresh backed Mills up with a few shots as he helped T-Bone to his feet. Flip and Cat Man begand firing off rounds again as well. Mills slipped behind a car as T-Bone and his boys were speeding off. Mills opened fire on the car before turning around and jogging to Buck's aid. Mek and Nesh were over his bloody body. The both of them were crying and screaming. Mek held Buck's head on her lap while crying out to God for help.

"Oh lord please no, not him, take me, its all my fault. Buck please don't leave me baby, I'm sorry I love you please no!!"

Her cries were to no avail, Buck was gone.

CHAPTER 20

Buck's death affected more than just his daughters and Mek's life. Deep down inside Mills blamed himself for his death, but on the surface he blamed Mek. He couldn't stand the sight of her. Mek was a wreck as well. She couldn't be trusted alone. She talked of taking her own life, Nesh didn't agree with her sister's actions and she was upset with her, but Mek was her only sister and she loved her. So she took care of her sister and her niece in their time of need. Mills didn't want Nesh to have anything to do with Mek so when Nesh went to her sister, he perceived it as betrayal.

He felt as though Nesh had chosen her side over his. Their relationship was failing, and Mills not answering his phone for two weeks didn't help it any. Mills refused to hustle or leave his grandmother's house until he found out who was responsible for Buck's death. He vowed to make his killer pay with their lives. He was an emotional wreck, and wanted no one to see him in such a state. Mills friends stopped by every day, but Mills refused to answer the door. The one time Nesh stopped by; she received the same treatment. No one beside Jimmy had seenMills since Buck's funeral. In a few short months Pimp had Long Street on lock. With Sonnny's connect, lessons and assistance, Pimp's boy house was doing numbers and hustlers before him didn't like it.

One day while walking, out to the corner store Pimp had a run in with Long Street's most feared hustler, Eazy. As Pimp reached the side of the store Eazy called after him.

"Aye homeboy let me take a look at you for a second," Eazy said as him and his two homeboys jogged across the street. Pimp didn't say anything, he just stood his ground while clutching his baby nine in his coat pocket. You the guy with the boy spot on

18th with that old man Sonny, right?" Eazy said while sizing Pimp up.

" Yeah that's me, what's happenin"

"What's happening is you fucking up my money, slowing down traffic. You in the wrong lane homie, my name Eazy and this is my strip. Pimp had a temper like his father and his blood got to boiling immediately. He held his composure though.

"Check it out, Eazy, for the record, my name is Pimp and I dig where you coming from, if this was my turf I'd probably be the same way, now I don't know if you thinking you about to run me off or what, but I can tell you now, ain't nothing like that happening, now we can come together and get this money,"

I ain't got no problem with that, its enough money out here for everybody, but other than that I don't know what to tell you."

Eazy could tell Pimp was packing by his calm demeanor. He also noticed Pimp never took his hand out his pocket. He wanted to shove his fist down Pimp's throat, but his better judgment told him to be careful.

"I thought we would be able to handle this the easy way but I see we won't be coming to an agreement, so keep it pimpin, Pimp and tell Sonny, Eazy said hey... later homeboy."

Eazy and his homies walked off, while Pimp backed away. Pimp wanted to wax Eazy, but it was too many witnesses out for his comfort. When Pimp made it back to his spot Sonny was in his favorite chair. For once he wasn't high, Pimp was glad because he wanted to talk to him about Eazy. Once sonny heard of Pimp's run in with Eazy, he wanted to handle the situation himself. Pimp didn't know it, but Sonny was an old school killer. He had took plenty of lives with his blade and just as many with revolver. Mostly everyone fromm the old school knew of Sonny and made it clear to all the young hustlers that he was not to be taken lightly. Pimp told Sonny he didn't want him to do anything to Eazy. He told Sonny, if Eazy wanted to go to war he had the right one.

And little did Sonny know; those words were back with an iron fist. It only took Eazy a few days to make his move. He marched around to 18th street with a chopper and three more gunmen. They unloaded over a hundred rounds into Pimp's spot. Pimp was gone, but Sonny was lucky he stood in the kitchen while his favorite chair got riddled up. Sonny hit the deck as bullets tore through his house, but his buddy Paul was too high to react with enough speed. The chopper shells tore through his skull and midsection. The gunshots seemed never to end, but when they finally did, Sonny didn't waste anytime dashing out the back yard headed for Liley's house two streets over.

After spending close to twenty days in solitude, confined in his grandmother's house, Mills was finally out of tears. After taking a shower and throwing on some clothes, Mills checked his messages on his cell phone. He had plenty from Nesh and they all touched him in his chest. Now that he had come to his senses, he knew he was inconsiderate and unfair. He missed Nesh and the sound of her tears cut him deep. He had messages from Brandy, Black, Shawn, Rio, Chico, B-Nut, H.T., and Peko as well. all of them were worried, but Black and Peko's messages seemed the most urgent. Before he could dial a number, Peko was calling . t=

"T-Money what the fuck man, why ain't you been answerin yo phone or the door, nigga we bro's yo pain is my pain and vise versa. That girl Nesh been callin me like I'm fucking her or something," Peko said.

My bad Pee, I just needed some time to pull myself together. Emotionally I was all over the place, you dig me,"

"Like a shovel. But I got some new that will brighten ya day,"

"Oh yeah try me. Black's lil cousin got word to us about who smoked Buck, he know where da niggas be at and all."

"Word nigga!"

"Word! We been trynna hit you up, Black's lil cousin fuck with the niggas, he was out there in the parking lot that night. You would never believe who all this shit is over."

" Who nigga? Listen bro, don't move I'm bout to call Black and we bought to be on our way over there."

"Hurry up, bro," Mills said before disconnecting.

A half-hour later the fellas were all in Mill's grandmothers living room. When Peko told Mills the whole story, it only made him feel worse. He blamed him self and Tameka for Buck's death when it was actually D-Roc and Walt's fault. He couldn't believe he slipped so much that night. Not only did he not notice D-Roc and Walt's g-ride in the lot, but T-Bone and his crew were in the VIP room next to theirs. Mills thought of how he cold he'd been acting towards Nesh for consoling her sister. He knew he owed her an apology, but it would have to come after avenging of Buck's death. The only thing that was on his mind was putting T-Bone in a casket. Later that night Black got all the information they needed from his little cousin. T-Bone and Deuce had an after hour on Cleveland and 16th, which served as a weight house as well. Not a night went by where they weren't there. Mills called H.T. for a throw away van, some artillery because tonight, vengence would be his. D-Roc and Walt pulled in front of Keisha's house in their newest ride. The Lincoln Navigator was doo doo brown, on gold hundred spokes. The pain't was dripping, with three wet coats of candy, while tinted windows hid them perfectly. The slap in the truck rattled the house as D-Roc called Keisha to inform the girls they were outside. Keisha and Iesha stepped out on the porch looking gorgeous. D-Roc killed the engine and the girls escorted them in the house. Black sat behind the wheel of the van. Mills rode shotgun, Shawn, Peko and Lil Mark rode in the back. They were dressed in all black, resembling a team of ninjas. Mills and Peko had tommy guns with hundred round drums, while mark and Shawn were equipped with 32 shot Mack Elevens. Black carried a sawed off pump, that rested across his legs, as they stalked the weight house. The place was packed while traffic still came in and out. Meanwhile, Pimp had already had enough of Eazy. Eazy made it clear that some one had to go, and Pimp refused to let it be him. After riding around for two hours looking for him, Pimp and Sonny had finally caght a break. Sonny caught an addict by the name of Wiz coming out of Eazy's boy house. The addict's money was short, and Eazy's worker refused to serve him, which worked in their favor. Pimp gave Wiz a few packs of his fire heroin and sonny drained him of all the info he needed.

Eazy was a the club on champion and Mt. Vernon while his homie ran the spot by him self. Sonny wanted to run in the boys spot, take Eazy money and kill his home boy, but Pimp didn't want his homeboy, he wanted Eazy's life. They sat across the street from the club, ducked off in the parking lot. Pimp was so furious and the wait was so long, he decided to smoke his first blunt. The weed had him tripping, it made him paranoid and impatient. Some females came walking out the club talking loudly. One of them held pieces of her weave in he hand, while anothers shirt was almost torn off her. It was clear they were drunk and had been in a cat fight. Shorty after the females came out, Eazy came out the club leaning on one of his homeboys shoulder. They were lit and were talking loudly about the way they sprayed Pimp's spot.

They staggered to the car parked a couple of vehicle in front of Pimp and Sonny. Pimp pulled his ski mask on and checked his gun. It was ready for action. Eazy stood outside the car taking a piss, while his homeboy enojoyed the nights air. Pimp popped up out of nowhere.

"Eazy look out!" His homeboy yelled as Pimp slid down on him.

"Die mutha fucka," Pimp said as he delivered a few shots to Eazy's upper body. His partner spun around and met Sonny's problem solver. His head exploded as his body hit the concrete. His homeboy ran towards the females as they ran and dove for cover. Bullets from Pimp's gun chased him down, a bullet to his back spun him around into a parked vehicle, while another went through his neck knocking him to the ground. His eyes were open, and he could see feet running, but his body couldn't move. Back at Keisha's, blunts were being lit and Walt was setting the mood as he rubbed on Iesha's ho ha! Keisha was in the kitchen on the phone telling T-Bone to hurry up. D-Roc and Walt were rocked to sleep.

"Bone hurry up cause these niggas is getting horny."

"Well, give them some pussy, give em sum head, I don't give a fuck, do what you gotta do to keep them their we on our way!" T-Bone said before diconnecting.

T-Bone and his crew came walking out the after hours. Deuce was walking slowly, still hunched over from his staples in his chest and stomach. He was supposed to be on bed rest but he refused to not be apart of killing D-Roc and Walt. Mills spotted the five walking out towards T-Bone's car.

"There go them niggas right there," He said while pulling his ski mask down and pulling his gloves on tight. Everyone in the van did the same thing. Fresh helped Deuce in the front of the car, while T-Bone unlocked the drivers door. Mills slid out the truck followed by Peko. He didn twaste any time, as soon as he hopped out the van he started blastting. He let the tommy rip through T-Bones body. Peko unloaded on the truck filling Deuce's body with holes. Mills walked over to T-Bones dead body and let off more shots. Mills then joined Peko with rearranging the Lexus truck. Fresh thumped back as he made a run for the after hour's front door. He made the wrong move, Black was creeping up and he ran right into the barrel of his gun. Boom! Once shot exploded Fresh's head, slumping his body immediately.

The rest of T-Bones crew dumped off a few rounds while taking off up the street. Shawn, and Lil Mark gunned them down, dropping them a few yards away from the after hours spot. Black was already back in the van, he whipped it on the side of the Lexus and yelled for Mills and Peko to get in the van. Shawn and Mark were already sliding in the back. Mills and Peko hurried into the van and Black put the pedal to the medal.

D-Roc and Walt had wrecked Keisha and Iesha's sheets. The girls let them have their way, no limits, as they tried their best to keep the guys their until T-Bone arrived. After a couple hours of banging head boards, D-Roc and Walt were in the wind. Keisha couldn't believe T-Bone and his crew missed an opportunity. She called his phone repitiously, angry that she had just gave her goodies away for free. Little did she know T-Bone wouldn't be answering his phone ever again. They say revenge is a dish served cold and the deaths of Buck's killers certainly cooled Mills off. He made amends with Nesh and finally had a talk with Chico. At Buck's funeral Chico had offered to have a few of his guys find and dispose of Buck's killers, but Mills declined his assistance. Chico understood. He knew that was blood mills wanted on his hands. Though he explained to Mills that he had reached a level of the game where his hands should never get dirty. His money not only talked for him, but it would also kill for him if he ordered it to. At Mills and Chico's meeting, Mills told chico he wanted the year of 99 to be his last year in the game. Normally Chico would of said no, because Mills hadn't worked fron him long enough, but out of love and respect he had for Buck, he made an exception. He told Mills that if he could get rid of 50 kilos a month for the next twelve months and payed him a fee of a million dollars he could walk away from the game.

He told Mills that he was family. But that there was still rules to the lifestyle that had to be followed. Mills understood and agreed to Chico's term. He also told Chico he wanted to introduce him to Peko, when the timing was appropriate. Chico agreed and the meeting was over. Mills had to grind hard, because he had to get rid of twenty more kilos a month. Chico wanted ten grand a kilo. Mills did the math in his head and realized that if he sold the kilos at fifteen grand a pop, he'd have three million dollars cash to go with 1.5 million he already had stashed and a few hundred thousand dollars in the streets. Mills couldn't believe how fast his life had changed. It seemed like yesterday, that Buck was taking care of him and his little brother and he was sneaking around smoking on blunts.

Now he was a millionaire, but the man who helped him reach his status and taught him everything he knew was gone. His grandmother was gone. Slim was dead and his once bestfriend was behind bars facing the death penalty. What he gained from the game seemed so little compared to what he had lost. The lord giveth and the lord taketh away. His grandmother once told him, he was starting to understand the mighty quote.

As the rained fell on his windowpane, he also though of some of Buck's words. Drugs didn't just end up in the black community, they were delivered there, as a secret weapon in the white man's genocide on the black race. The shit was bigger than pretty hustlers, if it wasn't presidency would have been riddled our country of drugs. We still sell this shit to make those mother fuckers more money than we could imagine. And what do they do? Make laws against the shit to send us to the modern day plantation called prison.

Don't let the money blind you T-Money, cause we lose more than we can ever gain. And if you survive through the losses, you'll one day ask yourself, was it all worth it. Mills thought of his mother, father, aunts, uncles, grandmother, Buck, and friends. He now knew the answer to that question. Black on black crime was at an all time high, don't you see the white man's plan working. We killing one another over this shit.

Give us blacks the guns and drugs and let us do their work for them. We just got to open our third eye. And we'll recognize the design. They've programmed us to hate one another. While they're thinking become employed, we're thinking become the employer, and when we start thinkig house, they start thinking land. And by then they will own the whole fucking world and we'll still be killing one another from crumbs! It took for Buck to die for Mills to really understand his words. The brother was deep and he never had the chance to shine his light on the world.

CHAPTER 21

Detective White and Brown sat behind their desk piecing together the vast amount of murders that had took place in the last couple of years. Detective Brown was furious behind the trail of bodies, but White could care less. White puffed on a Kool's Long, while his young partner shuffled through files on his desk.

"I'm telling you Whitey, a lot of these murders are linked together and we're just missing something", Brown said as the cases started to overwhelm him.

"I'd love to lock the mutha fuckers up and throw away the key Browny, but I'm not gonna wreck my fuckin brain behind the deaths of a bunch of low life, gang banging drug dealers. They can kill each other off, for all I care", White pulled hard on his cigarette before continuing. "Doing nothing make our jobs a lot easier, fucking pieces of shit!"

Brown searched through one file, while another sat in front of him wide open.

"Check this out Whitey, Fella Stargell is behind bars for the deaths of Chris Palmer and India Cypress. The key witness on the case is India Cypress friend Lisa Longley. She informed us that Fella and his cousin Anton "Slim" Stargell, along with some of his buddies robbed Chris Palmer about a year or so prior to Palmers death".

"And she knows this how?" White asked.

"She knows this because her friend India was present when the robbery took place, India was also involved with one of the robbers, which is Anton "Slim" Stargell".

"So this India whatshername may have been in on the robbery." White inquired.

"Maybe but that's not my point, here's my point…About a year after Palmer was robbed, Anton "Slim" Stargell was gunned down, while at a store in Palmers neighborhood".

"So Palmer was apart of Stargells death" White said.

"Exactly! And further proof of that is a month later Anton Stargells cousin and some of his buddies, probably the same ones form the robberies, went to Palmers apartment and killed him and the once again present India Cypress. All three murders are linked together like one big chain. But listen to this, the missing pieces to the puzzle are The Stargell boy's buddies, which we know without a shadow of a doubt has to be their all time running buddies"… White finished the sentence for Brown, "Derick "D-Roc" Sanders and Walt "Lil Walt" Burns".

"Exactly"! Brown yelled.

"Okay, so how do we prove that Sanders and Burns were involved and how does these murders link to Daylon "Buckshot" Draggs murder and the whole situation at the night club?" White asked.

"Well I'm getting to that, listen to this, Sanders, Burns, the Stargell boys, and check this out, Tony Mills are all apart of Draggs gang. Mills and a few others were present the night of Draggs death. As ususal they claim to know nothing. But after questioning the girl Keisha Smith, we know Mills and the rest of the crew are lying".

"Keisha Smith, who the fuck is she"? White asked.

"She's the girls whose phone number we found in Tydus 'Tibone' Carter's phone on the night of his death, we questioned her a few days ago. Brown reminded his partner.

"Oh okay, I remember , keep going," White said.

"Well Keisha Smith told us that Sanders and Burns robbed and shot T-Bones homeboys, Dustin Big Deuce Driver and his brother Michael Lil Mike Driver in the club's parking lot the same night of Dragg's death. And with T-Bone being dead she had no problem telling us that he was the shooter that killed Dragg that same night. In retaliation for his buddies driver boys." White added.

"Exactly!" Brown yelled again. He continued, "she also stated the night of T-Bones death she was apart of a scheme to set up D-Roc Sanders and Walt Burns up. She was calling T-Bone's phone because he was supposed to be on his way to her house, to catch Sanders and Burns, but never made it. Because some one killed him and his buddies before they could get there.".

"Exactly!"

"Sounds like a double set up to me," White said.

"My point exactly. That where Mills and his buddies come in.

"I don't get it," White said. While Ms. Smith, and Mr.Carter thought they were setting Saunders up, Saunders and Burns had some men camped outside and when they did," Brown said.

"And that's why Carter, Driver and those other guys never made it to Smith's house."

"So where does Mills come in at?" White asked.

"With both of the Stargell boys being out the picture and Carter and Burns have to team up with and why would Mills and others not cooperate in helping apprehend in killing Draggs killer unless they wanted revenge."

"And how do we prove all this?"

"Well Stargell boys and Palmer and Ms Cypress case is easy, but the thing with Buckshots Draggs, T-Bone Carter Mr. Mills and the rest of the guys are going to be tricky, we have two witnesses in Ms Smith and her friend, but we need a few more to put the puzzle all the way together," Brown said while rubbing his chin.

"Good luck finding them, everybody's dead! White said becoming irritated by the young detectives logic.

"Tell me something Brown, since you've put all that together, what ya got on the Detroit Boys homicides?" White asked in an irritated tone.

"I haven't got much on them, but what I do know is that the Detroit Boys on Oak Street are affiliated with the Detroit Boys on lLinwood, so the two cases could probably be connected. Word in the streets is some youngster by the name of Pimp and L's may be involved." Brown answered.

Clyde got a conituance on Fella's first hearing. Fella felt the walls closing in on him as he ran out of options to come up with Clyde's money. Unknowingly to Fella, Mills had a meeting with Clyde for later that evening. After thinking of all his loses, Mills thought of Fella's mother, who he had been neglecting through him and Fellas fall out. One evening Mills stopped by to check up on her and apologized for his absence. She cried her heart out to him about Fella's situation. Telling him of how D-Roc and Walt had been acting towards her and him, and how the lawyer needed twenty thousand dollars cash to defend her son. Mills peeled back a few dollars to help her out with her bills, then he left the lawyer's information assuring her that Fella would be okay. Mills asked Clyde to continue the case and assured him that he'd be to see him after court hours. Mills took Clyde ten grand and promised him the other ten grand in a few days. Clyde agreed and in return told mills the specifies about fellas case. He let Mills know about the only key witness in the case and Mills promised to have a talk wth her.

After promising Lisa twenty thousand, she agreed to lie on the stand for Fella. Mills gave her part of the money and promised her the rest when the job was done. Money moves everybody. Buck once told Mills and he was now seeing it happen. Mills couldn't understand why he was helping Fella, after the way he failed to watch over his grandmother and brother while he was on lock down and after choosing D-Roc and Walt over him.

Mills thought of the argument they had in front of his grandmother's house, when he told him he couldn't trust D-Roc and Walt and Fella defended them. Mills knew the average man would have let Fella fry, but he was taught that two wrongs don't make a right. Real niggas did real things. And loyalty was more than just a word, it was a way of life, and he lived by those lessons. No matter what he and Fella went through, Fella was family and he knew that now more than ever, that nothing is more impotant than family. Peko sat in his weight house clocking major dollars. It was the first of March and all the young hustlers were running through his packs faster than a New York minute.

D-Roc and Walt were parked a couple of apartments down from Peko's, contemplating their next move. They'd been planning to clean Peko for over a month now. Only problem was getting inside his apartment. They surely couldn't knock on the door, Peko would either not answer or open the door with his gun in his hand ready for action. They couldn't kick in the door because that ment they'd have to go in shooting,and they really didn't want to kill him. Just take him through the ringer, to show Mills and him they could be touched. As young Clarence got out his car and gravitated towards Peko's back door, the solution fell in their laps. By the time Clarence knocked on the door Walt had his Desert Eagle to his temple. "Don't say a word or I'm a knock ya noodles loose." Walt threatened.

D-Roc pressed his Glock 40 to the other side of Clarence's head, as Peko asked, "who is it?"

"Tell em who the fuck it is," D-Roc whispered.

"It's Clarence," Clarence mumbled.

"Who?" Peko asked while pressing his nine mm against the door. Walt pressed his gun into Clarence's temple with force. Reminding him that his noodles were at stake.

"Young Cee Clarence!" Clarence yelled.

Peko lowered his weapon after hearing Clarence's voice and name. He was waiting for Clarence to come and pick up his usual four and a half ounces. He yanked the door open with his gun held to his side. The sight of D-Roc's Glock 40 in his face, and Walt's Desert Eagle at Clarence's head froze him immediately.

"Don't be stupid nigga, drop the pistol on the floor and back the fuck up. Keep yo hands at yo side too nigga." D-Roc said while smiling a bedazzling smile.

They pushed their way inside, backing Peko into the kitchen counter. Walt kicked the door closed and made Clarence and Peko empty their pockets. Walt took Clarence's money, shoved him to the ground and told him not to move. He shot through the house while D-Roc handled Peko.

"You got anymore guns in here lil nigga?" D-Roc asked Peko while pressing his gun to his head. Peko didn't answer; he stared at D-Roc with a look of a killer. D-Roc cracked Peko upside his head, causing blood to leak instantly.

"When I ask you a fucking question, you better answer me nigga, and fix that look on ya face, you ain't no mutha fucking killer, now where the shit at?"

Peko wanted to go for D-Roc's gun, while he had him alone, but D-Roc quickly changed his mind and went upside his head again, and shoved him to the floor.

"I'm a ask you one more time, where the fuck is the dope?" D-Roc said while hovering over top of him and aiming his gun.

"It's in the drawer man."

"That's more like it, now get the fuck up and get it." D-Roc ordered. Peko did as he was told. Walt returned with a tech nine and several thousand of dollars in a bag. D-Roc shoved Peko back down to the floor and ordered him not to move. Peko did as he was told, but the look he gave them bothered Walt. Walt delivered a forceful kick busting Peko's mouth open.

"Who the fuck you looking at bitch! I'll blow yo shit lose and tell ya boy Mills he's next." Walt said before following D-Roc out the door. Peko jumped to his feet and called Mills immediately. Walt found his other gun so he didn't bother trying to impede on their get away. Young Clarence was shaking like drug store dice. Clarence ain't want Peko thinking he had anything to do with the robbery, so instead of running off, he begged for Peko's forgiveness. Peko knew Clarence was a victom of circumstance and robbery wasn't in his jacket. Clarence was a school boy trying to be a good hustler. Peko helped him reach the level he was on and he knew he looked up to him. He told Clarence not to worry about anything. He promised to put him back on his feet, but told him he needed him to leave right now. Peko was beyond mad, his pride was hurt, he was robbed even while holding a gun. His head and mouth both leaked blood and when Mills arrived with his artillery he was going to make sure his blood wasn't the only blood shed. Mils arrived quickly. He didn't know what to say, his ace Boone had been violated.

Peko's blood stained the floor and his clothing. Mills tossed him a vest, and an A.R 15. He decided to let his actions speak for him. All he could say was let's ride. D-Roc and Walt could be any where. The only place Mills could think of was their mother's houses. Mills pulled by D-Roc's mother first. A few of D-Roc's cars were parked out in front, but no sign of him.

"Fuck that T-Money, pull back by that bitch I'm lighting it up!" Peko ordered.

Mills busted a U-turn at the end of the block. When he neared D-Roc's mother house, he hung out the window and let off multiple rounds into the home and the vehicles. Peko's response wasn't over, Mills headed for Walt's mother's house and Peko laid an identical demonstration down there as well. The drive by shootings was the beginning of war! Peko didn't know it but one of those bullets almost hit D-Roc's baby sister, had D-Roc's mother not of been quick on her toes, the A.R 15 slug would have done more than gazed her. The next day, Peko's mother came home to a vandalized house. Her front door had been kicked in and the house was trashed. D-Roc and Walt riddled the inside of the house with A.K. holes, as a message for Peko. Had his mother of been home, she would of died. Peko and Shawn were in the process of moving their mother into a new two hundred and fifty thousand dollar home. They wanted it to be a surprise, but with the street war, it was clear they mother had to be out of her soon as possible. While Mills was helping Peko and Shawn with their mother's, Walt and D-Roc were ram sacking his grandmother's house. Mills didn't find out about his home until the following day. When Mills pulled in front the next morning, he instantly noticed his front door laying on the living room floor. He held his nine mm by his side as he crept in the house. Mills didn't keep any money or drugs in the house, because that was his grandmother's demand. Even with her resting in peace, he still honored and respected her home.

To his knowledge nothing was missing, but when he called his little brother to inform him of what had taken place, the first thing on his mind was the half a key of heroin and the thirty thousand cash he had stashed in his room. Mills knew things had gone beyond hood beef and it was best if he and Jimmy move in Nesh's apartment for a while. He had the door fixed, then headed for Peko and Shy's condo. When Jimmy arrived after school, his thoughts were confirmed, his stash was gone. He knew of his brother's beef with D-Roc and Walt. He wanted to interfere, but he couldn't chance getting recognized. At that moment he promised his self if the opportunity presented it self, he'd put a bullet through D-Roc and Walt's head. The money and drugs taken weren't a big problem.

Although the lost hurted, more was secretly stashed in Leslie's bedroom, and L's mother's house. He had Long Street on lock down and his name was both respected and feared. After a month of non stop shoot outs, Mills had to get back to his money. He had a goal to meet, and he couldn't let D-Roc and Walt's jealousy interfere with his mission. He knew he would catch them slipping sooner or later, and when he did, he'd finish the beef. Peko and Shawn weren't letting the beef rest. It was twelve O'clock in the afternoon, and they were out lurking. Little did they know, D-Roc and Walt had the same agenda. Peko pushed the Altima up Oak Street after checking for D-Roc and Walt at one of D-Roc's girlfriend houses. As he reached the stop sign at the corner of Oak and Kelton, he couldn't believe his eyes, D-Roc and Walt were coming his way. He knew their Bonneville from anywhere, D-Roc and Walt weren't aware that Peko had switched his rental car up so when they neared it, Peko caught them off guard. He stuck his hand out the window and blasted shots off at the Bonneville as it passed. D-Roc hit the brakes as the glass shattered in his face. Walt came out his window, unloading on the car as Peko made the U-turn. Walt fired his twin Desert Eagles, but they were no match for the chopper Shawn swung out the window. The rapid fire sent Walt sliding back in the window and D-Roc smashing the gas. Peko was on their tail and Shawn never stopped shooting. The chopper was tearing the car to smithereens, but the Bonneville's 350 turbo was too much for the Altima's small engine.

CHAPTER 22

It's late April and Pimp sat in his all white Bubble Lexus on he chrome eighteens. The windows are dark tinted which hid him perfectly as he watched King of New York on his flat screen television that rested on his dash board right above his C.D. deck. Leslie called and told him L's was calling back shortly and wanted to talk to him, so he rushed from his new spot to his partners call.

As he killed the television and exited the car, when he entered the house Sonny was nodding as usual. Liley had slowly pulled away from her Jones, after Pimp threatened to put her in a detox. Pimp was truly the man of the house, taking care of Leslie and her mother, along with furnishing the place and paying bills. Mills hated seeing Sonny with such a bad Jones. He respected and cared for Sonny like a father figure. The sight of Sonny nearly falling off the couch was all Pimp could take.

"Get the fuck up Sonny, c'mon man you gotta go to rehab and get some help." Pimp said while saving him from falling on the floor.

"C'mon Pimp, my life is over, you can't help a person that don't want help. I'm gone." Sonny whispered as his head nearly rolled off his neck.

"I ain't trynna hear that shit Sonny, you like a dad to me man, I can't watch you go out like this." Pimps words cut him deep, he had grown to the gangster, like he was his own.

"Don't waste your time youngin, I'm gone, just let me fade away."

"Naw fuck that, I tried this boy game out for you, now I'm asking you to try this rehab out for me, just give it ninety days, if you get out and cope, I'll leave you alone, but you have to at least try man. I did it for you, now do it for me…Tip for Tap Sonny." Pimp said

"Why are you doing this Pimp? I'm not worth it."

"To me you are, now we got a deal or what?" Pimp was adamant and Sonny had no response. It hurt him to let the youngster down but he just dropped his head.

"Pimp! Pimp!" Leslie yelled

"Hold up Bae."

"L's on the phone."

"This is an important call Sonny, but since you ain't say no, I'm taking that as a yes." He ran up the steps and grabbed the phone.

"What's up bro?"

"Shid you the one wit it, trynna get it." L's responded. Pimp laughed.

"I hear you talking slick, did you get them flicks?"

"Yes sir, that Lexus looking good, I know you copped me one, too." "Nah I ain't do that, but ya bro got it on lock and whatever you want when you get out, it's yours. Half of everything I own is you my nigga, I can't wait to show you this new game, its beautiful bro."

"Well you gone be showing me sooner or later cause I come home next month!" L's said enthusiastically.

"Get the fuck out of here, bro!"

"Real shit bro, I get out three months early for good behavior, so tell all my niggas the real Frank White is coming home and if a nickel bag get sold in the park I want in!

"Ha! Ha! Ha! Ha!" they both bursted out into laughter.

"Yea its on bro, I love you man!"

"I love you too bro, but I gotta go my time is up, you be careful." L's said before ending the call.

Pimp was pumped. He would have his partner back in a month and it couldn't be sooner. He was going to see his connect about giving him more weight. He recently started coping a half a kilo of heroin and got fronted the other half, but now he had enough cash to cop his own kilo and he wanted to be fronted another consignment. He'd have to be a little late for his appointment with his connect, because right now his mind was on Sonny. He told Leslie to bag up eighty thousand dollars and he'd be back to get it an hour. He left with Sonny and headed for the nearest rehab. Sonny signed his self over to the facility for ninety days. He placed him straight in a detox tank, where he'd clean his self up cold turkey, for two weeks.

They told Pimp everything he'd need for his stay and he immediately returned with the sweat suits, under clothing, and hygiene. He had to give his name for the visitors list and provider of the clothing. When they dropped Sonny's clothing off, he thought his name deceived him as he looked at the name on his property sheet. He was higher than a kite, but he knew saw the name with clarity. James Keys stood out like a stop sign. The only Keys he new was his old friend the notorious Tony Keys. He thought Pimp had a familiar face, but he couldn't pin point the identity. He thought of the youngsters temper and the way he handled Eazy and knew right then and there, who's child Pimp was.

Jimmy stood on the porch talking on his cell phone, while waiting on his cab. Mills pulled up with Rio in Rio's new car. Rio was only a few streets over from Long Street. He had Mt. Vernon on lock with the hard and soft. As close as he was to Pimp, he'd never saw the notorious youngster, though he's heard his name plenty of times. The youngster's name held weight in the streets and his unseen hands made him more of a legend. As Mills and Rio stepped on the porch, Jimmy quickly ended his call.

"What's up, bro?" Mills said while wrapping his arm around his little brother. Jimmy had a style of his own as he could without copycatting. Mills was smooth and easily attracted to.

"Nothing much," Jimmy replied.

"Rio this is my little bro. Jim this is my homie Rio, real good dude." Mills said while winking at Rio.

"This the genius slash football star?" Rio asked while giving Mills a playful elbow.

"The one and only." Mills said proudly.

"What's up lil bro, Mills talks about you all the time."

"Sup" Jimmy returned with a smile. Rio entered the apartment to the sound of Nesh's voice yelling for Mills to come upstairs. Mills left Rio in the living room alone. When he walked in the room the first thing he noticed was Tameka sitting on the bed. Although he no longer blamed her for Buck's death, he still hadn't forgiven her for cheating on him, in his book Tameka couldn't be trusted. The sight of Daylana going crazy to get in his arms made him over look Tameka.

"C'mere my baby." Mills said as he grabbed her out of Nesh's hands.

Nesh loved the sight of Mills with Daylana. Her niece loved Mills and he loved her.

"What's up bae? Why you screaming like somebody attacking you?" Mills said after kissing her soft lips.

Nesh looked at Tameka. "We'll sis, its about time for me and Day-Day to get going, I love you."

"I love you too; call me." Mills gave Daylana a big kiss before handing her over to her mother.

"Bye Mills take care."

Mills was caught off guard, they hadn't spoken in months, but he managed to respond in a timely fashion.

"You do the same, Mek."

Mills gave Nesh a look that asked where did that come from.

"Boy ain't no body mad no more, but you." Nesh said while playfully rolling her eyes.

"I know that's right…" Mills said playfully. "What's up bae, I got company downstairs." Nesh didn't know how to say it, so she just spit it out.

"Mills I'm pregnant."

"Damn bae, as much as I want us to have children, right now…it's real fucked up timing."

For a moment Nesh couldn't believe what she was hearing.

I know he not saying what I think he's saying. Nesh thought.

"Mills I know you're not asking me to kill our baby?" Nesh said with attitude while pulling back from his hold.

"C'mon bae, I love you too much to ever ask a thing like that of you, I want us to have our baby, I'm just saying the timing was off. I'm stuck in these streets moving this shit for about eight more months, which means I won't be able to go through the stages of pregnancy with you like I always imagined ,then I'm in the middle of a fucking war with them niggas Roc, and Walt, its on sight gun play and I don't want you and my baby in the middle of my bullshit, you know."

Nesh was once again speechless. Mills made some valid point, and the last one he made frightened her. She was well aware of D-Roc and Walt's craziness. Mills could see that worry in her face, so he pulled her closer to him and assured her that everything would be alright.

"Don't worry bae; I'll die before I let anything happen to you and our baby. As soon as I finish my business with Chico, we leaving this crazy-ass city."

Almost a month passed since Mills learned of his father hood. He owed Chico eight more months of the game before he could leave. Peko would take his position and Shawn would take Peko's when he retired. Chico was happy to be dealing with apples from the same tree, so to speak, because he knew what to expect. Buckshot gave Chico ten years of his life and Chico just needed another hustler like Buck who was in the game for the long haul. Mills knew Peko could possibly be that guy and the reason coupled with the fact that he was, Mills introduced him to Chico. Although Mills brought Peko and Shawn into the game, they were born to hustle and Mills couldn't think of anyone who actually hustled harder than those two.

Mills was in the middle of explaining their new positions when he spotted D-Roc a couple of cars ahead of them, riding shotgun with his girlfriend, Tasha.

"Pee, that's D-Roc a couple cars in front of us, keep it cool, but stay on his heels." Mills said from the back seat of Peko's low key Ford Contour.

One of the cars between them had turned off leaving one car between them. Tasha whizzed through the light as it turned red. Peko swerved around the car in front of him and thrust out into traffic behind her. D-Roc spotted them as Peko closed in the gap between them. Tasha smashed the gas swerving around a few a cars and making a quick turn. Peko was on her tail, but the quick turn put a little distance between them. When Peko made the sharp turn, D-Roc and Tasha were hurrying out the car.

"Stop! Stop!" Mills yelled.

Peko hit the brakes directly behind Tasha's Honda. Mills hopped out of the car and beat D-Roc to the punch. Mills squeezed of the first shots, as D-Roc shielded his self behind Tasha's car, while snatching her to the ground. D-Roc took a bullet to the hip and the hot one burned as he squatted for cover. D-Roc stuck his hand over the trunk of the car and squeezed off a few rounds. When he popped up he took another one of Mills 40 cal slugs. His arm felt like it was on fire as the bullet entered his bicep. Lucky for him, Mills had run out of bullets. D-Roc took advantage of that as he continued to squeeze off shots from his gun. Mills dove into the car as Peko hopped out and emptied his eleven shot clip from his Smith, and Wesson. D-Roc ran behind another car for cover and Shawn raised out the window splashing with his gun as Peko pulled away. D-Roc popped off a few times as Peko bent the corner.

"Get the fuck up and take me to the hospital." D-Roc yelled at Tasha, who was still on the ground covering her head. D-Roc hadn't crossed paths with Mills in over a month. He couldn't believe he was caught slipping, but the argument he was in with Tasha distracted him. If he wasn't checking to see if there were any police in sight, before he popped her in her mouth, he would of never seen the car zipping through the red light behind them. Mills, Peko, and Shawn had the last shot today, but those who blasted last usually the longest, and D-Roc promised his self the next time they traded shots he'd blast first and last.

Summer had arrived , and at seventy-five degrees, the weather couldn't of been better for L's return to the real world. L's loved all the respect Pimp had gained in his absence. Pimp was serving weight and bundles of boys, in every corner he and L's bent his name was being screamed. Pimp gave L's the low down on the boy game and caught him up on all the beefs he buried in the last nine months. By the time they reached 18th street, L's was up to date, and ready to play his position.

"So how we gone handle things now Pimp?" L's asked while enjoying his first time passing his ace a blunt.

"Like we always do it…together nigga. We family. All I got is you and my big bro, it ain't nothing we can't accomplish together. We bout to get rich bro." Pimp said as he inhaled the hydro smoke.

While Pimp and L's walked up 18th Street, Rio and his young homie Tiger were rolling in Rio's low key mobile. Rio did all his hustling out of the old school cutlass. He named it Brown Bomber, after its ugly brown pain't job. Tiger was a youngster who sold heroin and crack. He coped his boy from Pimp and his crack from Rio . Tiger was where Rio heard most of his stories of the notorious Pimp and as they rolled through the streets , Tiger was at it again with the stories of the young don.

"I'm telling you big homie, he done took Long Street over, if a mutha fucka selling boy they getting it from him, and he a young nigga like my age getting that one kind of paper," Tiger said as he puffed on a fat blunt.

"Yeah I been hearing about him a lot in the streets, but I ain't never seen the lil nigga, it's like he ghost or something."

"Yeah he be ducked off in those boy spots, he got like three of them shits, he here one day, there the next, and over there the next." Tiger said while using his hands to point all over the place.

Rio burst into laughter as he hit 18th Street . Tiger was surely fascinated with this Pimp guy. Tiger spotted Pimp and L's leaning up against Pimp's Lexus.

"There go Pimp right there," Tiger said. Rio stared through the tint as Tiger pointed Pimp out. Rio almost hit a parked car as he stared at Mills little brother Jimmy. Rio fumbled with his cell phone as he quickly called Mills. Meanwhile, Mills sat in a booth staring at Fella through the glass as the guards escorted him to an unexpected visit. When Fella reached the booth, he couldn't believe his eyes. His mother and lawyer told him everything Mills was doing for him, but Mills also told his mother not to give him his number. Mills wasn't being nasty, he just didn't want to talk to Fella over the phone, because he knew Fella's calls were being monitored. He knew he'd visit him one day, he just didn't know when. Mills and Fella grabbed the phone at the same time.

"What's up bro," they said in unison.

It was a moment of silence then Mills spoke.

"Man ain't nothing changed still grinding and tryna stay away from the law."

"I can dig it."

"So how things looking in the court room?"

"A lot better thanks to you."

"Don't worry about it bro, I told you if you ever needed, I'd be there for you, a lot has changed between us and I don't know if things will ever go back to the way they used to be, but it'll take more than what happened between us, for my loyalty to you to die. I got cha back like I'm following you bro." Mills said.

His words caused Fella to drop his head. Fella allowed his greed for street fame to cost him everything. His one true friend and possibly his life. He and Mills conversed for another fifteen minutes. He caught Mills up on the ups and downs in his case, and Mills caught him up on the streets, including the rift with D-Roc and Walt. When Mills spoke of his baby brother, Fella's mind went straight to the scene of Jimmy shooting the robbers on Oak Street .

"Mills listen bro, first I apologize for not telling you sooner, but ya lil bro, in them streets deep."

"What you mean Fells, not my lil bro, my lil bro in school handling his biz." Mills said with authority.

"T-Money listen man, I know you've been hearing about them lil niggas L's and Pimp?"

"Yea, but what that got to do with Jimmy?"

"Just think of the nick name we gave Jimmy when he was a youngin."

Mills blurted out, " J-Pimp!"

"We named him J-Pimp, cause he was a chick magnet, I seen it with my own two eyes bro, D-Roc's lil freak cousin was hooking us up with the low down on Pimp and L's, cause we was gone rob them niggas, but when I seen who it was, I cut that lick short ASAP. But then the wildest thing happened, as Jimmy and his dude came walking out the store, some nigga was robbing they spot and Jimmy and his partner got to blazing on them niggas, shit wig me out. Get yo lil bro before he fall too deep into the trap, we call street life."

Mills couldn't believe his ears. He was angry at Fella for not telling him sooner. He thought of all the murders Pimp and L's name was on. Then his mind shot to the massacre on Linwood and Fulton. He rose from his seat with out saying a word and rushed to county's visiting booth. He ran to his car, he was right on time too, the minutes meter had just ran out. He slid between the tint, removed his T-shirt and pulled his vest over top of his tank top, then pulled his t-shirt back on. Mills was in a rush, but he couldn't forget about D-Roc and Walt, who blast him if they seen him one sight. As he pulled his five hundred in to traffic, he reached for his cell, which sat on the passenger seat. Before he could dial his little brother's number, a call chimed in.

"Yea who dis?"

"This Rio , where you at bro?"

"I know man I just found out, I'll get wit you later." Mills clicked Rio off before giving him a chance to say another word.

He dialed Jimmy's number and Jimmy quickly answered.

"What up?"

"Where you at lil bro, I'm coming to get you, its important."

Jimmy couldn't let Mills come and get him. He and L's were sitting in one of his boy spots and Mills was coming to pick him up anywhere around Long Street was a bad idea. He had to think quickly because he could hear the urgency in his brother's voice.

"What's going on Mills, why you sound so serious?"

"Cause this is a serious situation, now where you at?"

"I'm with Leon and his mom, can she drop me off somewhere?"

Jimmy was lying to his brother and Mills knew he was being lied to but didn't have time to argue.

"Meet me at Nesh's right now Jim."

Jimmy didn't get a chance to respond, Mills hung up immediately after his demand.

"What's up bro?" L's asked.

"I don't know I think my bro is in some trouble." "
What kind of trouble?"

"I don't know man, but c'mon you gotta drop me off at his girl's apartment, he wants me to meet him at his girl's apartment, something ain't right bro." Pimp said as they headed for his Lexus. Mills was a wreck, he couldn't believe he let his little brother fall victim to the streets. He neglected his responsibilities as an older brother and as a guardian. If his brother is who he thinks he is, he had to get out of Columbus ASAP. Pimp's name ran through the streets, for over five murders. He couldn't imagine his little brother being a stone cold killer, but if he really was a spitting image of their father when he was younger, then maybe he'd inherited his rage, temper, and need for power. Mills thought of Detective White and Detective Brown who had been harassing him and his crew since they were young. The detectives were persistent and lately they had been back on the prowl. They've been working hard to piece Bucks murder together and the murder of the Detroit Boys. If he knew the detectives as good as he did, they've already been informed of the names Pimp and L's that had been floating through the streets. He grabbed a screw driver from his night stand as he rammed through his dresser drawers. Mills was paranoid and he easily broke a sweat, as he held a Mack eleven in one hand and unscrewed the wall in his closet with the other. He layed the Mack by his feet and removed his shirt, and vest. His tank top was drenched with sweat. He removed a duffle bag from the hole in the wall. He opened it up and glanced at the 50 kilos he'd got from Chico yesterday. He threw the bag on the bed. The sight of three million dollars and fifty kilo's of pure cane made him more paranoid. He paced the floor with his Mack in his hand until he figured out what to put all the cash in. He ran downstairs and returned with some large trash bags.

He piled the cash into the heavy duty garbage bags and carried them along with a duffle bag of cane downstairs. Mills knew he owed Chico six more months but, he needed to get his brother, his women, and their child on safe grounds first. He gave Chico his money and explained to him what was going on in his life and asked him to let Peko take over for him. He was sure Peko would do his last six months for him. He'd leave Peko his clientele and let him profit the $250,000 a month. D-Roc and Walt sat in Walt's girlfriend complex bobbing their head to Ja'rule, while smoking on a fat blunt and taking a hit of coke before hitting the road. Nesh was driving up the street in her new Infiniti. She drove right by the Navigator, never noticing D-Roc and Walt behind the tint.

"Look at that." D-Roc said as Nesh drove by.

"That's Mills little bitch ain't it?"

"Yes sir"

"Follow that bitch Roc, I bet she going to her and Mill's apartment, lets got dawg." Walt said as he rushed D-Roc to pull off. D-Roc quickly caught up to her, as she pulled into her and Mills complex. D-Roc and Walt watched her as she parked next to Mills.

"Looks like Mills got him some new wheels." D-Roc said. Nesh grabbed her back pack out the back seat and hurried into the apartment.

"Pull over there." Walt said while pointing to a spot a few spaces down from Nesh's Infiniti.

"We about to go get this one while we got it. I knew we would catch this nigga sooner or later, those who shoot last usually live longer." D-Roc said while pulling into the space.

"That nigga got money dope in there for sure," Walt said while checking his twin Desert Eagles. When Nesh walked in the door, Mills was pacing the living room floor while taking strong puffs from his hydro filled blunts. Nesh looked at Mills in his sweaty white beater, then she looked at the duffle bags full of drugs and three heavy duty garbage bags filled with money. Mills held one Mack eleven in his hand and another sat on the couch.

"Mils what's wrong with you?" Nesh asked as she froze in the middle of the floor.

"Bae shit fucked up right now, my lil bro maybe in big trouble and he is on his way here, we got to leave town bae."

Nesh was getting scared, and paranoid, but she tried to stay calm.

"Okay baby, just calm down, and put the gun down, do you want Jimmy to see you like this, do you want him to see all this money and drugs? C'mere baby." She grabbed Mills in her arms, and removed the gun from his hands.

"Let's sit down Mills, talk to me until your brother get here, what's the problem?" Nesh said, while directing Mills towards the couch. The front door hit the floor after two hard kicks. The first one startled Mills and Nesh, but the second caused Mills to grab his gun off the couch. By the time he raised up with his weapon D-Roc was coming through the front door. He spotted Mills and blasted shots immediately. The first bullet struck Mills in his shoulder knocking him backwards. He still sprayed off rapid shots from his gun. D-Roc took a few shells to his mid section, but continued to shoot back, hitting Mills in his gun hand. Walt burst through the door letting his Eagle's bullets clap. He hit Mills in his stomach causing him to drop his weapon. From there, Walt took control over the battle, he hit Mills a few more times knocking him to the floor. Mills hit the carpet hard, he couldn't move. He glanced to his left and noticed Nesh laying in a puddle of blood. He tried reaching for her hand as it rested on her protruding belly, but his arm wouldn't comply. Outside Pimp stopped his Lex at the entrance. He didn't want Mills to see how he arrived. When he exited the car, he noticed the apartment door wide open he couldn't tell but, a body appeared layed out on the door. He spotted Walt coming out of the house with two duffle bags in his hand. He took off running towards the apartment with his browning nine in hand. The closer he got the more he saw. Walt threw the bags in the back of the navigator and then headed back to the house for the final bag. Pimp let his nine roar from a distance. Hot ones tore through Walt's body dropping him immediately. One of his Desert Eagles flew from his hand. L's was right behind him, he didn't have a pistol, but that didn't stop him from helping his partner the best way he could. As Pimp ran for the apartment, L's spotted Walt reaching for his waist. L's picked up the Desert Eagle and finished him off before he could get off a shot. Pimp heard the shots and turned to see his partner standing over Walt's body with a forty four in hand. He knew L's had just saved his life. As he ran into the apartment, he stepped over D-Roc's dead body and ran to his brother's aid. Mills was leaking.

"Fuck no, not my brother!" Pimp said to him self. L's came running in. he looked at three bodies layed out, and then he noticed the bag of cash next to the couch.

"That nigga outside had two trash bags full of money and a duffle bag full of coke in the back seat, I loaded that shit into the Lex." L's said.

"That was my bro's shit L's, they was robbing my brother," Pimp said as tears ran down his cheek.

"Jim...Jim...Jimmy." Nesh whispered.

"Oh shit Nesh you still alive baby, don't worry we bout to get you and my brother out of here, don't talk," Pimp said.

"L's come grab her, I'm a get my bro, we gotta get them to the hospital." Pimp continued, as L's scooped Nesh up with ease and said,

"Bro C'mon we gotta hurry up, the cops is getting closer." Pimp grabbed Mills car keys off the table, scooped his brother up, and rushed out the door behind him.

"Put her in the front seat of my brother's Benz," Pimp yelled. L's put Nesh in the front seat and helped put Mills in the back. Pimp watched Mills move his fingers as he layed across the back seat. "He moving his fingers L's my bro still got some fight in him. Grab those guns and that bag of money in the apartment, put em in the Lex with the rest of the shit and let's bang out." Pimp ordered.

L's rushed in the apartment and quickly returned with the guns and the bag of cash.

"Keep fighting bro, don't you leave me now," Pimp said, as he looked down at his brother in the back seat. He pulled the Benz out, and sped out the complex with L's right behind him in the Lexus.

TO BE CONTINUED